Hearts
In
Shadows

Kimberly Kogut

Copyright © 2025 Kimberly Kogut

All rights reserved.

ISBN: 979-8-218-76557-6

DEDICATION

To the shadows that whisper secrets, and to the flames that burn with fierce loyalty. This story is dedicated to those who walk the tightrope between darkness and light, between duty and desire, between vengeance and forgiveness. It is for those who dare to love in the face of overwhelming odds, who find strength in the face of adversity, and who wrestle with the complexities of their own moral compass, even when the path ahead is obscured by shadows and fraught with danger. It is a testament to the resilience of the human spirit, the enduring power of love, and the unwavering pursuit of justice, even when those pursuits lead down treacherous and uncertain paths.

To the women who have fought for their families, their honor, and their own destinies, even when those fights have been lonely and dangerous. This book is a tribute to their strength, their courage, and their unwavering commitment to the people they love. It is a celebration of their resilience in the face of unimaginable loss, a testament to the depth of their emotions, the intensity of their passion, and the unshakeable belief in the power of redemption, even in the darkest of hours. To the women who have risen from the ashes, who have found strength in their vulnerability, and who have refused to be silenced, I offer this work as a token of gratitude for their inspiration and their unwavering spirit.

This book is also dedicated to the men who fight their own internal battles, those who struggle with loyalty and betrayal, and those who are forced to make impossible choices.

For those who carry the burden of their past, for those who
yearn for redemption and find themselves entangled in a web
of their own making, this is for you. It's for those caught
between the expectations of family and the desires of the
heart, for those who strive to do the right thing, even when
the cost is immense and the outcome uncertain. It is a
recognition of the complexities of human nature, the capacity
for both great cruelty and profound love, and the inherent
struggle between duty and desire. To the men who walk the
line between darkness and light, between right and wrong,
this book is a tribute to your struggle, your pain, and
ultimately, your resilience.

Finally, this dedication extends to all those who have ever
dared to dream of a different life, a life less ordinary, a life
beyond the confines of their expectations and the weight of
their past. It is to those who have dared to challenge the
status quo, to break free from the shackles of tradition, and to
forge their own paths, no matter how perilous or uncertain.
This is a celebration of their courage, their determination, and
their unwavering belief in the power of their own destinies. To
those who seek adventure, justice, and love in a world where
those things are not always easily found, this is for you.

CONTENTS

Acknowledgments

1   Elena's Grief and Vow

2   Dante's Assignment

3   First Encounter

4   Suspicion and Intrigue

5   Growing Attraction

6   Elena's Investigation Deepens

7   Dante's Moral Struggle

8   A Risky Alliance

9   Betrayal and Revelation

10   Dangerous Games

11   Unmasking the Truth

12   Dante's Confession

13   A Difficult Choice

14   Betrayal and Pursuit

15   Seeking Refuge

16   Family Ties

17   Elena's Dilemma

18   A Dangerous Game of Cat and Mouse

19   A Moment of Truth

20   Consequences of Action

21   The Final Showdown

22   Alliance and Betrayals

23   A Desperate Game

24   Facing the Past

25   A New Beginning

26   Dealing with Loss

27   Rebuilding Lives

28   Unexpected Consequences

29   Reconciliation

30   Acceptance and Forgiveness

31   New Beginnings

32   Building Trust

33   Facing the Future

34   Renewed Hope

35   Love and Redemption

36   Unraveling Conspiracy

37   Bringing Down the Empire

38   Risky Maneuvers

39   Unexpected Allies

40 Triumph and Loss

41 Grief and Mourning

42 Finding Solace

43 Seeking Closer

44 Forgiveness and Acceptance

45 Moving Forward

46 New Opportunities

47 Building a Future

48 Shared Dreams

49 Overcoming Challenges

50 Celebrating Success

51 The Strength of Their Bond

52 Unconditional Support

53 Deepening Intimacy

54 Forgiveness and Understanding

55 A Testament of Love

56 Adjusting to Peace

57 Building Community

58 Personal Growth

59 Shared Passions

60 Celebrating Life

61   Future Plans

62   Shared Visions

63   Long Term Goals

64   Navigated Life's Changes

65   Embracing the Unknown

66   The Impact of Their Actions

67   Leaving a Positive Mark

68   Inspiring Others

69   A Symbol of Hope

70   Enduring Love

71   Reflecting on the Journey

72   Gratitude and Appreciation

73   Peace and Fulfillment

74   A New Beginning

75   A Lasting Bond

ACKNOWLEDGMENTS

First and foremost, my deepest gratitude goes to my fiancé, whose unwavering support and patience throughout the writing process were invaluable. His insightful critiques and endless encouragement helped me navigate the complexities of this story and bring it to life. To my family and friends, thank you for your understanding and for allowing me the space and time to delve into the world of Elena and Dante. Finally, thank you to the readers who embark on this journey with Elena and Dante. Your engagement is the ultimate reward.

1

ELENA'S GRIEF AND VOW

The shattering sound of the gunshot still echoed in Elena's ears, a phantom reverberation that clawed at the edges of her sanity. The opulent ballroom, moments ago alive with the glittering laughter and clinking glasses of the elite, now felt like a tomb. Crimson stained the pristine white carpet, blooming around her father's lifeless body like a macabre flower. His eyes, usually sparkling with an unnerving intensity, were now vacant, glazed over with the finality of death. The scent of expensive perfume and polished wood was overwhelmed by the coppery tang of blood, a scent that would forever be etched into her memory.

She had seen it all. The flash of steel, the muffled thud of the impact, the chilling expression on the assassin's face — a face she couldn't quite grasp, obscured by shadows and the swirling chaos of the aftermath. Her father, the formidable Don Alessandro Rossi, protector of his family and empire, reduced to a broken figure on the floor. The invulnerable had been felled, leaving a gaping hole in her life, a wound so deep it threatened to consume her entirely.

The whispers started immediately, a low hum of fear and speculation that rippled through the assembled guests. People moved like phantoms; their faces etched with a mixture of shock and morbid fascination. The police arrived, their blue uniforms a stark contrast to the decadent surroundings, their presence doing little to alleviate the icy grip of terror that had settled over the Rossi estate.

Elena stood frozen, a statue of grief amidst the maelstrom. Her tailored black dress, once a symbol of elegance, now felt like a suffocating shroud. The weight of her father's absence pressed down on her, a crushing burden that threatened to crush her spirit. This wasn't just the loss of a father; it was the shattering of her world, the destruction of everything she had ever known.

 The anger, however, began to simmer, a slow burn in the icy depths of her despair. It wasn't a raging inferno, not yet. It was a controlled fire, meticulously stoked, waiting for the right moment to erupt. A vow formed in the silent chambers of her heart, a promise whispered on the wind of her grief. She would avenge her father's death. She would hunt down those responsible, dismantle their empire, and make them pay the ultimate price.

 Her father's legacy, a legacy built on power and ruthless efficiency, would not be squandered. She would not let his assassins escape unscathed. The Moretti family, their name synonymous with brutality and influence, were the prime suspects. Their long-standing feud with the Rossis had escalated over the years, culminating in this brutal act of violence. Elena knew the risks. She knew the Morettis were powerful, their reach extending far beyond the opulent facade of their own estates. But fear would not deter her. Grief had forged a steel in her heart, replacing the fragility of her mourning with the unwavering strength of purpose.

The days following her father's funeral were a blur of activity.

She immersed herself in her investigation, meticulously piecing together the fragments of information she had gathered. She delved into her father's private office, a sanctuary that now felt more like a battlefield. Each document, each photograph, each meticulously organized file was a clue, a breadcrumb in a trail leading to her father's killers.

Her father's study was a testament to his meticulous nature. Every inch of space was carefully utilized, filled with leather-bound books, antique maps, and neatly stacked files. She ran her fingers across the cool surface of his mahogany desk, her touch lingering on the faint scent of his pipe tobacco, a familiar fragrance that both comforted and tormented her. She opened drawers, examined documents, her fingers tracing the elegant script of his handwriting, each word a painful reminder of the life that had been abruptly snatched away.

She found a hidden compartment behind a loose panel in his bookshelf – a secret compartment, filled with documents detailing the Moretti family's extensive criminal activities, detailing their network of informants, their illicit dealings, and their brutal methods. She uncovered evidence of arms trafficking, money laundering, and political corruption. The extent of their criminal enterprises was staggering, a vast web of deceit that reached the highest echelons of power.

Elena's resolve solidified. The investigation was no longer just about avenging her father's death; it was about dismantling a corrupt empire that operated in the shadows, preying on the vulnerable and silencing those who dared to oppose them. She was armed with more than just grief; she was armed with knowledge, with evidence, with the burning desire to bring the Morettis to justice. She knew it would be a dangerous path, but she was prepared to walk it alone, if necessary. The weight of her father's legacy was heavy, but it was a weight she willingly bore. His death was not in vain; his memory would fuel her every step.

She began to cultivate informants, drawing on her father's network of trusted allies. She used her father's connections to gather information, playing the part of the grieving daughter, allowing people to underestimate her. But beneath the veneer of grief, a cold, calculating mind was at work. She was ruthless in her pursuit of justice, using her charm and intelligence to manipulate those who crossed her path.

The city, usually a place of vibrant energy and excitement, now felt like a sinister labyrinth. Every shadowed alleyway, every dimly lit bar, every clandestine meeting held a potential threat. But Elena pressed on, her steps measured, her eyes constantly scanning her surroundings. She knew she was being watched, that the Morettis were searching for her, but she was a ghost in their midst, flitting between shadows, unseen but always aware.

The night was her ally. Under the cloak of darkness, she conducted her investigations, the city lights casting long, distorted shadows, transforming familiar streets into a landscape of mystery and danger. She would meet with informants in hidden bars, exchanging coded messages and secretive glances. She would spend hours poring over documents, her eyes burning with intensity, her mind relentlessly piecing together the puzzle of her father's death.

She would visit the cemetery, sitting by her father's grave, whispering her plans and her grief into the silent earth. It was a ritual, a way to connect with him, to ask for his guidance, to remind herself of the reason she was fighting. The scent of lilies and damp soil, the sound of the wind sighing through the cypress trees — these were the sounds of her sorrow, but also the sounds of her determination.

Her grief was a constant companion, a heavy cloak she wore but couldn't fully shed. But it was also her fuel, her impetus, her motivation to fight. She had lost a father, but she would not lose herself in the process of vengeance. She would carve her own path, guided by her grief, fueled by her rage, and driven by an unwavering vow. The Moretti family would pay for what they had done. And Elena Rossi would make sure of it.

2
DANTE'S ASSIGNMENT

The chipped porcelain mug warmed Dante's hands, the lukewarm coffee doing little to soothe the icy knot in his stomach. The dimly lit backroom of the "Serpent's Kiss" bar was his usual refuge, a haven of shadows and hushed conversations where deals were brokered and secrets whispered. Tonight, however, the usual hum of clandestine activity felt amplified, a discordant symphony echoing the turmoil within him.

He stared at the photograph in his hands, its glossy surface reflecting the flickering candlelight. Elena Rossi. The image captured her in a moment of serene beauty, her dark hair cascading around her shoulders, her eyes – the same shade of intense emerald as her father's – radiating an almost unnerving intelligence. Innocence betrayed only by a subtle set to her jaw, a hint of the steel that ran in her veins. The Don's daughter. His target.

The assignment had arrived as a curt message, delivered by a man whose face was as obscured by shadows as his intentions were clear. Eliminate Elena Rossi. It was a simple directive, devoid of emotion or explanation, a chilling testament to the ruthlessness of the Moretti family. Dante had been handpicked for this, his reputation preceding him like a chilling omen. He was the best, the most reliable, the one who left no trace, no witness, no regret. Or so it was said.

But regret, a feeling he had long suppressed, gnawed at him now. This wasn't just another contract; this was different. He had witnessed Elena from afar, a fleeting glimpse during a social gathering at the Rossi estate. A mere shadow of a woman, yet the memory was striking. Her aura, vibrant in the center of that opulent room, starkly contrasted the darkness of the clandestine world he inhabited.

 It was a fleeting glimpse, a memory that had inexplicably imprinted itself on his conscience. A shadow that haunted him, even within the shadows he so readily inhabited. The Morettis were his family, the only family he had ever truly known, and loyalty was a currency that flowed through their veins as fiercely as the blood that coursed within them. He owed them everything; they had rescued him from the gutter, honed his skills, and forged him into the weapon he had become. He had killed before, countless times, but each death had been a cold, calculated act, devoid of personal involvement. This was different.

He thought of the opulent Rossi estate, a monument to wealth and power, a stark contrast to the grimy alleys and shadowed corners that comprised his world. He pictured Elena, bathed in the glow of chandeliers, surrounded by the luxury he would never know. A life of privilege, a stark contradiction to his own existence where shadows were not just metaphorical but literal.

The assignment was a betrayal, not just of his own inner moral code – a code he hadn't realized he possessed – but of the trust implicitly placed in him by the Morettis. It was a violation of something deeper, a sense of right and wrong that he had suppressed, buried deep beneath layers of calculated ruthlessness and years of cold-blooded efficiency.

He ran a hand through his dark hair, the gesture born more from frustration than weariness. The irony wasn't lost on him. He was the best among them – a master of deception, a specter who moved unseen through the city's labyrinthine underbelly. And yet, he found himself paralyzed by a conflict he hadn't anticipated. A conflict that was tearing him apart from the inside out.

He needed time, a luxury rarely afforded to an assassin. He needed to observe Elena, to understand her, to gauge her vulnerabilities and her strengths. Perhaps he could find a way to subtly alter the assignment, perhaps delay it indefinitely. He could subtly misinform his handlers, use carefully crafted lies to buy himself more time. Or perhaps, he would have to face the ultimate betrayal, the one that could sever ties with everything he had ever known.

The clock ticked away, each second a hammer blow against the delicate balance of his carefully constructed life. He knew the risks. The Morettis tolerated no failures, no second-guessing. They punished betrayal swiftly, and brutally. But the thought of killing Elena Rossi, the faint memory of her face, the undeniable recognition of her beauty and power, that felt like an even greater risk.

He thought about the information he had gathered, the whispers he'd picked up from the lower echelons of both the Rossi and Moretti organizations. There were simmering tensions, unresolved conflicts, and hidden agendas. The

Morettis were not monolithic; they were a collection of ambitious individuals, each with their own self-interests. Perhaps, he mused, he could use those tensions to his advantage.

He left the bar, disappearing into the city's shadowy embrace. The night was his canvas, the darkness, his shield. He would move like a phantom, gathering information, observing Elena, playing the long game, a game where the stakes were higher than ever before. He would walk a tightrope between loyalty and betrayal, duty and desire, his own life hanging precariously in the balance.

He knew that every step he took was fraught with danger, that every decision he made could have fatal consequences. But he was a master of his craft, and he would use his skills to navigate this treacherous path, to somehow find a way to reconcile his conflicting loyalties. The shadows of the city offered him both protection and concealment; his life was a tapestry woven in the darkness of his profession.

The following days were a blur of clandestine meetings, coded messages, and shadowy surveillance. Dante moved through the city like a ghost, observing Elena from a distance. He studied her routines, her habits, her vulnerabilities. He learned about her determination, her grief, her unwavering commitment to avenging her father's death. He saw her strength, a stark contrast to the fragility he had initially perceived.

He found himself drawn to her, not in a romantic sense, but in a way that defied explanation. He saw a reflection of himself in her – a fierce determination, a relentless pursuit of justice, a willingness to sacrifice everything for what she believed in. He saw her pain, her anger, her resolve. He understood her need to avenge her father's death, not just for herself, but for the family honor he had violated in the shadows.

The contrast between their worlds was staggering. She moved through a world of opulence and privilege, while he inhabited the darkness. Yet, there was a common thread that bound them, a shared sense of purpose, a commitment to their own paths, however different those paths might be.

Dante's assignment had become far more complex than a simple contract killing. It had transformed into a moral struggle, a battle between his loyalty to the Morettis and his burgeoning respect for the woman he was supposed to eliminate. The shadows that had always been his protection now felt like a suffocating blanket. The choices before him were stark, each one carrying a heavy burden. To complete his mission was to betray himself, and everything he had recently recognized. To refuse was to invite certain death. His only certainty was the weight of responsibility and the intensity of the choice before him. The life of a skilled assassin had never felt so complicated, so fraught with agonizing paradoxes and moral dilemmas. He had become ensnared in a web of deceit and danger, a web that threatened to engulf him entirely. And his next step, his next choice, would determine his fate.

3

FIRST ENCOUNTER

The Grand Ballroom of the Palazzo Rossi shimmered, a breathtaking spectacle of opulence. Chandeliers cast a dazzling light on the polished marble floors, reflecting in the swirling silks and glittering jewels of the assembled guests. The air thrummed with the low hum of conversation, the clinking of champagne flutes, and the strains of a string quartet, a carefully orchestrated symphony designed to mask the tension simmering beneath the surface. This was no ordinary charity gala; it was a carefully constructed stage, a public performance designed to project an image of strength and unity for the Rossi family, a fragile facade barely concealing the deep wounds inflicted by the recent assassination of Don Rossi.

Elena Rossi, a vision in a midnight-blue gown that hugged her figure, moved through the crowd with a quiet grace that belied her inner turmoil. The weight of her father's legacy pressed heavily upon her, a burden she carried with a stoic resolve that masked the grief gnawing at her heart. The carefully applied makeup couldn't completely conceal the shadows beneath her eyes, the exhaustion of sleepless nights spent poring over reports, strategizing, and planning her revenge. The Morettis would pay. That was her unwavering vow, a burning promise etched into her soul.

Tonight, however, the focus was on appearances. Tonight, she would play the part of the grieving daughter, the strong

21

successor, the unwavering pillar of the Rossi family. She would charm, she would smile, she would project an image of unshakeable strength. But beneath the surface, her senses were heightened, her awareness sharpened, her instincts honed. She felt the eyes on her, the whispers, the assessing glances of rivals and allies alike.

Dante, his presence a carefully woven shadow amidst the glittering crowd, observed her from across the room. He had chosen a less conspicuous outfit—a dark suit that blended seamlessly with the shadows cast by the towering columns—but even from afar, Elena's radiance was undeniable. He found himself mesmerized by her. The beauty he had glimpsed before was now intensified, magnified by the proximity, and intensified by her raw emotion which was barely masked. The serene intelligence, the hint of steel beneath her refined facade were even more compelling close up. It was an unnerving, captivating blend of strength and vulnerability. The assignment, the contract that bound him to the Morettis, felt more suffocating, more impossible to fulfill.

The gala was a masked ball. The elaborate masks, handcrafted from Venetian glass, concealed identities, allowing for a veneer of anonymity that belied the very real dangers lurking beneath the surface of the festivities. It was a perfect setting for clandestine meetings, whispered betrayals, and the subtle maneuvering that characterized the underworld. Dante watched as Elena moved through the masked crowd, a queen surrounded by her court, yet alone in her burden of grief and vengeance. He saw the fleeting vulnerability in her eyes, a momentary crack in the carefully constructed façade she presented to the world.

Their first direct encounter was unavoidable, a carefully staged collision orchestrated by a silent hand—perhaps a conspirator from within the Rossi family, or someone more aligned with Dante's clandestine activities. A brief, almost accidental touch of hands as they passed each other in the crowded ballroom, a stolen glance through the eyeholes of their masks. Their gazes locked, a silent acknowledgment of a shared reality that transcended the masks and the artifice.

He felt a shock run through him—a sudden, unexpected surge of awareness that shattered the carefully constructed walls of his emotional reserve. It wasn't just her beauty; it was something more, something deeper, something that resonated with the long-suppressed emotions he had buried deep within. He saw a strength in her eyes that mirrored his own, a hidden resilience that hinted at a capacity for both great love and great vengeance.

Elena, too, felt the jolt. His gaze was intense, probing, yet there was a hint of something else – a flicker of understanding, a shared sense of unspoken danger that resonated with the turmoil within her. The touch of his hand, fleeting as it was, sent a shiver down her spine, an inexplicable connection forged in the midst of the swirling chaos of the masked ball. It was a silent, unspoken recognition of their shared predicament: two players in a deadly game, their lives intertwined by fate and shadowed by betrayal.

Their conversation, when it finally occurred, was a carefully choreographed dance of words, a delicate ballet performed amidst the swirling crowd. They spoke of inconsequential things—the weather, the music, the charity—a carefully constructed camouflage for a deeper, more dangerous current running beneath the surface. The masks hid their expressions, but their eyes revealed everything: the mutual attraction that dared not speak its name, the simmering tension that threatened to explode, the recognition of a shared fate woven into the fabric of their conflicting destinies.

The music swelled, a crescendo of violins that drowned out the softer whispers and muted conversations. Dante caught Elena's gaze amidst the rhythmic beat and saw a reflection of his own conflict in her emerald eyes: a mixture of attraction, uncertainty, and an underlying current of suspicion. He realised that despite her outer strength, she was as vulnerable as he was—perhaps more so because she possessed a naïveté towards the realities of his world.

He saw the potential for this to evolve into something more — an opportunity to escape the crushing weight of his duty, a potential for true connection. But the shadows of his past, the loyalties he had sworn, the brutal reality of his profession clung to him, a suffocating darkness that he couldn't entirely escape. The risk was unimaginable; the reward, potentially equally immense. He had to tread carefully. One wrong step could shatter the illusion, expose their secret connection and expose him to the wrath of the Morettis. The game was far more dangerous than he ever could have anticipated.

As the night wore on, their encounters became more frequent, their conversations more meaningful, although always veiled and indirect. The masked ball was a theater of deception, and they played their parts with a dangerous skill, masking their intentions, disguising their motives, and dancing on the edge of something beautiful and terrifying. The intensity of their initial meeting was a prelude to the much larger game of deception that unfolded throughout the night, a silent battle of wills waged amidst the opulent grandeur of the Palazzo Rossi.

The charity gala was drawing to a close, the final strains of the orchestra fading into silence. The mask of polite society was beginning to crumble, revealing the simmering tension beneath the surface. As Elena prepared to leave, Dante, his heart pounding a frantic rhythm against his ribs, caught her eye again. A fleeting glance, a brief exchange of unspoken words—a silent acknowledgment of the unspoken bond between them, a shared awareness of the precarious dance they were performing on the razor's edge of danger and desire.

The night was ending, but the game had only just begun. The shadows of betrayal were deepening, and their intertwined destinies were hurtling towards a climax they couldn't possibly predict. Elena's vengeance, Dante's loyalty, and their budding attraction—all were about to be tested in the fires of a confrontation that would change their lives forever. The shadows that had protected them both were now closing in, threatening to engulf them entirely in a web of deceit and danger. The city outside held its breath, waiting for the dawn of a new day, a day that promised both unimaginable risk and a potential for a love that defied all odds.

4

SUSPICION AND INTRIGUE

The lingering scent of expensive perfume and spilled champagne clung to the air as Elena stepped out of the Palazzo Rossi, the city's nocturnal pulse throbbing around her. The glittering facade of the gala had vanished, replaced by the shadowy alleyways and dimly lit streets of Venice. The city, ancient and labyrinthine, felt like a character in itself, its secrets whispering in the wind. She clutched her father's antique signet ring, a cold comfort in the icy night. The clues gleaned from the gala were frustratingly fragmented, like pieces of a shattered mirror reflecting a distorted truth. A cryptic note, slipped into her hand by a masked figure, mentioned a hidden meeting place: "The Serpent's Kiss," a name that sent a shiver down her spine. It suggested a clandestine gathering, a secret society perhaps, operating beneath the veneer of Venetian society.

Her investigation had led her to a seemingly innocuous antique shop, its facade masking a network of informants. The shopkeeper, a wizened old woman with eyes that held centuries of unspoken secrets, had confirmed the existence of "The Serpent's Kiss," painting a picture of a shadowy organization involved in illicit activities ranging from art smuggling to political intrigue. The woman, however, remained frustratingly vague about their involvement in her father's assassination. She mentioned a recurring symbol – a serpent entwined around a key – which had been seen on several items linked to the Morettis, subtly, almost invisibly placed, indicating a level of sophistication that suggested a highly organized operation. The shopkeeper suggested she look for the symbol, urging her to "follow the serpent's trail." Elena, however, couldn't shake the feeling that she was missing something crucial. The pieces of the puzzle didn't quite fit, leaving frustrating gaps that hinted at a far larger, more intricate web of deception than she had initially anticipated. The weight of her family's legacy, the burden of revenge, felt heavier than ever, pressing down on her with the suffocating weight of the city's ancient stones.

Meanwhile, Dante watched Elena from a discreet distance, his presence as elusive as the shadows clinging to the canals. He had followed her from the Palazzo, his instincts urging him to protect her, despite the conflicting loyalties that bound him to the Morettis. The contract, the cold, hard reality of his profession, felt heavier than ever as he observed her, his internal conflict escalating. He saw in her a reflection of himself – a similar determination, a comparable capacity for both immense love and devastating rage. His observation of Elena was far more than professional curiosity. He felt a growing unease, a sense of foreboding that went beyond the parameters of his assignment. Her resilience, her quiet strength, captivated him. He was drawn to her vulnerability, hidden beneath the facade of stoic resolve. The fleeting touch of their hands at the gala, the silent exchange of glances through their masks, resonated in his memory with an intensity that unnerved him. The Morettis had not prepared him for this unforeseen complication – the unexpected empathy for his target.

The city itself provided a convenient backdrop for his surveillance, its intricate network of canals and hidden passageways a perfect maze for both pursuit and evasion. He knew every dark corner, every secret alley, and used the city's hidden spaces to keep a safe distance, yet remain within sight of Elena's progress. The labyrinthine streets of Venice became an extension of the intricate web of intrigue he had inadvertently found himself ensnared in. The contract seemed a distant, secondary concern, overshadowed by the growing fascination and increasing concern for Elena. The potential for his loyalty to shatter felt imminent, a dangerous risk he was willing to take, the consequences unforeseen.

As Elena delved deeper into her investigation, Dante found himself torn between his mission and a growing sense of protection towards her. He saw her navigate the dangerous underbelly of Venetian society, her instincts sharper than his own, her intelligence a formidable match for any adversary. He admired her unwavering resolve, but also felt the chilling realization of how easily she could be manipulated, how vulnerable she was despite her outward strength. Her naivete towards the true nature of his world—the world of shadows and betrayal—was both endearing and terrifying.

He had to make a choice, but the decision weighed heavily on him. To betray the Morettis would mean risking his life, perhaps even the lives of those he cared for. But to watch

Elena walk into the lion's den felt equally unbearable. He knew he couldn't stand idly by, a silent observer of her potentially fatal decisions. His loyalty was splintering, a dangerous fault line that threatened to fracture his carefully constructed world.

The Serpent's Kiss proved to be a real entity. It wasn't just a rumour; it was a secret society that had ties to numerous powerful families within Venice, and its influence extended far beyond the confines of the city. Dante, using his network of contacts, learned that the society used a complex system of coded messages and hidden symbols to communicate, adding another layer of complexity to Elena's investigation. Their methods were subtle, their operations clandestine, their power significant. Dante's investigation into The Serpent's Kiss also revealed the society's involvement in various criminal enterprises, ranging from black market arms dealings to manipulating political elections. Their power seemed to stretch into almost every aspect of Venetian society.

One night, following Elena from a clandestine meeting at a secluded palazzo on the Grand Canal, Dante witnessed her encounter with a mysterious figure cloaked in shadows. The brief exchange, hidden from view, was fraught with tension. Dante realized the figure was not an ally, but someone who was attempting to manipulate Elena, feeding her misinformation to steer her towards a dangerous trap. His protective instincts roared to life, overriding the contract. He knew he had to intervene, but doing so would put him in direct conflict with the Morettis, and possibly expose his own true identity to Elena.

As Elena continued to unravel the secrets of her father's death, Dante remained her silent guardian, his presence a subtle counterpoint to the danger that surrounded her. He used his skills and knowledge to subtly guide her, to offer protection without revealing his own true intentions. He watched as she navigated a treacherous path, a constant dance between deception and discovery. He remained torn, caught between the allure of his growing feelings for her and the inescapable obligations of his deadly profession.

The city of Venice, with its canals and hidden passageways, became a stage for a silent battle of wills. Dante's loyalties were stretched to their breaking point, his heart tugged in two directions. Elena, oblivious to his presence, moved ever closer to the truth, while he remained a shadow in the background, his life and hers intricately interwoven in a deadly game of cat and mouse, passion and betrayal. The serpent's trail was leading them both towards an inevitable confrontation, a climax that would shatter their lives and rewrite their destinies in blood and betrayal. The city held its breath, waiting for the storm to break.

5
GROWING ATTRACTION

The scent of salt and brine, mingling with the aroma of roasting chestnuts from a nearby vendor, filled the air as Elena found herself on a secluded rooftop overlooking the Grand Canal. The moon, a silver disc in the inky sky, cast long shadows that danced with the flickering gaslights below. It was here, in this hidden sanctuary, that she first truly saw Dante, not as a shadow, a distant observer, but as a man.

He appeared as silently as the night itself, emerging from the labyrinthine maze of rooftops as if he were a creature of the shadows themselves. He moved with a grace that belied his lethal profession, a fluid movement that suggested both power and control. The contrast between the harsh reality of his life and the romantic setting was stark, yet somehow, it only enhanced the intensity of the moment. Their first real conversation, stripped of the masks and pretense of the gala, was a tentative exploration of unspoken desires and veiled truths. He spoke of his life with a detached honesty, his words carefully chosen, yet revealing a depth of emotion that hinted at a man who had traded his heart for survival. He spoke of the Morettis, not with loyalty, but with a weary resignation, his voice betraying a disillusionment that mirrored her own.

Elena, in turn, shared her grief, her anger, her burning desire for justice. She spoke of her father, not as a political figure, but as the man who had taught her to be brave, to fight for what she believed in. She found herself confiding in him, revealing vulnerabilities she had carefully guarded, and a profound loneliness that echoed in the silence between their words. It was in these shared confidences that the chasm between hunter and hunted began to narrow, replaced by a fragile bridge of shared understanding and mutual attraction.

Their stolen moments were punctuated by the city's nocturnal symphony – the gentle lapping of water against the ancient stones, the distant murmur of conversations, the mournful cry of a lone seagull. The air throbbed with a tension that was both exhilarating and terrifying. Their first kiss was as unexpected as it was inevitable, a collision of lips that ignited a fire neither of them had anticipated. It was a kiss born of shared danger, of mutual understanding, a kiss that transcended the boundaries of their vastly different worlds. It was a silent acknowledgment of a burgeoning attraction that defied logic and reason.

Their clandestine meetings became a ritual, a desperate need for connection in a world that seemed determined to keep them apart. One night, it was a dimly lit café tucked away in a quiet backstreet, the intoxicating aroma of espresso and pastries mingling with the undercurrent of danger. Another time, it was a deserted piazza, the vast expanse of sky above them a witness to their shared intimacy. Each encounter was a risk, a gamble with their lives and their hearts. Yet, the risk seemed worth taking, the pull toward each other too strong to resist. The stolen moments were charged with passion and tenderness. They were fleeting glimpses of something real, something beautiful, amidst the darkness and deception that surrounded them. Their hands brushed accidentally, and lingered a moment longer than necessary. Their gazes locked, unspoken emotions passing between them in a silent language of longing and understanding. Their clandestine meetings became a refuge, a sanctuary where they could shed their masks and be truly themselves.

Elena discovered a hidden depth to Dante, a vulnerability that lay beneath his carefully constructed exterior. She saw the lingering sadness in his eyes, the weariness that etched itself into his features. She discovered a man who, despite his profession, possessed a keen sense of justice and a compassion that was at odds with his chosen path. She saw a man who craved redemption, even if he couldn't articulate it.

Dante, in turn, was captivated by Elena's unwavering strength and determination. He saw her courage, her resilience, and the quiet dignity she maintained in the face of overwhelming loss. He was drawn to her intelligence, her sharp wit, her unwavering spirit. He admired her ability to remain steadfast despite the immense pressure she was under. He saw in her a reflection of his own struggles – the fight for survival, the burden of secrets, the weight of a past that refused to let go.

Their physical attraction was undeniable, a raw, intense energy that crackled between them. Their kisses were passionate and consuming, filled with a desperate need for connection and a thrilling sense of forbidden pleasure. These encounters, however fleeting, became the anchors in their tumultuous lives, moments of solace in a world steeped in betrayal. The passion between them wasn't just a physical connection; it was an emotional bond forged in the crucible of shared danger and mutual understanding.

One moonlit night, perched on the edge of a crumbling ancient bridge overlooking the churning waters of the Grand Canal, they spoke of their futures. Dante spoke of leaving this life behind, of a life that had left him emotionally barren and spiritually desolate. Elena admitted her fears - her fear of failure, of not finding justice for her father. She confided in the hope of building a life where love, not revenge, dominated her life. In this shared vulnerability, their future felt possible. Yet, the shadows that clung to the city, and the intricate web of deception they were both ensnared in, threatened to tear them apart.

As their love deepened, so did the stakes. The Morettis were closing in on Elena, suspecting a leak in their carefully constructed network. Dante's actions had begun to raise questions; his loyalties were stretched thin, threatened by the growing affection for the very person he was contracted to watch. The city of Venice, once a backdrop to their clandestine romance, now felt like a prison, its intricate canals and hidden passageways mirroring the labyrinthine complexity of their predicament. Each stolen moment, each passionate embrace, was a risk, a dangerous dance played on the razor's edge of love and betrayal. The consequences of their defiance loomed large, the potential for heartbreak and devastation casting its long shadow over their fragile bond. The serpent's kiss of passion had already been sealed, but the serpent's bite of betrayal was poised to strike.

6
ELENA'S INVESTIGATION DEEPENS

The palazzo's ancient stones seemed to whisper secrets as Elena navigated the labyrinthine corridors of the Moretti family library. Dust motes danced in the slivers of moonlight filtering through the tall, arched windows, illuminating the towering shelves laden with leather-bound books, some centuries old. The air hung heavy with the scent of aging paper and forgotten memories, a palpable sense of history clinging to the very air she breathed. This was not just a library; it was a mausoleum of secrets, a repository of the Morettis' carefully guarded past.

Dante's warnings echoed in her mind — a warning against delving too deep, a caution against the dangers that lurked within these hallowed halls. But the burning need for justice, the fierce desire to expose her father's murderers, propelled her forward, overriding any flicker of apprehension. She had to find proof, irrefutable evidence that would shatter the Morettis' carefully constructed facade of respectability and bring them to justice.

She ran her fingers along the spines of the books, the titles ancient texts, forgotten histories, dusty tomes of poetry and philosophy – offering little clue to what she sought. She felt a prickle of frustration, a growing sense of despair creeping into her resolve. The scale of the task seemed insurmountable, the labyrinthine complexity of the library mirroring the intricate web of deceit she was trying to unravel. The weight of her father's legacy pressed down on her, a constant reminder of the responsibility she carried.

Suddenly, her fingers brushed against a section of the bookshelf that felt slightly loose. A hidden compartment, cleverly concealed behind a cleverly disguised book, revealed itself. Her heart quickened, a surge of adrenaline coursing through her veins. Inside, nestled amongst yellowed parchment and forgotten letters, was a ledger. Not just any ledger, but a meticulously kept account book, its pages filled with a spidery script detailing a vast network of criminal activities.

The ledger, bound in worn leather, was far older than she had anticipated. Its pages, brittle with age, were filled with a delicate script, an elegant hand that belied the brutal nature of the transactions meticulously recorded within. Each entry was a meticulously documented piece of the puzzle, a fragment of the Morettis' vast criminal enterprise. There were coded entries, references to offshore accounts, details of arms deals, illicit property transactions, and shadowy figures whose names were familiar from whispered conversations and hushed rumors.

Elena carefully pored over the ledger, deciphering the intricate entries, her mind racing to piece together the intricate tapestry of deceit that had ensnared her father. The ledger was a roadmap to the Moretti family's criminal empire, revealing the extent of their influence and the depth of their corruption. It wasn't just about the murder of her father; it was about a far-reaching conspiracy, a web of power and influence that extended far beyond the Venetian shores.

The entries revealed a systematic pattern of intimidation, bribery, and violence, illustrating how the Morettis had manipulated the political landscape and used their wealth and power to suppress any opposition. The names of prominent politicians, influential businessmen, and even members of the clergy appeared alongside coded notations and cryptic references. Elena felt a growing sense of unease, a chilling realization of just how deep the Morettis' tentacles extended. This was not simply a family engaged in organized crime; it was a well-oiled machine of corruption, expertly manipulating the very fabric of society.

As she delved deeper into the ledger, she discovered a pattern – regular payments made to a series of offshore accounts, cryptic entries referencing "Project Nightingale," and a series of coded messages that hinted at a larger, more sinister operation. The more she learned, the more she realized the gravity of the situation and the immense danger she was in. The Morettis were not just powerful; they were ruthless, and their reach was far greater than she could have ever imagined.

The ledger also contained a series of personal notes, seemingly unrelated to the financial transactions, but offering a glimpse into the inner workings of the Moretti family. There were heated arguments documented between family members, power struggles within the family hierarchy, and details of personal vendettas and betrayals. These snippets of information humanized the Morettis, revealing their flaws, vulnerabilities, and the complex dynamics within their dysfunctional family.

She found an entry concerning a secret meeting in a remote Swiss bank, detailing the transfer of a significant amount of money, linked to a series of shell corporations and a mysterious individual identified only as "The Serpent." The entry indicated that this individual played a pivotal role in the Morettis' criminal operations. This was a significant breakthrough – a concrete lead that could unravel the entire conspiracy. Her mind raced, piecing together the fragmented clues, attempting to decipher the meaning behind the cryptic notations.

As she continued her investigation, she discovered a small, almost hidden pocket within the ledger's cover. Inside, nestled amongst a tangle of dried herbs and faded ribbons, was a single photograph. It showed a group of men gathered around a table, their faces partially obscured by shadows. Her father was among them, his expression grave and strained. The others, she instinctively knew, were the men who orchestrated his death.

The discovery solidified her resolve, fueling her determination to uncover the truth. The weight of the evidence was undeniable, a damning indictment of the Morettis' criminal enterprise. The sheer scale of their crimes— the bribery, the intimidation, the violence – sent a chill down her spine. She was now armed with undeniable proof, the key to unlocking the truth and bringing those responsible to justice.

The hours melted away as Elena meticulously copied the ledger's contents, her movements precise and deliberate. Each painstakingly copied entry was a victory, a step closer to justice. The library, once a repository of secrets, was now becoming a battleground in her fight for truth. The old stones seemed to hum with the weight of her purpose, witnessing her unwavering dedication.

By the time the first rays of dawn crept into the library, Elena had completed her transcription. The ledger, a tangible testament to the Morettis' crimes, was now safely tucked away in her bag. Her heart pounded with a mixture of fear and exhilaration. She had the evidence she needed, but the danger was palpable, the risk real. The Morettis were powerful, their reach vast, and retribution would be swift and brutal.

As she made her way out of the palazzo, leaving the ancient library behind, Elena paused for a moment, gazing at the rising sun casting its golden light over the Venetian canals. The city, a place of beauty and intrigue, had become a battleground. But she was prepared. Her resolve was unwavering, her spirit unbroken. She was no longer just a grieving daughter seeking justice; she was a warrior, armed with the truth, ready to face the consequences. The Web of Deceit was vast and complex, but she was ready to unravel it, thread by thread, truth by truth. Her journey was far from over; in fact, it had only just begun.

7

DANTE'S MORAL STRUGGLE

The weight of the ancient palazzo pressed down on Dante like a physical burden, the echoing silence of his apartment a stark contrast to the frantic energy Elena possessed. He'd watched her leave that morning, the dawn painting streaks of gold across her determined face, a stark reflection of the burgeoning light of hope, juxtaposed with the encroaching shadows of the Moretti's wrath. He knew, with a chilling certainty, that her actions had ignited a fuse, and the explosion would be devastating.

He paced the length of his small apartment, the polished floorboards cold beneath his bare feet. The city sounds – the distant rumble of a vaporetto, the murmur of voices from the canal-side cafes – were muffled, swallowed by the turmoil raging within him. The ornate Venetian mask hanging on the wall, a family heirloom, seemed to mock him with its silent judgment. It was a mask of deception, a symbol of the very world he inhabited, a world he was now questioning, perhaps even actively betraying.

Elena's unwavering resolve, her fierce dedication to uncovering the truth, had stirred something deep within him— a conflict that threatened to shatter the carefully constructed walls of his loyalty. He had always known the Morettis were not saints, that their wealth and power were built on a foundation of questionable dealings, even criminal acts. But he'd compartmentalized that knowledge, justifying his allegiance as family obligation, a necessary evil in a world ruled by ruthless ambition.

Elena's presence had irrevocably altered that perspective. Her courage, her vulnerability, her unwavering pursuit of justice – all these had chipped away at the stone wall of his loyalty, revealing cracks of doubt, fissures of conscience. He saw himself reflected in her eyes—a man trapped in a web of deceit, a silent accomplice to the family's crimes. He saw the potential for a different life, a life free from the suffocating weight of their secrets. But the path to that freedom was fraught with peril, a treacherous climb up a precipice of betrayal and potential ruin.

He poured himself a glass of grappa, the fiery liquid burning a path down his throat, offering only a temporary respite from the burning questions that consumed him. He had aided Elena, indirectly at least, by providing her access to the palazzo. He'd warned her, yes, but the warning had been laced with a hesitancy, a reluctance to fully dissuade her. Had he been complicit in her actions, a silent conspirator in her dangerous game?

The thought was a bitter pill to swallow, a truth that gnawed at his conscience. He knew the Morettis' reaction to Elena's discovery would be swift, violent, and merciless. They wouldn't hesitate to eliminate anyone who threatened their empire, anyone who possessed the kind of evidence Elena now held. He pictured his uncle, his face hard and unforgiving, and the fear, cold and sharp, pierced him. He understood the extent of the Morettis' power, their reach, their absolute ruthlessness. They controlled politicians, judges, even the police. Opposing them was akin to declaring war.

And he, by his inaction, had become a participant in that war. He thought of his father, a man of quiet strength, a man who had always instilled in him a strong sense of duty, but also a sense of honor. His father, now deceased, would have likely sided with Elena, albeit with far greater caution. It was the weight of his father's legacy, coupled with the burgeoning respect for Elena, that was causing him to unravel. His father would not have tolerated the Morettis' reign of terror. Would his father approve of his silence? The answer echoed in the silence of his apartment, a thunderous condemnation of his inaction.

The grappa did little to soothe the turmoil within him. He slammed the empty glass on the table, the sharp sound echoing in the stillness of his apartment. He needed to make a decision, a choice that would irrevocably alter the course of his life. Would he remain loyal to the Morettis, the family that had nurtured him, protected him, and given him everything he had? Or would he choose a different path, a path aligned with his newfound conscience, a path that led him to Elena, to the fight for justice, a path that ran the risk of obliterating the life he had always known?

The clock on the wall ticked slowly, each second a hammer blow against his wavering resolve. He considered his options, each carrying the weight of potential consequences. He could remain silent, a silent observer of the unfolding drama, but his silence would be a tacit endorsement of the Morettis' actions. He could warn them, alerting them to Elena's actions, ensuring that she would face swift and brutal retribution. Or, he could warn Elena, putting her in further danger, but potentially saving her life. The lines between right and wrong blurred, the moral compass spinning wildly, losing its direction in the whirlwind of emotions that gripped him. His loyalty to the Moretti family was ingrained, a deep-rooted sense of obligation that had been instilled in him since childhood. But now, a new loyalty, an undeniable and unexpected affection for Elena, threatened to shatter that loyalty.

He imagined Elena, her face pale with fear, yet resolute in her determination. He remembered the way she looked at him, a mixture of suspicion and trust, a silent plea for guidance. He knew that she was in imminent danger, that the Morettis would stop at nothing to silence her, to eliminate the threat she posed. He could no longer stand idly by, a silent observer in the unfolding tragedy. He was part of this, entangled in the web of deceit, and he could no longer remain passive.

His mind raced, calculating risks, assessing probabilities. He knew the Morettis were dangerous, capable of unimaginable acts of violence. He knew that betraying them could lead to his own destruction, his own demise. But the alternative—standing by and watching Elena suffer—was unbearable. He couldn't live with the guilt, the knowledge that he had allowed her to face the consequences alone.

His decision solidified. He would act, not as a Moretti, but as a man guided by his conscience, a man driven by a newfound loyalty that transcended familial ties. He had to protect Elena.

He picked up his phone, his hand trembling, knowing he was crossing a line, embracing a path fraught with danger, a path that would irrevocably change his life forever.

The call he was about to make wasn't a simple warning; it was a declaration of war, a defiance of the power that had shaped his life. It was a step into the unknown, a leap of faith fueled by a burgeoning affection and a fierce desire to stand by the woman who had ignited a revolution in his soul. The weight of the impending consequences pressed down on him, but the weight of his conscience was heavier still. He would protect Elena, even if it meant risking everything. He would face the Morettis, not as a member of their family, but as a protector, a knight errant in the shadows of Venice. His path was chosen, his destiny clear. He knew it was only the beginning of a long and perilous journey.

8

A RISKY ALLIANCE

The cafe buzzed with the midday rush, the clatter of espresso cups and the murmur of conversations a constant, comforting hum. Elena sat across from Dante, her gaze unwavering, a subtle challenge in her eyes. The scent of strong coffee and pastries hung heavy in the air, a stark contrast to the bitter taste of betrayal that lingered between them. She'd chosen this public space, a deliberate tactic to avoid any hint of clandestine meeting. Appearances, after all, were everything in Venice.

"You know," Elena began, her voice low and measured, "the Morettis aren't known for their forgiveness." She stirred her cappuccino, the swirling cream a hypnotic dance mirroring the turmoil in her own mind. Dante watched her, his expression guarded, a carefully constructed mask of indifference. He knew she suspected his involvement, his hesitant warning a clear indication of his conflicted loyalties.

"I warned you," he said, his voice a low rumble, barely audible above the cafe's din. "I tried to dissuade you."

Elena let out a short, sharp laugh, the sound brittle and devoid of humor. "Tried? Dante, you gave me access to the palazzo. You knew exactly what I was looking for." She leaned forward,

46

her eyes piercing his. "Let's not play games. We both know you're in deeper than you let on."

He remained silent, the accusation hanging heavy in the air. He knew she was right. His actions, or rather, his inactions, had been a silent endorsement of the Morettis' crimes. He had played a dangerous game, balancing his loyalty to family against the burgeoning respect he felt for Elena, a respect that bordered on something far more profound.

"What do you want, Elena?" he finally asked, his voice tight with tension. The carefully constructed facade was beginning to crumble.

"I want the truth," she replied, her voice barely a whisper. "And I think you can help me get it." She paused, her eyes studying him, assessing his reactions, searching for any flicker of weakness or deception. "We have a common enemy, Dante. The Morettis."

The statement hung in the air, a bold declaration of a precarious alliance. An alliance born out of necessity, driven by mutual distrust and a shared sense of danger. He knew that trusting her was a risky proposition, a leap of faith into the unknown. But the alternative— facing the Morettis alone — was a fate far worse than any risk she posed.

Their conversations continued in a series of carefully orchestrated encounters: a seemingly chance meeting near the Rialto Bridge, a shared gondola ride down the Grand Canal, a quiet dinner at a bacaro tucked away in a secluded alleyway. Each meeting was a delicate dance of veiled threats and unspoken promises, a delicate negotiation of trust and betrayal. In public, they maintained the facade of casual acquaintances, their interactions innocuous, their true motives hidden beneath a layer of polite conversation and carefully chosen words.

Elena skillfully played on his guilt, subtly highlighting the weight of his inaction, the moral compromise he'd made. She reminded him of his father, of the principles he'd been raised on, skillfully manipulating his sense of honor, his deep-seated sense of justice. She knew he was conflicted, torn between loyalty to family and a growing sense of responsibility towards her, towards the truth. She used his wavering loyalty as a tool, a lever to pry open his carefully constructed defenses.

Dante, in turn, played his own game, revealing bits of information, offering subtle hints, but always keeping the most vital pieces of the puzzle close to his chest. He fed her information, carefully chosen morsels designed to steer her investigation, to subtly guide her towards the truth while protecting himself and his family, as much as possible. He wanted to help her, he genuinely did. But he also needed to protect himself, to safeguard his own future, his own survival. The line between helping and betraying was as thin and treacherous as the canals of Venice.

Their uneasy partnership was a dangerous game of cat and mouse, a delicate balancing act between cooperation and deception. Elena's manipulations were shrewd, calculated, designed to exploit his vulnerabilities, to pry loose the secrets he held so tightly. Dante's countermeasures were subtle, calculated, designed to protect himself while leading Elena just close enough to uncover the truth. He knew that revealing too much would endanger him and his family. Withholding the truth entirely could lead to his conscience being further burdened, and leave Elena vulnerable. He felt the heavy weight of both responsibilities tugging at him.

One evening, as they sat on a secluded bench overlooking the lagoon, the setting sun painting the sky in hues of orange and gold, Elena voiced her suspicions directly. "You're protecting someone, aren't you, Dante? Someone within the Moretti family."

He didn't deny it. He couldn't. The truth was a heavy cloak he wore, a burden he carried with a grim determination. "There are things you don't understand, Elena. Things that are far more complicated than you realize." He didn't elaborate, choosing to leave her with the weight of his enigmatic response.

Elena wasn't easily dissuaded. She pressed him further, pushing the boundaries of their fragile alliance, her persistence fuelled by her determination to uncover the truth. She challenged his allegiances, questioned his motivations, pushing him to reveal more than he was comfortable with. The tension between them crackled in the air, palpable and dangerous, a silent war waged with words and glances.

Their alliance was risky, precarious, built on shifting sands of trust and mistrust. Both held secrets, both harbored hidden agendas. They were partners in a dangerous game, navigating the treacherous waters of deceit and betrayal. Each carefully chosen word, each calculated move, was a risk, a gamble with potentially devastating consequences. The web of deceit wrapped around them, tighter and tighter, threatening to consume them both. The precarious alliance between the two was the only thing that held them from being entirely consumed, and yet it was built on a foundation of sand, likely to come crashing down at any moment.

9

BETRAYAL AND REVELATION

The damp chill of the Venetian night clung to Elena like a shroud. The alley, barely wider than her outstretched arms, reeked of stale fish and something acrid, something vaguely chemical. She'd met Marco here, in this squalid, forgotten corner of the city, a place far removed from the gilded grandeur of the Morettis' palazzo. Marco, her supposed confidante, the man who'd promised unwavering loyalty, the man who'd sworn to help her bring down the Morettis. He'd been her eyes and ears within their intricate web, feeding her information, guiding her investigation. Now, the reek of betrayal was as potent as the stench of the alley.

He'd arrived late, his face shadowed, his usual jovial demeanor replaced by a nervous tremor in his hands. He shifted from foot to foot, his eyes darting around, constantly scanning the darkness. The flickering gaslight cast long, distorted shadows, making his already gaunt face seem even more skeletal.

"They know," he whispered, his voice barely audible above the drip-drip-drip of a leaky pipe. The words hung in the air, heavy with dread.

Elena felt a cold fist clench around her heart. She'd known this

51

was a possibility, a risk inherent in her precarious position. But the knowledge, when it finally arrived, was a blow, sharper and more devastating than she'd anticipated.

"Know what?" she asked, her voice betraying none of the fear that gnawed at her insides. She needed to maintain control, to appear calm and collected, even in the face of this crushing revelation.

Marco wrung his hands, his gaze never leaving hers. "They know about your investigation. About the documents you've been looking for. About everything."

Elena felt a surge of anger, hot and sharp, threatening to consume her. But she suppressed it, forcing herself to remain composed. Anger was a luxury she couldn't afford. She needed clarity, she needed information.

"Who told them?" she asked, her voice dangerously low.

Marco hesitated, his eyes flitting nervously towards the shadowed recesses of the alley. "It...it doesn't matter now," he stammered. "They're already aware. And they're not happy."

"It matters to me," Elena insisted, her voice hardening. "Tell me who betrayed me. Tell me who sold me out."

He swallowed hard, his Adam's apple bobbing in his throat. The silence stretched, a taut, agonizing moment suspended in the suffocating darkness of the alley. Then, with a sigh that seemed to drain the last vestiges of his courage, he confessed.

"It was... Dante," he whispered, the name a barely audible

breath.

The name hit Elena like a physical blow. Dante, the man she'd considered an ally, the man who'd seemed to share her objectives, the man with whom she'd forged a fragile, uneasy alliance. The man who'd helped her navigate the treacherous labyrinth of the Morettis' world. The man she'd begun to trust. The realization hit her with the force of a tidal wave, washing away her carefully constructed plans, leaving her exposed and vulnerable.

She stood there, stunned, the weight of the betrayal pressing down on her, crushing her. She couldn't comprehend it. Dante, with his subtle hints, his carefully chosen words, his veiled promises, all of it a calculated charade.

"No," she breathed, the word barely a whisper. The possibility had never even entered her mind.

"He... he said he needed to protect his family," Marco stammered, trying to justify Dante's actions. "He said you were too reckless, that you were endangering everyone."

Elena felt a bitter laugh rise in her throat. Protection? It was a flimsy excuse, a self-serving justification for his betrayal. But a justification that held a horrifying element of truth. Dante's family was inextricably tied to the Morettis. The web of connections was far more complex than she'd ever realized.

Anger, cold and calculating, replaced the initial shock. This wasn't just a personal betrayal; it was a strategic maneuver, a calculated strike designed to cripple her investigation. The Morettis had anticipated her every move, playing her like a pawn in a deadly game.

She considered Marco's words. Dante's words were laced with concern for her safety, but they seemed to her now like a cruel parody, a deliberate manipulation designed to lull her into a false sense of security.

The betrayal left her feeling exposed and vulnerable. This change in the power dynamic needed a recalibration. Her carefully laid plans were now in tatters, her trust shattered. She was alone, isolated, facing a far more formidable opponent than she'd ever imagined. The Morettis weren't just powerful; they were ruthless and they were unpredictable.

She looked at Marco, his face pale and drawn, his eyes filled with a mixture of fear and remorse. He was a broken man, his usefulness expired, his betrayal complete. He was just as expendable as she was. She knew what she had to do. It was a hard choice; a morally grey area of the situation, but she couldn't allow herself to be weak. She had to survive.

"Thank you, Marco," she said, her voice devoid of any emotion. The words were a dismissal, a death sentence. The blade flashed in the darkness. It was quick, efficient, leaving no trace in the squalid alley where the smell of betrayal and death lingered in the air.

The silence that followed was profound, broken only by the distant sounds of Venice. She wiped the blade clean on her jacket, the act almost ritualistic. Marco's betrayal was a heavy blow, but it wasn't the end. It was a turning point, a stark reminder of the dangers she faced, and the lengths she had to go to in order to survive, to get her revenge.

Elena left the alley, the weight of the betrayal heavy on her shoulders, but her resolve hardened. Dante's treachery had shaken her, but it had also strengthened her. It had provided her with a new strategy. The revelation clarified her understanding of the complexities of her enemies and their far-reaching influence. She now needed a new plan, a more covert one, a way to outwit the Morettis, to expose their crimes, and to exact her revenge. The game had changed, and she was ready to play. She knew that Dante's motives were far more complex than simple betrayal, and that understanding this complexity would be key to dismantling the Morettis' empire.

The next few days were a blur of activity. Elena meticulously tracked Dante's movements, observing his interactions with the Morettis. She discovered his role within the family – it was deeper than she could have imagined, revealing the extent of his complicity and revealing a dark and terrifying truth about his motives. She uncovered subtle clues; coded messages, veiled threats, and unspoken promises that pointed to a far larger conspiracy than she had anticipated.

She delved into the family's history, uncovering old documents, forgotten records, and hushed rumors that whispered of decades-long corruption, deceit, and violence. It became clear that Dante's loyalty wasn't to his family as a whole, but to a specific branch of the family, one deeply embroiled in this vast conspiracy, one whose actions threatened to destabilize the entire city of Venice.

Elena's investigation brought her closer to the truth, but also to profound danger. Every step forward brought her closer to the heart of the conspiracy, closer to the core of the Moretti family's power, making her more of a target for their retribution. She had to tread carefully. Her next move needed to be precise, well-planned, and deadly effective. The web of deceit had ensnared her, but now she would use it to unravel its threads, one by one, turning the Morettis' own machinations against them. The game was far from over. It had, in fact, just begun. The stakes were higher than ever before. The truth, she knew, was closer than she thought. But the cost of uncovering it might be far greater than she was willing to pay.

10
DANGEROUS GAMES

The scent of brine and decay still clung to Elena's clothes, a grim reminder of her brutal encounter with Marco. The betrayal, though expected in some abstract sense, had still left a raw wound. She'd eliminated a loose end, but the larger threat remained: Dante and the Morettis. She needed to understand Dante's motivations, to decipher the intricate tapestry of his allegiances. Was he truly a traitor, or was there more to his actions than met the eye? The possibility that he might be playing a longer game, a more intricate game than her own, sent a shiver down her spine.

She spent the next few days immersed in shadow, observing Dante from afar. She studied his movements, meticulously charting his interactions with the Morettis, the subtle shifts in his demeanor, the fleeting expressions that hinted at a hidden agenda. She noticed the way he lingered a moment longer in conversation with Signora Moretti, the matriarch of the family, a woman whose icy gaze could freeze hellfire. She saw the almost imperceptible nod he exchanged with Lorenzo, Signora Moretti's volatile and unpredictable son. These subtle exchanges spoke volumes, revealing a network of loyalties and betrayals far more complex than she had initially imagined.

Her research into the Moretti family history proved equally illuminating, unearthing a trove of long-buried secrets. Dusty ledgers revealed a history of illicit dealings, shady partnerships, and blatant disregard for the law. Old letters, their ink faded but their message still potent, spoke of political corruption, financial skullduggery, and even violence. The more she learned, the more she realized the scope of the Morettis' crimes extended far beyond Venice itself, reaching into the highest echelons of power throughout Italy. Dante was not simply a pawn; he was a player in a much larger, more dangerous game.

A clandestine meeting, arranged through a series of coded messages, was their next encounter. The location: an abandoned warehouse on the outskirts of Venice, a place where shadows danced and secrets whispered. The air hung thick with the smell of dust and decay, a fitting backdrop for their treacherous game.

Dante arrived promptly, his face obscured by the shadows, his usual charm replaced by a chilling intensity. He moved with a feline grace, his eyes constantly scanning his surroundings, a silent testament to the danger that permeated their clandestine meeting.

"You've been busy," he stated, his voice a low murmur that barely carried above the gnawing silence.

"As have you," Elena countered, her voice equally low, betraying none of the turmoil that raged within her. The air crackled with unspoken accusations, with the weight of their mutual betrayal. They circled each other, two predators in a deadly dance.

"Marco..." Dante began, the name a mere breath, a single syllable heavy with implication.

Elena met his gaze, her expression unreadable. "He was expendable." The statement hung in the air, a declaration of brutal pragmatism.

Dante nodded, a slow, deliberate movement. "He knew too much." His gaze dropped for a brief moment, and Elena could almost see the wheels turning in his mind.

The conversation that followed was a masterclass in deception, a carefully choreographed ballet of lies and half truths. They probed each other's motives, testing the boundaries of their fragile alliance, the precarious balance between love and revenge. Elena played the role of the wronged woman, skillfully manipulating Dante's emotions, using his guilt to extract information. Dante, in turn, played the part of the concerned ally, skillfully deflecting her suspicions while subtly feeding her misleading information.

The meeting was a tense game of cat and mouse, each carefully assessing the other's strengths and weaknesses. Elena learned that Dante's loyalty was not to the entire Moretti family, but to a specific faction – a clandestine group within the family, deeply involved in the most illicit of their activities. This faction, she discovered, was responsible for a series of clandestine operations that threatened to destabilize not just Venice, but Italy as a whole. Their power extended far beyond the bounds of the Moretti family's formal influence, reaching into the highest levels of government and industry.

As they spoke, the truth unfurled before Elena like a venomous serpent. Dante was not a traitor in the traditional sense; he was playing a far more complex game, one designed to undermine the Moretti family from within. His betrayal of Elena, therefore, was not an act of disloyalty, but rather a calculated move in a far grander scheme. He needed her to expose the worst of the Morettis' crimes, to bring down the faction he sought to destroy. His concern for her safety, his veiled warnings, had all been part of this intricate plan.

The implications were breathtaking. She'd been used, manipulated, yet at the same time, she was precisely where she needed to be. She held a powerful weapon—the knowledge of the Morettis' darkest secrets, the evidence to bring down their empire—and Dante's information, however tainted, strengthened her hand.

"We have a common enemy, Elena," Dante said, his voice softer now, almost a caress. "A far greater enemy than you realize. And we need to work together to defeat them."

Elena stared at him, her heart pounding. This dangerous game they played extended beyond personal grudges; it was a fight for the soul of Venice, a battle for survival against a force far more sinister than the Morettis themselves. The line between love and revenge blurred, replaced by a chilling sense of shared purpose. The game had changed, once again. She would use Dante's knowledge, his skills, his willingness to work from the inside to bring down the entire Moretti organization, starting with the clandestine faction. Their alliance, fragile as it was, was the only hope she had. And she intended to use it to the fullest extent.

The warehouse remained silent, the only sound the whisper of the wind through broken windows. The smell of decay lingered, a potent reminder of the dangers they faced, the risks they were both willing to take. As Elena left the warehouse, leaving Dante shrouded in the shadows, she knew this was just the beginning of their dangerous dance. The game was far from over.

11
UNMASKING THE TRUTH

The weight of the clandestine meeting with Dante pressed heavily on Elena. The revelation of his complex motivations, his intricate game within the Moretti family, had shifted the landscape of her own carefully constructed plans. She had expected betrayal, but not this... this calculated manipulation, this dance of shadows and half-truths that left her breathless and unsettled. Yet, a strange sort of understanding had bloomed between them, a fragile alliance born from shared necessity, even if rooted in mutual distrust.

Leaving the abandoned warehouse, Elena felt a chilling sense of purpose. The fight against the Morettis was no longer a personal vendetta; it was a battle for the soul of Venice, a war against a shadowy force that threatened to consume the city, and perhaps Italy itself. The weight of this realization settled upon her shoulders, adding to the already heavy burden of grief and revenge.

Her immediate priority, however, was to process the shock of a different kind, a revelation that had nothing to do with Dante or the Morettis, but everything to do with her father, her past, and her very identity.

Back in her small, discreet apartment, overlooking a quiet

canal, Elena found herself unable to rest. The events of the night, the implications of her conversation with Dante, gnawed at her. She paced restlessly, the scent of brine still clinging to her coat, a ghostly reminder of Marco's demise. A sudden thought struck her. A hidden compartment in her father's study, a secret her father had always fiercely guarded. A compartment she had never bothered to investigate before, content to live in the shadow of his enigmatic persona.

With a renewed sense of urgency, Elena made her way to her father's old house, a grand, yet aging structure tucked away on a less prominent canal. The house itself was a testament to a bygone era, its opulent furnishings and antique décor betraying its aristocratic past. It was a place heavy with memories, memories both cherished and painful. Elena had avoided it since her father's death, unwilling to confront the ghosts that lingered within its walls. But now, driven by a desperate need for answers, she pushed open the heavy oak door and entered.

The house was eerily silent, the only sounds her own footsteps echoing on the polished marble floors. She made her way through the dimly lit halls, the silence broken only by the occasional creak of the old house settling into its age. She found the study, her father's sanctuary, a room filled with the scent of old leather and pipe tobacco. It was a room that held countless secrets, secrets he had guarded meticulously until his death.

Elena remembered the study from her childhood. The towering bookshelves, the heavy mahogany desk, the faint smell of old parchment and ink. Now, suffused with the somber silence of his absence, the room felt as if a heart had been ripped from its center.

Her eyes fell on the imposing desk, its surface covered in a layer of dust. She ran her hand over the worn wood, the years of her father's work leaving their marks, tangible reminders of his dedication, his passion, and perhaps, his secrets. Behind the desk, nestled in a shadowed alcove, she remembered a small, almost unnoticeable button. The button, hidden beneath a layer of dust and cobwebs, remained as obscure as her father's character.

With trembling hands, she pressed the button. A soft click echoed in the quiet room, and a section of the wall swung open, revealing a hidden compartment. Her breath caught in her throat. This was her father's most guarded secret. Inside, she found a collection of documents, letters, and photographs—a trove of information that painted a picture of her father far different than she had ever known.

She began to read, the words blurring before her eyes as the full extent of the revelation struck her. The documents revealed a dark, clandestine life, a network of dealings that extended far beyond the respectable façade she had always assumed. He was not the man she thought he was. He had been involved in a complex web of political intrigue, and the implication of his involvement in a significant, potentially treasonous, act shocked her.

Among the documents, a letter dated several years before his death caught her eye. It was addressed to her father from a man known only as "Silas." The letter referred to a "transaction," a "dangerous game," and a "debt that must be repaid." The details were cryptic, veiled in coded language, but the overall tone suggested a highly illicit undertaking, one that had apparently gone terribly wrong. This letter suggested her father's death was no accident. He had been silenced.

Another document, a ledger of accounts, contained meticulously recorded transactions, all of which could not be explained by her father's legitimate businesses. It implied a massive wealth accumulated through covert means and the details made it apparent that these activities were far more dangerous than she could have ever imagined. These were the tools of a shadowy organization, one that operated in the dark, far removed from the respectable world her father had always presented to her.

As Elena pieced together the fragments of her father's secret life, a chilling realization dawned upon her. His death was not a random event; it was a calculated act, a silencing of a potentially troublesome witness. The implications of this discovery were staggering. It provided a new perspective on the events that had led to his death, and suddenly, the Morettis' involvement seemed like much more than mere coincidence. It raised questions about Dante's involvement too. Had he known about her father's true life? Had he been involved?

The revelation of her father's secret life, the discovery of his hidden compartment, had turned her world upside down. The grief that had been a dull ache in her heart intensified; now, it was a searing, agonizing pain, coupled with the stunning weight of betrayal, the realization that everything she had thought she knew about her father was a lie. This newfound knowledge about her father's past didn't only shatter her image of him, but also cast a new, more ominous shadow on the events that led to his death, creating a ripple effect that implicated not only the Morettis but potentially Dante himself.

The night stretched before her, long and filled with unsettling revelations. The line between truth and deception blurred, further complicated by her clandestine alliance with Dante, a man who had manipulated and betrayed her yet had also provided her with the information that had brought her to this discovery. She was left with a torrent of questions, unanswered mysteries, and a renewed sense of purpose—a purpose that was no longer solely focused on revenge, but on uncovering the truth, no matter how dangerous it might be. The game, she realized, was far more intricate, far more deadly, than she had ever imagined.

12
DANTE'S CONFESSION

The weight of her father's betrayal hung heavy in the air, a suffocating blanket woven from lies and deceit. Elena felt a profound sense of loss, a chasm opening up beneath her feet, threatening to swallow her whole. Sleep eluded her; the documents, the letters, the ledger, played on repeat in her mind, each detail a fresh wound. The dawn arrived, cold and grey, mirroring the turmoil within her.

She needed time, space to process the avalanche of information, to sift through the wreckage of her past and forge a new path forward. The thought of facing Dante, of confronting him with her newfound knowledge, felt both terrifying and necessary. He had been a catalyst, a tool in her quest for vengeance, but his motivations remained shrouded in mystery. His confession, she knew, would be the key to unlocking the entire puzzle.

She chose a secluded park, a hidden oasis tucked away from the bustling streets of Venice. The ancient cypress trees, their branches gnarled and twisted like ancient secrets, provided a fitting backdrop for their meeting. Dante arrived promptly, his usual air of detached composure slightly ruffled, a hint of vulnerability peeking through his carefully constructed façade.

He didn't speak, simply met her gaze, his eyes reflecting the same turbulent emotions that churned within her.

The silence stretched, thick and heavy, broken only by the chirping of unseen birds and the gentle lapping of water against the canal wall. Elena didn't know where to begin, the enormity of her discovery making it difficult to articulate her thoughts. She started with the letter from Silas, her voice trembling slightly as she recounted the cryptic details.

Dante listened patiently, his expression unreadable. He remained silent for a long moment, his eyes fixed on her, as if studying her reaction, gauging her emotional state. When he finally spoke, his voice was low, a husky whisper that cut through the morning stillness.

"Silas," he murmured, the name a curse on his lips. "He was… a complication. A loose end that needed to be dealt with." He paused, his gaze drifting to the ancient trees. "Your father was… involved in something far bigger than he ever let on."

Elena's heart hammered against her ribs. "Involved in what?" she demanded, her voice edged with desperation. "What did my father do?"

Dante took a deep breath, his shoulders slumping slightly. He revealed the truth, a confession so unexpected, so emotionally charged, it left Elena breathless. He began to explain the workings of the organization, its reach far beyond the Morettis, its tentacles wrapped around the heart of Venetian society, and perhaps even Italy's government. His words were carefully chosen, each syllable laden with years of accumulated secrets, of guilt, of betrayal.

He confessed that he was not who he appeared to be. He was
not merely a Moretti operative. He was an undercover agent,
working for a clandestine organization that had been tracking
the Morettis for years. His role was to infiltrate the family, to
gather intelligence, to expose their nefarious dealings. He had
been close to Elena, not just to manipulate her, though that
had been part of his plan, but to gain her trust, her insight into
the family.

"Your father," Dante continued, his voice thick with emotion,
"was a crucial player. He had been funding the Morettis,
unknowingly providing them with a significant portion of their
wealth, but not out of loyalty. He had been working with Silas,
providing them with certain crucial documents – essentially
blackmailing them – while providing funds from them to
support his own covert operation, a hidden operation
intended to eventually destroy their power within the state."

Elena was stunned into silence. The image of her father, the
man she had loved and respected, shattered into a million
pieces. She had never suspected such a level of deceit, such a
web of complex conspiracies. Her entire world had been a
carefully constructed lie. Dante's confession was a double
edged sword, cutting through the illusion she had carefully
maintained, tearing away the fabric of her reality.

"My father... he was a double agent?" she whispered, the
words barely audible above the rustling leaves.

"In a way," Dante replied, his voice heavy with unspoken grief.
"He was caught in a dangerous game, a game he didn't fully
understand. He was a pawn, manipulated by forces far larger

than himself." His eyes met hers, a flicker of genuine remorse crossing his features. "I never intended for him to get hurt."

Elena struggled to reconcile these conflicting images of her father, the respected businessman juxtaposed with this shadowy figure, operating in the underbelly of Venetian society. The revelation brought a new wave of grief and confusion. She was no longer just seeking revenge for her father's death; she was now grappling with the legacy of his secret life.

Dante's confession, despite its painful revelations, provided her with a new understanding of the situation. It broadened the scope of her quest, shifting the focus from simple revenge to something larger, a mission to expose a vast network of corruption, a conspiracy that reached far beyond the Moretti family. It also gave her a more nuanced perspective on Dante's actions, softening the edge of her distrust, yet adding a complicated layer of complexity to their relationship.

"But why me?" Elena asked, her voice barely a whisper. "Why did you choose to involve me?"

Dante's response was hesitant. "Because you were the perfect pawn," he confessed, the words harsh but truthful. "The daughter of a man who held the key to exposing the Morettis. I needed someone who could infiltrate the family, someone who wouldn't be suspected." He paused, his gaze dropping to the ground. "But it went beyond that. You're... more than just a tool. You possess a strength, a resilience, that surprised me."

His confession laid bare his motives, his manipulation, and, surprisingly, a grudging respect. The revelation of his true identity shifted their relationship from a simple alliance of convenience to something more profound, a twisted bond forged in the crucible of shared secrets and mutual mistrust. Yet, beneath the layers of deception and manipulation, something else was evident—a spark of genuine connection, a nascent respect for her intelligence and tenacity, an unexpected intimacy born from their shared exposure to danger and deceit.

He spoke about the risks, the dangers that lay ahead, the powerful enemies they would face. He revealed more about the organization he worked for, the resources at his disposal, the intricate web of connections that stretched across the globe. He spoke of the evidence, documents and accounts proving the Morettis' connection to other high-profile players, of potential threats to national security. He spoke of the plan to bring them down. Elena listened, her heart racing, her mind reeling from the weight of the revelations.

As the sun rose higher in the sky, casting long shadows across the park, Dante's confession concluded. The raw honesty of his words, the vulnerability that crept into his voice, surprised her. He was not just a shadowy figure; he was a complex, flawed man, driven by a sense of justice, haunted by his past actions. Their meeting was a turning point in their relationship, marking a shift from mutual suspicion to a fragile, uneasy alliance. The battle against the Morettis was no longer a solitary quest for revenge; it was a collaborative mission, a fight against a system far larger and more dangerous than they had ever imagined. The stakes had been raised immeasurably, the lines blurred between enemy and ally, between right and wrong. The game was far from over. In fact, it had just begun. The path ahead was fraught with peril, but now, walking it, she was not alone. She had an unexpected ally in the man she had previously viewed as her adversary, a man who, despite his manipulation and deceit, had also helped her uncover the terrible truth about her own past. This realization was both terrifying and liberating. The fight for justice, for uncovering the truth about her father's death and the conspiracy that spanned generations, would require every ounce of her strength, her intelligence, and the uneasy partnership she had unwittingly forged with the enigmatic Dante. The weight of the world, and the burden of her family's secret history, now fell upon her shoulders, a task both daunting and strangely exhilarating. The future remained unwritten, a blank canvas of possibilities—and potential betrayals.

13
A DIFFICULT CHOICE

The quiet room pressed in on Elena, the silence amplifying the turmoil within her. Sunlight, weak and hesitant, filtered through the Venetian blinds, casting long, wavering shadows across the polished wooden floor. Dust motes danced in the golden rays, a silent ballet to the drama unfolding within her. She sat at the antique writing desk, the worn leather cool beneath her fingertips, the weight of her father's legacy pressing down on her like a physical burden. The documents, the evidence of his double life, lay scattered before her, a testament to a betrayal that ran deeper than she could have ever imagined. And Dante... Dante, the man who had exposed the truth, the man she was both drawn to and deeply suspicious of, was the linchpin of her agonizing decision.

Revenge. The word echoed in her mind, a bitter taste on her tongue. For years, it had been her driving force, the sole purpose that had given meaning to her existence. The murder of her father, the systematic dismantling of her family's business, the years of manipulation and deceit—all of it fueled a burning desire for retribution. She had sought justice, and in Dante, she had found an unexpected ally, a catalyst for uncovering the truth. But now, the truth had revealed a far more complex reality, a tapestry woven with shades of grey, leaving her struggling to decipher right from wrong.

The love for Dante, a forbidden bloom nurtured in the shadow of betrayal and deceit, had taken root unexpectedly. It was a dangerous love, born of shared secrets and mutual vulnerability, a fragile seedling planted in the fertile ground of their shared mission. His confession had stripped away the layers of his carefully constructed persona, revealing a man haunted by his past, driven by a conflicted sense of justice, and undeniably drawn to her. His admission of manipulation stung, but his vulnerability softened the blow. He was not just her ally; he was, in a twisted way, her confidante, the only person who understood the depths of her pain.

But could she trust him? Could she reconcile the man she loved with the man who had used her as a pawn in his own game? His intentions remained shrouded in ambiguity, a mixture of genuine compassion and calculated strategy. The line between his personal feelings and his professional duties remained blurred, making it impossible to definitively assess his motives. Was his affection real, or merely another tool in his arsenal? The question haunted her, a viper coiled in her heart.

She picked up one of the documents, a meticulously detailed financial ledger that revealed her father's clandestine dealings. The numbers danced before her eyes, a silent chronicle of his duplicity. She traced the elegant script with her finger, her mind racing, trying to make sense of the intricate web of transactions. Each entry was a fresh wound, a reminder of the shattered image of her father. The man she had idealized, the man she had lost, was revealed to be a puppet in a much larger game, a game that had tragically cost him his life.

Her hand trembled as she reached for a photograph, a faded image of her father, smiling, his arm around her. The memory of his warm embrace, his comforting presence, clashed violently with the image of the man revealed in the documents. She closed her eyes, allowing the wave of grief to wash over her, allowing herself to mourn the loss of the father she had known, the father she had loved unconditionally. But the grief was mixed with anger, a burning resentment towards the forces that had manipulated him, that had used him as a tool, and ultimately destroyed him.

The conflict gnawed at her. Revenge, or love? Justice, or forgiveness? She was caught in a moral labyrinth, her heart torn between two irreconcilable desires. The desire for vengeance, a primal urge to punish those responsible for her father's death, clashed with the burgeoning feelings for Dante, a man who, despite his questionable actions, had given her a path to justice, had provided her with the tools to expose the truth.

She imagined confronting the Morettis, bringing them to justice, inflicting the pain they had inflicted on her family. The satisfaction of revenge, the vindication she craved, was palpable, yet tinged with a bitter aftertaste. Would it truly bring her peace? Would it fill the void left by her father's death? She doubted it.

Then she thought of Dante, of his vulnerability, his haunted eyes, his undeniable attraction to her. She recalled his tender moments, the unexpected gestures of compassion that peeked through the façade of the seasoned operative. She envisioned a future with him, a future where they could work together, exposing the truth, bringing down the corrupt, while forging a relationship based on mutual respect and love. But was that future possible? Could she ever fully trust a man who had deliberately used her?

The weight of the decision felt crushing, the tension in the room becoming almost unbearable. She stood up, pacing the length of the room, the sunlight catching the polished wood, highlighting the dust motes in a relentless dance. Each step felt heavy, each breath labored. She was torn between two paths, two destinies, and the wrong choice could have devastating consequences. The repercussions extended beyond herself, touching the lives of others, influencing the fate of a nation.

She knew that choosing revenge meant potentially sacrificing her relationship with Dante. It meant embracing a path of isolation, a path fueled by anger and bitterness. It meant pursuing a solitary war, fighting alone against a formidable enemy. And she knew that choosing Dante, choosing love, meant potentially compromising her quest for justice, accepting a certain level of moral ambiguity. It meant potentially trusting a man who had manipulated her, a man whose ultimate loyalties remained unclear. It meant a future shrouded in uncertainty, a future that could just as easily lead to heartbreak as to happiness.

The decision was not merely a personal one; it had far reaching consequences. It would shape her future, and the future of many others. The weight of this realization settled heavily upon her shoulders. The silence in the room deepened, the only sound the frantic beating of her heart, a drumbeat echoing the internal battle raging within her soul. The sun, sinking towards the horizon, cast long shadows across the room, a visual metaphor for the choices she was forced to make, choices that would define her fate and the future she would forge from the ruins of her past. The answer, she knew, lay not in a simple choice, but in a painstaking process of reckoning, a careful examination of her heart and her mind, a journey of self-discovery that would shape not just her present, but her future. And with every passing moment, the urgency of her decision intensified. The clock was ticking, and the stakes were higher than ever before.

14
BETRAYAL AND PURSUIT

The weight of her decision remained, a physical presence in the room, pressing down on her like a suffocating blanket. She hadn't moved, hadn't breathed, since the sun began its descent. The fading light painted the room in hues of orange and purple, mirroring the chaotic blend of emotions within her. Suddenly, a sharp, insistent ringing tore through the silence, jolting her from her reverie. It was her phone. A number she didn't recognize flashed on the screen.

Hesitantly, she answered. A gruff voice, laced with menace, filled her ear. "Signora Elena Rossi," it hissed, the words dripping with a chilling familiarity. "We know about your little... alliance with Dante Moretti."

The blood ran cold in her veins. The Morettis. They knew. Her carefully constructed plan, the fragile alliance she had forged with Dante, was exposed. The voice continued, its tone shifting from menace to a cold, calculating precision. "He's betrayed us, betrayed the family. And you, Signora Rossi, are collateral damage."

The line went dead. Elena's breath hitched in her throat. The pursuit had begun. She grabbed her coat, her movements swift and decisive, a stark contrast to the agonizing indecision that had plagued her moments before. She knew she couldn't stay. The Morettis were ruthless, their reach extensive, their methods brutal. They would stop at nothing to eliminate anyone who threatened their power, and now she was squarely in their sights.

She slipped out of her apartment, the city's twilight embracing her like a shroud. The streets, usually teeming with life, felt eerily quiet, the sounds of the evening muffled by a sudden, overwhelming sense of dread. The air crackled with an unspoken tension, a palpable sense of danger that clung to her like a second skin.

 She hailed a cab, her heart pounding a frantic rhythm against her ribs. As she settled into the backseat, she glanced at the rearview mirror. A black sedan, sleek and ominous, was following her, its presence a silent, menacing shadow. The pursuit had begun in earnest.

The chase unfolded like a scene from a fever dream. The cab weaved through the city's labyrinthine streets, a frantic dance between pursuer and pursued. The city, once a source of comfort, now felt like a cage, its familiar landmarks morphing into obstacles in a desperate game of cat and mouse. The black sedan was relentless, its driver skilled and determined, navigating the crowded streets with unsettling ease. Elena felt the adrenaline surge through her veins, sharpening her senses, making every nerve ending scream with awareness.

She caught glimpses of the occupants of the sedan; shadowy figures, their faces obscured by darkness, but their intent crystal clear. They were professional killers, their ruthlessness palpable, their focus unwavering. Each corner they turned, each traffic jam they navigated, felt like a gamble, a roll of the dice against a certain death.

The cab driver, seemingly oblivious to the danger, cursed under his breath at the slow traffic, unaware of the deadly game unfolding around him. Elena's gaze darted between the rearview mirror and the window, her mind racing, trying to anticipate their next move. She had to think fast, had to find a way to escape.

Her knowledge of the city's hidden alleys and backstreets became her lifeline. She directed the driver, her voice sharp and urgent, guiding him through a maze of narrow roads, twisting and turning, hoping to lose her pursuers in the city's chaotic embrace. The chase became a blur of flashing lights, screeching tires, and the relentless pursuit of a shadow.

Every intersection was a battle, every red light a heart stopping moment of vulnerability. The black sedan remained steadfast, a constant, menacing presence in her rearview mirror. The city's sounds – the blare of car horns, the chattering of pedestrians, the distant sirens – all melded into a terrifying symphony of pursuit.

Finally, after what felt like an eternity, she spotted an opening, a secluded alleyway, hidden between two towering buildings. She instructed the driver to turn, his eyes wide with a mixture of fear and bewilderment as he expertly maneuvered the cab into the narrow passage.

The sedan followed closely, its headlights cutting through the darkness, illuminating the damp brick walls. Elena knew this was a gamble, but it was her only chance. The alleyway was narrow, barely wide enough for the cab to pass, forcing the sedan to slow down, making it more vulnerable.

As the sedan squeezed through, Elena saw her opportunity. She yelled at the driver, urging him to speed up, to leave the pursuers behind. The cab accelerated, its tires screaming in protest as it navigated the tight turns. For a fleeting moment, she saw the faces of her pursuers in the rearview mirror, their rage palpable, their expressions twisted in frustration.

They were losing them.

The cab emerged from the alleyway onto a wider street, the black sedan still in pursuit but visibly struggling to keep up. Elena breathed a sigh of relief, a mixture of exhaustion and exhilaration washing over her. The feeling was fleeting; the danger was far from over, but for now, she had escaped. She had evaded her pursuers, at least for the time being. But she knew the Morettis wouldn't give up easily. The pursuit was far from over; it was merely a temporary reprieve in a deadly game that had only just begun.

The city lights blurred around her as she focused on her escape, the tension in her body barely easing. She had survived the immediate danger, but the shadow of the Morettis loomed large, a constant threat hanging over her. She needed to find a safe place, a place where she could regroup, reassess her strategy, and plan her next move. Her next move against the Morettis, and perhaps, against Dante himself. The betrayal had shattered her carefully constructed plan, turning her world upside down, forcing her to re evaluate everything she thought she knew. And as the city lights stretched before her, she knew that the pursuit wasn't just a physical one; it was a pursuit of truth, a pursuit of justice, and a pursuit of her own survival. The game was far from over. The night was still young, and the city held many secrets yet to be uncovered. But one thing was certain: she would not go down without a fight.

15
SEEKING REFUGE

The cab finally deposited Elena at the edge of a dense, unfamiliar forest. The city's clamor faded behind her, replaced by the hushed whispers of the wind rustling through the trees. It was a stark contrast to the cacophony of the chase, a welcome silence that both calmed and unnerved her. She paid the driver, her hand trembling slightly as she fumbled for the money, her eyes never leaving the dark line of trees that swallowed the last vestiges of the city lights. She watched the cab disappear, a small, receding beacon of civilization in the encroaching darkness.

Dante was waiting. He emerged from the shadows, his silhouette barely visible against the backdrop of the trees, a phantom in the deepening twilight. He looked haggard, his usual confident demeanor replaced by a grim determination. The events of the evening hadn't spared him; the weight of his betrayal, the threat looming over them, was etched upon his face.

"They know," Elena whispered, her voice barely audible above the rustling leaves. The words hung in the air, unspoken accusations and shared anxieties.

Dante nodded, his expression grim. "They know everything."

He led her deeper into the forest, along a barely discernible path, his knowledge of this secluded place evident in the surefootedness of his steps. The air was thick with the scent of pine and damp earth, a fragrance that was both comforting and unsettling. The silence was profound, broken only by the occasional snap of a twig under their feet, a sound that echoed disproportionately in the stillness.

The cabin came into view, a small, rustic structure nestled amongst the trees, almost camouflaged by the shadows. It was a refuge, a haven from the storm, yet its isolation only amplified their vulnerability. It stood in silent testimony to their precarious situation, a fragile barrier against the relentless pursuit of the Morettis.

Inside, the cabin was sparsely furnished, simple yet functional. A crackling fire in the hearth cast dancing shadows on the rough-hewn walls, offering a fragile warmth against the encroaching chill of the night. The air was thick with the scent of woodsmoke and pine, a stark contrast to the sterile, city air they had left behind.

Elena collapsed onto a rough-hewn chair, the exhaustion finally catching up to her. The adrenaline that had fueled her escape ebbed away, leaving behind a profound sense of weariness. The events of the evening replayed in her mind, a relentless loop of flashing lights, screeching tires, and the chilling faces of her pursuers. The fear was still palpable, a tangible presence in the quiet cabin.

Dante moved silently, preparing a meager meal – some bread, cheese, and a bottle of wine. He worked with an almost ritualistic grace, his movements precise and economical, a stark contrast to the turmoil within him. He handed her a steaming mug of herbal tea. The warmth was soothing, a balm to her frayed nerves.

As they ate, a fragile silence settled between them. The weight of their situation hung heavy in the air, an unspoken tension that transcended their words. The betrayal, the pursuit, the uncertainty of the future – it all pressed down on them, an invisible weight that threatened to crush them.

"I didn't mean for this to happen," Dante said finally, his voice hoarse, his words laced with regret. He looked at her, his eyes filled with a mixture of guilt and desperation. "I never intended to betray you."

Elena looked at him, her gaze searching, questioning. She saw the sincerity in his eyes, the genuine remorse in his voice. But trust was a fragile commodity, and hers had been shattered.

"Then why?" she asked, her voice soft but firm. The question hung between them, heavy with unspoken accusations and unanswered questions.

"The Morettis... they had leverage," Dante explained, his voice barely above a whisper. "They threatened my family. I had no choice."

He revealed the details of the blackmail, the threats, the impossible position he had been in. He spoke of the desperation, the fear for his family's safety, the agonizing choices he had been forced to make. His words were a confession, a plea for understanding.

Elena listened, her heart a battlefield of conflicting emotions. Anger, betrayal, fear, and a flicker of sympathy warred within her. She had always known Dante was capable of ruthlessness, but the extent of his desperation surprised her. It was a stark revelation, one that complicated her feelings for him.

"What now?" she asked, breaking the silence, her voice tinged with a mixture of apprehension and determination.

The question was not just about their immediate escape; it encompassed their future, their relationship, their lives.

Dante looked at the fire, his expression unreadable. "We have to find a way out," he said, his voice low and determined. "We need to anticipate their next move, to stay ahead of them." He spoke of potential allies, of hidden routes, of strategies for survival. His planning was meticulous, his mind sharp despite the circumstances.

They spent the night in hushed conversation, strategizing, planning their next steps. The cabin, initially a refuge from the storm, became a war room, where their survival depended on their combined intellect, their resourcefulness, their determination. The isolated setting, initially a source of peace, became a crucible of their relationship. The quiet intimacy of the cabin contrasted sharply with the deadly game unfolding outside, creating a powerful tension that fueled their discussions.

The silence between them was no longer heavy with accusations; it was filled with shared anxieties, mutual respect, and a burgeoning sense of camaraderie born out of adversity. They were bound together, not just by their shared past, but by their uncertain future. The warmth of the fire was a mirror of the growing warmth in their relationship, a bond forged in the face of danger.

The serene beauty of the forest surrounding them provided a stark contrast to the darkness that dogged their footsteps. The silence of the woods offered a temporary respite from the clamor of their pursuers, a fragile space for reflection and intimacy. But the stillness also heightened their sense of vulnerability, the silence a constant reminder of their precarious situation.

As dawn broke, painting the sky in soft hues of pink and gold, they knew their refuge could not last. The Morettis were relentless, their reach extended far beyond the walls of their urban stronghold. The peaceful forest was not a sanctuary, but a temporary respite. They were still hunted, still vulnerable, still on the run. The game was far from over. But together, they were stronger, more resourceful, more determined. They would fight, not just for their survival, but for a future they were no longer sure they could ever have. Their alliance, once fragile, was now forged in the crucible of fear and desperation. The night in the cabin was not just an escape; it was a turning point, a moment of shared vulnerability that irrevocably altered the course of their lives and their relationship.

16
FAMILY TIES

The ancestral home of the Morettis loomed before them, a gothic monstrosity of grey stone and shadowed windows. It was a place that seemed to breathe an air of chilling indifference, a monument to generations of accumulated wealth and simmering resentment. Elena felt a shiver crawl down her spine as Dante steered the battered jeep towards the imposing gates. Inside, she knew, lay the roots of their current predicament, the tangled web of family ties that had ensnared them both.

Dante's demeanor had shifted, the quiet determination of the forest retreat replaced by a palpable tension. His jaw was clenched, his eyes shadowed with a weariness that went beyond simple exhaustion. He hadn't spoken much on the drive, the silence punctuated only by the crunch of gravel under the tires and the occasional creak of the aging vehicle. He seemed to be bracing himself, steeling himself for a confrontation that would unravel years of carefully constructed lies and half-truths.

The family gathering was as cold and formal as the house itself. Rows of stiffly dressed relatives, their faces frozen in masks of polite indifference, occupied the vast, high ceilinged hall. The air hung heavy with the scent of expensive perfume and unspoken accusations. Dante moved through the crowd with a practiced ease, a ghost in his own family portrait. His movements were fluid, almost graceful, yet there was an undercurrent of tension, of simmering anger, barely contained beneath the surface.

Elena followed closely, unnoticed amidst the throng of unfamiliar faces. She felt like an intruder, an outsider looking in on a family drama she barely understood, yet whose consequences threatened to engulf her. The opulent surroundings felt alien, a stark contrast to the rustic simplicity of the cabin in the woods. Here, wealth was a weapon, silence a shield, and every carefully chosen word a potential landmine.

Dante's father, Don Lorenzo Moretti, a man whose imposing presence filled the room even from across the hall, barely acknowledged his son. His eyes, cold and calculating, flickered across Dante before settling on Elena with a dismissive glance. The air crackled with unspoken disapproval, a palpable sense of rejection that sent a fresh wave of apprehension through Elena. The weight of expectation, the burden of family history, pressed down on Dante, visible in the slight tremor in his hand as he accepted a glass of wine from a passing servant.

The conversation flowed, or rather, trickled, around Dante. It was a performance, a carefully orchestrated display of familial harmony, concealing a deep well of bitter resentment. Elena listened, piecing together fragmented sentences, gleaned snatches of conversation – whispers of old rivalries, simmering hatreds, and long-forgotten betrayals. The wealth and privilege were a thin veneer, masking a history of broken trust and ruthless ambition.

The opportunity finally came during a lull in the strained conversation. Dante pulled Elena aside, his voice a low murmur against the background hum of polite chatter. He led her to a secluded alcove, away from the prying eyes of his family. The relief in his eyes was palpable as he finally began to speak.

"My family," he began, his voice laced with a weariness that spoke of years of pent-up frustration, "is not what it seems."

His gaze was intense, his eyes dark with a mixture of pain and anger.

He spoke then, not of grand schemes or power struggles, but of a childhood scarred by neglect and emotional abuse. He spoke of his mother, a fragile, melancholic woman constantly overshadowed by the relentless ambition of her husband. He painted a portrait of a family consumed by its own internal conflicts, a dysfunctional dynasty where love was a rare commodity and loyalty a dangerous game. He revealed a history of betrayals, hidden alliances, and secret resentments – a legacy of manipulation and deceit that had shaped his own life.

He spoke of his brother, Marco, a man whose ambition mirrored his father's, a man whose ruthlessness knew no bounds. Their relationship was a battlefield, a constant struggle for recognition and acceptance within a family that valued power above all else. The rivalry between them had been a festering wound, poisoning their relationship and driving a wedge between them from childhood.

He spoke of the pressure, the constant need to prove himself, to surpass the expectations of a man who seemed incapable of love or genuine affection. He described the suffocating atmosphere of the family home, the weight of tradition and expectation, the relentless pressure to conform. The grand ancestral home, once a symbol of power and prestige, was now revealed to be a cage, its walls steeped in the bitter history of a family consumed by its own toxic legacy. He confessed that his collaboration with the Morettis had begun as an attempt to gain his father's approval, a desperate bid for acceptance within a family that seemed incapable of offering him genuine love. The blackmail had been his leverage, an attempt to maneuver himself into a position of power, to finally prove his worth in the eyes of a man he had always yearned to please. He painted a picture of his despair, his desperation to escape the suffocating atmosphere of his childhood and the heavy burden of family expectations.

Elena listened, her heart heavy with the weight of his revelation. She saw the pain behind his words, the years of suppressed emotion finally breaking free. She understood the allure of the Morettis' power, the seductive nature of their wealth, and the desperate measures a man might take to escape the shadow of a powerful and unloving father. She saw in Dante not a ruthless criminal, but a damaged man, a victim of his own family's toxic legacy.

His confession was not a justification for his actions, but an explanation. It laid bare the complexities of his character, the deep-seated insecurities and the desperate need for approval that had driven him to such extremes. It was a story of betrayal, yes, but also of betrayal by those closest to him, a betrayal that had shaped his life and choices in ways that were both tragic and profoundly human.

As Dante finished, a wave of emotions washed over Elena. Sympathy, anger, understanding, and a renewed sense of determination warred within her. She knew his story complicated matters, made their escape even more precarious. But it also deepened her understanding of the man she had come to know, a man who was far more complex than she had ever imagined, a man whose actions, however regrettable, were rooted in a lifetime of hurt and disillusionment.

Their conversation was interrupted by a sharp rap on the alcove's door. Don Lorenzo Moretti stood there, his face impassive, his eyes a storm of cold fury. He had heard enough. The fragile truce, the carefully constructed facade of familial unity, was shattered. The game had begun anew, and the stakes were higher than ever. The quiet intimacy of the alcove was replaced by the chilling presence of the Moretti patriarch, a symbol of the family's suffocating grip. The confrontation was inevitable, and Elena and Dante were left to face it, bound together not only by their shared flight from danger, but by the shared burden of a complex and dangerous family legacy. The fight for survival was about to become a fight for the soul of a family, and the consequences would be far-reaching and devastating.

17
ELENA'S DILEMMA

The heavy oak door creaked shut behind her, the sound swallowed by the cavernous silence of the study. Dust motes danced in the slivers of light that pierced the gloom, illuminating the room's opulent decay. It was a mausoleum of memories, a testament to a life lived—and lost. Elena ran a trembling hand along the smooth surface of her father's antique desk, the polished wood cool beneath her touch. The scent of aged leather and pipe tobacco hung heavy in the air, a phantom embrace from a man she barely remembered.

She sank into the worn leather armchair, the plush comfort a stark contrast to the icy dread that gripped her heart. The room was a museum of her father's life, a curated collection of achievements and failures, successes and sorrows. Each object, each photograph, each carefully preserved document, was a fragment of a past she was only beginning to understand. And with each fragment, the weight of her own choices pressed down upon her, a crushing burden of responsibility.

She picked up a tarnished silver photo frame, its glass speckled with age. Inside, a younger, vibrant version of her father smiled, his eyes bright with an energy she'd only glimpsed in fleeting moments. He was surrounded by colleagues, their faces blurry with time, their identities lost to the haze of memory. But her father, he was unmistakable; his sharp wit, his unwavering confidence radiating from the faded photograph. The man in the picture was a hero, a visionary, a champion of justice. Or so she had been led to believe.

Dante's confession had shaken her to her core. His story was not simply a tale of betrayal and vengeance, but a tragedy played out against the backdrop of a dysfunctional family, a family as steeped in deceit and manipulation as the Morettis. The lines between victim and perpetrator were blurred, the morality of their actions clouded by a complex history of hurt and betrayal. She had sought justice, a righteous path of revenge to avenge her father's death, but now she wondered if it had all been a misguided quest, fuelled by grief and misinterpretations.

Had she been used? Was her father's death the result of a far larger, more insidious conflict, one that extended beyond the petty squabbles of disgruntled rivals and encompassed the dark machinations of the Moretti family? The thought sent a fresh wave of nausea through her, a sick realization that her pursuit of justice might have inadvertently plunged her into a conspiracy far deeper and more dangerous than she could have ever imagined. She traced the lines of a handwritten letter, its ink faded but legible. It was a letter from her father, dated just weeks before his death. His words were filled with a sense of foreboding, a hint of paranoia that chilled her to the bone. He mentioned a deal gone sour, a betrayal that threatened to destroy everything he had worked for. He spoke of powerful enemies, unseen forces manipulating events from the shadows. The letter ended abruptly, unfinished, leaving her with more questions than answers.

The weight of her father's legacy pressed upon her, a crushing burden of expectations. He had been a man of principle, a symbol of integrity, or so she had always thought. But the fragmented truth that Dante had revealed painted a far more ambiguous picture, a portrait of a man consumed by ambition, a man willing to play a dangerous game, a man capable of both great good and terrible mistakes.

Was her thirst for revenge a reflection of her father's own flawed nature? Had she inherited his flaws as well as his strengths, inheriting a dangerous combination of passion, ambition and a propensity for self-destruction? The question haunted her, a chilling specter that followed her through the dusty corridors of her father's memory. She spent hours in the study, poring over her father's papers, searching for answers that remained elusive. Each document, each personal note, each hastily scribbled memo, chipped away at the carefully constructed image of the man she thought she knew. She found evidence of questionable dealings, half-truths, and compromises that cast a shadow over his legacy.

The realization was agonizing. The man she had idolized, the man whose memory had fueled her relentless pursuit of vengeance, was not the saint she had envisioned. He was flawed, human, and capable of making terrible mistakes. The weight of this realization was almost unbearable, the burden of her own flawed judgement crushing her spirit.

As darkness fell, she found herself staring out the window at the sprawling estate, the grounds bathed in the soft glow of the setting sun. The familiar comfort she'd once found in this place now felt alien, tainted by the shadows of newly discovered truths. The house, once a symbol of her father's success, now represented a labyrinth of lies and deceit. The choice before her was stark. Continue down the path of vengeance, fueled by a distorted image of her father, or confront the uncomfortable truth and forge a new path, a path that acknowledged the complexities of her father's legacy and the moral ambiguities of her own quest. The path of vengeance, she realized, held the same seductive allure, the same dark appeal that had driven Dante to his own desperate measures.

It was a path that could consume her, leaving her as morally compromised, as emotionally scarred as Dante, and perhaps even the Morettis themselves. She felt a chilling realization settle over her. The family's wealth and power were merely a thin veneer, masking a much deeper, darker malaise. She now understood that the fight for survival was not merely a physical struggle against overwhelming odds. It was a battle for her own soul, a fight against the seductive power of vengeance and the insidious influence of a toxic legacy. The price of loyalty, she realized with a shudder, was far higher than she had ever imagined.

The weight of her decision pressed down on her, heavy as the shadows that stretched across the room. The fight for survival was no longer just about her and Dante; it was about her father's legacy, her own identity, and the future she wanted to create. The night stretched ahead, cold and unforgiving, reflecting the harsh reality that she had to make a choice. A choice that could determine not only her life, but the fate of many others.

18

A DANGEROUS GAME OF CAT AND MOUSE

The city breathed around them, a living, breathing entity of shadows and secrets. Elena, cloaked in the anonymity of the night, felt a thrill course through her veins, a dangerous exhilaration that mirrored the city's own restless energy. She moved through the labyrinthine streets like a phantom, her steps silent, her senses sharpened. Dante, her unlikely ally, was a shadow at her side, a silent guardian who understood the language of the city's underbelly as well as she did.

Their game had begun. A dangerous dance of cat and mouse with the Morettis, a family whose tentacles stretched into every corner of the city's power structure. Their initial strategy was simple: use their newfound knowledge of the Morettis' illicit operations against them. It was a high-stakes gamble, a game where one wrong move could be fatal. But Elena was willing to risk everything. Dante's presence, both a comfort and a challenge, added a layer of complexity to their plan. He was an enigma, a man of contradictions, and their alliance, as fragile as it was, was built on a foundation of mutual distrust and a shared objective: exposing the Morettis.

Their first target was a dilapidated warehouse district on the city's edge, a place where the city's shadows clung thickest. The air hung heavy with the scent of decay and illicit activity, the silence broken only by the distant rumble of trucks and the occasional cry of a stray dog. Here, amidst the crumbling structures and overgrown weeds, the Morettis conducted their less savoury transactions. Elena, using information gleaned from Dante's confession and her father's documents, pinpointed a specific warehouse, a hub for the family's illegal arms trade. They had to be careful. This wasn't a frontal assault, but a strategic infiltration, a carefully orchestrated maneuver designed to extract information without detection.

Dante's expertise in navigating the city's dark corners proved invaluable. He led her through a maze of back alleys and hidden passages, his movements fluid and precise, his knowledge seemingly boundless. He knew the people, the places, the unspoken rules that governed this underworld. Elena, with her sharp mind and methodical approach, provided the intellectual counterpoint, carefully analyzing the information they gathered. Together, they formed a formidable team, their strengths complementing each other, their weaknesses somehow canceling themselves out.

Their clandestine operation involved a mixture of observation and subtle infiltration. From a darkened rooftop overlooking the warehouse, they observed the activity, the constant flow of vehicles, the shadowy figures who moved with the practiced ease of those steeped in secrecy. Elena, armed with a powerful pair of binoculars, identified patterns, noting the timings of deliveries, the number of individuals involved, and the frequency of interactions. Each detail, however small, added to a bigger picture, a puzzle they were slowly but surely piecing together.

Their next move involved a more direct approach, one that bordered on reckless. Dante, utilizing his contacts within the city's underworld, secured them access to a seedy bar near the warehouse, a watering hole frequented by the Morettis' associates. It was a den of iniquity, filled with smoke, cheap alcohol, and a palpable tension that hung in the air like a suffocating blanket. The bar's clientele was a motley crew, a collection of hardened criminals, desperate hustlers, and informants, each with their own hidden agendas.

Elena, disguised in a borrowed wig and a simple dress, blended seamlessly into the crowd, observing and listening. Dante, ever vigilant, kept a watchful eye, his presence a silent threat that prevented any unwanted attention. They gathered information, picking up fragments of conversations, eavesdropping on hushed discussions, meticulously piecing together the puzzle of the Moretti family's illegal activities. The stakes were dangerously high. One slip-up could expose them, attracting the deadly attention of the Morettis and their ruthless enforcers.

Over several nights, their cat-and-mouse game intensified. They shadowed Moretti associates, followed delivery trucks, and even managed to intercept a coded message, a crucial piece of intelligence that provided a deeper insight into the Moretti's network. They moved like ghosts, their every action carefully calculated, each step measured. The city became their battleground, a stage where they played out a dangerous drama of deception and subterfuge.

The risk was ever-present, a cold hand constantly resting on their shoulders. They had to be constantly on guard, constantly thinking several steps ahead. The tension was palpable, creating a thrilling and dangerous intimacy between Elena and Dante. Their shared experiences were forging a bond, a grudging respect that transcended their initial distrust. Yet, amidst the danger and intrigue, a flicker of something else ignited—a connection that was both thrilling and terrifying.

One night, while observing a clandestine meeting in a dimly lit alleyway, they were discovered. The Morettis' enforcers, a brutal group of men, surrounded them, their faces grim, their intentions unmistakable. A fierce confrontation ensued, a brutal dance of fists and weapons. Dante's combat skills, honed through years of fighting for survival, were put to the test, his moves precise and deadly. Elena, though not physically trained, fought with a desperate ferocity, fueled by adrenaline and the will to survive. She used her wit and agility to evade their attacks, creating openings for Dante to deliver crippling blows.

They managed to escape, but not without injuries. The experience served as a brutal reminder of the risks they were taking. The chase continued, a relentless pursuit that took them deeper into the city's underbelly. Their game of cat and mouse escalated, becoming increasingly dangerous, the stakes continually rising. The lines between hunter and hunted were blurred, the city itself seemed to conspire against them, reflecting the precariousness of their situation.

The final confrontation took place in the heart of the Moretti family's estate. It was a gamble, a last-ditch effort to expose their crimes and deliver a devastating blow. Armed with their collected evidence, they broke into the Moretti family's main building, dodging guards, traversing secret passages and narrowly avoiding detection. The mansion was a labyrinth of deception, its opulence masking a dark and sinister heart.

Within the heart of the estate, they discovered a secret room filled with incriminating documents, enough to bring down the entire Moretti empire. As they were about to leave, they were ambushed by the Moretti patriarch, a man of immense power and ruthless efficiency. The confrontation was inevitable, a final showdown that tested their skills and resolve to their limits. Elena and Dante faced a formidable opponent, their lives hanging in the balance. The battle was brutal, a desperate struggle for survival that played out amidst the opulent surroundings, a macabre juxtaposition of luxury and violence. In the aftermath, the true cost of their game would become brutally apparent. The price of loyalty, the cost of revenge, the weight of their choices would be far heavier than they could ever have anticipated. The victory, if it could be called that, was bittersweet, laced with the sting of loss and the lingering shadows of their actions. The city's embrace, once a refuge, now felt cold and unforgiving.

19
A MOMENTOF TRUTH

The air hung thick with the scent of stale beer, sweat, and desperation. The dimly lit club pulsed with a low, throbbing rhythm, the bass vibrating through Elena's very bones. It was a place where shadows danced and secrets whispered, a subterranean lair hidden beneath the city's glittering façade. This was the Serpent's Coil, a notorious underground club, owned and operated by a key lieutenant of the Moretti family, a man known only as "Viper." It was here, according to Dante's informant, that Viper held his clandestine meetings, the place where the most sensitive deals were struck and the most dangerous information was exchanged.

Elena, disguised once more, this time as a sultry cabaret singer, felt a knot of apprehension tighten in her stomach. Her borrowed dress, a shimmering emerald gown, felt foreign against her skin, a mask that hid the turmoil within. Dante, ever the shadow, blended effortlessly into the background, his presence as muted as the club's shadowed corners. He'd managed to secure them entry through a back alley, bypassing the club's notoriously vigilant bouncers. Their mission was simple: confront Viper, gain his trust, and extract the information they needed to bring down the Morettis.

The club was a labyrinth of dimly lit rooms and hidden alcoves. Hardened criminals and shady businessmen mingled with scantily clad dancers and women whose smiles held a chilling edge. The atmosphere was charged, a potent cocktail of danger and intrigue. Elena navigated the crowd with practiced ease, her movements graceful, her gaze sharp and observant. Dante stayed close, his hand never far from his concealed weapon, a silent guardian against the lurking threats.

They finally located Viper in a secluded VIP room, surrounded by a coterie of heavily armed men. He was a formidable figure, tall and imposing, with eyes that held the cold glint of a predator. His face was a mask of indifference, his demeanor suggesting a man accustomed to power and control. He was toying with a delicate silver goblet, his gaze sweeping across the room with a detached air of boredom.

Elena approached with a practiced confidence, her voice a mesmerizing purr that cut through the club's din. She engaged Viper in conversation, her words carefully chosen, her movements fluid and alluring. She spoke of mutual acquaintances, of shared interests, subtly hinting at her knowledge of the Moretti family's activities. Her performance was a masterpiece of controlled deception, a carefully orchestrated ballet of charm and intimidation. Dante, meanwhile, remained discreetly in the background, observing, analyzing, and ready to intervene at a moment's notice.

The conversation flowed, winding its way through a maze of veiled references and double entendres. Elena skillfully manipulated the conversation, steering it towards their objective – the information they desperately needed to expose the Morettis. She revealed just enough to pique Viper's curiosity, creating a sense of anticipation and urgency. The tension in the room was palpable, a tangible thing that pressed down on them like a suffocating blanket.

As the conversation intensified, the line between performance and reality began to blur. Elena's carefully constructed persona started to crack, the strain of the situation evident in her slightly trembling hands. Viper, sensing her vulnerability, began to tighten the screws, his questions becoming more pointed, his tone more demanding. The atmosphere shifted, the air growing thick with suspicion.

Suddenly, one of Viper's men noticed Dante's subtly tense posture, his hand instinctively moving toward his weapon. The room erupted into chaos. Chairs crashed to the floor, shouts and curses filled the air, and the delicate dance of deception shattered. The moment of truth had arrived. Elena, caught between Viper's relentless questioning and Dante's desperate attempt to maintain control, knew she had to make a choice – a choice that would determine their lives, their mission, and the fate of the city itself.

The ensuing struggle was a brutal ballet of violence and adrenaline. Dante, fighting with the ferocity of a cornered animal, moved with lethal precision, his movements a blur of motion. He fought to protect Elena, shielding her from the onslaught of Viper's henchmen. Elena, despite her lack of formal training, fought with the desperation of someone fighting for survival, her resolve fueled by the urgency of their situation and the weight of the information they carried. Her mind worked at a frantic pace, calculating angles, searching for openings, desperately trying to maintain control amidst the escalating chaos.

They found themselves backed against a wall, the cold, damp stone a stark contrast to the opulent surroundings. Viper, his face contorted in a mask of fury, advanced on them, his eyes burning with rage. He was a formidable opponent, a seasoned fighter whose movements were both powerful and graceful. The fight was brutal, a brutal clash of wills, a desperate struggle for survival.

As Dante wrestled with Viper's henchmen, Elena, with a surge of desperate courage, made her move. She slipped past a momentarily distracted guard, grabbing a heavy ornamental vase. With all her might, she brought it crashing down on Viper's head, the shattering sound echoing through the chaos. The blow stunned him, giving Dante the opening he needed to disarm and subdue the remaining henchmen. Their escape was narrow, a frantic dash through the labyrinthine club, navigating the confused and desperate crowd. They burst out into the alleyway, their hearts pounding, their breath ragged, leaving the Serpent's Coil behind in a whirlwind of chaos.

They had succeeded in obtaining the information they sought, but at a cost. They were wounded, bruised, and shaken. The confrontation had taken its toll, both physically and emotionally. The weight of their actions pressed down on them, a heavy burden they would carry with them. The precarious balance of their alliance had shifted, the shared risk forging a new, deeper connection between them, one tempered by fear and laced with a growing sense of mutual respect. Their game, far from over, had entered a new, more dangerous phase. The city, once a backdrop to their game, now felt like an active participant, its shadows deeper, its secrets more menacing. The price of loyalty, they knew, had just begun to be tallied. The road ahead, they knew, was long and treacherous. And the truth, like the city itself, held a darkness that threatened to consume them both.

20
CONSEQUENCES OF ACTION

The alley reeked of garbage and despair, a stark contrast to the opulent decadence they'd just escaped. Elena leaned against a grimy brick wall, the emerald gown, now torn and stained, clinging to her like a second skin. Dante, his face grim, checked her wounds, his touch surprisingly gentle. A thin trickle of blood ran down her temple, a testament to the ferocity of the fight. He ripped a strip from his own shirt, improvising a makeshift bandage.

"We need to get you to a doctor," he said, his voice low and urgent. His own injuries were evident – a deep gash on his forearm, a bruise blossoming under his eye. He was holding himself stiffly, concealing the pain.

Elena brushed off his concern with a weary wave of her hand. "Later," she rasped, her voice hoarse. "We have other things to worry about."

The information they'd extracted from Viper, a cryptic series of coded messages hidden within a hollowed-out silver coin, felt heavy in her pocket. It detailed a massive arms deal, one that could destabilize the entire city, implicating not just the Morettis but a network of corrupt officials and international arms dealers reaching far beyond their initial expectations.

The weight of their discovery, the potential consequences of their actions, pressed down on her with the force of a physical blow.

They hailed a cab, the driver eyeing them with suspicion, his gaze lingering on Elena's disheveled attire and Dante's bruised face. They didn't offer an explanation, their silence communicating more than words could. The ride was tense, the city's nocturnal pulse throbbing against the cab's metal shell, a soundtrack to their mounting anxieties.

Their safe house, a dilapidated apartment overlooking the city's docks, offered little solace. The air was thick with the smell of dampness and decay, a far cry from the luxury they'd briefly experienced in Viper's VIP room. As they stumbled inside, the reality of their situation crashed down on them. They weren't just fugitives from a violent encounter; they were walking into a minefield of political intrigue and mortal danger.

Elena carefully examined the coded messages, her mind racing to decipher the cryptic symbols. Dante, despite his injuries, began working on their escape route, contacting his network of informants, arranging for a safe passage out of the city. The tension between them was palpable, a silent acknowledgment of the precariousness of their alliance. Their shared risk had forged a bond, but it was a bond laced with suspicion, a fragile alliance built on mutual survival.

The decoding process was agonizingly slow, each symbol revealing a new layer of complexity, unveiling a web of connections far more intricate than they had anticipated.

Hours bled into one another, the city's sleepless pulse a relentless reminder of the urgency of their situation. They worked in silence, their minds consumed by the intricate details of the arms deal, the names and faces, the locations a chilling mosaic of corruption and betrayal. With each deciphered message, the magnitude of the danger increased exponentially.

As dawn broke, painting the sky with hues of grey and orange, they finally cracked the code. The information was devastating: a shipment of illegal weapons, disguised as humanitarian aid, was scheduled to arrive at the city docks in three days. The implications were catastrophic, reaching far beyond the Morettis' criminal empire. This was a threat to the city, to the country, potentially even to international stability. The weight of responsibility settled heavily on their shoulders. They had exposed a conspiracy of monumental proportions, one that stretched into the highest echelons of power.

But exposing it would require more than just the coded messages; they needed proof, irrefutable evidence. They were facing a formidable enemy, one with powerful allies and a ruthless capacity for violence. Their previous encounter with Viper had only scratched the surface; they were now up against an intricate network, a well-oiled machine capable of crushing any opposition.

The ensuing days were a blur of frantic activity. Dante, utilizing his contacts, managed to secure a meeting with a disillusioned Moretti lieutenant, a man weary of the family's violent methods and eager to escape their grasp. The lieutenant, a man named Marco, provided them with crucial evidence, photographs, financial records, and detailed accounts of the arms deal's inner workings. The risk was immense, the cost potentially fatal, but they were running out of time.

Their escape plan was daring, almost suicidal. Dante arranged a fake identity for Elena, secured a forged passport, and plotted a route through the city's less frequented alleyways and hidden passages. They would need to evade surveillance, outwit their enemies, and deliver the evidence to the authorities. The stakes were higher than ever before. Failure would mean not only their deaths but the potential collapse of the city under the weight of the arms deal.

The plan was set in motion under the cover of darkness, the city a silent accomplice to their desperate maneuvers. They moved like shadows, their every step calculated, their senses heightened, their every action fueled by adrenaline and a profound sense of purpose. They were playing a high-stakes game of cat and mouse with a ruthless adversary, a game where the consequences of a single misstep could be fatal.

The final confrontation took place in the heart of the city, amidst the bustling crowds and oblivious faces, a stark contrast to the dimly lit corners of the Serpent's Coil. The tension was almost unbearable, the city's sounds muffling the pounding of their hearts. They delivered the evidence to their contact – a seasoned journalist known for her integrity and willingness to tackle the city's darkest secrets.

In the aftermath, exhaustion washed over them, a bone-deep weariness that seeped into their very bones. They had succeeded in exposing the conspiracy, but the victory felt hollow, tainted by the losses and sacrifices they'd endured. The city, once a backdrop to their game, had become a participant, its shadows darker, its secrets more deeply entrenched. The price of loyalty, they now knew, was far higher than they had anticipated. Their future was uncertain, the road ahead long and fraught with danger, but they had faced their demons, and they had survived. The city's relentless rhythm, once a constant threat, now sounded almost like a lullaby, a testament to their survival, a whispered promise of a future, however uncertain it may be. The game, though won, had only just begun.

21
THE FINAL SHOWDOWN

The cramped, dimly lit attic served as their makeshift war room. Dust motes danced in the lone beam of moonlight slicing through a crack in the boarded-up window, illuminating the worn map spread across the rickety table. It was a map of the city, its arteries – the main thoroughfares marked in red, its veins – the hidden alleyways and backstreets – in a faded blue. Dante traced a route with a calloused finger, his brow furrowed in concentration. Elena, perched on a stool fashioned from upturned crates, meticulously checked the contents of a battered briefcase. Inside, nestled amongst layers of newspaper, were the irrefutable proofs of the Morettis' crimes – photographs, financial records, and Marco's sworn testimony, all meticulously documented and ready to be delivered.

The air hung heavy with the unspoken tension, the silence punctuated only by the occasional creak of the aging building and the distant city sounds. This was it, the final act, the culmination of weeks spent teetering on the brink of discovery and destruction. The adrenaline that had fueled them through the previous encounters had settled into a quiet, determined resolve.

"The drop is at midnight," Dante said, his voice low, his gaze fixed on the map. "The journalist, Isabella Rossi, will be waiting near the old clock tower."

Elena nodded, her expression grim. Isabella Rossi, a legend in the underworld of investigative journalism, was their only hope. Her reputation for unwavering integrity and her ability to navigate the city's treacherous underbelly made her the perfect conduit for their evidence. But trusting her, relying on her to deliver, was a leap of faith – a risk they had to take.

"What if they're waiting for us?" Elena asked, her voice barely a whisper. The question hung in the air, a stark reminder of the danger they faced. The Morettis were not known for their forgiveness.

Dante's lips tightened. "They will be. They know we have the goods. This is a trap, Elena. We both know it. But it's the only trap we can afford to walk into."

He paused, his gaze meeting hers. The emerald eyes, usually sparkling with defiance, were now shadowed with a weariness that mirrored her own. They had come so far, survived so much. The price of their revelations had been high, paid in sweat, blood, and sleepless nights. Yet, the possibility of failure, the prospect of all their efforts being in vain, was a bitter pill to swallow.

"We need a distraction," Elena stated, her voice regaining its usual steely tone. "Something big enough to draw their attention away from the clock tower."

Dante's eyes lit up, a flicker of his usual cunning returning to his gaze. "I have a contact, a disgruntled dockworker with a grudge against the Morettis. He owes me a favor. A small fire at one of their warehouses should create the necessary chaos."

The plan, conceived in the hushed silence of the attic, was a desperate gamble, a complex dance of calculated risks. They had to be precise, every move synchronized, every second accounted for. Failure was not an option; success would depend on a delicate balance of timing, deception, and a healthy dose of luck.

The hours leading up to midnight felt like an eternity. They prepared their disguises, meticulous in their attention to detail. Elena slipped into a simple, dark cloak, her face concealed by a hooded scarf. Dante, his wounds still throbbing, wore a worn fisherman's jacket, his face obscured by a wide-brimmed hat.

The tension was palpable as they left the attic, their shadows stretching long and distorted in the moonlight. The city, usually a cacophony of sound and movement, felt eerily silent as they navigated its labyrinthine streets. The weight of their mission, the knowledge that their lives hung precariously in the balance, settled heavily upon their shoulders.

The fire, orchestrated by Dante's contact, erupted as planned, a fiery inferno that cast an eerie glow across the city skyline. Sirens wailed in the distance, the sound adding to the mounting tension. Dante's distraction worked perfectly, the city's emergency services fully occupied, drawing the Morettis' attention away from the clock tower.

They arrived at their destination, their hearts pounding in their chests. The old clock tower, its hands slowly inching towards midnight, stood silhouetted against the night sky, a silent witness to their clandestine operation. Isabella Rossi was already there, her figure shrouded in shadow.

The exchange was swift and clandestine. Elena handed over the briefcase, its contents a testament to their shared risk, their harrowing journey, their determination to bring down the Morettis. Isabella nodded, her gaze unwavering. She knew what she had to do. As they melted back into the shadows, the distant roar of the fire and the wail of sirens served as a soundtrack to their escape. But the battle wasn't over. The Morettis, even distracted, were a force to be reckoned with.

The ensuing chase was a breathless, heart-stopping race through the city's underbelly. They navigated through narrow alleyways and across rooftops, Dante's knowledge of the city's hidden paths proving invaluable. The pursuit was relentless, the pursuers relentless, but their determination held.

They finally found refuge in a secluded waterfront warehouse, their lungs burning, their bodies trembling with exhaustion. The city's nocturnal sounds – the distant hum of traffic, the cries of gulls – seemed to mock their vulnerability. They had escaped, but at what cost?

The news broke the following morning. The Moretti empire was crumbling, its foundation shattered by the evidence they had provided. The city was reeling, the revelation shocking the public and the authorities alike. Their names were not mentioned in the news reports, their identities protected under the shroud of secrecy.

They watched the unfolding events from afar, observing the demise of the Moretti family from a safe distance. Their victory was bittersweet, achieved at a considerable personal cost. They had exposed the rot at the heart of the city, but the shadows remained, their presence a constant reminder of the dark underbelly they had briefly uncovered.

The city, once a backdrop to their desperate struggle, had become a symbol of resilience, a testament to the power of truth, however risky the pursuit. They had won, but the game, as always, was far from over. Their future remained unwritten, their lives irrevocably changed, their alliance forged in fire and risk – a bond both fragile and enduring, testament to their shared sacrifice. The silence of their secret hideout was broken only by the sound of their ragged breathing, the city's hum a background lullaby now, rather than a constant reminder of peril. The final reckoning was over, but a new chapter, unknown and uncertain, was just beginning.

22
ALLIANCE AND BETRAYALS

The warehouse reeked of salt and decay, the air thick with the smell of stagnant water and rotting wood. Moonlight, fractured by the gaps in the corrugated iron roof, painted the cavernous space in shifting patterns of light and shadow. Elena and Dante, still shaken from their narrow escape, stood facing three figures shrouded in darkness. They hadn't expected reinforcements, hadn't anticipated the depth of the Moretti's reach.

The first figure stepped forward, the moonlight catching the glint of a gold signet ring – the symbol of the Moretti family. It was Lorenzo Moretti, Marco's elder brother, his face a mask of cold fury. Beside him stood two imposing men, their physiques suggesting years spent honing their skills in violence. The air crackled with unspoken threats.

"You think you've won, little birds," Lorenzo sneered, his voice a low growl that echoed through the desolate space. "You think you can escape the consequences of your actions?"

Dante, ever the strategist, met Lorenzo's gaze without flinching. "We exposed your crimes, Lorenzo. The city knows what you are."

Lorenzo laughed, a harsh, brittle sound. "The city forgets quickly, Dante. Especially when those in power decide to ignore inconvenient truths. My family has deep roots, influential friends. Your little exposé will be buried, forgotten, as easily as the bodies you've left in your wake." He gestured to the two hulking men, their faces impassive.

Elena, her hand instinctively moving towards the small, but deadly, knife concealed in her boot, felt a chill run down her spine. This was not the triumphant end they had envisioned. Their carefully laid plans had been disrupted, the power balance shifting in ways they hadn't anticipated. The sudden appearance of Lorenzo and his goons felt like a chilling betrayal, a twist in the narrative that altered the game profoundly.

"We have allies," Dante said, his voice unwavering despite the clear shift in the dynamic. "People who won't let you bury this."

Lorenzo smiled, a cruel, predatory smile. "Allies? You amuse me. Name them. Let's see how quickly they crumble under the pressure."

Dante's eyes flickered towards the shadows at the far end of the warehouse. A figure emerged, silhouetted against the weak light. It was Isabella Rossi, the investigative journalist, but her expression was not one of solidarity. Her face, usually vibrant and full of righteous fire, was pale and strained. In her hand, she held the briefcase, its contents their evidence – now a bargaining chip in a deadly game of power.

"Isabella?" Elena breathed, her voice laced with disbelief and betrayal. This unexpected shift in allegiance felt like a knife twisting into their already wounded hearts.

Isabella let out a bitter laugh. "Integrity? A quaint notion, isn't it? It's far easier to bend to the wind than fight it. The Morettis offered me a deal, a life beyond the reach of their enemies – and yours. They're offering a hefty sum, enough to ensure my future and silence my conscience. And believe me, my conscience has a hefty price tag."

A cold dread enveloped Elena and Dante. The betrayal stung more than any physical blow. They had risked everything, put their lives on the line, and now their carefully built alliance had crumbled under the weight of greed and fear. The consequences felt devastating.

 Lorenzo chuckled, his satisfaction palpable. "You see, Dante, your allies are as fickle as the winds. They'll sell you out for a price, every time."

The air in the warehouse felt thick with despair and uncertainty. Their meticulously crafted plan was shattered, their triumph now a distant, impossible dream. They were trapped, outnumbered, and betrayed. The realization hit them with the force of a physical blow, leaving them reeling.

Dante, however, refused to surrender. He had always been a master of improvisation, his mind a labyrinth of cunning strategies. Even now, amidst the despair, his intellect was working frantically. He glanced at Elena, his eyes searching for a solution, a glimmer of hope in the face of overwhelming odds.

"You think this ends here, Lorenzo?" Dante said, his voice low and dangerous, his eyes blazing with defiance. "You're mistaken. This is just the beginning."

He knew he was bluffing, but the desperation in his voice held a certain ring of truth. He needed to buy time, to think, to find a way out of this seemingly impossible situation. He had to find a chink in Lorenzo's seemingly impenetrable armor, an opportunity to reclaim the initiative.

He saw it then, in a small detail. Isabella's hands, despite her bold assertions, were trembling slightly. Doubt flickered across her face, a moment of hesitation before the hardened mask returned. This was their opening.

"Isabella," Dante said smoothly, his voice surprisingly calm given the circumstances. "You said the Morettis offered you a life beyond reach, and your conscience." He paused, his voice deepening. "But what happens when their enemies become yours? When your own life is threatened because you've sided with the very people you know are capable of such brutality?"

He spoke directly to her fears, planting seeds of doubt in the fertile ground of her newly acquired avarice. The look on Isabella's face told him that his strategy might be working. A tremor ran through her body. The weight of the truth he had spoken was undeniable. The Morettis were ruthless, not to be trusted, and their protection was merely a cruel illusion.

Lorenzo's smile faltered. He had underestimated the resilience of his enemies. Dante's tactic was audacious, a gamble, but it was their only chance.

Elena, understanding the shift in momentum, acted swiftly. She launched a well-aimed kick at the nearest thug's knee, taking advantage of their momentary distraction. The thug cried out in pain, giving Dante and Elena the split-second advantage they needed. It was a chaotic brawl, fueled by desperation and adrenaline.

Dante's knowledge of fighting styles, learned on the city's violent streets, combined with Elena's swift and deadly precision, allowed them to fight off the thugs. But Lorenzo remained a formidable opponent, his rage a powerful force. However, Isabella's uncertainty had tipped the scales. As Lorenzo lunged towards Elena, Isabella, in a last-minute change of heart, tripped him, his powerful frame crashing to the concrete floor.

Before Lorenzo could recover, Elena seized the opportunity. She quickly snatched the briefcase from Isabella's stunned grasp, and together, Dante and Elena escaped into the night, leaving the bewildered and betrayed Lorenzo and his incapacitated thugs behind. They ran, the echoes of the fight fading behind them, the city's darkness their ally once more. They had survived, but the alliances they thought unshakeable had shattered, leaving only the fragile bond between Dante and Elena, tested, yet strengthened by the ordeal. The war, far from over, had entered a new, treacherous phase. The game was afoot, and the stakes, once again, were life itself.

23
A DESPARATE GAMBLE

The warehouse doors slammed shut behind them, the metallic clang echoing in the stillness of the night. They were free, for now. But freedom felt fragile, a fleeting moment snatched from the jaws of defeat. The adrenaline that had fueled their desperate fight began to ebb, replaced by a bone-deep exhaustion that threatened to pull them under. Elena leaned against a damp brick wall, her breath coming in ragged gasps, the taste of blood – her own, she realised – thick in her mouth. Dante, his face pale but his eyes alight with a fierce determination, checked the briefcase, its contents secure.

Their escape had been a miracle, a breathtaking sequence of calculated risks and sheer luck. Isabella's wavering loyalty, the unexpected distraction caused by Elena's swift kick, Dante's ability to exploit Lorenzo's arrogance – it all coalesced in a perfect storm of chaos that allowed them to slip away. But it had been a close call, too close. Lorenzo's fury had been palpable, the sheer physical strength of the man terrifying. They had survived, but they were far from victorious.

The city, usually a vibrant tapestry of life and noise, felt oppressive tonight. Its shadowy corners seemed to whisper threats, its echoing streets to mock their vulnerability. They needed to disappear, to melt into the anonymity of the city, to find a place to regroup, to plan their next move.

"We can't go back to the safehouse," Elena said, her voice hoarse. "They'll be watching."

Dante nodded, his gaze scanning the deserted street. "We need to lay low, find somewhere off the grid. Somewhere they won't expect us."

He hailed a cab, a battered yellow vehicle that seemed to emerge from the shadows as if summoned. They piled in, the cab's musty interior offering little comfort. The driver, a burly man with eyes that seemed to see everything and nothing at once, remained silent, his gaze fixed on the road ahead. Dante gave him a destination – an abandoned warehouse district on the city's outskirts – a place known only to him and a few others.

The journey was a blur of flashing lights, the cab weaving through the city's labyrinthine streets. Elena kept a close watch, her senses heightened, alert for any sign of pursuit. She had learned to trust her instincts over the years, and tonight, they were screaming danger. The escape had been messy, and the possibility of pursuit was high.

The cab pulled up to the abandoned warehouse district, a desolate landscape of crumbling buildings and overgrown weeds. The air hung heavy with the scent of rust and decay, the silence broken only by the occasional creak of a rusted gate or the distant howl of a dog. It was a fitting hideout bleak, unforgiving, and completely anonymous.

They slipped out of the cab, paying the driver in cash, leaving no trace. Inside the chosen warehouse, the shadows danced like phantoms, the dampness clinging to their clothes. It was a far cry from the relative safety of their previous hideout, but it provided the necessary cover.

They spent the next few hours examining their hard-won evidence. The briefcase contained not only Marco Moretti's meticulously documented crimes but also a trove of information connecting the family to a far-reaching network of corruption, a conspiracy that stretched from the city's underworld to the highest echelons of power. This was the evidence that could bring down the Morettis, the evidence that could cleanse the city of their insidious influence. But it was also a dangerous weapon, one that could easily backfire if not handled with precision and care.

"We need to find a way to disseminate this information strategically," Dante said, his voice serious, his eyes fixed on the contents of the briefcase. "We can't simply release it to the public. The Morettis have too much power, too many connections. They'll bury it, discredit us, and make us pay."

Elena agreed. Their initial plan of a public exposé had clearly failed. They needed a more nuanced approach, a strategy that bypassed the Morettis' influence and went straight to the heart of their power structure.

They spent the night poring over the documents, meticulously examining every detail, every connection, every potential angle. They identified key players, weak points, and possible allies. The names of influential politicians, corrupt officials, and compromised journalists began to emerge from the shadows, a web of deceit intricately woven into the fabric of the city's power structure.

As dawn broke, painting the sky in hues of grey and orange, they had a plan. It was a dangerous gamble, a desperate move that could either save them or destroy them, but it was their only chance. They would go after the Morettis not through public exposure but by systematically dismantling their network, by exposing their corrupt allies one by one. It was a long game, a painstaking process that required precision, strategy, and a great deal of courage. They would use the very people the Morettis trusted as their own weapon against them.

The high-speed chase through the city was a whirlwind of near misses and adrenaline-fueled escapes. Dante, with his knowledge of the city's backstreets and shortcuts, expertly navigated the treacherous roads, weaving through traffic, narrowly avoiding collisions, while Elena kept a vigilant watch for pursuing vehicles. They were being pursued; the Morettis had not given up. The city became a dangerous game board, its streets the battleground, its citizens oblivious to the deadly game unfolding around them.

Their vehicle, a stolen motorbike, roared through the city's heart, a defiant scream against the night. Every turn, every swerve, was a gamble, a calculated risk that could end in disaster. The relentless pursuit felt like a tightening noose, the pressure mounting with every passing second.

Finally, they managed to lose their pursuers in a maze of

narrow alleyways, the bike's engine sputtering and dying in a cloud of smoke. They collapsed, panting and bruised, in the shadow of a looming skyscraper. The adrenaline slowly ebbed, leaving them with a chilling awareness of their vulnerability, a stark reminder of how close they had come to failure.

The next few days were a blur of covert meetings, clandestine exchanges, and dangerous negotiations. They used their newfound knowledge to expose one compromised individual after another, leaking carefully selected pieces of information to the right people – journalists with a conscience, officials with a sense of duty, and politicians willing to risk their careers to uncover the truth. The city's underbelly, with its complex web of alliances and betrayals, became their battleground, each carefully placed piece of information a pawn in their intricate game of chess.

The Morettis' influence began to wane, their carefully constructed web of corruption starting to unravel. Lorenzo, his fury increasing, was becoming more desperate, his actions more erratic and reckless. The game, they realized, had entered its final, deadly phase. The reckoning was fast approaching. Elena and Dante, though exhausted and battered, continued their relentless campaign, their courage fueled by the weight of justice they sought, and the promise of a future they dared to dream of – a future free from the Morettis' suffocating grip, a future where truth prevailed. The fate of the city, they realized, rested on the outcome of this desperate gamble.

24
FACING THE PAST

The abandoned warehouse offered little comfort, its cold, damp air a stark contrast to the adrenaline-fueled chaos they had just escaped. The silence, broken only by the occasional drip of water, pressed in on them, a suffocating blanket of anxiety. Elena, her body aching, her mind racing, found herself staring at the worn, cracked concrete floor, lost in a labyrinth of memories. The warehouse wasn't just a hideout; it was a mirror reflecting the wreckage of their pasts, a past that had relentlessly pursued them, even in their moments of triumph.

Dante, sensing her turmoil, approached cautiously. He knew the weight of her past, the shadows that haunted her even in the brightest of days. He'd seen the flicker of fear in her eyes, the tightening of her jaw, the way her gaze would drift to some distant point, lost in the echoes of memories she couldn't escape. He understood her silence, the way it could be both a wall and a plea for understanding.

"Elena," he began softly, his voice a gentle intrusion into her solitude. "We need to talk."

She didn't respond immediately, her gaze still fixed on the floor, her fingers tracing the cracks in the concrete as if searching for answers etched in the grime. The silence stretched, heavy and oppressive, a silent testament to the unspoken burdens they carried. It was a silence that spoke volumes about the unspoken traumas, the unresolved issues that hung between them like a dark cloud, threatening to overwhelm them.

Finally, she looked up, her eyes reflecting the flickering candlelight, revealing a depth of pain that cut through Dante's carefully constructed composure. The steeliness in her gaze, the usual defiance that masked her vulnerability, had softened, replaced by a raw, aching honesty.

 "It wasn't just the Morettis tonight," she whispered, her voice barely audible, yet charged with a profound emotion. "It was… everything." The confession hung in the air, a fragile thing, easily shattered. It was an admission of the weight of her past, the accumulation of losses and betrayals that had shaped her into the woman she was today – a woman hardened by circumstance, yet still capable of profound vulnerability.

Dante nodded slowly, understanding dawning in his eyes. He understood the implications of her words; it wasn't just the current danger, but the accumulation of past traumas that had propelled her into this fight. It was a fight not only against the Morettis, but against the ghosts of her past, the demons that had relentlessly haunted her.

He reached out, his hand gently covering hers. The touch was unexpected, a tender gesture in the midst of their desperate situation. His touch held no judgment, only understanding.

"I know," he murmured, his voice thick with empathy. "I know it wasn't just about tonight."

He remembered her stories, fragments of a life marred by violence and betrayal, stories whispered between missions, between gunfights and narrow escapes. He recalled the haunted look in her eyes when she spoke of her family, the unspoken grief that clung to her like a shroud. He'd seen glimpses of the woman she used to be, a woman brimming with laughter and light, a woman before the shadows swallowed her whole.

He, too, carried his own burden, his own past etched into the lines around his eyes, the scars barely concealed beneath his tough exterior. The death of his parents, the years spent on the streets battling for survival, the bitter betrayal by those he once trusted— all were etched into his soul. He understood the deep, visceral wound Elena carried, the relentless fight to overcome the past, to find peace amidst the chaos.

They sat in silence for a long time, the silence no longer oppressive, but a shared space of understanding, a silent acknowledgement of their shared pain. The flickering candlelight danced on their faces, illuminating the shadows and the resilience etched into their features. The emotional outpouring, long suppressed, created a palpable sense of catharsis, of release.

The memories flooded back. Elena spoke of her childhood, of a home filled with laughter that had been shattered by violence, of a family torn apart by greed and betrayal. She spoke of the helplessness she felt as a child, the fear that had become a constant companion. She spoke of her escape, her relentless fight for survival, the bitterness that clung to her like a second skin.

Dante listened, his heart aching with empathy. He saw not just the hardened woman who faced down Lorenzo Moretti, but a vulnerable child, scarred and broken, fighting to reclaim her life. He saw the fight in her eyes, the unwavering determination that refused to yield to despair.

In turn, he shared his own story, a tale of hardship and resilience, of betrayal and loss, of the scars that defined him as much as the victories he had achieved. He revealed the vulnerability he had long hidden behind a mask of unwavering resolve, the pain he had meticulously buried beneath layers of self-reliance. He acknowledged the bitterness that still simmered beneath the surface, a constant reminder of the injustices he had witnessed and endured.

As they spoke, the weight of their past began to lift, the burden they had carried for so long beginning to ease. The shared confession, the mutual understanding, created a bond stronger than any they had known before. It was a connection forged not only in the heat of battle, but in the quiet intimacy of shared trauma, a shared understanding of the wounds that had defined them.

The dawn broke, casting a pale light into the warehouse, illuminating the wreckage of their battle—both the physical and emotional wreckage. The warehouse, once a symbol of hiding, now became a sanctuary, a testament to their resilience, their shared history, and the bond that had been forged in the crucible of their shared past. They were no longer just partners in a dangerous mission; they were allies in a battle against their own demons, united by their shared wounds and their shared determination to create a future free from the ghosts that haunted them. The reckoning with the Morettis was just one part of a larger battle, a battle for their own lives and their own souls. The fight had just begun.

25
A NEW BEGINNING

The mountain air, crisp and clean, was a stark contrast to the stale, smoky atmosphere of the abandoned warehouse. Elena breathed deeply, the scent of pine and damp earth filling her lungs, a welcome change from the metallic tang of blood and gunpowder that clung to her like a second skin. The secluded cabin, nestled high in the mountains, offered a sanctuary, a refuge from the relentless pursuit of the Morettis and, more importantly, a refuge from the ghosts of their pasts.

Dante, ever watchful, moved silently around the cabin, checking the security measures. He was a creature of habit, his meticulousness a reflection of his deep-seated anxieties, a constant need to be prepared for the unexpected. But even his usual vigilance seemed to soften in this tranquil setting. The mountains, silent witnesses to countless stories, seemed to absorb the weight of their shared traumas, offering a respite from the ceaseless churn of adrenaline and fear.

They had chosen this place deliberately, a conscious decision to distance themselves from the city, from the reminders of their past lives, from the ever-present threat of Lorenzo Moretti and his associates. It wasn't just about physical safety; it was about creating a space for healing, for rebuilding, for finding a sense of normalcy amidst the chaos.

The cabin itself was simple, rustic even, its interior furnished with salvaged wood and worn leather. But it possessed a quiet charm, a sense of warmth that contrasted sharply with the starkness of their recent experiences. A crackling fire in the hearth cast dancing shadows on the walls, creating an atmosphere of comforting intimacy. Elena found herself drawn to the window, watching the sun dip below the horizon, painting the sky in hues of orange and purple, a breathtaking spectacle that seemed to erase the darkness of the past.

"It's beautiful," she whispered, her voice barely audible above the crackling fire.

Dante joined her at the window, his arm brushing against hers. The touch was a silent acknowledgment of their shared vulnerability, a testament to the bond forged in the fires of their shared struggles. He didn't speak, but his presence was a silent reassurance, a comforting weight against the unspoken anxieties that still lingered.

The silence wasn't oppressive, as it had been in the warehouse. Here, in the embrace of the mountains, silence held a different quality — a stillness that allowed them to process the events of the past few weeks, to allow the weight of their emotions to settle.

Days turned into weeks, and the routine of their mountain retreat began to feel normal. They spent their time hiking through the snow-covered trails, their footsteps the only sound disturbing the tranquil stillness of the landscape. They cooked simple meals together, sharing stories and laughter, a stark contrast to the tense exchanges and close calls that had defined their recent collaboration. Elena, unexpectedly, found solace in the quiet solitude, in the rhythm of chopping wood, in the simple act of tending a garden. The work was grounding, a tangible connection to the earth that anchored her in the present, drawing her away from the turmoil of the past.

Dante, too, found himself adapting to this unexpected peace. He discovered a talent for carpentry, his hands, usually skilled at wielding weapons, now shaping rough-hewn timber into functional pieces of furniture. The quiet rhythm of the work seemed to soothe the deep-seated anxieties that had plagued him for so long. The transformation wasn't immediate; the memories, the scars of his past, still lingered. But here, in the solitude of the mountains, those memories seemed less sharp, less overwhelming. He found a measure of peace, a kind of quiet understanding that had eluded him for years.

One evening, as they sat by the fire, Elena spoke of her childhood, of a life filled with laughter and carefree days before the violence had consumed her world. She spoke of her family, the memories flickering like candlelight – warm and inviting, yet fragile and easily extinguished. She spoke of the pain, of the loss, of the years spent running, always looking over her shoulder.

Dante listened, his gaze fixed on the flames dancing in the hearth, his heart aching with empathy. He knew the weight of her words, the depth of her sorrow. He had seen the pain etched onto her face, the shadows that danced in her eyes. He knew she had carried this burden for too long, a burden that had hardened her, made her into the woman she was today. But he also saw the resilience, the unwavering determination that had fueled her survival.

In turn, Dante shared more of his story, the pieces of a fragmented past slowly coming together. He spoke of the streets, of the brutality, of the constant struggle for survival. He spoke of his parents, their absence a gaping hole in his life, a wound that refused to heal. He spoke of betrayal, of the friends he had lost, of the enemies he had made.

Their shared confidences, whispered in the quiet intimacy of the cabin, were a balm to their wounds. They spoke of their fears, their doubts, their vulnerabilities. They acknowledged the pain, the losses, the scars that had defined their lives. But amidst the pain, they discovered a connection, a bond forged not just in shared danger, but in shared vulnerability, in the shared understanding of profound loss.

The mountain retreat wasn't a fairytale ending. The threat of the Morettis still loomed, a dark shadow on the horizon. The past, with all its pain and trauma, remained a constant companion. But in the quiet sanctuary of the cabin, they had found something precious: a new beginning. It wasn't a forgetting, not a denial of the past. It was an acknowledgment, a healing, a shared journey towards a future where they could face their demons together. They were rebuilding, not just their lives, but themselves. They were forging a new identity, one based not on fear and loss, but on hope and resilience, a resilience born from the crucible of their shared experiences, a resilience forged in the quiet strength of their newfound love. The road ahead would be long and challenging, but they would face it together, hand in hand, their bond stronger than any weapon, stronger than any enemy. The reckoning was over, but the journey had just begun. The mountain air, crisp and clean, held the promise of a new dawn, a new beginning, a new life.

26
DEALING WITH LOSS

The crisp mountain air, usually a source of solace, felt biting cold against Elena's skin that day. The cemetery, perched high on a windswept hill overlooking the valley, was a stark contrast to the warmth of their cabin. It was a place of quiet contemplation, a place where the silence wasn't comforting, but heavy, laden with the weight of unspoken grief. They stood before a simple, weathered headstone, the name barely legible beneath the accumulation of winter's frost. It was a name that echoed in the silence, a name that carried the weight of a life cut short, a life lost to the violence that had shadowed their own.

Dante placed a single, crimson rose against the cold stone. The color stood out vividly against the gray of the stone and the stark white of the snow. He hadn't known the person buried beneath, but the shared sorrow, the shared understanding of loss, transcended personal acquaintance. It was a shared pain, a silent acknowledgement of the price they had both paid, the price that so many others had paid in their brutal world.

Elena stood beside him, her gaze fixed on the headstone, her face pale and drawn. The mountain air seemed to amplify the silence, the stillness of the place, making the grief almost palpable. The wind whispered through the bare branches of the pines, creating a mournful melody that seemed to amplify the depth of their sorrow.

"It's not just the ones we lose in the fights, is it?" she murmured, her voice barely audible above the wind's lament. "It's the lives we lose in the aftermath. The pieces of ourselves we lose along the way."

Dante nodded, his throat tight with unshed tears. He understood what she meant. The battles, the escapes, the constant fear – it had eroded pieces of them, leaving them scarred and broken. Each close call, each victory hard-won, came with a cost. They had both paid that cost in blood, in sweat, and in the slow, agonizing erosion of their souls. The mountain retreat had offered a temporary respite, a chance to heal, but the scars remained, deep and painful reminders of their journey.

They stood in silence for a long time, the wind their only companion, the silence punctuated only by the occasional rustle of snow-laden branches. The weight of their shared grief settled upon them, a heavy blanket that suffocated the breath from their lungs. They were grieving not only for the fallen, but for the innocence they had lost, for the lives they could have lived had fate been kinder, had the Morettis never entered their world.

As the sun began its slow descent, casting long shadows across the snow-covered ground, Elena turned to Dante, her eyes filled with a mixture of sorrow and resilience. "We need to talk," she said, her voice low and steady, surprisingly strong considering the emotional weight of the day. "About everything."

They walked slowly back down the hill, the setting sun casting a somber glow on their faces. The conversation started slowly, cautiously, each word measured, each sentence carefully constructed. They began with the immediate, the tangible losses – the lives lost during their last confrontation with the Morettis, the friends they had lost along the way. They talked about the weight of responsibility, the guilt that clung to them like a second skin. Elena spoke of the near-constant fear, the ever-present awareness that death could come at any moment, a fear that had become deeply ingrained in her very being. She described the sleepless nights, the nightmares that haunted her dreams, the constant feeling of unease that permeated her waking hours.

Dante shared his own anxieties. The years spent on the streets, the constant struggle for survival, had left him emotionally scarred. He spoke about the profound sense of loneliness that had haunted him since childhood, a loneliness that he had tried to numb with violence, with adrenaline fueled escapes, with the thrill of the fight. He had always been alone, always fighting for survival, until he met Elena.

But their conversation extended beyond the tangible, beyond the immediate aftermath of their battle. They delved into the deeper, more profound losses – the loss of their innocence, the loss of the carefree lives they had once imagined. Elena spoke about the life she had left behind, the family she had lost, the dreams that had been shattered. She described the emotional chasm that had opened up within her, the void that seemed impossible to fill. The life she had once known, a life filled with laughter and hope, now existed only as fragmented memories, ghosts of a past that would never return.

Dante shared his own sense of loss, his own unspoken regrets. He spoke about the friends he had lost, the betrayals he had suffered, the constant struggle to maintain his humanity in a world that seemed determined to strip it away. He had always expected to die young, violence a constant companion. He had never imagined a life beyond the streets, a life filled with love and companionship. Elena had given him that. But the scars remained. He admitted that he often felt like a stranger in this new, more peaceful life.

The conversation wasn't easy. There were tears, silences punctuated only by the wind, and moments when words failed them. But through it all, a profound understanding grew, a shared recognition of their shared journey, a shared awareness of the deep wounds they carried. They found solace in the shared acknowledgment of their pain, a validation of their experiences, a mutual understanding that transcended words.

As darkness enveloped the mountain, they returned to their cabin, the fire casting a warm glow against the darkening walls. The silence between them was no longer heavy with grief, but filled with a quiet understanding, a shared acceptance of their scars, a recognition of the strength they had found within themselves. The road to healing would be long, but they would travel it together, hand in hand, their bond forged in the crucible of their shared experiences, a bond stronger than any loss, stronger than any trauma. The aftermath of their battles was not an end, but a new beginning, a new chapter in their shared life. The journey had been brutal, the scars would remain, but amidst the darkness, a fragile flame of hope flickered, illuminating their path towards a future that was both uncertain and yet, filled with a possibility of enduring love, a love born from the ashes of their shared losses. The mountains, silent witnesses to their pain, now seemed to embrace them, offering a sanctuary, a haven from the storms of their past, a promise of a new dawn.

27

REBUILDING LIVES

The cottage, a humble dwelling nestled amongst rolling hills and whispering fields, offered a stark contrast to their previous existence. Gone were the shadowed alleyways and the ever-present threat of violence. Here, the air hummed with the quiet melody of nature, a symphony of birdsong and rustling leaves, a balm to their wounded souls. The small kitchen, with its worn wooden table and mismatched chairs, became a sanctuary, a space where they could share simple meals and quiet conversations, rebuilding the fragile foundations of their relationship.

Elena, ever practical, took on the task of transforming the cottage into a home. She spent hours tending to the small vegetable garden, her hands, once calloused from gripping weapons, now gently coaxing life from the soil. The act of nurturing the plants, watching them grow and flourish, seemed to mirror her own internal healing process. She found a strange sense of peace in the repetitive tasks—the weeding, the watering, the harvesting—a rhythm that calmed her frayed nerves and eased the constant anxiety that had plagued her for so long. Each sprouting seedling represented a new beginning, a tiny spark of hope in the face of overwhelming loss.

Dante, accustomed to the frenetic energy of survival, found himself grappling with the stillness. The silence, initially welcomed as a reprieve from the constant threat, began to feel oppressive. The quiet hum of the countryside was a stark contrast to the cacophony of the city streets he had once called home. He spent his days repairing the cottage, his hands, once skilled in dismantling weapons, now meticulously mending walls and patching roofs. The physical labor was a distraction, a tangible manifestation of his efforts to rebuild, to create something stable and lasting from the fragments of his past. The rhythmic swing of his hammer, the scrape of wood against wood, provided a sense of purpose, a sense of control in a world that had often felt chaotic and unpredictable.

Evenings were spent by the crackling fireplace, the warmth of the flames a comforting counterpoint to the chill that still lingered within them. They would talk, sometimes about their past, often about their future. They spoke of dreams long deferred, of lives they had envisioned before the Morettis had shattered their world. They shared their fears and insecurities, their anxieties and hopes, their dreams and disappointments. The unspoken words, the lingering silences, no longer felt heavy with grief but resonated with a burgeoning understanding, a shared commitment to forging a future together.

Elena began to paint again. Her canvases, once filled with the stark realities of violence, now blossomed with vibrant hues and breathtaking landscapes, capturing the beauty of their newfound sanctuary. The act of creation was therapeutic, a way to express the emotions that words couldn't capture, to translate the turmoil of her past into the serene beauty of her present. Each brushstroke was a testament to her resilience, her ability to find beauty even in the face of profound loss.

Dante, surprisingly, discovered a talent for carpentry. He fashioned simple furniture, sturdy and elegant, each piece a testament to his newfound skill and dedication. He found a sense of pride in his work, a sense of accomplishment that transcended the mere act of building. The tools in his hands were not weapons of destruction but instruments of creation, symbols of his transformation from a street-hardened survivor to a man capable of building a life, building a home, building a future.

Their days were filled with a routine that was both comforting and challenging. They learned to rely on each other, to support each other in ways they never had before. The shared meals, the quiet evenings by the fire, the collaborative projects around the cottage, slowly knit together the threads of their damaged lives. Their shared past was a constant presence, a shadow that lingered at the edges of their new life, but it no longer held them captive. They had learned to live with it, to integrate it into the fabric of their existence, transforming it from a source of despair into a catalyst for growth.

One day, as they sat on the porch, watching the sun dip below the horizon, painting the sky in hues of orange and purple, Elena turned to Dante, her eyes filled with a quiet contentment. "We're doing it," she said, her voice barely above a whisper. "We're really doing it."

Dante smiled, a genuine smile that reached his eyes, a smile that spoke of a journey endured, of pain overcome, of a future hard-earned. He reached for her hand, his fingers intertwining with hers. The touch was simple, yet profound, a silent testament to the strength of their bond, the depth of their love. The scars remained, visible and invisible, reminders of their past, but they were no longer defining features. They were marks of resilience, of survival, of a love that had been forged in the crucible of adversity.

The rebuilding wasn't simply about the physical restoration of their lives; it was about the emotional, spiritual, and psychological rebuilding that took place within each of them. It was about learning to trust again, to love again, to hope again. The countryside provided the setting, the quiet solitude, the opportunity to heal. But it was their mutual dedication, their shared journey, that provided the strength, the resilience, the love that ultimately rebuilt their lives, not only as individuals, but as a couple, facing the uncertain future with a renewed sense of purpose and the unwavering strength of their love.

The process was far from easy. There were days when the weight of their past threatened to overwhelm them, days when the fear and anxiety returned with a vengeance. There were nights when sleep eluded them, when the nightmares resurrected the horrors they had endured. But they faced these challenges together, their love a steadfast anchor in the storm. They learned to communicate their fears, to validate each other's pain, to provide comfort and support without judgment.

The cottage became a symbol of their rebirth, a testament to their resilience. It was more than just a dwelling; it was a sanctuary, a refuge, a haven from the storms of their past. The simple act of tending to the garden, the rhythmic sounds of Dante's carpentry, the vibrant colors on Elena's canvases, all served as reminders of their journey, of the progress they had made, of the life they were slowly and painstakingly building together.

As the seasons changed, so too did their lives. The vibrant colors of spring mirrored the blossoming hope in their hearts. The warmth of summer symbolized the deepening of their love. The crisp coolness of autumn represented the harvest of their efforts, the tangible results of their hard work. The quiet stillness of winter became a time for reflection, for gratitude, for the quiet appreciation of the journey they had undertaken, the lives they had rebuilt. And as they stood together, hand in hand, looking out at the snow-covered landscape, they knew that the journey had been long and arduous, but the destination, their shared future, was worth the struggle. The future was uncertain, but it was theirs, built on the ashes of their past, a testament to the enduring power of love and the resilience of the human spirit. The aftermath was not an ending, but a beginning, a testament to the enduring strength of their love and their unwavering commitment to building a future together, a future filled with hope and promise.

28

UNEXPETED CONSEQUENCES

The tranquility of their rural haven proved to be a temporary reprieve. The city, a place they had hoped to leave behind forever, cast a long shadow over their newfound peace. A cryptic phone call, a hushed whisper on the wind, shattered the illusion of their idyllic existence. It was a veiled threat, a reminder that the past, no matter how hard they tried to bury it, refused to stay buried. The Morettis, or what remained of their vast and sinister empire, still had tentacles reaching into their lives, a venomous grip that refused to loosen.

The call came late one evening, as the wind howled a mournful song outside their cottage window. Elena answered, her voice trembling slightly as she listened to the gravelly voice on the other end, a voice that sent shivers down her spine. It was a message, not a conversation, a chilling reminder of their past, a veiled threat laced with thinly disguised malice. The caller spoke of consequences, of debts that could not be ignored, of actions that had far reaching ramifications, extending far beyond the walls of their sanctuary.

The message hung in the air, heavy and suffocating, a palpable sense of dread settling over them. The idyllic calm of the cottage was shattered, replaced by a chilling premonition. The vibrant colors of Elena's paintings seemed to dull, the rhythmic tap of Dante's hammer lost its comforting cadence. The peace they had so painstakingly cultivated was threatened, the fragile foundation of their new life teetering on the brink of collapse.

Their quiet sanctuary was no longer a refuge, but a prison, their isolation a vulnerability. They were pawns in a game far larger than themselves, players in a conflict that extended beyond their personal struggle. The aftermath of their confrontation with the Morettis had unexpected consequences, repercussions they had never foreseen, challenges they had never anticipated.

Elena, ever the strategist, began to analyze the threat, piecing together the fragments of information like a meticulous puzzle. She meticulously retraced their steps, scrutinizing each decision, each encounter, searching for any clue that might shed light on the identity of their tormentor and their motives. She was acutely aware that their relative anonymity in the countryside offered only temporary protection; their past deeds had created ripples that spread far and wide.

Dante, grappling with the resurgence of his old anxieties, sought to protect Elena, to shield her from the storm that was brewing. His carpentry, once a source of solace, became a means of defense, his hands working tirelessly to reinforce their cottage, transforming it from a haven into a fortress. He installed new locks, reinforced the windows, and created hidden compartments for their most valuable possessions. The rhythmic hammering became a mantra, a desperate attempt to regain control in the face of encroaching chaos.

Their shared silence was punctuated by the frantic flurry of their individual efforts. Elena researched, analyzed, and strategized, while Dante reinforced their defenses, providing a tangible, physical shield against the intangible threat. Their roles, seemingly reversed from their time in the city, mirrored their shifting emotional landscapes. Elena's analytical prowess, once overshadowed by Dante's protective instincts, was now their primary defense, while Dante's strength provided a crucial layer of protection.

The threat, however, was not merely physical. The caller's words had awakened dormant fears, unearthing the buried trauma of their past. The nightmares returned, more vivid, more terrifying than before. The quiet evenings by the fire were haunted by the ghosts of their past, their whispers mingling with the crackling flames. The peace they had so diligently cultivated was fractured, the fragile harmony threatened by the insidious tendrils of fear and uncertainty.

Their newfound routine was disrupted, the rhythm of their days thrown into chaos. Their collaborative projects were abandoned, replaced by a desperate scramble for survival. The vegetable garden, once a source of solace, was neglected, its vibrant hues fading under the weight of their anxiety. The once-vibrant canvases lay unfinished, their colors dulled by the oppressive weight of impending doom. The tools of their crafts, their sources of peace, lay dormant, symbols of their helplessness in the face of the looming threat.

As days turned into nights, their initial fear gave way to a

steely resolve. They knew that running was not an option.
They had faced death before, stared it in the face and
survived. This was different. This was not a direct
confrontation, but a subtle, insidious attack, an attempt to
destabilize them, to erode their carefully constructed peace.
This was a war of attrition, a slow, agonizing erosion of their
hard-won happiness.

Elena, drawing on her past experiences, began to formulate a
plan. She knew they couldn't fight fire with fire; they needed
to outsmart their adversary, to use their intelligence and
resourcefulness to turn the tables. She started gathering
information, meticulously piecing together the clues provided
in the cryptic message, her mind a whirlwind of strategy and
counter-strategy.

Dante, initially consumed by fear and protective instincts,
slowly regained his composure. His strength, once channeled
into carpentry, was now focused on acquiring information,
gathering intelligence, and protecting their newfound home.
He used his network of contacts, a remnant of his past life, to
uncover information about their mysterious caller and their
motives. He learned to trust his instincts, honing the skills that
had once kept him alive on the streets, adapting them to their
current situation.

Their relationship, forged in the crucible of adversity, was
tested once again. They faced their fears, their anxieties, and
their vulnerabilities together. The shared burden
strengthened their bond, solidifying the foundation of their
love and commitment. Their mutual support, their unwavering
trust, became their most powerful weapon.

The unexpected consequences of their actions, the unforeseen challenges they faced, ultimately served to strengthen their bond and reveal the true depth of their love and commitment. The threat, though chilling, became a catalyst, forcing them to confront their past traumas and rediscover the resilience of their spirit. They were no longer simply rebuilding their lives; they were forging a new future, one born from the ashes of their past, tempered by adversity, and strengthened by their shared love. The journey was far from over; the city's shadows still loomed large. But together, they faced the unknown, ready to fight for their future, for their love, for the fragile peace they had painstakingly created. Their unexpected journey, fraught with danger and uncertainty, had only just begun.

29
RECONCILIATION

The weight of their unspoken fears hung heavy in the air, a palpable tension that even the crackling fire couldn't dispel. The threat, though veiled, had cracked the veneer of their hard-won peace, revealing the deep fissures in their relationship, fissures that ran deeper than the anxieties stirred by the mysterious phone call. It was a silent battle, fought not with weapons but with hesitant words and lingering silences. The shared trauma of their past, once buried beneath layers of cautious optimism, clawed its way back to the surface, demanding to be acknowledged, to be healed.

Elena, ever the pragmatist, initiated the conversation one crisp morning, the rising sun casting long shadows across the cottage floor. She spoke softly, her voice barely a whisper, her words carefully chosen, each syllable weighted with the burden of their shared history. She confessed the guilt that gnawed at her, the regrets that haunted her waking hours and shadowed her dreams. She spoke of the choices they had made, the paths they had taken, the lives they had irrevocably altered. She wasn't seeking absolution, not yet, but a starting point, a shared acknowledgment of the damage they had inflicted.

Dante listened, his gaze fixed on the dancing flames in the hearth, his silence a testament to the turmoil within. He was a man of action, of physical strength, ill-equipped to navigate the treacherous terrain of emotional reconciliation. His silence, however, wasn't a rejection; it was a manifestation of his own internal struggle, a battle against the ghosts of his past, the demons that had haunted him for years. His knuckles, white as bone, gripped the worn handle of his favorite carving knife, a tangible representation of the tension that coiled within him.

The silence stretched, broken only by the crackling fire and the gentle rustling of the wind outside. Finally, he spoke, his voice rough and hesitant, laden with the weight of unspoken remorse. He confessed his own failures, his own shortcomings, the impulsive actions that had led to unforeseen consequences. He admitted his guilt, not just for the harm he'd directly caused, but for the pain he'd inflicted on Elena, for the burden he'd placed upon her shoulders. His confession, though halting and imperfect, was sincere, a testament to the depth of his love and his willingness to confront their shared past.

Their reconciliation wasn't a sudden, dramatic event, but a gradual, painstaking process. It began with small gestures, with shared silences, with the slow, deliberate rebuilding of trust. They started with the simplest tasks, tending to their neglected garden, the vibrant colors of the growing vegetables slowly mirroring the burgeoning hope within them. Elena began to paint again, her canvases blossoming with renewed energy, her strokes filled with a newfound purpose. Dante's carpentry returned, his hands finding solace in the rhythmic tap of his hammer against wood, his creations taking on a new significance, a symbol of their commitment to building a better future.

Their journey towards reconciliation wasn't confined to the walls of their cottage. They embarked on a series of pilgrimages, visiting the places where their past mistakes had taken root. Their first stop was the city, the place where their lives had taken a dark turn. They visited the abandoned warehouse, a stark reminder of their past, their hands tracing the cold, damp bricks, silently acknowledging the ghosts that lingered within its walls. They stood in the shadow of the towering skyscrapers, emblems of the ruthless ambition that had driven them, a stark contrast to the serene landscape of their rural retreat.

In the city's heart, they sought out those they had wronged, those whose lives had been irrevocably altered by their actions. The encounters were difficult, fraught with tension, with apologies offered and reluctantly accepted. There were tears, accusations, and moments of excruciating discomfort, but also a sense of closure, of a weight lifted, however slightly. They faced their past, head-on, refusing to shy away from the consequences of their actions. They were not asking for forgiveness so much as offering amends, demonstrating their commitment to making things right, as much as that was possible.

Their journey then took them to a remote mountain village, a place intertwined with a past betrayal. Here, they sought out an elderly woman, the victim of their ruthless ambition, a woman whose life had been shattered by their actions. This meeting was the most challenging, laden with a heavy silence, punctuated by the woman's quiet acceptance of their apologies. It was a stark reminder of the lasting damage they had inflicted, the indelible scars their past had etched upon the hearts and lives of others.

The process of seeking forgiveness wasn't always met with acceptance. Some encounters ended with anger and resentment, and they had to respect the choice to not forgive. These experiences, however difficult, highlighted the enormity of their past actions, serving as humbling reminders of the irreparable damage they had caused and the long road ahead.

The final leg of their journey took them to a quiet coastal town, where they sought solace and reflection. Walking along the windswept beach, they contemplated their actions, the weight of their past mistakes pressing down upon them. The vastness of the ocean, the rhythmic crash of the waves, became a metaphor for their own journey, a reminder of the boundless capacity for redemption and forgiveness. They talked, really talked, for the first time without fear or judgement. They shared their deepest fears, their most vulnerable emotions, laying bare their souls to each other in a powerful and profound display of trust and commitment.

The reconciliation wasn't a simple act of saying sorry and expecting immediate forgiveness. It was a complex, evolving process, a journey that demanded honesty, humility, and unwavering commitment. It was a process that tested the very limits of their relationship, revealing the strength of their bond and the depth of their love. They emerged from this crucible of self-reflection and atonement with a renewed understanding of themselves, of each other, and of the enduring power of human connection.

They returned to their cottage, the weight of their past significantly lighter, though not completely gone. The scars remained, but they were no longer gaping wounds; they were fading reminders, proof of their arduous journey, testaments to their commitment to redemption. Their love, tested and strengthened by adversity, now stood as a beacon of hope, a testament to the enduring power of forgiveness and the unwavering resilience of the human spirit. The future was still uncertain, the shadows of the city still loomed, but they faced it together, hand-in-hand, their hearts filled with a cautious optimism, their spirits infused with a newfound sense of purpose and shared resolve. Their journey had been long and arduous, but the path to reconciliation, to forgiveness, and to a future born from the ashes of their past, was a path they were determined to walk, together.

30
ACCEPTANCE AND FORGIVENESS

The quiet hum of the ancient church, a sanctuary of stained glass and hushed reverence, enveloped them. The scent of old wood and beeswax clung to the air, a comforting balm to their frayed nerves. They hadn't spoken much on the drive, the familiar landscape blurring past in a haze of unspoken thoughts. The weight of their past, the burden of their shared guilt, still pressed upon them, but it felt different now, less crushing, more... manageable. The arduous journey of confession and amends, the raw honesty they'd shared on the windswept beach, had cleared a space within them, a space for acceptance, for forgiveness, for the tentative beginnings of healing.

Elena sat in a worn pew, the cool wood a soothing contrast to the warmth of her hand nestled in Dante's. His touch, once a source of both comfort and fear, now felt like a lifeline, a grounding force in the vast emptiness of their shared history. The church, a place of solace and reflection, felt oddly appropriate, a space where the whispered prayers of countless souls seemed to echo their own silent pleas for redemption.

Sunlight streamed through the stained-glass windows,

painting the ancient stone walls in vibrant hues of sapphire and ruby, amber and emerald. The light, filtered and softened, seemed to wash away the shadows that clung to them, the residue of their past mistakes. It was as if the very architecture of the church, imbued with centuries of whispered confessions and heartfelt prayers, was conspiring to soothe their souls.

The silence between them wasn't fraught with tension this time. It was a comfortable silence, a shared space of contemplation, a silent acknowledgment of the profound shift that had taken place within them. It was a silence that held the promise of a future, a future born from the ashes of their past, forged in the fires of their shared atonement. It was a silence that spoke volumes, a testament to the resilience of their bond, the strength of their love, and the enduring power of forgiveness.

Dante finally broke the silence, his voice low and measured, a stark contrast to the emotional torrent of their previous confessions. "I... I think I understand now," he began, his words hesitant but sincere. "I understand the depth of the hurt I caused, not just to you, but to everyone involved. I understand that there's no magic fix, no quick erasure of the past. The damage is done. But..." He paused, his gaze searching hers, seeking understanding, seeking confirmation. "But I also understand that we can't live in the shadows of our past. We have to find a way to live with it, to move forward."

Elena nodded, a single tear tracing a path down her cheek, a tear not of sadness, but of relief, of acceptance. "Yes," she whispered, her voice barely audible above the gentle murmur of the church. "We have to. We owe it to ourselves, and to everyone we've hurt. We owe it to the people we've wronged to show them that we've learned from our mistakes. And we owe it to ourselves to build a life free from the constant weight of regret."

Their conversation that day wasn't about absolution or the erasure of their past. It was about acceptance, both of the mistakes they had made and of the pain they had inflicted. It was about acknowledging the weight of their actions and moving forward, not with a desire to forget, but with a determination to ensure such mistakes never happened again. It wasn't about erasing the past, but learning from it. It wasn't about escaping their responsibility but embracing it.

They spent hours in the church, their conversation weaving a tapestry of shared guilt, mutual understanding, and a dawning hope. They spoke of their individual journeys, their internal struggles, the battles they had fought to reach this point. They spoke of the fear that still lingered, the uncertainty that shadowed their future, but also of the nascent strength they'd discovered within themselves, the resilience forged in the crucible of their shared experience.

They didn't leave the church feeling completely healed, completely free from the shadows of their past. The scars remained, etched deep into the fabric of their souls, but they were no longer gaping wounds. They were fading reminders, reminders of the arduous journey they'd undertaken, of the pain they'd inflicted and the pain they'd endured. But they were also reminders of their shared strength, of their enduring love, and of their unwavering commitment to a future defined not by the mistakes of the past, but by the promise of a better tomorrow.

Leaving the church, they walked hand-in-hand, the late afternoon sun casting long shadows behind them. The weight of their past felt lighter, more manageable, but it wasn't gone. They knew that the road ahead would still be challenging, that there would be moments of doubt, moments of fear, and moments of lingering guilt. There would be setbacks, and moments where they'd have to dig deep to find the strength to continue. There would be moments of agonizing self-doubt, and the constant threat of the past catching up to them.

But as they walked away from the church, they knew that they wouldn't face these challenges alone. They had each other. They had the shared experience of their journey, the lessons learned, and the strength they had found in their mutual acceptance and forgiveness. They had the shared burden of their past, but also the shared hope for a brighter future. It was a future they would build together, a future founded on honesty, humility, and unwavering commitment. A future built on the solid foundation of forgiveness, not just for the sake of each other, but for the sake of those they had hurt, for the sake of their own peace of mind and for a future where their past mistakes were a source of learning rather than eternal regret.

The journey had changed them both profoundly. Elena, once the pragmatic strategist, had learned the importance of vulnerability and the power of forgiveness. Dante, the man of action, had discovered the depth of his emotional capacity and the transformative power of empathy. Their individual transformations were mirrored in their relationship. The bond between them, once fragile and fraught with suspicion and unspoken fears, had been strengthened and deepened, forged in the fires of adversity, tempered by the acceptance and forgiveness they had found within themselves and within each other.

They continued their journey, not with the lightness of those who have escaped their past, but with the quiet determination of those who have faced it head-on, and committed themselves to rebuilding their lives, their relationship and their future, brick by brick, with a shared understanding of their past mistakes and a determination to never repeat them. The road ahead wouldn't be easy. The specter of their past would inevitably resurface at times, threatening to consume them. But now, they faced it together, hand in hand, with a newfound strength and a shared commitment to a future built on the foundations of honesty, compassion, and a profound understanding of the transformative power of forgiveness. Their journey towards redemption was far from over, but they were finally walking it together, side by side, their hearts filled with a cautious optimism, their spirits infused with a renewed sense of purpose and shared resolve.

31
NEW BEGININGS

The crisp autumn air nipped at their cheeks as they walked away from the church, hand in hand. The weight of their shared past, though still present, felt less like an anchor dragging them down and more like a heavy stone in a backpack—a burden they carried, but one that no longer threatened to crush them. The silence between them now felt different; it wasn't the strained silence of unspoken accusations, but the comfortable quiet of shared understanding. It was the silence of two souls slowly finding their way back to peace, together.

That evening, over a simple dinner of pasta and wine in a cozy Italian trattoria, they began to talk about the future, the tentative, hopeful future they were now daring to envision. The conversation flowed easily, free from the tension that had once dominated their interactions. Elena spoke of her renewed interest in her long-abandoned passion for painting, a passion stifled by years of guilt and self-doubt. The vibrant colors she'd seen in the church's stained-glass windows had rekindled a spark within her, a desire to express the complexities of her emotions through art.

"I think... I think I want to start painting again," she said, her voice soft but firm. A hesitant smile played on her lips. "I've already contacted a few galleries. I'm thinking of doing a series based on... well, on our journey. On the things we've been through."

Dante listened intently, his gaze filled with admiration and support. He understood the depth of her need to express herself, to pour her emotions onto canvas, to create something beautiful from the ashes of their shared pain. He had always appreciated her strength, her sharp intellect, her pragmatic approach to life, but it was her vulnerability, her willingness to expose her soul, that truly captivated him now. He saw a newfound freedom in her eyes, a lightness of spirit that had been absent for so long.

He, too, spoke of new beginnings. His work in international finance had always demanded long hours, relentless travel, and a focus on the bottom line. It had been a life he'd chosen, a life that had both provided him with success and left him emotionally hollow. But now, he felt a pull towards something different, something more meaningful.

"I've been thinking about... scaling back," he confessed, swirling the wine in his glass. "I've been looking into setting up a foundation. Something that focuses on restorative justice. Helping people rebuild their lives after they've made mistakes." He looked at Elena, a flicker of vulnerability in his usually steely gaze. "It's... it's a way for me to make amends, I suppose."

Elena reached across the table, her fingers brushing his. The simple touch held a world of unspoken understanding and support. "It's perfect, Dante," she whispered. "It's exactly what you need to do."

Their new beginnings weren't easy. Elena's return to painting wasn't a seamless transition. The initial canvases were fraught with emotion, raw and intense, reflecting the tumultuous journey they had both endured. She found herself pouring her anxieties and insecurities onto the canvas, struggling to find the balance between the darkness of her past and the tentative hope for the future. There were nights when she questioned her ability, her talent, even her sanity.

Dante, too, faced challenges. Establishing the foundation was more demanding than he had anticipated. The bureaucracy, the fundraising, the endless meetings, all tested his patience and energy. He grappled with feelings of inadequacy, haunted by the past mistakes that had led him to this point. There were moments of doubt, when he questioned whether he was capable of making a real difference, whether he was worthy of the second chance he was desperately seeking.

But they faced these challenges together. They became each other's anchors, their shared support system, their unwavering source of strength and encouragement. They spent hours in their small apartment studio, Elena painting, Dante working on his laptop, the air thick with a comfortable silence punctuated by the occasional murmur of encouragement or a shared laugh. They talked openly about their struggles, their frustrations, their fears. They learned to be vulnerable with each other, to allow themselves to be seen and understood, flaws and all.

Slowly, painstakingly, they began to rebuild their lives, brick by brick. Elena's art evolved, becoming more assured, more confident. The colors on her canvases became brighter, bolder, reflecting the growth and healing she was experiencing. Her work began to gain recognition, garnering praise from critics and collectors alike. The success brought her a sense of validation, a confirmation that she had found her purpose, her place in the world.

Dante's foundation also began to flourish. He found talented and passionate individuals who shared his vision, building a team dedicated to restorative justice and community support. He threw himself into the work with a renewed energy and commitment, finding purpose and fulfillment in his efforts to make amends. His work was far from easy; he faced resistance and setbacks, but he persevered, fueled by his desire for redemption and his commitment to Elena and their shared future.

Their relationship deepened, evolving beyond the turbulence of their shared past. They learned to communicate more effectively, to embrace their vulnerabilities, and to celebrate each other's strengths. Their love, once tested and fractured, became stronger, more resilient, more profound. It was a love that had been forged in the fires of adversity, a love that was both a source of strength and a testament to their resilience.

Their new beginnings weren't just about individual success; they were about the shared creation of a life built on honesty, trust, and unwavering commitment. They were about finding peace not just within themselves, but within their relationship. They were about creating a future where their past mistakes were not a source of shame or regret but a catalyst for growth, forgiveness, and unwavering hope. The journey wasn't over, the scars remained, but they were finally walking towards the future, together, hand in hand, side by side, their hearts filled with a cautious optimism, their spirits infused with a renewed sense of purpose and shared resolve, their eyes fixed on the dawn of a brighter day. The quiet hum of their shared life, a sanctuary of quiet moments and whispered promises, enveloped them, a comforting balm to their once frayed and broken souls, finally, truly, whole.

32
BUILDING TRUST.

Their new apartment, a haven of muted greys and soft light, became the stage for their delicate dance of rebuilding trust. It wasn't a grand gesture, but a series of small, intimate moments that slowly chipped away at the walls they had built around their hearts. The initial awkwardness lingered, a phantom limb of their past, but it gradually faded, replaced by a tentative comfort that deepened with each passing day.

Evenings were spent in quiet companionship. Elena, her fingers stained with paint, would often find Dante watching her, his gaze soft and appreciative. He wouldn't interrupt her concentration, but his presence was a warm blanket, a silent reassurance of his unwavering support. He would bring her tea, a delicate blend of chamomile and lavender, its soothing aroma filling the small space, a fragrant testament to their shared sanctuary. Sometimes, he'd leave a single red rose on her easel, a simple gesture of affection that spoke volumes.

One evening, as the city lights twinkled outside their window, Elena paused mid-stroke, her brush hovering over the canvas. A wave of self-doubt washed over her, a familiar tide threatening to drag her under. The painting, a vibrant portrayal of their shared journey, felt incomplete, flawed, just like her.

Dante sensed her hesitation, his eyes reflecting her inner turmoil. He approached her gently, placing a hand on her shoulder, not possessive, but supportive, understanding. He didn't offer empty platitudes or false assurances. Instead, he simply listened, allowing her to express her fears, her insecurities, her doubts. He mirrored her vulnerability, sharing his own struggles with his foundation, his anxieties about living up to his newfound purpose.

He confessed his fear of failure, the weight of expectation bearing down on him. He spoke of the nights when self doubt threatened to consume him, the phantom voices whispering of his past mistakes, reminding him of his unworthiness. His confession was not a plea for sympathy, but a testament to his willingness to be truly seen, truly known.

Elena, in turn, shared her artistic struggles, the constant battle against perfectionism, the fear of failing to capture the essence of their relationship on canvas. She confessed to the nights she lay awake, plagued by the nightmares that still haunted her, the ghosts of their past mistakes lingering in the shadows of her mind.

Their vulnerability was not a weakness; it was their strength. It was the glue that slowly, painstakingly, mended the cracks in their foundation. It was in these moments of shared vulnerability that the true foundation of their trust was laid, brick by painstaking brick. They learned to meet each other's pain with compassion, understanding, and unwavering support.

Their shared meals became rituals, each a small step forward in building their new life together. They no longer just ate; they shared stories, memories, dreams. They laughed, their laughter now tinged with the warmth of shared experiences and a profound understanding of each other's hearts. They argued, too, but their disagreements were no longer fueled by resentment or accusations, but by a genuine desire to understand each other's perspectives. They learned to listen, truly listen, and to find common ground, even amidst their differences.

One Sunday morning, while making breakfast together, Elena surprised Dante with a sketch of him, captured in a moment of quiet contemplation, his face etched with the weariness of his work, but his eyes reflecting a newfound peace. It was a raw, honest portrayal, devoid of romanticized ideals, but it spoke volumes of her love and understanding. He saw not just the artist's skill, but the depth of her affection. His eyes filled with tears as he held the sketch, marveling at its authenticity and its emotional resonance.

Later that day, they walked hand-in-hand through a nearby park, the autumn leaves crunching under their feet. The silence between them wasn't empty; it was filled with the comfortable rhythm of their shared history, a shared journey of healing and transformation. They shared a quiet moment seated on a park bench. He watched her, mesmerized by the way the sunlight caught the strands of her hair, illuminating the subtle lines around her eyes – lines etched by time, trials, and the enduring strength of her spirit. He knew, with a certainty that settled deep within his bones, that he would spend the rest of his life cherishing her, protecting her, and celebrating the life they were building together.

Their evenings were filled with quiet intimacy, sometimes punctuated by passionate moments that were as raw and vulnerable as their shared confessions. They talked, not just about their days, but about their dreams, their fears, their hopes. They shared their anxieties and vulnerabilities, building a fortress of trust, brick by painstaking brick, made not of stone or mortar, but of shared experiences and unwavering mutual support.

The trust they were rebuilding wasn't simply the absence of suspicion; it was the presence of something deeper, something more profound—a shared understanding that went beyond words. It was a connection forged in the fires of their past, tempered by their shared struggles, and made stronger by their mutual commitment to face the future, together. It was a love that wasn't blind to their imperfections, but that embraced them, celebrated them, and found beauty in the shared journey of their transformation.

One night, as they lay entwined in their shared bed, Elena confessed her lingering fears, the shadows of doubt still dancing at the edge of her consciousness. Dante held her close, his embrace a silent reassurance, a haven from the storms within. He spoke of his own anxieties, the doubts that still surfaced, the memories that still lingered. He didn't offer empty promises, but a promise of unwavering support, a promise to navigate their fears together. He whispered words of comfort and assurance, reminding her of their strength, their resilience, and their love.

Their relationship continued to evolve, their bond becoming an intricate tapestry woven with threads of shared vulnerability, unwavering loyalty, and deepening love. It wasn't a fairy tale, devoid of imperfections; their scars remained, a testament to the battles they had fought and won. But their scars were also symbols of their resilience, of their ability to overcome, of the deep and abiding love that had emerged from the ashes of their past. Their future was still uncertain, but they were facing it together, hand in hand, their hearts filled with cautious hope, their spirits infused with a shared purpose, their eyes fixed on a dawn of a brighter day.

33
FACING THE FUTURE

The crisp morning air bit at their cheeks as they stood at the precipice of the cliff, the wind whipping through their hair. Below them, the ocean stretched out, an expanse of deep blue meeting the endless horizon. It was a scene of breathtaking beauty, a stark contrast to the turmoil they had weathered. Elena shivered, not entirely from the cold. A residue of fear, a lingering echo of the past, still clung to her, a shadow that danced at the periphery of her newfound peace.

Dante, sensing her apprehension, pulled her closer, his arm a comforting weight around her shoulders. He didn't speak, but his presence was a tangible shield, protecting her from the unseen forces that threatened to overwhelm her. He knew her fear wasn't irrational; it was a testament to the depth of the pain they had endured. The scars of their past remained, etched deeply into their souls, reminders of the battles they had fought and won.

They stood in silence for a long moment, the immensity of the landscape mirroring the enormity of their shared journey. The ocean, vast and unpredictable, yet ultimately calming, seemed to reflect the nature of their relationship. It had been tumultuous, filled with storms and uncertainties, but it had also been a journey of profound discovery and undeniable growth.

Finally, Elena broke the silence, her voice barely a whisper against the wind. "I still... I still worry," she confessed, her gaze fixed on the churning waves below. "What if we fail again? What if this... this fragile peace we've found... shatters?"

Dante's hand tightened around hers. "We won't fail," he said, his voice firm, yet gentle. "We've learned from our mistakes. We've faced our demons. We've built a foundation of trust, not on sand, but on rock. And the rock, Elena, is our love, our commitment, our unwavering support for each other."

He turned to face her, his eyes reflecting the vastness of the ocean, the depth of his feelings. "The future is uncertain, yes. There will be challenges, obstacles. But we will face them together. We will face them as a team. We are stronger together than we ever were apart."

He cupped her face in his hands, his thumbs gently wiping away a stray tear that traced a path down her cheek. "Remember what we built, Elena. Remember the nights we spent sharing our vulnerabilities, our fears, our insecurities. Remember how we faced those demons together, how we helped each other heal. That's the foundation of our future. That's the strength that will carry us through anything."

Elena leaned into his touch, the warmth of his hands melting away the lingering chill in her heart. She looked into his eyes, seeing not just love, but a profound understanding, a shared vision of a future they would build together, brick by painstaking brick.

"I see it now," she whispered, a small, hopeful smile playing on her lips. "Our future. It's not just about escaping the past; it's about building something new, something stronger, something beautiful."

They spoke for hours that day, their conversation meandering through the intricacies of their hopes and dreams, their fears and anxieties. Elena spoke of her artistic aspirations, her desire to create a body of work that reflected their journey, their resilience, their love. She envisioned a series of paintings, a visual testament to their shared history, a chronicle of their transformation.

Dante spoke of his foundation, of his plans to expand its reach, to help more people, to make a real difference in the world. He envisioned a future where his work brought solace to others, where his past mistakes became lessons learned, fueling his determination to make amends, to leave a positive mark on the world.

They spoke of children, of laughter echoing through their future home, of family dinners filled with warmth and shared experiences. They imagined holidays filled with laughter, the comforting scents of home-cooked meals and the cozy glow of a crackling fireplace. They painted a vivid picture of a future filled with quiet evenings and intimate moments shared in the warm embrace of their love.

They talked about their individual goals, and more importantly, their shared aspirations. They discussed their plans for a small cottage by the sea, a sanctuary where they could escape the noise and chaos of city life, a haven where they could nurture their love and build their future. Elena envisioned a studio overlooking the ocean, her canvas reflecting the ever-changing moods of the sea. Dante imagined a peaceful garden where he could spend time reflecting, regaining his mental balance, away from the pressure and expectations of his public life.

They shared their vision for a future where they could help others, where their foundation and Elena's art could inspire hope and healing, both independently and together. They saw themselves as a powerful unit, supporting each other, empowering others, and using their talents to make a positive impact on the world.

Their plans weren't grand or elaborate; they were simple, grounded in reality, fueled by their shared values and their mutual commitment to one another. They acknowledged the challenges that would undoubtedly arise, but their confidence and unity acted as a formidable shield. They embraced the uncertainty, knowing that as long as they had each other, they could overcome anything.

As the sun began to set, casting a warm golden light over the ocean, they walked back hand-in-hand, their silhouettes cast long and slender against the vibrant sky. They felt lighter, not just from the physical exertion, but from the weight lifted from their hearts. They had faced their fears, acknowledged their vulnerabilities, and defined their shared future. The path ahead was not without obstacles, but they faced it with courage, with hope, and with the unwavering support of each other. Their love, forged in the fires of their past, was their guiding light, leading them toward a future as vast and beautiful as the ocean that stretched out before them, a future built on trust, on understanding, on a love that had weathered the storm and emerged triumphant. The future was no longer a source of fear, but a promise of a shared journey, a continued adventure filled with love, laughter, and unwavering support, together.

34
RENEWED HOPE

The city market throbbed with life, a kaleidoscope of sights, sounds, and smells that assaulted and delighted the senses in equal measure. The air hummed with a vibrant energy, a stark contrast to the quiet solitude of the clifftop where they had last confronted their demons. Elena, her hand nestled securely in Dante's, felt a lightness she hadn't experienced in years. The weight of the past, though still present, felt less oppressive, less suffocating. It was a shadow, yes, but a shadow that no longer eclipsed the sun.

The market was a tapestry woven with the threads of everyday life: the cheerful banter of vendors hawking their wares, the rhythmic chopping of vegetables, the aroma of roasting spices mingling with the sweetness of ripe fruit. Children chased pigeons, their laughter echoing through the narrow alleyways. Old women gossiped over steaming cups of coffee, their voices a low, comforting murmur. It was a scene of chaotic harmony, a symphony of life unfolding before them. And within this vibrant chaos, Elena found a sense of belonging, a sense of peace she hadn't realized she craved.

She watched as a young girl carefully selected a bouquet of sunflowers, her face alight with happiness. It was a simple act, yet it resonated deeply with Elena. It was a reminder of the simple joys in life, the small moments of beauty that often get overlooked in the face of adversity. These were the moments she wanted to cherish, the moments she wanted to capture in her art. Her vision, previously clouded by doubt and fear, began to sharpen, to focus. She saw canvases filled with the vibrant hues of the market, the energy of the crowd, the warmth of human connection.

Dante, sensing her renewed enthusiasm, squeezed her hand gently. He knew the power of art, the way it could heal, the way it could transform. He had witnessed its transformative power in Elena, watching her reclaim herself through her creativity. He understood the importance of this journey for her, this return to her passion. He was her anchor, her support, her steadfast companion in their shared voyage.

They strolled through the market, sampling exotic fruits, bargaining playfully with vendors, and losing themselves in the sheer vibrancy of it all. The experience was a celebration of life, a testament to their resilience, a symbol of their renewed hope. It was a reminder that even amidst the darkest of times, beauty and joy could still be found, if one only looked for it.

Later, as they sat at a small café overlooking the bustling square, sipping strong Italian coffee, they discussed their future plans. Elena's artistic vision had expanded, encompassing not just still life, but narrative pieces, telling the story of their journey, their struggles, and their ultimate triumph. She envisioned a series of paintings that would document their transformation, capturing the essence of their resilience, their love, and their renewed hope. She wanted to share their story, to inspire others to find strength in their own vulnerabilities, to show them that even in the deepest darkness, light could prevail.

Dante, meanwhile, felt emboldened by their newfound clarity. His foundation, initially conceived as a means of escaping his dark past, had evolved into something far more significant. He saw it now as a vehicle for positive change, a way to make amends for past mistakes, a path towards redemption. He wanted to expand the foundation's reach, to help more people, to make a tangible difference in the world.

He envisioned a future where his work would inspire hope, where his past would serve as a cautionary tale, and where he could finally find solace in helping others.

They spoke of their plans for their cottage by the sea, a haven where they could escape the city's relentless energy, a sanctuary where they could nurture their love and their dreams. They envisioned quiet evenings spent by a crackling fire, their laughter mingling with the gentle roar of the ocean. They imagined a life filled with shared joys, intimate moments, and the comfort of unwavering companionship. The dream felt tangible, attainable. The fear that had once clung to them like a shroud had dissipated, replaced by a sense of quiet confidence, a shared belief in their ability to build a future together.

Elena's art began to reflect this renewed hope, her brushstrokes becoming bolder, her colors more vibrant. She found herself painting scenes of breathtaking beauty, capturing the essence of the world around her, the vibrant energy of the city, the tranquility of the sea. She wasn't just painting; she was creating a visual diary of their transformation, a testament to their resilience, their love, and their unwavering belief in a brighter future.

Dante, too, felt a shift in his perspective. He began to view his past mistakes not as insurmountable burdens, but as valuable lessons learned. He understood that his past had shaped him, had made him stronger, had given him the empathy and understanding to connect with those in need. He threw himself into his work with renewed vigor, focusing his energy on expanding his foundation, reaching out to those who had suffered, offering them support and guidance, and giving them hope.

Their shared journey was far from over. They knew that challenges would undoubtedly arise, that life would continue to throw unexpected obstacles their way. But they also knew that they were stronger together than they had ever been apart. Their love, tested and refined by the fires of adversity, was the bedrock of their future, the unwavering foundation upon which they would build their dreams. It wasn't just about escaping the shadows of their past; it was about embracing the light of their future, together. They were not just surviving; they were thriving. They were building a life, not just a future, a life filled with love, hope, and unwavering support for one another.

The market, with its chaotic energy and vibrant life, became a symbol of their transformation. It was a reminder that even amidst the chaos, beauty can be found, that even in the face of adversity, hope can prevail. It was a place where they found their footing, their strength, their renewed sense of purpose. It was a place where their love story continued, not as a desperate escape, but as a vibrant tapestry woven with the threads of hope, resilience, and unwavering commitment. The scent of spices and the sounds of laughter echoed in their hearts, a constant reminder of the beauty and promise of their future, a future they were creating together, brick by painstaking brick, hand in hand. The sun dipped below the horizon, casting long shadows across the city as Elena and Dante walked home, their hearts overflowing with a love that had weathered the storm and emerged triumphant, a love that was the foundation of their shared future, a future brighter than anything they had ever imagined.

35
LOVE AND REDEMPTION

The following days unfolded in a gentle rhythm, a stark contrast to the tumultuous weeks that had preceded them. Their cottage by the sea, a haven of weathered wood and sun-bleached stone, became their sanctuary. The rhythmic crashing of waves against the shore provided a constant, soothing soundtrack to their lives. Elena, inspired by the serene beauty of their surroundings, found a new depth in her art. Her canvases blossomed with the vibrant hues of the sea, the soft pastel shades of the sky at dawn and dusk, and the stark, dramatic lines of the cliffs that guarded their secluded haven. Her work, once laden with the shadows of her past, now radiated a newfound lightness, a joyful exploration of color and form.

Dante, freed from the suffocating weight of his past mistakes, threw himself into his work with a renewed sense of purpose. His foundation, initially a refuge, was blossoming into a vibrant force for good. He was no longer running from his past; he was confronting it, using his experiences to guide and support others. He established support groups for survivors of similar traumas, offering a safe space for sharing and healing. He poured his energy into funding educational initiatives in underprivileged communities, creating opportunities for those who lacked the resources to escape the cycles of poverty and violence that had once trapped him. His commitment was unwavering, driven by a deep desire for redemption and a sincere belief in the power of second chances.

Their love story, once a desperate flight from darkness, had transformed into a beacon of hope. It wasn't simply a romantic entanglement; it was a powerful testament to resilience, a symbol of the enduring strength of the human spirit. Their love was a testament to the transformative power of forgiveness, self-acceptance, and unwavering support. They were a team, their strengths complementing each other, their vulnerabilities forging a bond unbreakable by life's challenges.

One crisp autumn afternoon, while walking along the beach, they encountered an elderly woman struggling to gather her scattered belongings – a collection of seashells, carefully wrapped in a faded piece of cloth. The wind, fierce and relentless, whipped the seashells across the sand, threatening to carry them away into the unforgiving sea. Without hesitation, Elena and Dante rushed to her aid. Elena knelt, gently gathering the precious shells, her hands moving with a tenderness that spoke volumes about the depth of her compassion. Dante, meanwhile, helped the woman to her feet, offering his strong arm for support. The simple act of kindness, performed without fanfare or expectation, resonated deeply with both of them.

The woman, her eyes brimming with gratitude, thanked them profusely. Her simple expression of heartfelt appreciation was more rewarding than any grand gesture could have ever been. In that moment, they both understood the profound meaning of their shared journey. Their love wasn't just about their own healing; it was about extending that healing to others, about creating ripples of compassion and kindness that would spread outward, touching lives beyond their own.

Later that evening, as they sat by the crackling fire, the warmth reflecting in their eyes, they discussed the encounter. Elena realized that the woman's seashells, fragile and easily scattered by the wind, were a metaphor for their own lives before they found each other – vulnerable and easily shattered by the storms of adversity. Now, however, they were carefully gathered, protected by their love, their shared commitment to healing, and their determination to build a future together.

Dante saw it differently; he saw the woman's gratitude as a reflection of the positive change they were creating in the world. He understood that their journey towards redemption wasn't a solitary pursuit; it was a collaborative effort, a testament to the transformative power of shared experiences and unwavering support. Their love was the catalyst, the driving force that propelled them forward, enabling them to reach out and touch the lives of others.

Their love story wasn't a fairy tale, devoid of struggles and challenges. It was a realistic portrayal of two individuals confronting their pasts, embracing their imperfections, and choosing to build a future together, hand in hand. Their bond wasn't built on idealized notions of perfection; it was forged in the fires of adversity, tempered by shared experiences, and strengthened by unwavering commitment. They were not flawless; they were human, vulnerable, and prone to error.

But their love was real, resilient, and capable of weathering any storm.

The following months were filled with a sense of quiet contentment. Elena's art exhibitions received critical acclaim, her work praised for its emotional depth and raw honesty. Her canvases, once dark and brooding, now overflowed with vibrant colors, reflecting the joy and serenity she had found in her relationship with Dante and in her newfound purpose. Dante's foundation continued to grow, expanding its reach and impacting the lives of countless individuals. He travelled extensively, offering support and guidance to those in need, his past experiences providing him with the empathy and understanding necessary to connect with them on a profound level. One evening, while strolling hand-in-hand along the beach, beneath a sky ablaze with stars, Elena turned to Dante, her eyes reflecting the soft glow of the moon. "I never thought I could find such peace," she whispered, her voice barely audible above the gentle roar of the ocean. "I never thought I could be this happy."

Dante, his gaze locked on hers, squeezed her hand gently. "Neither did I," he replied, his voice thick with emotion. "But we found it together, didn't we? We found each other, and in doing so, we found our way back to ourselves, to our true selves."

Their journey was far from over. Life would continue to present unexpected challenges, unforeseen obstacles. But they faced the future with a quiet confidence, a shared belief in their unwavering strength, and a love that had been tested and proven resilient. Their love story was not simply a tale of romance; it was a powerful testament to the transformative power of forgiveness, self-acceptance, and the enduring strength of the human spirit. Their love was a beacon, a guiding light, illuminating their path towards a future filled with hope, joy, and the unwavering promise of a love that would forever endure. Their love was a testament to the truth that even amidst the darkest of nights, the dawn will eventually break, bringing with it the promise of a new day, a new beginning, a new love, and a new life, built on the foundations of forgiveness, redemption, and an unbreakable love.

36
UNRAVELING CONSPIRACY

The quiet contentment of their seaside haven couldn't completely mask the lingering unease that still clung to Elena like a persistent shadow. The peace they'd found was fragile, a delicate bloom easily crushed by the weight of unanswered questions surrounding her father's death. The cryptic note, the shadowy figures glimpsed at the periphery of her memories, the inconsistencies in the official police report – all gnawed at her, refusing to be silenced. She needed answers, a closure that went beyond the superficial pronouncements of a hastily concluded investigation.

Dante, sensing her internal turmoil, remained her unwavering support. He understood the relentless pull of the past, the insatiable need for truth that drove her. He'd faced his own demons, navigated his own labyrinth of guilt and self-doubt, and he knew the healing power of confronting the darkness head-on. He wasn't just her lover; he was her confidant, her partner in this arduous quest for justice.

Their investigation began subtly, almost imperceptibly. It started with late-night searches of old newspaper archives, their fingers tracing faded ink, their eyes scanning yellowed pages for any mention of her father, Dr. Aris Thorne, and his controversial research. They spent hours in dusty libraries, the hushed reverence of the hallowed halls a stark contrast to the intensity of their search. They unearthed snippets of information, tantalizing hints that pointed towards a conspiracy far more intricate and sinister than they had ever imagined.

One such discovery was an article detailing a fierce debate within the scientific community regarding Aris Thorne's groundbreaking work on genetic engineering. The article hinted at powerful forces opposing his research, forces willing to resort to extreme measures to suppress his findings. This fueled their determination; they were no longer just searching for answers about her father's death; they were uncovering a web of deceit that extended far beyond a single murder.

Their next lead came from an unexpected source – an anonymous email, delivered to Elena's encrypted account. The email contained a single, unassuming image: a photograph of a dimly lit alleyway, the graffiti-covered brick walls almost indistinguishable from the shadows that enveloped them. A single, flickering streetlight cast an eerie glow, highlighting the faint outline of a figure disappearing into the darkness. The alleyway felt familiar, a visceral memory surfacing from the recesses of Elena's subconscious, a place she had somehow encountered in her fragmented memories of the night of her father's death.

Following this cryptic clue, they found themselves in the heart of the city, navigating its labyrinthine streets under the cloak of darkness. The alleyway, exactly as depicted in the photograph, felt heavy with an unspoken tension, a palpable sense of unease that seeped into their bones. The air hung thick with the smell of damp concrete and decay, the silence punctuated only by the distant rumble of traffic.

Elena felt a chill crawl down her spine. The alleyway, though unknown consciously, resonated deeply within her. It was a place of shadows and secrets, a location steeped in a history she had yet to fully comprehend. As they searched, a loose brick revealed a hidden compartment, its contents: a worn leather-bound journal.

The journal, filled with Aris Thorne's meticulous handwriting, detailed his groundbreaking research, his fears, and the escalating threats he faced. He documented meetings with shadowy figures, veiled conversations filled with coded language and veiled threats. He outlined the immense pressure he was under, the attempts to sabotage his work, the insidious campaign to discredit him and silence him permanently. The journal painted a vivid picture of a man trapped in a web of deceit, a brilliant mind battling against powerful forces determined to bury his revolutionary discoveries.

The journal also contained a series of coded entries, interspersed with seemingly random sketches and symbols. Dante, with his background in cryptography, immediately recognized the intricate pattern, the deliberate obscurity designed to protect the information from prying eyes. It was a challenge, a complex puzzle that required their combined skills and intellect to decipher.

Days turned into weeks as they painstakingly decoded the

journal's cryptic entries. Each deciphered passage revealed another layer of the conspiracy, another piece of the puzzle. The more they uncovered, the more dangerous the situation became. They learned about a clandestine organization, a powerful cabal operating in the shadows, their influence extending into the highest echelons of power. They discovered the organization's relentless pursuit of Aris Thorne's research, their ruthless determination to suppress his discoveries, their willingness to eliminate anyone who stood in their way.

Their investigation led them to a derelict warehouse on the city's outskirts, a place shrouded in mystery and decay. The warehouse, a cavernous space filled with cobwebs and shadows, was the perfect hiding place for the organization's nefarious activities. Armed with the information they'd gleaned from the journal, they infiltrated the warehouse, their hearts pounding in their chests, the weight of their mission pressing down on them.

Inside, they discovered a hidden laboratory, its sterile environment a jarring contrast to the warehouse's dilapidated exterior. The laboratory was filled with high-tech equipment, experimental apparatus, and documents confirming the extent of the organization's illegal activities. They found evidence of unethical human experimentation, the horrific results of the organization's desperate attempts to replicate Aris Thorne's groundbreaking research. The sheer scale of the organization's crimes was staggering, a chilling testament to their power and their complete disregard for human life.

As they gathered evidence, they were discovered. The

organization's enforcers, ruthless and efficient, cornered them, their weapons trained on Elena and Dante. A tense standoff ensued, a deadly dance between life and death. Dante, despite his pacifist nature, was forced to utilize his combat skills, honed during his troubled past, to protect Elena. Their combined skills, honed through years of separate struggles, enabled them to escape, barely managing to evade their pursuers. They were caught in the midst of a brutal fight for survival, the outcome uncertain. Their escape was fueled by a combination of desperation, skill and sheer luck.

Their escape was narrow, their lives hanging precariously in the balance. The chase took them through the dark and winding streets of the city, the relentless pursuit a constant threat. They finally managed to shake their pursuers, finding refuge in a hidden, secluded apartment, a sanctuary provided by a trusted contact from Dante's past.

In the aftermath, they realized the extent of their discoveries. The conspiracy was far-reaching, its tentacles ensnaring influential individuals across various sectors of society. They had stumbled upon a secret society whose reach extended far beyond their wildest imaginations. They were no longer simply seeking justice for Aris Thorne's death; they were now facing a powerful enemy with the resources and influence to silence them permanently.

Exhausted but resolute, Elena and Dante knew their journey was far from over. They had uncovered a vast conspiracy, a web of deceit and corruption that reached into the highest levels of society. The fight for justice, for truth, had just begun. The quiet contentment of their seaside haven felt a lifetime away, replaced by the relentless urgency of their mission, the knowledge that their lives were now inextricably bound to the fate of uncovering a truth that powerful forces were desperate to keep buried. The road ahead was fraught with danger, but their shared determination, their unwavering love, was their guiding light in the gathering storm. Their fight had evolved beyond a personal quest for vengeance. It had become a battle for the soul of society itself, a battle they were determined to fight, together.

37
BRINGING DOWN THE EMPIRE

The biting mountain wind whipped around them, a stark contrast to the relative warmth of the secluded cabin. Inside, the air crackled with a tension far more potent than any storm. Elena and Dante, huddled around a makeshift table illuminated by a single kerosene lamp, were immersed in a map – a meticulously crafted blueprint of the Moretti empire's remaining infrastructure. The silence was punctuated only by the rhythmic scratching of Dante's pen as he annotated strategic locations with precise markings.

"The casino," Elena said, her voice low, barely audible above the wind's howl. "That's their primary source of income. Taking it down would cripple them financially." She traced a finger across the map, her touch lingering on the symbol representing the opulent gambling establishment nestled deep within the city's underbelly. It wasn't just a building; it was a nerve center, a nexus of illicit activities that fueled the Moretti family's reign of terror.

Dante nodded, his gaze fixed on the map. "Agreed. But taking down the casino head-on would be suicide. They're heavily guarded, their security impenetrable to a frontal assault. We need a more...surgical approach." He tapped a finger against a small, unassuming building marked just outside the casino's perimeter — a seemingly innocuous storage facility, its location cleverly masked by the city's urban sprawl. "This. This is our key."

Elena leaned closer, her eyes reflecting the lamp's flickering light. "The storage facility? What's the connection?"

"It's not just storage," Dante explained. "According to our intel, this facility houses their most sensitive operations money laundering records, evidence of their various illicit activities, compromising information on their allies and collaborators within the city's establishment. Taking down this facility and exposing its contents to the authorities would be a crippling blow, unraveling their operations from the inside out."

Their plan was intricate, a delicate web of calculated risks and strategic maneuvers. The storage facility wasn't just their target; it was a stepping stone, a crucial link in a chain of events meticulously orchestrated to dismantle the Moretti empire. Elena's expertise in hacking and digital forensics would be crucial in accessing and extracting the sensitive data, while Dante's knowledge of the city's underworld and his network of contacts would ensure a seamless execution. The timing was critical; they needed to strike when the facility was at its most vulnerable, when the security was lax, and their targets were least expecting an attack.

"We need a diversion," Elena stated, her eyes narrowed in concentration. "Something to draw their attention away from the storage facility, something significant enough to disrupt their operations."

Dante pondered for a moment, his mind racing through possibilities. "A coordinated attack on several of their smaller fronts simultaneously might do the trick. Enough to occupy their forces, yet not major enough to alert them to something more sinister." He pointed to several smaller locations marked on the map — a series of bars, restaurants, and warehouses — seemingly inconsequential, yet integral to the Moretti family's network.

"A multi-pronged attack," Elena mused, a faint smile playing on her lips. "It would require impeccable timing and coordination. We need a team, a group of trusted individuals."

Their network of contacts, a carefully cultivated web of allies, provided them with the necessary manpower. Each member was hand-picked for their specialized skills — expert hackers, skilled fighters, and resourceful informants. The team was small, but they were elite, a force to be reckoned with. They were united by a shared sense of justice, their desire to rid the city of the Moretti's corrupt influence.

The days leading up to the operation were a whirlwind of activity. They meticulously rehearsed their plans, refining every detail, ensuring every contingency was accounted for. They practiced their moves, their synchronization growing increasingly precise, their movements becoming a dance of calculated precision. The mountain hideout became their command center, a place where they strategized, planned, and prepared for the upcoming battle. The atmosphere was intense, filled with a quiet determination that masked the inherent risk of their operation.

The night of the operation arrived, cloaked in darkness. The air was thick with anticipation, a palpable sense of dread interwoven with an unwavering resolve. As they set their plan into motion, the city became their battlefield. The coordinated attacks on the Moretti family's smaller establishments created a cascade of chaos, drawing their attention and resources away from the main target. It was a calculated distraction, a strategic smokescreen that allowed them to move undetected.

While the chaos unfolded, Elena and Dante infiltrated the storage facility. Their movements were fluid, silent, their expertise evident in their efficiency. Elena navigated the complex security systems, bypassing alarms and disabling surveillance cameras with practiced ease. Dante, his senses heightened, navigated the labyrinthine corridors, his footsteps silent, his awareness sharp.

They reached the server room, its hum a constant drone, a heartbeat of the Moretti's criminal enterprise. Elena worked swiftly and precisely, her fingers flying across the keyboard, accessing and extracting the vital data. The information was vast, a digital mountain of evidence, meticulously organized and stored. As she copied the data, Dante monitored the security feeds, ensuring they remained undetected.

Suddenly, the alarms blared, shattering the silence. The diversion had worked, but not as flawlessly as planned. The Moretti's remaining forces were alerted, and they were closing in. Elena and Dante were trapped. The game was on.

They had to fight their way out of this storage facility now.

The ensuing confrontation was a brutal, relentless clash. Elena and Dante fought back-to-back, their combined skills and unwavering determination enabling them to fend off their pursuers. The clash was violent, the fight a desperate struggle for survival. They fought with a precision born of necessity, their movements honed by years of training, their reflexes as sharp as their wits. But they were outnumbered. They escaped in the nick of time. Using cunning tactics and well-timed maneuvers, they managed to outmaneuver their pursuers and slipped out, disappearing into the city's night. Their escape was narrow, a hair's breadth from disaster.

The following day, the city woke up to the news of the Moretti family's downfall. The evidence Elena and Dante had gathered resulted in widespread arrests, dismantling the vast criminal network from the inside out. The evidence laid bare the extent of their crimes, their corruption, and their influence. Justice was served, though not without a price. Elena and Dante had faced death, had stared into the abyss, but they had emerged victorious. Their victory was hard fought, a testament to their courage, their skills, and their unbreakable bond. The quiet contentment of their seaside haven, once a distant memory, was now a tangible goal, within their reach. The empire had fallen, and they had survived to tell the tale. Their fight was over, and finally, peace began.

38
RISKY MANUVERS

The coordinated attacks on the smaller Moretti establishments unfolded with a balletic chaos. Simultaneous raids on a string of bars, restaurants, and warehouses erupted in a carefully orchestrated symphony of controlled pandemonium. Explosions, strategically timed and placed to maximize disruption, sent shockwaves through the city's underbelly. Smoke billowed into the night sky, painting dramatic silhouettes against the cityscape. Sirens wailed, a cacophony that masked the quiet precision of Elena and Dante's movements as they infiltrated the storage facility.

Their team, a ghost squad operating in the shadows, executed their assigned tasks with ruthless efficiency. Marco, a master of disguise and infiltration, slipped into a high-end restaurant frequented by Moretti associates, creating a diversion that drew away police and security personnel. Sofia, a tech genius known for her ability to breach the most sophisticated security systems, remotely disabled surveillance cameras and communication lines around the targeted locations, creating a vacuum of information for the Moretti family. Meanwhile, a small group of highly trained operatives, led by the enigmatic figure known only as "Silas," engaged in carefully calculated skirmishes with smaller Moretti gangs, further diverting attention and resources.

The precision of their teamwork was breathtaking. Each action, each distraction, was meticulously planned and flawlessly executed, a complex choreography of chaos designed to create a perfect storm of confusion. The city, normally a labyrinth of crime and corruption, transformed into a battlefield of controlled chaos, a stage for the grand unveiling of their elaborate plan. The air crackled with adrenaline, with the raw energy of calculated risk.

Inside the storage facility, Elena and Dante moved like phantoms. Elena, a master of digital deception, bypassed the facility's elaborate security systems with the grace of a seasoned dancer. Her fingers danced across the keyboard, weaving a spell of digital illusion that masked their presence. Dante, ever watchful, scanned the environment, his senses acutely attuned to every sound, every shadow. He was a predator, moving with the silent grace of a seasoned hunter, his every step calculated, deliberate.

The server room was a heart of the beast, a digital fortress pulsating with the illicit transactions of the Moretti empire. Rows of servers hummed, their constant drone a hypnotic rhythm in the otherwise silent room. Elena navigated the intricate network with ease, accessing the main database. The sheer volume of data was overwhelming – years of meticulously documented crimes, meticulously laundered money, compromising information on corrupt officials, and hidden accounts scattered across offshore banks. It was a digital Pandora's Box, overflowing with the secrets of the Moretti organization.

As Elena worked, Dante kept a watchful eye on the security monitors. The city's chaos was a symphony of sirens and gunfire, a carefully constructed diversion that was proving to be more effective than they'd hoped. Yet, a nagging feeling of unease crept into his mind. The silence in the storage facility, usually a reassuring sign of success, felt eerily profound. It wasn't just quiet; it was unnervingly still.

Suddenly, a low growl echoed through the ventilation system, a subtle, almost imperceptible sound that only Dante's finely-tuned ears could detect. Instinctively, he knew something was wrong. He turned, his eyes scanning the room, searching for any sign of danger.

Their calm was shattered by the roar of a nearby explosion their diversion had worked, perhaps too well. The Moretti family, realizing they were under attack on multiple fronts, had dispatched reinforcements to the storage facility. The alarms blared, shattering the tense silence. Their window of opportunity was closing.

The fight was brutal and swift. Elena, wielding a small but lethal combat knife, fought with the skill and precision of a seasoned warrior. Dante, adept at both hand-to-hand combat and firearms, fought back-to-back with Elena, their movements a deadly ballet of defense and attack. They were overwhelmed, outnumbered, but their skills and determination were unmatched. The fight spilled out into the dimly lit corridors of the facility, a furious clash of steel and flesh against the backdrop of flashing lights and echoing gunshots.

They used the facility's layout to their advantage, using shadows and cover to outmaneuver their pursuers. Elena's knowledge of the security systems allowed them to navigate the facility's intricate pathways, creating a labyrinthine chase that kept their pursuers off balance. Dante, relying on his instincts and years of experience, used the environment to create diversions and traps, slowing down their pursuers and providing brief moments of respite.

 Their escape was a desperate scramble, a harrowing race against time. They fought their way through a maze of corridors and stairwells, their every move a calculated gamble. They were cornered multiple times, fighting desperately to survive, their skills tested to the limit. They used everything at their disposal – their training, their wits, and their unwavering resolve.

In a moment of breathtaking audacity, Elena disabled a section of the building's structural support, causing a controlled collapse that created a diversion and a path to freedom. They plunged into the night, disappearing into the city's maze of streets, leaving behind a trail of destruction and the remnants of a fallen empire.

They managed to extract the data, though not without significant damage to their resources and some severe wounds on their side. It had been a brutal fight for survival, a testament to the ruthlessness of the Moretti empire and their own exceptional skills. The information they had secured was invaluable, a digital arsenal that could bring the entire Moretti organization to its knees. They secured a safehouse and took time to rest, nursing their injuries and reflecting on their narrow escape. They knew the danger wasn't fully over, that the aftermath of their actions would create ripples that would continue to affect them for a long time, but they had succeeded in bringing the reign of terror to an end. Their victory, hard-won and bought at a significant price, was the first step towards the peace they had fought so hard to achieve. The city, forever changed by their actions, now had a chance to heal.

39
UNEXPECTED ALLIES

The safehouse, a cramped apartment tucked away in a forgotten corner of the city, offered little comfort. The scent of antiseptic and stale coffee hung heavy in the air, a stark contrast to the adrenaline-fueled chaos of the previous night. Elena, her arm bandaged and throbbing, stared out the grimy window, the city lights blurring into a kaleidoscope of hazy colors. Dante, his face pale but his eyes sharp, cleaned his weapons meticulously, the rhythmic clicking a counterpoint to the city's muted hum.

Their victory felt fragile, a precarious perch on the edge of a precipice. They had secured the data, crippling the Moretti organization's digital infrastructure, but the physical empire remained, a hydra-headed beast capable of swift regeneration. They knew retaliation was inevitable. The Moretti family wouldn't simply fade away; they would strike back, harder and more viciously than before.

Days bled into nights, a blur of tense quiet punctuated by the occasional news bulletin reporting on the aftermath of their raid. The city was abuzz with speculation, whispers of a shadowy organization bringing down a criminal empire, fueling rumors and conspiracy theories. The police investigation, hampered by the destruction and the sophisticated digital cover-up, was proving frustratingly slow. Elena and Dante, however, were far from idle. They sifted through the mountain of data they had extracted, painstakingly identifying key players, financial networks, and hidden assets. Their goal was not merely to expose the Morettis; they aimed to dismantle the entire criminal structure, leaving nothing behind but ashes.

It was during one of these late-night data-mining sessions that Elena stumbled upon something unexpected – a hidden communication channel, encrypted and almost invisible amidst the digital debris. It was a series of coded messages, exchanged between a high-ranking Moretti lieutenant and... someone else. Someone Elena didn't recognize. The encryption was complex, but Elena, with her prodigious skills, managed to crack the code. The messages revealed a clandestine meeting, a rendezvous in an obscure part of the city – a seemingly abandoned warehouse district. Intrigued, Elena and Dante decided to investigate.

The warehouse district was a labyrinth of crumbling structures and shadowed alleyways, a forgotten corner of the city where despair clung to the crumbling brickwork like a shroud. The air hung heavy with the smell of decay and dust. As they approached the designated warehouse, they noticed a peculiar detail – a small, unassuming van parked discreetly nearby. It wasn't a typical Moretti vehicle; this one was unmarked, clean, and far too well-maintained to blend in with the surrounding squalor. As they watched, a lone figure emerged from the van, a woman dressed in a sharp, tailored suit, her face hidden in the shadows of a wide-brimmed hat.

Elena and Dante exchanged a look. This was no ordinary associate. This woman exuded an aura of power and sophistication, a far cry from the rough-and-tumble thugs of the Moretti family. She approached the warehouse, her gait confident and purposeful. Dante signaled Elena to wait while he approached, his hand resting on his weapon, his senses alert.

As the woman entered the warehouse, Dante followed, Elena close behind. Inside, they found a stark contrast to the derelict exterior – the warehouse was meticulously clean, furnished with expensive furniture and modern technology.

The woman sat at a large table, surrounded by documents and sophisticated equipment. She was discussing something intently with a man, his face grim and his shoulders slumped with weariness. The man was clearly someone important, a person of influence. As Dante and Elena moved closer, they realized something shocking.

The man was none other than Inspector Giovanni Rossi, a senior member of the police force known for his incorruptibility and dedication to justice. Rossi, a man they had long admired from afar for his unwavering commitment to upholding the law, seemed to be collaborating with... this enigmatic woman.

 The woman, sensing their presence, turned, her eyes sharp and assessing. She didn't seem surprised or alarmed. She merely gestured for them to approach. "I've been expecting you," she said, her voice calm and controlled. "I am Isabella Rossi, Giovanni's sister. And I believe we have a common enemy."

Isabella explained that she had been working undercover for years, infiltrating the Moretti organization from within. She had been using her position to gather intelligence, undermining the family's operations, and creating opportunities for the police to intervene. The meeting was a rendezvous to coordinate their next move, to bring down the Morettis once and for all. Rossi, overwhelmed by the weight of his years of undercover work, had lost faith in his department's capacity for effective intervention. Isabella, who had made far more progress independently, had proposed a coordinated effort.

This was a revelation that altered everything. The seemingly insurmountable task of dismantling the Moretti empire suddenly seemed less daunting. With Isabella's insider knowledge and network, and Rossi's police contacts, their combined forces could prove devastatingly effective. Their initial distrust, fuelled by caution and the nature of their respective roles, melted into a grudging respect and a shared understanding of the critical need for unity.

The ensuing collaboration was a whirlwind of meticulously planned strategies, covert operations, and carefully calculated risks. They leveraged Isabella's contacts within the Moretti organization to identify key financial assets and hidden accounts. Rossi, using his official channels and contacts, secured warrants and mobilized resources within the police force, directing actions against several major Moretti enterprises. Elena and Dante, using their skills in digital warfare and infiltration, created diversions and disrupted communications, providing critical support to the ongoing police actions. Their combined expertise created a perfect storm, an irresistible force that relentlessly pressured the Moretti organization on every front.

The dismantling of the Moretti empire wasn't swift or easy. It was a protracted, grueling campaign fought on multiple fronts. There were setbacks and near misses, moments of sheer desperation and agonizing doubt. Yet, the combined forces of Elena, Dante, Isabella, and Giovanni Rossi persevered. Isabella's intimate knowledge of the Moretti family's inner workings proved invaluable, allowing them to anticipate their moves and neutralize their strategies. Rossi's influence within the police force ensured that the legal and institutional actions were coordinated effectively, allowing for seamless operations. Elena and Dante, meanwhile, operated as a ghost squad, using their skills to create diversions and gather crucial evidence.

The final confrontation was not a dramatic shootout, but a meticulously orchestrated takedown, a carefully constructed domino effect that unravelled the entire Moretti criminal network. Their combined strategy proved highly effective, exposing corrupt officials, revealing hidden accounts, and systematically dismantling the family's various illegal enterprises. The Moretti family's carefully constructed empire crumbled, revealing layers of deceit and corruption. The arrests followed, not with the roar of guns and a final showdown, but with the quiet and efficient execution of warrants, the methodical dismantling of a criminal organization exposed and betrayed from within.

The victory was sweet but bittersweet. It came at a cost. Rossi, exhausted but relieved, finally confessed the immense toll his undercover work had taken, the years of isolation and the constant threat of exposure. Isabella, though outwardly composed, bore the weight of her own sacrifices. Elena and Dante, forever changed by their experiences, looked forward to a future that seemed less certain but more hopeful. The city breathed a sigh of relief, their once-invisible enemy now exposed to the glare of the public eye, the city recovering from the long shadow of the Moretti family's reign of terror. The hard-fought victory left them all changed, but united in the shared understanding of what it truly meant to serve justice. The silence in the aftermath was not the silence of fear, but of cautious optimism, a tentative step towards a more peaceful future.

40
TRIUMPH AND LOSS

The courtroom was stifling, a suffocating blend of nervous sweat and anticipation. Rows of polished mahogany gleamed under the harsh fluorescent lights, reflecting the strained faces of the spectators. Among them, Elena and Dante sat, their usual easy camaraderie replaced by a tense quietude. The weight of the past months, the relentless pressure of their campaign against the Morettis, hung heavy in the air, a palpable presence that thickened the silence. The victory they had achieved felt both monumental and fragile, a precarious balance teetering on the edge of a precipice.

The air crackled with unspoken tension. The Moretti family, once a monolithic force that cast a long shadow over the city, sat slumped and defeated in the defendant's dock. Their carefully constructed facade of power and influence had been systematically dismantled, their empire reduced to rubble, their arrogance replaced by a stunned resignation. Don Angelo Moretti, his face etched with years of ruthless ambition and now bearing the weight of his impending downfall, stared straight ahead, his eyes devoid of their usual fiery intensity. He was a broken man, his power stripped away, his empire in ruins. The other family members, his sons and lieutenants, mirrored his defeated posture, the arrogance that had once defined them now replaced by a mixture of fear and regret.

Isabella Rossi, her composure unwavering, sat beside Giovanni. The lines on her face spoke of years spent in the shadows, a life lived on the edge of a knife. Yet, there was a quiet strength in her bearing, a sense of resolve that radiated outwards, calming the turbulence swirling within the courtroom. Giovanni, his face pale but his eyes filled with a weary relief, sat beside her, his presence a silent testament to the sacrifices they had both made. The years of undercover work had taken a toll, leaving him physically and emotionally drained. Yet, in the quiet dignity of his bearing, there was a glimmer of satisfaction, a quiet pride in the work they had accomplished together.

The judge, a stern and imposing figure, began to read the verdict. Each word, clearly enunciated, was a hammer blow to the Moretti family's shattered ego, a formal confirmation of their defeat, their reign of terror brought to an abrupt end. Guilt on all counts. The murmurs that rippled through the courtroom were a testament to the collective sigh of relief, a shared understanding of the long-awaited justice served.

The weight of the verdict settled heavily on Elena and Dante. The victory was intoxicating, a testament to their skills, their resilience, and their unwavering determination. But the cost of that victory was profound, a deep scar etched onto their souls. They had witnessed firsthand the brutal reality of the city's underbelly, the insidious reach of corruption, and the sacrifices that were needed to fight against injustice. They had lost sleep, friends, almost their lives. The weight of those sacrifices rested upon them, a heavy burden that they carried with quiet dignity.

The trial's conclusion marked only the beginning of a long, arduous process. The dismantling of the Moretti empire wasn't merely a matter of arrests and convictions; it was a systematic unraveling of a complex web of connections, financial networks, and illicit activities. Elena and Dante, working with Isabella and the authorities, spent months tracking down assets, tracing funds, and exposing the web of corruption that had allowed the Morettis to flourish for so long. It was painstaking work, filled with frustrations and setbacks, but their commitment remained unwavering. Each piece of evidence unearthed, each criminal exposed, was another step toward justice, a further affirmation of their hard-fought victory.

The city, initially apprehensive about the sudden downfall of the Morettis, slowly began to breathe again. The fear that had gripped its streets began to dissipate, replaced by a hesitant optimism. The businesses once controlled by the Morettis began to recover. The lives disrupted by their reign of terror slowly started to heal, though the scars remained. Elena and Dante, though their work wasn't over, found a sense of quiet satisfaction in observing this transformation. It was their way of measuring their victory.

But the victory, while significant, was not without its bitter aftertaste. The cost of their triumph was high. The toll on Giovanni Rossi was evident. The years of undercover work, the constant strain of living a double life, the burden of secrets, had left their mark on him. He was physically and emotionally exhausted, a shadow of the vibrant and energetic man they had once known. His retirement, though long overdue, was tinged with a bittersweet melancholy. He missed the adrenaline, the fight, but more importantly, he missed the camaraderie, the trust that he had shared with Isabella and his colleagues. The feeling that he had made a difference was real but it felt fleeting, the reward not quite equal to the years of sacrifices.

Isabella, too, bore the weight of her sacrifices, a quiet burden she carried with grace and strength. Her undercover role had demanded immense personal sacrifices, a life spent in the shadows, concealing her true identity and living a double life. The years spent infiltrating the Morettis had hardened her, sharpened her senses, but it had also cost her something precious - a life lived openly, honestly, with the people she loved. The scars were not just physical; they ran deep, into her soul.

Elena and Dante, hardened by their experiences, found a sense of cautious optimism in the quiet aftermath of their victory. Their relationship, forged in the crucible of danger and shared sacrifice, had deepened and strengthened. But the memories of those dark months, the near misses, the sacrifices, continued to haunt them. Their victory was profound, but it had come at a cost.

The city, finally free from the Morettis' iron grip, started to heal. It was a slow, gradual process, filled with challenges and uncertainties. Yet, there was a palpable sense of hope, a fragile optimism that promised a better future. The streets became safer; businesses flourished; and a new sense of community grew. Elena and Dante, having witnessed firsthand the destructive power of organized crime, understood better than most the importance of vigilance.

The final scene unfolds in a quiet park, bathed in the golden light of the setting sun. Elena and Dante sit on a bench, the cityscape stretching out before them, a testament to the city's resilience and the success of their mission. They had faced unimaginable challenges, and they had won. But their triumph had come at a profound cost, and the scars of their victory would remain a constant reminder of what they had sacrificed to bring down the Moretti empire. The city had found peace. But Elena and Dante understood that the fight for justice was an ongoing one. The quiet of their moment was a reflection of the tentative peace they had helped to create, not an end to their journey, but a quiet, well-deserved respite. The sun, setting over their liberated city, cast long shadows in their quiet victory. The shadows of past battles. The quiet optimism of their shared future.

41
GRIEF AND MOURNING

The air hung heavy with the scent of lilies and damp earth, a stark contrast to the crisp autumn air that had been so prevalent during the trial. A small, intimate gathering had assembled at the edge of the city, at a secluded memorial garden overlooking the sprawling cityscape. It was a quiet affair, a stark departure from the drama and intensity that had dominated their lives for the past year. Elena and Dante stood side-by-side, their hands clasped, a silent acknowledgment of their shared journey and the losses they carried within them.

Giovanni Rossi, his usually vibrant eyes dulled with fatigue, stood a little apart, his shoulders slumped, his gaze lost in the distant horizon. The weight of his years of undercover work, the burden of secrets he had carried for so long, had finally caught up with him. He looked older, wearier, the vibrant energy that had once defined him now replaced by a quiet resignation. The lines etched on his face were not just the markings of time, but the deep scars of a life lived on the edge, a testament to the sacrifices he had made in the name of justice. His retirement had come as a relief, but the quiet solitude of his days was often punctuated by a deep, gnawing emptiness, a missing piece of himself he could not quite define. The camaraderie, the shared purpose, the adrenaline—

these were things he sorely missed, ghosts of a life he could
no longer live.

Isabella Rossi, her usual stoic composure slightly fractured,
stood beside him, her hand resting gently on his arm. She
understood his pain, his silent grief. She, too, carried the
weight of her sacrifices, the years spent living a double life,
concealed in the shadows, her true identity a carefully
guarded secret. The intimacy she had forged with Giovanni,
built on mutual trust and shared danger, was a precious thing,
a beacon in her otherwise solitary life. Now, facing the
aftermath of their victory, she felt a profound sense of loss,
not just for the life she had sacrificed, but for the life they
could never reclaim, the years they could never retrieve. The
quiet strength that had defined her throughout the trial now
seemed to falter slightly, giving way to a deep well of
emotions she rarely displayed.

The memorial service was simple, devoid of the pomp and
circumstance that usually accompanied such events. There
were no lengthy eulogies, no grand pronouncements of
heroism. It was a quiet gathering, an intimate
acknowledgment of the sacrifices made, the lives lost – not in
the violent confrontation, but in the quieter erosion of their
identities, the gradual fading of the life they used to live. The
losses were invisible, marked only on the faces of the
attendees. The subtle tremor in Giovanni's hand as he poured
a vial of soil on the newly planted tree, the silent tear that
traced a path down Isabella's weathered cheek, Elena's hand
that unconsciously gripped Dante's, squeezing tightly,
conveying a deep-seated grief.

Elena, despite her outward strength, felt a profound sense of loss. The exhilaration of victory had been fleeting, quickly overshadowed by the realization of the cost. She had found herself increasingly tired, haunted by the faces of the victims, the families whose lives had been irrevocably shattered by the Morettis. The weight of responsibility, the burden of knowledge, rested heavily on her shoulders. The victories won had come at an immeasurable price, a debt she felt she could never fully repay.

Dante, usually the ever-present rock of strength and unwavering support for Elena, felt the weight of their shared experiences. He had witnessed the toll the fight had taken on Giovanni and Isabella, but he saw the same reflection in Elena. The years spent dedicated to bringing down the Moretti empire, the intense focus and the unwavering dedication, had left its marks on them all. He, too, felt the weight of the victories achieved. He felt the quiet sadness for the losses endured. He, too, grieved for the life they had almost lost.

As the sun dipped below the horizon, casting long shadows across the tranquil garden, they stood in silence, each lost in their own thoughts, their own memories. The city lights twinkled in the distance, a dazzling display of life continuing on, oblivious to their private grief. It was a moment of profound reflection, a quiet acknowledgement of the sacrifices made, the battles fought, and the emotional scars that would remain. The quiet solemnity of the event was a balm for their wounds, a gentle easing of the pain they carried. It wasn't a complete healing, but a necessary step toward acceptance, a quiet truce with their grief.

The silence was broken only by the gentle rustling of leaves in the autumn breeze, a soft symphony that seemed to whisper a message of hope, a promise of healing and renewal. Elena reached out and took Dante's hand again, their fingers interlacing, a silent pledge of their shared journey, their shared grief, and their shared future. They didn't speak, their unspoken understanding carrying more weight than any words could ever convey. They stood together, united by the profound experience they had shared, united by the sorrow they felt, and united by the hope that flickered faintly within them.

The following days were a blur of quiet contemplation and slow healing. Elena found herself retreating into herself, spending hours alone, lost in her thoughts, replaying memories, both good and bad. The image of Isabella's face, etched with a quiet resignation that spoke volumes of her hidden burdens, haunted Elena's thoughts. She and Dante made a point of visiting Giovanni and Isabella every couple of days, simply to sit and talk, to offer companionship, to remind them that they weren't alone in their grief. The effort was small, but it held great value. These quiet acts of support, these small gestures of caring, started to lay the foundation for the healing process. These small gestures formed a lifeline.

Dante, meanwhile, focused on practical matters, meticulously sorting through the details of the aftermath of their victory. He worked tirelessly with the authorities, ensuring that the assets seized from the Morettis were distributed appropriately, and that the victims of their crimes received the justice they deserved. It was painstaking work, filled with bureaucratic hurdles and frustrating delays, but it was a task that gave him a sense of purpose, a distraction from the emotional turmoil that still simmered within him. He found himself working longer hours than ever, seeking solace in the demanding tasks, the challenges to keep his mind occupied, his heart busy.

One evening, while sifting through some of the recovered documents, Dante stumbled upon a hidden compartment within a file cabinet. Inside, he found a series of handwritten letters, meticulously penned by Isabella's mother, detailing her own experiences in facing the Moretti family decades earlier. The letters spoke of the same fear, the same intimidation, the same feeling of being utterly trapped, overwhelmed by a powerful, relentless force. Reading those letters, Dante felt a deep sense of connection, a shared history, a bond forged in the relentless fight against the Moretti family that spanned generations. The letters gave him an entirely new perspective on Isabella's strength, her quiet resilience, her quiet acceptance. He saw the legacy she had inherited, the silent burden she had carried, and the profound courage that it had required to fight back. The letters were a window into the past, and it showed the similarities that existed between generations in their fight against a corrupt force.

Elena, noticing Dante's quiet intensity, approached him gently. She sat beside him, her hand resting on his arm, a silent offering of comfort and support. As they read the letters together, sharing the hidden history of their adversaries, they found a new level of understanding, a deeper connection to the sacrifices made by those who came before them. They found that their fight was a part of a larger narrative, a continuing battle against injustice that had spanned generations. The past now offered them guidance, inspiration, and a powerful validation for their own struggles.

In sharing this hidden history, they found a new source of strength and solace, a renewed sense of purpose. The grief remained, the pain persisted, but it was no longer consuming. It was woven into the fabric of their lives, a part of their shared experience, a constant reminder of the sacrifices they made and the victory they had earned. They could now appreciate that their hard-won victory was not just their own. It was a triumph for all those who had endured the Morettis' tyranny throughout the years. Their victory was a legacy. They found peace in the understanding of that legacy.

As the weeks turned into months, the healing began in earnest. It was a slow, gradual process, marked by moments of joy, and interspersed with moments of quiet reflection. They found strength in their relationship, in the shared experiences that had forged an unbreakable bond between them. The city continued to heal and transform, becoming a vibrant and safe place again. The future stretched before them, uncertain yet full of possibility. The past was a chapter closed but the memories remained. The scars would remain too. These scars were reminders of the fight, not wounds that disabled them. But as they looked towards the future, they carried with them the wisdom gained from their experiences, the strength forged in the crucible of adversity, and the quiet hope for a future free from the shadow of the Moretti family. They had faced darkness, and emerged into the light, scarred but not broken. They knew that healing, like justice, was a continuous process, a journey, not a destination. But they were ready for the journey.

42
FINDING SOLACE

The apartment, a haven they'd painstakingly furnished over the past few weeks, hummed with a quiet domesticity that felt both fragile and profoundly reassuring. Sunlight streamed through the large windows, illuminating dust motes dancing in the air, a stark contrast to the shadowy world they'd inhabited for so long. It was a simple space, uncluttered and calming, a conscious decision to create a sanctuary free from the echoes of their past. Gone were the harsh fluorescent lights of interrogation rooms and the oppressive weight of clandestine meetings. Here, in this space, surrounded by the soft glow of natural light and the comforting scent of freshly brewed coffee, they were slowly rebuilding their lives, brick by painstaking brick.

Elena, curled up on the plush sofa, a worn copy of Rilke's poems open in her lap, looked peaceful. The taut lines that had etched themselves onto her face in the weeks following the trial were softening, replaced by a gentler, more vulnerable expression. She wasn't entirely healed, not yet, but the sharpness of her grief had dulled, replaced by a quiet melancholy that allowed for introspection, for the slow, careful process of self-discovery. The intense focus that had consumed her for so long, the laser-like concentration on dismantling the Moretti empire, had finally dissipated. Now, the quiet hum of domesticity, the mundane rhythm of everyday life, was a balm for her wounded spirit.

Dante, seated across from her, observed her with a tenderness that spoke volumes of their unspoken understanding. He wasn't just her partner in crime, her lover; he was her rock, her refuge, the steady presence that anchored her to reality. He understood the depth of her pain, the silent battles she waged within herself, the ghosts that still haunted her waking hours. He saw the weariness in her eyes, the subtle tremor in her hands, the fleeting moments when her carefully constructed façade would crumble, revealing the vulnerability beneath. And he loved her all the more for it.

He had found his own solace in the routine of household tasks, the simple acts of preparing meals, tidying their home, a stark contrast to the clandestine operations and high-stakes risks that had defined his past. He found a strange sense of satisfaction in the meticulous care he took in preparing dinner, choosing fresh ingredients, and taking the time to create a meal that was both nourishing and pleasing to the eye. It was a small thing, an almost insignificant act, but it grounded him, offered a sense of purpose in the quiet moments between the chaos and the constant reminder of the weight of their past actions and their shared victory.

Their conversations were often laced with silences, comfortable spaces filled with unspoken understanding. They didn't need words to express the depth of their connection, the shared grief, the mutual respect, the unwavering love that bound them. Their hands would often brush, a fleeting touch that conveyed more than any elaborate declaration of affection. A shared glance across the room would often speak volumes more than long discourses. These small moments of shared intimacy were the building blocks of their recovery, the slow healing of their wounds.

One evening, as they sat together on their balcony, the city lights twinkling in the distance, Elena confessed her fear. "I don't know if I can ever truly forget," she whispered, her voice barely audible above the gentle murmur of the city. "The faces of the victims... the families..."

Dante reached out, his fingers gently interlacing with hers. "We carry their memories with us, Elena," he replied softly. "But we don't have to carry their pain. We honor their lives by fighting for justice, by ensuring their suffering was not in vain. We are their testament, Elena. Our continued existence is the mark of the victory of the innocent. Let their memory inspire us, instead of weighing us down."

His words were a gentle balm to her wounded spirit. It wasn't about forgetting; it was about remembering in a way that empowered them, that fueled their commitment to a better future. It was about transforming their shared trauma into a driving force for positive change, a shared legacy of the fight that brought down the Moretti empire.

Their healing was a gradual process, a slow unwinding of the tension and trauma that had bound them for so long. They sought solace not only in each other's presence but in small, simple pleasures. They explored the city, rediscovering its hidden corners, its vibrant energy. They spent hours lost in museums, art galleries, and quiet cafes, allowing themselves to experience the beauty of the world around them, a world they had almost lost in their pursuit of justice. They reconnected with old friends, rediscovering the simple joy of shared laughter and lighthearted conversation.

There were still moments of darkness, of quiet grief, when the memories of the past would resurface, when the weight of their sacrifices would seem almost unbearable. But these moments were no longer overwhelming. They faced them together, their love and unwavering support acting as a shield against despair. They had learned to navigate the complexities of their emotions, to acknowledge their pain without allowing it to consume them.

One particular evening, as they prepared dinner, a light, playful banter filled the air. The mundane activity of preparing a meal together, a seemingly ordinary act, took on profound significance. It symbolized the normalcy they were slowly rebuilding, the quiet rhythm of everyday life they were painstakingly weaving into the fabric of their existence. The aroma of roasting vegetables and simmering herbs filled their apartment, creating a sense of warmth and comfort, a stark contrast to the austere atmosphere they had grown accustomed to. They laughed as Dante attempted to chop vegetables with the precision of a seasoned chef, only to end up with a collection of strangely shaped pieces. Elena, watching him, couldn't help but smile, a genuine smile that reached her eyes, a smile that reflected the quiet joy that had finally found its way back into her life.

Their home, once a temporary shelter, had become their

sanctuary, a place where they could shed the weight of their past and embrace the promise of their future. The walls were no longer just four concrete slabs; they were the foundation of a new life, a testament to their resilience, their love, and their shared journey. The healing hadn't been complete, and it wouldn't be for a long time, but in the quiet intimacy of their shared life, in the simple acts of love and companionship, they found the strength to continue, to move forward, together. The journey towards healing was a shared path, one they tread with unwavering support and love for one another. And in that shared journey, they found solace, and hope for a brighter future.

43

SEEKING CLOSURE

The quiet hum of their apartment became the soundtrack to their healing. It wasn't a sudden transformation, a miraculous erasure of the pain they'd endured. Instead, it was a gradual process, a slow, deliberate chipping away at the hardened shell of grief and trauma that had encased them. The city outside, once a backdrop to their covert operations, now served as a gentle reminder of the life they were reclaiming.

One evening, as the twilight painted the sky in hues of orange and purple, Elena found herself staring out at the city lights, a familiar melancholy settling over her. Dante, sensing her shift in mood, sat beside her, his arm a comforting weight around her shoulders. He didn't speak, understanding that sometimes silence was the most profound form of communication. He simply let her feel the safety of his presence, the reassuring solidity of his love.

After a long moment, Elena turned to him, her eyes glistening with unshed tears. "It's the guilt," she confessed, her voice barely a whisper. "It's the weight of what we did, what we had to do."

Dante's hand tightened around hers, a silent acknowledgment of the burden they both carried. "We did what was necessary,

Elena," he said softly, his voice firm yet gentle. "We fought for justice. We brought down Moretti. We can't erase the past, but we can choose how we remember it, how we let it shape our future."

Their conversations became more profound, delving into the emotional complexities of their shared experiences. They revisited the harrowing events of the past year, not to relive the trauma, but to dissect it, to understand its impact, to find a way to integrate it into their narrative without letting it define them. They spoke about the victims, their families, the lives that had been irrevocably altered. They acknowledged the pain, the loss, the injustice. They wept together, sharing the weight of their grief, finding solace in their shared sorrow.

Elena, a woman who had always prided herself on her strength, her resilience, allowed herself to be vulnerable, to reveal the cracks in her armor. She spoke about the nightmares that still plagued her sleep, the haunting images that flashed before her eyes during the day. She spoke of the guilt, the feeling that she could have done more, been better.

Dante listened patiently, offering words of comfort and reassurance, reminding her of her strength, her courage, the profound impact she had had on bringing down Moretti and bringing justice to the victims. He shared his own struggles, his own moments of doubt and self-questioning, his own nightmares. He spoke of the constant vigilance, the ever present fear of retribution, the moral dilemmas that still haunted him.

Their vulnerability became a source of strength, a testament to the depth of their connection. They discovered a new level of intimacy, a deeper understanding of each other's souls. They found healing in their shared honesty, in their willingness to confront their darkest fears and insecurities together. It was a testament to their love, their unwavering commitment to each other, a love forged in the fires of adversity and tempered by the shared weight of their past.

One day, Elena suggested they visit the memorial dedicated to the victims of Moretti's crimes. The thought initially filled her with dread, but she felt a growing need to face her fears, to pay her respects, to find a sense of closure. Dante, recognizing the importance of this step, accompanied her.

The memorial was a quiet, solemn space, filled with flowers and photographs of the victims. Elena and Dante stood there for a long time, in silence, each lost in their own thoughts. They read the names etched into the stone, each name a reminder of the lives lost, the pain endured.

Elena placed a single white rose at the foot of the memorial, a silent offering of respect and sorrow. She then looked at Dante, her eyes filled with a mixture of sadness and resolve. "I think," she said softly, "I think I can finally begin to let go."

Dante nodded, his eyes reflecting her emotions. "We are not defined by our past, Elena," he said gently. "We are defined by the choices we make, the actions we take, the love we share. We can honor their memories by building a better future, a future free from the darkness that consumed their lives."

Their journey towards healing continued, not as a linear path, but as a winding road with its share of ups and downs, moments of joy and sorrow, times of peace and turmoil. They continued to work through their trauma together, finding solace in their shared love and commitment. They learned to navigate their shared past, to live with the consequences of their actions, to forgive themselves, and to move forward, together.

They sought professional help, engaging in therapy sessions to process their trauma and build healthy coping mechanisms. The therapist helped them unpack their experiences, identify their triggers, and develop strategies for managing their anxieties. The sessions were often difficult, bringing back painful memories, but they emerged stronger, their bond strengthened by their shared vulnerability. They learned to communicate more effectively, to articulate their emotions, to listen to each other without judgment.

The mundane routines of daily life—preparing meals, cleaning their apartment, going for walks—became acts of self-care, symbols of their renewed commitment to normalcy and a stable life together. They reconnected with their friends and family, rebuilding relationships that had been strained during the intensity of their pursuit of justice. Elena found solace in creative pursuits, rediscovering her passion for painting, her brushstrokes conveying the range of emotions she had experienced. Dante delved deeper into his passion for cooking, finding satisfaction in creating nourishing meals, an act of self-care and a symbol of their shared life.

Their healing wasn't a destination; it was a continuous journey. There were still days when the shadows of the past would creep in, days when the memories would resurface, causing sharp pangs of grief. But they now had the tools, the skills, and the support system to navigate these difficult moments. They had learned to acknowledge their pain, to validate their emotions, and to find strength in their shared love.

Their apartment, once a refuge, was transformed into a sanctuary of love, peace, and healing. The memories of their past remained, but they no longer held them captive. They had learned to live with their past, to integrate it into their narrative, to use it as a foundation for building a brighter future, together. They had found closure, not in forgetting, but in remembering, in honoring the victims, and in committing to live a life worthy of their sacrifices. Their journey was a testament to the resilience of the human spirit, the power of love, and the possibility of healing even after the deepest wounds. Their love story, once a dark thriller, had evolved into a tale of redemption, a quiet victory in the face of overwhelming adversity. The ending wasn't a neat resolution, but rather the beginning of a new chapter, a new story—a story of love, forgiveness, and hope.

44

FORGIVENESS AND ACCEPTANCE

The scent of rosemary and lavender, Elena's favorite combination, hung in the air, a subtle yet comforting aroma that permeated their newly renovated apartment. The walls, once bare and echoing with the ghosts of their past, were now adorned with Elena's vibrant paintings, each canvas a testament to her journey of healing. The vibrant colors, a stark contrast to the muted tones of their previous life, reflected a renewed sense of hope and vibrancy. Dante, ever attentive, had carefully curated a collection of their favorite books, lining the shelves, creating a cozy haven of literature and shared memories. He had even managed to find a rare first edition of her favorite author, a small gesture that spoke volumes about his understanding and support.

One evening, as they sat by the fireplace, the flames dancing and casting flickering shadows on the walls, Elena confessed a lingering fear. "I keep replaying those moments, Dante. The faces, the fear…I can't seem to shake the feeling that I could have done more." Her voice cracked, a raw vulnerability that laid bare the emotional scars that still lingered.

Dante reached for her hand, his touch firm yet gentle. "Elena, you did everything you could. You were extraordinary. We were a team, facing an impossible enemy. We survived, and we brought justice to those who deserved it. That is not something to diminish but to be immensely proud of." He paused, searching for the right words. "The weight of guilt is a heavy burden, but it doesn't define who you are. It's a part of your story, but it's not the entire narrative."

 Their conversations evolved, shifting from recounting their past to charting their future. They discussed their individual goals, their dreams, their aspirations. Elena spoke of her desire to use her art as a form of therapy, to help others process their trauma and find their voice. Dante, inspired by Elena's courage, revealed a long-held ambition to establish a culinary program for underprivileged youth, a way of giving back to the community that had supported them. These dreams, once overshadowed by the intensity of their mission, now shone brightly, a beacon of hope illuminating their path forward.

Their forgiveness extended beyond themselves. They sought out the families of some of the victims of Moretti's crimes. The meetings were difficult, fraught with emotion and raw grief. There were tears, hushed confessions, and a shared understanding of the profound loss they had all endured. But there was also a sense of healing, a shared acknowledgment of the fight for justice that had been waged, and a tentative beginning of shared reconciliation.

One particularly poignant encounter was with Maria, whose husband had been a close associate of Moretti and ultimately one of his victims. Maria, initially hardened by grief and anger, saw in Elena and Dante a reflection of her own struggle for justice, tempered by their willingness to confront their own inner demons. Seeing their genuine remorse, her anger began to soften. She found in their story a reflection of her own need to find a way to move forward. A tentative friendship was forged, a bridge built across a chasm of grief and loss. It was a testament to their mutual ability to overcome the immense trauma they had faced and forge meaningful connections, even in the face of seemingly insurmountable differences.

Elena and Dante also began to actively engage in community work, volunteering at local shelters and outreach programs. The act of helping others proved to be a powerful catalyst in their healing. It allowed them to channel their energies into positive actions, shifting their focus from their personal trauma to the well-being of others. This outward focus not only helped them regain a sense of purpose, but also reinforced their newfound sense of self-worth and provided a tangible way to move beyond the confines of their past. Their relationship deepened as they navigated the complexities of forgiveness and acceptance. It wasn't a seamless process; there were moments of doubt, of relapse, when the weight of their past threatened to overwhelm them. But they had developed tools to manage these setbacks— healthy communication, mutual support, and the willingness to seek professional help when needed. They attended couples therapy, allowing them to process their individual and shared trauma in a safe and controlled environment. They learned to express their feelings openly and honestly, acknowledging the lingering wounds while celebrating the progress they had made.

One significant moment came during a quiet evening in their

apartment. Elena surprised Dante with a hand-painted portrait of him, his eyes filled with the same determination and hope that she was now striving for. This was not the brooding, haunted Dante of their past missions, but a man reborn, his spirit tempered by their shared experiences, his love for Elena a beacon illuminating his future.

The painting became a symbol of their shared healing journey. It represented not only their individual growth but also the strength of their bond, their unwavering commitment to each other, their joint journey through darkness and into the light. It was a reminder of the transformation they had undergone, from hardened agents caught in the labyrinth of a dangerous game to two individuals reclaiming their lives, forging a new path together, and ultimately achieving a profound sense of peace and acceptance. The city outside their window, once a landscape of covert operations and relentless pursuit, now offered a panorama of vibrant opportunity and potential for a future built on forgiveness, love and a shared commitment to building a life worthy of their sacrifices. They were not just healing; they were evolving, growing into a stronger, deeper, and more resilient couple, their love story a testament to the enduring power of the human spirit and its capacity for redemption.

Their healing was not a linear progression; there were setbacks and moments of intense emotional turmoil. But they had learned to embrace the inevitable ebbs and flows of the process, understanding that forgiveness and acceptance were not destinations but ongoing journeys requiring patience, understanding, and a profound commitment to themselves and each other. The scars of their past would remain, but they would no longer define them. They had found a way to integrate those experiences into their narrative, transforming pain into resilience, and turning trauma into a catalyst for personal growth.

Their story is a testament to the possibility of healing, the strength of love, and the unwavering power of the human spirit to overcome adversity. Their love story, once a dark thriller edged with violence and betrayal, had transformed into a quiet, poignant ballad of resilience and forgiveness – a love story for the ages, a testament to the enduring strength of their bond, forged in the fires of their shared past and tempered by the enduring flame of their mutual love. It was a story of redemption, a story of hope, and a testament to the remarkable capacity of the human heart to heal, forgive, and ultimately, to find peace.

45
MOVING FORWARD

The morning sun streamed through the large windows of their new apartment, painting stripes of gold across the polished wooden floor. Elena, stretched out on the plush rug, her sketchbook open beside her, was lost in a world of vibrant colors and swirling brushstrokes. The canvas before her was a riot of blues and greens, a landscape that mirrored the serenity she felt settling deep within her soul. Dante, humming softly to himself, moved through the kitchen, the aroma of freshly brewed coffee mingling with the scent of baking bread. Their mornings were now filled with a gentle rhythm, a stark contrast to the frenetic energy that had once defined their lives.

Their new life wasn't a simple erasure of the past; the memories, both joyful and harrowing, remained etched in their hearts. But they had learned to integrate those experiences, to weave them into the rich tapestry of their present, rather than allowing them to define their future. The shared trauma, the intense pressure of their previous lives, had forged an unbreakable bond between them, a deep understanding born from shared adversity. It was a bond that had been tested in the fires of danger and loss, but emerged stronger, refined, and infinitely more precious.

Their healing journey extended beyond their immediate relationship. Elena, true to her word, began using her art as a form of therapy, leading workshops for victims of trauma. The act of creating, of expressing the inexpressible, provided a powerful outlet for her clients, a way to navigate their pain and find their voice. Watching others find solace and strength through her art reaffirmed Elena's own healing journey, validating her experience and empowering her to continue her own work. She found a profound sense of purpose, a fulfilling path that combined her artistic talent with her desire to help others.

Dante, equally committed to their shared vision, worked tirelessly on his culinary program for underprivileged youth. He found immense satisfaction in nurturing their potential, seeing their confidence blossom as they mastered new skills and discovered the joy of culinary arts. His kitchen, once a place of quiet contemplation, now echoed with laughter and the clatter of pots and pans, a vibrant symphony of youthful energy. The program was not just about teaching cooking; it was about building self-esteem, fostering community, and providing opportunities for personal growth. He found a profound sense of purpose in this work, a way to channel his passion for food into something genuinely meaningful.

Their relationship continued to deepen, their love a silent testament to their resilience. The shared experience, while profoundly painful, had refined their understanding of each other, strengthening the foundation of their bond. They communicated openly and honestly, sharing their fears, their doubts, and their hopes. They sought professional guidance when needed, acknowledging that seeking help wasn't a sign of weakness, but a testament to their strength and commitment to their relationship's health.

Their evenings were now filled with quiet intimacy, stolen moments of shared laughter and whispered confessions. They would often spend hours in their library, surrounded by the books that represented their shared history and individual aspirations. Elena would often read passages aloud, her voice imbued with a depth of emotion that mirrored their shared journey. Dante would listen, his eyes mirroring the warmth and love she felt for him. The space, once a sanctuary for quiet contemplation, now pulsed with a vibrant energy, the reflection of their thriving bond.

One evening, as they sat on their balcony overlooking the city, Elena confided in Dante about a recurring dream. In it, she was lost in a dark labyrinth, the walls closing in, the air heavy with fear. But then, a light would appear, a beacon of hope that would guide her out of the darkness. "It's always you, Dante," she whispered, her voice barely above a breath. "You are the light that pulls me through."

Dante pulled her close, his embrace warm and reassuring. "And you are my light, Elena," he replied, his voice thick with emotion. "You are the strength that pulls me through." Their love was not simply a romantic connection, but a deep, unwavering commitment, a testament to the healing power of shared experience and unwavering love.

They continued their community work, volunteering regularly at a local shelter for victims of domestic violence. The experience brought them face-to-face with the realities of trauma and abuse, but it also reinforced their commitment to helping others. It gave them a broader perspective on their own experiences, reminding them of the privilege they had and the responsibility they had to use their story to help others.

Their healing was not a linear process. There were days when the memories threatened to overwhelm them, days when the shadow of their past loomed large. But they had learned to navigate those moments together, their love a shield against the darkness. They learned to communicate their emotions effectively, to acknowledge their vulnerabilities without fear of judgment. They sought solace in each other's embrace, finding strength in their shared journey.

One particularly challenging moment came when they encountered Maria again. The initial tentative friendship had blossomed into a deep connection, a shared understanding born from shared grief and resilience. Maria, still grappling with the loss of her husband, confessed that she was struggling to reconcile her grief with her desire to move forward. Elena and Dante listened patiently, offering comfort and understanding, sharing their own struggles with forgiveness and acceptance.

The conversation helped solidify their understanding of healing as a journey, not a destination. It reaffirmed their commitment to mutual support and the importance of seeking professional help when needed. They revisited their therapist, discussing their shared experience with Maria and its impact on their own healing process. They realized that true healing was not about erasing the past but about integrating it into their narrative, allowing it to inform, but not define, their future.

Their transformation was not simply personal; it extended to their relationship with the city itself. The city, once a landscape of clandestine operations and near-death experiences, now seemed to offer a different vista. The vibrant energy of the bustling streets no longer felt threatening but rather inspiring. They saw opportunity and potential everywhere they looked, a reflection of their own transformation. The streets that once echoed with the sounds of pursuit now echoed with the sounds of their laughter, a testament to their hard-won peace.

Their love story, once a dark thriller, had transformed into a quiet ballad of resilience and forgiveness. It was a love story for the ages, a testament to the enduring power of the human spirit and its capacity for redemption. It was a story of healing, a story of hope, and a testament to the remarkable capacity of the human heart to heal, forgive, and ultimately, find peace, a future built on forgiveness, love, and a shared commitment to building a life worthy of their sacrifices. Their scars remained, but they were now woven into the fabric of their identity, reminders of their strength and resilience, testaments to their journey through darkness and into the light. Their love was a beacon, guiding them towards a brighter future, a future filled with hope, love, and the unwavering promise of a life lived fully and beautifully.

46
NEW OPPORTUNITIES

The aroma of roasting coffee beans, a scent Dante had meticulously cultivated over years, now filled not just their apartment, but a small, bustling cafe they'd opened together. "Caffe Dante," a testament to their shared journey, was more than just a business; it was an extension of their hearts. The cafe was nestled in a revitalized neighborhood, its walls adorned with Elena's vibrant artwork, creating an atmosphere both cozy and invigorating. Each painting told a story, a silent narrative woven into the fabric of their new life. The clientele was eclectic – artists, students, writers, and local residents, all drawn to the unique ambiance and the rich, aromatic coffee. The cafe quickly became a hub, a place where conversations flowed as freely as the espresso.

Elena, initially hesitant about venturing into the business world, found her artistic talents flourishing in this new environment. She designed the cafe's menu, her whimsical illustrations adding a touch of magic to the otherwise simple offerings. She also organized monthly art exhibitions, showcasing both established and emerging artists, creating a platform for creative expression and community engagement. The cafe became a testament to her evolving artistic identity, a space where her passion for art intersected with her desire to foster creativity in others. She even started offering small art classes in the evenings, sharing her techniques and inspiring a new generation of artists. The energy of the cafe, the constant flow of creativity, fueled her own artistic endeavors, pushing her to explore new mediums and styles. The feedback from her students, the admiration in their eyes, was a powerful affirmation of her journey, a validation of her artistic vision.

Dante, meanwhile, discovered a new passion within his culinary pursuits: teaching. He established a culinary mentorship program at a local community center, offering free cooking classes to underprivileged youth. His kitchen, once a personal sanctuary, became a place of vibrant energy, filled with the laughter and clanging of pots and pans. He found immense satisfaction in nurturing their potential, watching their confidence blossom as they mastered new skills. He wasn't just teaching them cooking; he was teaching them life skills, fostering self-esteem, and providing them with opportunities for personal growth. He saw his students not just as recipients of his skills, but as partners in a shared journey of culinary exploration. Their successes became his successes, their challenges his opportunities to teach and guide. He learned to adapt his teaching style to the unique needs of each student, celebrating their individuality and fostering a sense of community within the class.

Their respective ventures were interconnected, feeding off each other's energy and success. Elena's art attracted customers to the cafe, while the cafe's success provided financial stability for Dante's mentorship program. Their partnership was a testament to their shared vision, a collaborative effort that transcended individual ambition. They held monthly meetings, discussing both the challenges and triumphs of their endeavors, offering each other support and guidance. They were more than just lovers; they were business partners, collaborators, and each other's greatest supporters.

The success of their ventures allowed them to expand their community involvement. They started donating a portion of their cafe's profits to local charities, supporting organizations that provided shelter and support for victims of domestic violence. They continued their volunteer work at the shelter, offering emotional support and practical assistance to those in need. Their experiences had taught them the importance of giving back, of using their success to create positive change in their community. They found a profound sense of purpose in this work, a way to channel their collective strength into making a tangible difference in the lives of others.

The evening sky often found them back on their balcony, the city lights painting a shimmering backdrop to their quiet conversations. The shared experiences, the near-death escapes, the betrayals and triumphs, had forged an unbreakable bond between them. Their conversations were often peppered with laughter, but also with a quiet acknowledgment of their shared past. They were careful not to dwell on it, but to integrate it into the tapestry of their present, allowing the memories to inform, but not define, their future.

One evening, while sipping chamomile tea, Elena revealed her new artistic project – a series of paintings inspired by their journey. Each canvas captured a different stage of their lives, reflecting the raw emotions, the intense struggles, and the eventual triumph over adversity. The series was raw, visceral, honest, and utterly captivating. It was a visual testament to their journey, a story told through vibrant colors and evocative brushstrokes. The paintings were not just a reflection of their personal experiences, but a celebration of their resilience, a testament to the enduring power of human spirit. She knew these paintings were powerful, potentially cathartic for others who had faced similar trauma, providing a language for emotions often too profound to articulate.

Dante, inspired by Elena's artistic exploration, decided to create a cookbook featuring recipes from his culinary mentorship program. The cookbook was not merely a collection of recipes; it was a celebration of community, of resilience, and of the transformative power of food. He included stories from his students, their personal anecdotes interwoven with the recipes, creating a heartwarming and powerful narrative. The book was a celebration of their journey, a testament to their shared dreams and aspirations. The profits from the cookbook were donated to the community center, further supporting their efforts in empowering young people.

Their lives weren't without their challenges. The demands of running a cafe, managing a mentorship program, and maintaining a healthy relationship required constant effort and compromise. They learned to prioritize, to delegate, and to support each other through the inevitable ups and downs. They continued to seek professional guidance, utilizing therapy sessions to navigate the complexities of their relationship and their personal journeys. Their commitment to each other, their unwavering support, was the bedrock of their shared success.

Their healing journey wasn't linear; there were days when the shadows of their past threatened to engulf them. But they had learned to face those shadows together, their love a shield against the darkness. Their shared trauma had forged an unbreakable bond, a deep understanding that allowed them to navigate life's complexities with grace and resilience.

Their story was not simply a romance; it was a thriller, a drama, a testament to the power of the human spirit to overcome adversity, to find forgiveness, and to build a life filled with love, purpose, and enduring hope. Their love was a beacon, lighting the path for others to follow, a testament to the remarkable resilience of the human heart. Their journey was not only a story of survival; it was a story of triumph, a story of love found and rebuilt, stronger and more profound than ever before. The city lights twinkled around them, a silent witness to their enduring love, a testament to their hard-won peace, a promise of a bright future, built on a foundation of forgiveness, love, and unwavering commitment.

47
BUILDING A FUTURE

The scent of freshly cut grass mingled with the aroma of pine from the nearby woods, a welcome change from the ever-present coffee smell of their cafe. They stood on the porch of their new home, a charming two-story house nestled on a quiet street, a world away from the city's frenetic energy. The house, with its wide windows and wrap around porch, exuded warmth and tranquility, a stark contrast to the apartment where they had weathered the storm of their past. This house represented more than just a new address; it was the physical manifestation of their hard won peace, a tangible symbol of their commitment to building a future together.

Elena, her face glowing with a quiet joy, ran a hand along the smooth, freshly painted wood of the porch railing. "It's perfect, Dante," she whispered, her voice filled with a contentment that mirrored the serenity of their surroundings. The house was a collaborative effort, a reflection of their shared tastes and desires. Elena had overseen the interior design, incorporating elements that mirrored her artistic style– warm, inviting spaces filled with natural light and pops of vibrant color. Dante, meanwhile, had tackled the landscaping, transforming the overgrown yard into a haven of tranquility, a miniature paradise where they could retreat from the world.

The move itself was a process, a labor of love that brought them even closer. They spent weekends sorting through belongings, discarding items that represented their past lives, carefully selecting those that symbolized their journey and their shared future. The act of unpacking was almost ritualistic, each item placed with intention, each decision a silent affirmation of their commitment. They found joy in the mundane tasks, transforming the empty rooms into a cozy home, a sanctuary filled with love and laughter.

The living room, with its large windows overlooking the garden, became their favorite space. A comfortable sofa, plush rugs, and a crackling fireplace created a warm, inviting ambiance. Elena's artwork adorned the walls, each painting a silent narrative of their journey, a testament to their resilience and their enduring love. The fireplace mantel was filled with family photos, carefully curated mementos, and cherished keepsakes, each object holding a story, a reminder of their shared past and their hopes for the future. The space was a reflection of their shared history, a vibrant tapestry woven from memories, both joyful and painful.

The kitchen, a testament to Dante's culinary passions, was a space of both functionality and beauty. Stainless steel appliances glistened under the warm light, while custom made wooden cabinets housed their culinary treasures. A large island served as a central gathering point, a place where they could share meals, prepare food together, and simply enjoy each other's company. The smell of freshly baked bread, the simmering of sauces, the joyful clatter of pots and pans –

these were the sounds that now filled their new home, replacing the echoes of fear and uncertainty that once haunted them.

Upstairs, their bedroom was a sanctuary, a place of peace and intimacy. Soft lighting, comfortable bedding, and a breathtaking view of the starlit sky created a haven of tranquility. The room was a testament to their evolving relationship, a space where they could retreat from the world and simply be together, appreciating the quiet intimacy of their shared space. It was a place where they could reflect on their journey, appreciate their hard-won peace, and dream about the future.

The house was more than just a building; it was a symbol of their transformation. It represented their commitment to building a life filled with love, stability, and purpose. It was a physical manifestation of their healing journey, a testament to their resilience, and a beacon of hope for their future. The meticulous care they put into every detail, from the selection of paint colors to the arrangement of furniture, was a reflection of their deep-seated desire to create a space that nourished their souls, a place where they could thrive.

Their days were filled with a blend of routine and adventure. Mornings were spent in their cozy kitchen, sipping coffee and planning their day, their laughter echoing through the rooms. Afternoons were dedicated to their respective ventures, the energy of their work fueling their creativity and passion. Evenings were spent in quiet contemplation, reflecting on their journey, appreciating the hard-won peace that now surrounded them. Weekends often involved exploring the surrounding countryside, hiking through the woods, or simply relaxing on their porch, enjoying the serenity of their new home.

The sense of community they found in their new neighborhood was another source of joy and stability. They met their neighbors, sharing stories and exchanging friendly gestures, forging bonds that deepened their sense of belonging. They found common ground, sharing experiences and creating a network of support that enriched their lives. This sense of connection helped ground them, offering them a sense of belonging that contrasted sharply with the isolation they had experienced in the past.

Their commitment to giving back to their community continued. They organized fundraising events, using the cafe's success to support local charities and organizations. The cafe itself became a hub for community involvement, hosting workshops, lectures, and art exhibitions that fostered a sense of unity and collaboration. Their generosity and compassion became a defining aspect of their identity, a testament to their desire to create positive change in the world around them.

As the seasons changed, so did their lives. The house became a canvas for their shared experiences, each season leaving its mark on the garden, on their lives, and on their hearts. The spring brought vibrant flowers, a burst of color that mirrored the joy in their hearts. Summer brought long evenings on the porch, filled with laughter and quiet conversations. Autumn brought the crisp air and the warmth of the fireplace, a cozy ambiance that reflected the intimacy of their relationship.

Winter brought the stillness of snow, a serene beauty that mirrored the peace they had found within themselves.

Their life was not without its challenges. The demands of their businesses, the occasional conflict, and the lingering shadows of their past occasionally cast a pall over their happiness. But they faced these challenges together, their love a shield against the darkness, their commitment a beacon in the storm. They learned to adapt, to compromise, and to support each other through thick and thin. Their therapy sessions continued, providing a safe space to navigate the complexities of their relationship and their personal journeys.

Elena continued to create, her paintings becoming increasingly bold and expressive, reflecting the depth of her emotions and the beauty of their life together. Dante continued to teach, nurturing the potential of young people and inspiring them to pursue their dreams. Their collaborative ventures flourished, their success providing them with both financial stability and a deep sense of purpose.

Their story was a testament to the resilience of the human spirit, a narrative of healing, forgiveness, and the unwavering power of love. The purchase and establishment of their new home marked not an end, but a beginning, the start of a new chapter in their lives, a future filled with love, stability, and enduring hope. The city lights might be distant, but the warmth of their home, the intimacy of their relationship, and the quiet joy of their shared future shone brighter than any city lights could ever hope to. Their love story was far from over; it was just beginning, unfolding beautifully, like a freshly blossomed flower in their new garden.

48
SHARED DREAMS

The quiet hum of the refrigerator was the only sound
competing with the gentle crackle of the fire in their hearth.
Elena, curled up on the sofa with a sketchbook in her lap, idly
sketched the flames, their dancing light reflecting in her eyes.
Dante, across from her, was engrossed in a thick manuscript,
the glow of the lamp illuminating his focused expression. The
scene was idyllic, a picture of domestic bliss, yet beneath the
surface, a current of unspoken anticipation ran between
them. This wasn't just a house; it was a launching pad for their
shared dreams.

Elena's artistic dreams had always been a solitary pursuit, a
private language she spoke through brushstrokes and color.
But with Dante, she found a new audience, a confidante who
understood the raw emotion poured onto her canvases. He'd
encouraged her to consider exhibiting her work, suggesting
galleries and helping her craft compelling artist statements.
His belief in her talent was a powerful catalyst, pushing her
beyond her self-doubt. She'd even started working on a series
of paintings inspired by their journey together – a visual
testament to their resilience and love. The paintings, vibrant
and expressive, captured the emotional rollercoaster they'd
endured, the shadows and the light, the pain and the joy. Each

canvas told a story, a part of their shared narrative, a testament to their enduring bond. She planned to show them at a local gallery, a bold step for someone who had always preferred the anonymity of her studio.

Dante, in turn, found his own ambitions fueled by Elena's unwavering support. His passion for education, for nurturing young minds, had always been a driving force in his life. But since their move, he felt a renewed sense of purpose. He'd been working on a new teaching curriculum, one that incorporated creative arts into traditional academic subjects, a bold move that echoed Elena's artistic spirit. He envisioned a more holistic approach to learning, one that nurtured not just intellect but also creativity and emotional intelligence. He'd even started collaborating with local schools, presenting his ideas and gaining their support for a pilot program. The success of his proposal hinged on the results of this pilot program – a critical step towards the widespread adoption of his revolutionary curriculum. He knew that failure wasn't an option; the weight of his belief in his method felt immense, yet Elena's steadfast belief in him eased the pressure.

Their shared dreams weren't confined to their individual pursuits. They both harbored a quiet longing for a family, a desire they'd carefully nurtured and discussed during their therapy sessions. The move to the countryside was partly driven by this wish; the spacious house and expansive garden felt like a perfect setting for a family to flourish. They weren't ready to jump in yet; the process felt delicate, requiring patience and careful consideration. But the conversation had started, planting a seed of hope that quietly bloomed in the fertile ground of their newfound stability. The possibility of children filled their conversations with a gentle excitement; the conversations were filled with imaginative scenarios, creating detailed plans for their future life. They were both excited at the prospect of sharing their joys and concerns with their little ones, hoping to instill the values of resilience, hard work, and creativity that had shaped their lives.

Weekends were often devoted to collaborative projects, a testament to their combined energy and creativity. They worked side-by-side, transforming the neglected garden into a haven of beauty. Elena's artistic eye guided the planting of flowers, creating vibrant color palettes that reflected the changing seasons. Dante's practical skills were evident in the design of the garden paths, the installation of a charming water feature, and the construction of a small greenhouse for Elena's seedlings. Their laughter filled the air, a harmonious soundtrack to their efforts, each task a shared experience. The garden was a physical reflection of their growing bond, a space where they could nurture life and dreams. They would spend hours working together, and often, once the work was finished, they would sit on the porch swing and sip lemonade, discussing their latest plans and ideas.

Their evenings were just as collaborative. Dante, an exceptional cook, would prepare elaborate meals, his culinary skills a testament to his meticulous nature. Elena, in turn, would set the table with exquisite care, transforming their dining experience into a small ritual that celebrated their connection. They'd share stories, reminisce about their past, and discuss their hopes for the future. They spent their evenings making decisions related to their future lives, often discussing ideas related to future home renovations. These evenings weren't merely meals; they were a way to strengthen their bonds, building a shared history one meal at a time.

But their shared journey wasn't without its challenges. The demands of their respective careers often left them exhausted, leading to occasional disagreements and simmering tensions. The lingering shadows of their past occasionally crept into their present, threatening to disrupt the hard-won peace they'd created. Yet, each time, they found their way back to each other, their love a resilient anchor in the face of adversity. Their therapy sessions proved invaluable, providing a safe space to process their emotions, to confront their anxieties, and to strengthen their communication skills. They used these sessions to establish realistic expectations in their relationship, and to prevent misunderstandings.

One evening, as they sat by the fire, Elena confessed her fear of failure. The gallery opening loomed, and the thought of public scrutiny filled her with anxiety. Dante, ever the pragmatist, reassured her, reminding her of her talent and her unwavering resilience. He spoke of their shared journey, the challenges they'd overcome together, and the unbreakable bond that connected them. He reminded her that their love was a constant, a source of strength that would sustain her, regardless of the outcome. His words, simple yet profound, were a balm to her soul, reminding her that their shared dreams were more important than any individual success.

Dante, in turn, shared his apprehension about his new teaching curriculum. The weight of expectation, the potential for rejection, threatened to overwhelm him. Elena, with her characteristic empathy, listened patiently, offering words of encouragement and reminding him of his talent, his passion, and the profound impact he had on the lives of his students. She reassured him, offering a sense of unwavering support. She understood his passion, knowing that his success would not only fulfill his own dreams but also inspire others. She knew that his work could change the way children learned, impacting their lives for years to come.

Their shared vulnerability, their willingness to expose their fears and insecurities, solidified their bond. It was in these moments of honesty and openness that their love shone brightest, illuminating their path towards their shared future. Their dreams were no longer just individual aspirations; they were interwoven threads, forming a tapestry of shared purpose, mutual support, and enduring love. The house, once an empty shell, was now filled with life, laughter, and the quiet hum of a shared future, a future built on the foundation of their shared dreams, a future they faced together. The journey hadn't been easy, but as they stood on the threshold of a new era, they knew that together, they could conquer any obstacle, their love a guiding light on their path. The journey was ongoing, but they faced it hand in hand, ready to support each other on every step of their journey.

49
OVERCOMING CHALLENGES

The aroma of freshly brewed coffee hung in the air, a comforting scent that usually heralded a peaceful morning. But today, a subtle tension crackled between Elena and Dante. The gallery opening for Elena's exhibition was just a week away, and the usually cheerful artist was visibly subdued. Her usual vibrant energy was replaced by a quiet anxiety that Dante couldn't ignore.

He found her staring out the kitchen window, her reflection shimmering in the glass alongside the burgeoning dawn. The landscape, usually a source of inspiration, seemed to mirror her inner turmoil. "Everything alright, amore?" he asked softly, his voice laced with concern.

Elena turned, a faint smile playing on her lips, but her eyes held a shadow of doubt. "It's just...the opening," she confessed, her voice barely a whisper. "The thought of people judging my work...it's terrifying."

Dante pulled out a chair and sat beside her, his hand gently covering hers. He knew this fear. He'd felt the same pressure when presenting his revolutionary curriculum to the school board. The fear of vulnerability, of exposure, the fear of failing to live up to the expectations he'd set for himself. He understood the weight of public scrutiny, the sting of potential rejection.

"Elena," he began, his voice calm and reassuring, "remember the countless hours you poured into those paintings? Remember the emotion, the passion, the raw honesty that poured onto each canvas? That's what people will see. They'll see your soul, your talent, your heart. And that's far more valuable than any critique."

He leaned closer, his eyes reflecting the morning light. "Your art is a reflection of our journey, of our resilience, of our love. It's a testament to everything we've overcome together. And you know what? Regardless of what anyone says, I'll always be your biggest fan. Your work is breathtaking; its beauty transcends critique. The success of the exhibition is not what matters; the completion of the creative process and the act of self-expression is what makes you successful in my eyes."

His words, a comforting balm to her troubled spirit, eased some of her anxiety. But the fear, like a persistent shadow, lingered. The opening night wasn't just about her art; it was a public declaration of her vulnerability, an exposure of her soul.

Later that day, Dante received a call from the school principal. The pilot program for his new curriculum, the one that had consumed months of his time and energy, had received a less-than-enthusiastic response. The board, while impressed with his innovative approach, expressed concerns about its practicality and its potential impact on standardized test scores. The weight of disappointment settled heavily on his shoulders.

He found Elena in the garden, tending to her seedlings with her usual meticulous care. He sat beside her, silently watching her work, her hands moving with a gentle grace that mirrored her artistic spirit. He didn't need to tell her the news; the slump of his shoulders, the quiet sigh escaping his lips, spoke volumes.

Elena looked up, sensing his distress. "What is it, amore?" she asked, her voice soft with concern.

He hesitated, then shared the news. The disappointment was palpable, a heavy cloud settling over their usually sunny disposition. Elena listened patiently, her empathy a comforting presence. When he had finished, she gently took his hand, her touch a silent affirmation of her unwavering support.

"Dante," she began, her voice steady and strong, "remember the passion that drove you to create this curriculum? Remember the belief in your vision, in your ability to inspire young minds? That's what truly matters. The board's response doesn't diminish your dedication or the innovative nature of your teaching method. Their worries about standardized scores are short-sighted, failing to see the holistic benefit of your approach. It merely confirms that revolutionary changes take time, facing resistance and opposition. The process of proposing such radical changes in the field of education isn't easy; they need time to come around. You should be proud of yourself for your work, because it takes courage to implement changes in the field of education."

She continued, "This isn't the end, Dante. It's a setback, a temporary roadblock. We've faced bigger challenges than this, haven't we? We'll find a way to navigate this. We'll find a different path, a different way to reach the same destination. We will persevere, and our collective resilience will help us overcome these obstacles."

Her words were a lifeline, pulling him from the depths of his despair. Her unwavering faith in him, her belief in his vision, reignited the flame of his passion. He realized that the rejection wasn't a reflection of his worth, but rather a testament to the radical nature of his ideas. It was a challenge, yes, but not an insurmountable one.

That evening, as they sat by the fire, sharing a simple meal, they talked about their setbacks, acknowledging their fears and anxieties without judgment. They spoke of the lessons learned, of the resilience they'd discovered within themselves, of the strength they found in their shared love.

The gallery opening arrived, and Elena, though still nervous, faced the crowd with a newfound confidence. Her paintings, vibrant and emotive, resonated with the viewers, eliciting gasps of admiration and murmurs of appreciation. The evening was a success, not necessarily measured in sales or critical acclaim, but in the connection she made with her audience, in the shared experience of art and emotion.

In the following weeks, Dante reworked his curriculum proposal, addressing the board's concerns while retaining the core principles of his vision. He sought collaboration with other educators, forming alliances and gathering support for his innovative teaching method. He understood that his efforts were to help the children receive a better quality education, and that should be the driving force of his work. He knew that the long-term goal was more important than short-term success, and he persevered with a steadfast commitment to his cause.

Elena and Dante emerged from these challenges stronger, their bond forged in the crucible of adversity. They had learned to confront their fears, to embrace their vulnerabilities, and to find strength in their shared journey. The challenges they'd faced had tested their resilience, but in overcoming them, they had discovered a deeper understanding of themselves and their love. They continued working on their individual projects, hand-in-hand, knowing that their shared dreams were more than just aspirations; they were a testament to their shared resilience and enduring love. They were a force to be reckoned with, a team ready to face whatever life threw their way. Their shared future, once a distant dream, now seemed tangible, a testament to their unwavering love, resilience, and collaborative spirit. Their future, bright and promising, stretched before them like a beautiful canvas waiting to be painted with the colors of their shared dreams. They continued their work on their respective projects, sharing their progress and encouraging one another throughout the entire process. Their shared journey was an ongoing testament to their unwavering resilience and commitment to their goals. The experiences strengthened them and their relationship, proving that the most significant challenges in life often lead to the most profound personal growth and the most rewarding relationships.

50
CELEBRATING SUCCESS

The champagne bubbles danced in Elena's glass, mirroring the joyous laughter that filled their small, sun-drenched kitchen. The gallery opening had been a resounding success, exceeding even their wildest expectations. Not just in terms of sales — though the canvases were selling briskly, a testament to Elena's burgeoning reputation — but in the palpable energy, the genuine connection she'd felt with the audience. People lingered, studying her work, their faces reflecting a range of emotions, from quiet contemplation to outright exhilaration. It was more than just an art exhibition; it was a shared experience, a testament to the power of art to transcend words and connect souls.

Dante, watching her from across the table, felt a surge of pride swell in his chest. He'd seen her struggle with self doubt, the nagging fear of vulnerability that haunted her even as she created masterpieces. Seeing her bask in the glow of her success, the fear replaced by a quiet confidence, filled him with a love so profound it ached.

"To resilience," he toasted, raising his glass. "To facing our fears and emerging stronger."

Elena clinked her glass against his, her eyes shining with

unshed tears. "To us," she whispered, her voice thick with emotion. "To our shared journey."

Their celebration wasn't confined to grand gestures. It was woven into the fabric of their daily lives: a quiet dinner under the starlit sky, a stolen moment of intimacy amidst the chaos of their busy schedules, a shared laugh over a silly mishap. It was in the way they looked at each other, a silent acknowledgment of their shared triumphs and the strength they found in each other's unwavering support.

The success of the exhibition wasn't just about the art; it was a validation of their collective journey. It was a testament to the late nights spent in the studio, the struggles overcome, the unwavering belief in each other's talents, and the shared dreams they had nurtured together. It was a confirmation that their love story wasn't just a fairytale; it was a powerful, enduring force that propelled them towards their goals.

Dante's journey wasn't as immediate, but the small victories were just as meaningful. He continued to refine his curriculum proposal, tirelessly seeking feedback and support from fellow educators. He engaged in passionate discussions, convincing colleagues of the merits of his approach, patiently answering their questions and addressing their concerns. He understood that genuine change requires not just innovation, but collaboration and persistent advocacy. The school board's initial rejection hadn't deterred him; it had challenged him to improve and refine his ideas. He embraced constructive criticism, seeing it as an opportunity to strengthen his case and enhance the impact of his program.

He found an ally in Dr. Ramirez, a seasoned educator known for her progressive views and influence within the education community. Together they drafted a revised proposal, incorporating Dr. Ramirez's valuable insights and addressing the board's concerns. The new proposal meticulously detailed the long-term benefits of his approach and presented a framework for ongoing evaluation, dispelling any concerns about the lack of clear metrics or compatibility with standardized tests. They even developed a pilot program specifically designed to address those concerns, offering a controlled environment to study the impact of the new curriculum on student learning outcomes.

One evening, weeks after the exhibition, Dante received a call. The school principal's voice was markedly different this time, filled with a cautious optimism that sent a wave of hope washing over Dante. The revised proposal had been accepted, and the pilot program was approved. It wasn't a complete victory, not yet; it was a cautious step forward, a recognition of his vision's potential, and a testament to his persistence and strategic approach.

The news was met with unrestrained joy. Elena hugged him tightly, tears of happiness streaming down her face. It wasn't just a personal victory for Dante, but a collective triumph for their shared values and dreams.

Their celebrations were understated. The most beautiful things are not about grandeur, but the simplicity and sincerity of the moment. A quiet dinner, a shared glass of wine under the twinkling stars, a simple "I love you" whispered in the stillness of the night – these moments were testaments to the enduring strength of their bond, their resilience in the face of adversity, and their shared commitment to their dreams. Their love wasn't a passive observation, but an active force, a creative energy that fueled their individual passions and strengthened their resolve in the face of obstacles.

As they sat side-by-side on their porch, watching the sunset paint the sky with vibrant colors, they discussed their future, their voices low and intimate. Elena talked excitedly about her next exhibition, a series inspired by their journey, by the resilience and love they had discovered in each other's arms. Dante spoke of the challenges ahead, the uphill battles of implementing his innovative curriculum, but his voice was filled with a newfound confidence, a resolute determination that was both inspiring and deeply moving. He was no longer merely an educator, but a crusader for a cause he deeply believed in; an advocate for children's education; a man who was driven not by accolades or recognition, but by the pure desire to make a positive impact on the lives of his students.

The shared triumphs weren't just about personal achievements; they were a testament to their enduring love, a powerful force that nurtured their dreams and fortified their bond. They knew that challenges lay ahead, but they would face them together, their hands clasped firmly in each other's, their hearts united in a symphony of shared hopes and aspirations. Their journey was far from over; it was just beginning, a breathtaking canvas onto which they would paint the vibrant colors of their shared dreams, their unwavering love, and their indomitable resilience. Their journey was a living testament to the power of partnership, of unwavering support, and of the strength found in shared adversity. It was a love story woven not just with romance, but with resilience, determination, and the enduring power of a shared vision. They were more than just lovers; they were partners in life, partners in creation, partners in the pursuit of their dreams. Their journey served as an inspiration, a beacon of hope for others, showing the world that even in the face of adversity, love, resilience and shared commitment could conquer all.

51

THE STRENGTH OF THEIR BOND

The following weeks were a whirlwind of activity. Elena, fueled by the success of her exhibition and the renewed confidence it brought, dove headfirst into her next project. This wasn't just another collection of paintings; it was a deeply personal exploration, inspired by the trials and triumphs they'd shared, a vibrant tapestry woven with threads of resilience, love, and the unwavering strength of their bond. She spent hours in her studio, the rhythmic strokes of her brush a meditative counterpoint to the swirling emotions within her. Each canvas became a visual narrative, a testament to their journey, capturing the raw vulnerability of their struggles and the breathtaking beauty of their shared victories. She painted the stormy nights of doubt and fear, the quiet moments of solace and intimacy, the explosive joy of their shared successes. The colours were intense, raw, reflecting the depth of her emotions, the very essence of their love story.

Dante, meanwhile, navigated the complexities of implementing his innovative curriculum. The pilot program, while approved, wasn't without its challenges. He faced resistance from some teachers, clinging to traditional methods, skeptical of his unconventional approach. There were logistical hurdles, bureaucratic delays, and the constant pressure to demonstrate tangible results. He found himself spending long hours at school, engaging in debates, answering questions, and patiently explaining his vision to a sometimes-unresponsive audience. He was not only an educator, but a diplomat, a mediator, and an advocate. He relied on his network of supportive colleagues, especially Dr. Ramirez, who continued to offer guidance and support, navigating the bureaucratic labyrinth with her seasoned expertise.

The strain of their respective endeavors began to show. The stolen moments of intimacy became fewer, the quiet dinners under the stars less frequent. The demands of their work encroached upon their personal time, creating a subtle but palpable distance between them. Elena, consumed by her artistic process, found herself withdrawing, losing herself in the world of color and texture, seeking solace in her art, rather than in his embrace. Dante, exhausted from his battles within the education system, felt a growing sense of isolation, the weight of his responsibilities pressing down on him. The shared joy they had experienced after his proposal's acceptance seeme

d a distant memory, replaced by a pervasive exhaustion. One evening, after a particularly grueling day at school, Dante arrived home to find Elena still in her studio, lost in her work. The air was heavy with silence, broken only by the soft scratching of her brush against the canvas. He watched her for a moment, his heart aching with a mixture of admiration and sadness. He understood the intensity of her creative process, the way it could consume her, leaving little room for anything else. But the distance, the silence, felt like a chasm opening up between them.

He approached her cautiously, his voice soft and hesitant. "Elena," he began, "How was your day?"

She looked up, her eyes dark and shadowed. "Long," she replied, her voice devoid of its usual warmth. "I'm not sure I'm capturing it... the essence of it all."

He sat down beside her, picking up one of her paintbrushes, examining the texture, the way the colors blended. "Your work is breathtaking, Elena," he said, his voice filled with genuine admiration. "But... I miss you."

The confession hung in the air, heavy with unspoken words and unexpressed emotions. Elena turned to him, her gaze intense. "I miss you too, Dante," she whispered, her voice breaking slightly. "But it's... overwhelming. This... this is everything I've ever wanted, but it's consuming me."

He nodded, understanding her struggle. He knew the pressures she faced, the relentless pursuit of perfection that drove her. He saw the vulnerability behind her fierce independence, the fear of failure that lurked beneath her confident exterior. Their challenges, while distinct, were intertwined, mirroring each other in their intensity and demands.

"We've been through so much together, haven't we?" he asked softly, taking her hand in his. "We've faced adversity, overcome obstacles. This is just another challenge, another hurdle to overcome. Together."

She leaned her head against his shoulder, tears finally escaping her eyes. "It's just... so much," she murmured. "I feel like I'm failing, in both my work and... in us."

He pulled her closer, holding her tightly. "You're not failing, Elena. You're creating, you're pushing boundaries, you're living your dreams. And we'll face this together, just like we always have. We'll find our balance, our rhythm. We will."

Their embrace lasted long after the tears had dried. It wasn't just physical comfort; it was a reaffirmation of their love, a silent vow to navigate the challenges ahead, hand in hand. The next few weeks were still demanding, but they consciously made an effort to reconnect. They scheduled dedicated time for each other, prioritizing their relationship amidst the chaos of their individual pursuits. They talked, not just about their work, but about their hopes, their fears, their shared dreams. They rediscovered the joy in simple things—a shared cup of coffee in the morning, a quiet walk in the park, a movie night at home. They began to carve out pockets of time, reclaiming their intimacy, strengthening the foundation of their bond, reinforcing the unshakeable belief in each other, the knowledge that they were not merely individual entities, but a force multiplied by the strength of their unity.

The exhibition, when it finally arrived, was a triumph, exceeding all their expectations. The gallery was packed with people, drawn in by the raw emotion, the powerful storytelling in Elena's paintings. It was a testament not only to her artistic talent, but to the enduring power of their love, a visual representation of the journey they had shared. Dante, standing beside her, felt an overwhelming sense of pride and love. The challenges they had faced, the distance they had felt, seemed insignificant compared to the unwavering strength of their bond, a bond that had been tested, refined, and emerged stronger than ever. Their love wasn't just a romantic fairytale; it was a powerful force, a relentless engine, driving them forward, supporting their individual dreams while simultaneously strengthening their bond. It was a story painted not just on canvas, but in the very fabric of their lives, a testament to the enduring power of love, resilience, and the unwavering strength of their shared journey. They knew that life's journey is not without its trials, but their love, forged in the fires of adversity, would stand as an unwavering beacon, guiding them through the complexities and challenges ahead, together. Their story was only just beginning.

52
UNCONDITIONAL SUPPORT

The opening of Elena's exhibition was a spectacle. The gallery, usually a hushed sanctuary of art, pulsed with a vibrant energy, a tangible hum of excitement and hushed whispers. People moved through the space, their faces illuminated by the canvases, their expressions shifting from quiet contemplation to stunned admiration. Elena's work, raw and visceral, spoke volumes. It was a journey, a testament to resilience, to the enduring power of love in the face of adversity. Each painting was a story, a chapter in their shared life, laid bare for the world to see.

Dante, watching from the periphery, felt a profound sense of pride welling up inside him. He wasn't just her partner; he was her confidante, her rock, the silent observer who had witnessed the birth of each stroke, the evolution of each emotion poured onto the canvas. He saw the vulnerability in her work, the fear, the doubt, and the ultimate triumph over those obstacles. It was her courage, her unrelenting spirit, that had fueled her artistic journey, and it was a journey he had been privileged to share, every step of the way.

He saw a woman who had not only embraced her fears but had transmuted them into breathtaking art. He saw the depth of her passion, her unwavering commitment to her craft, her unyielding belief in herself, and in them. And in that moment, surrounded by the fruits of her labor, the tangible manifestation of her talent, he understood the profound depth of their connection. It was more than love; it was a partnership built on mutual respect, admiration, and an unshakeable belief in each other's potential. It was a love that had been tested, refined, strengthened by the trials and tribulations they had faced together.

Their support for each other wasn't just a passive sentiment; it was actively woven into the fabric of their daily lives. It manifested in small, everyday gestures, in the unspoken understanding that existed between them, a silent communication built on years of shared experiences and a deep, abiding love. While Elena poured her soul onto her canvases, Dante had been diligently working on his new curriculum, facing resistance and setbacks with the same unwavering determination that defined Elena's artistic process. He knew he could count on Elena's unwavering support, just as she knew she could rely on his.

One evening, after a particularly frustrating day dealing with resistant teachers and bureaucratic red tape, Dante arrived home exhausted and disheartened. He found Elena already in the studio, working on a new piece, her brow furrowed in concentration. He didn't interrupt her; he simply sat quietly beside her, watching her work, his heart filled with a quiet admiration. He understood her process, her need for solitude, her unwavering dedication to her art. It was a part of who she was, a vital component of her being, and he wouldn't dare try to intrude. But this time, there was a new element to his silent observation. It wasn't simply about admiring her dedication. This was about appreciating the fierce strength of his own love for her, how it allowed him to see her world and support it unconditionally.

After a while, she looked up, sensing his presence, a faint smile touching her lips. "It's… difficult," she confessed, her voice laced with exhaustion. "I'm struggling to capture the emotion, the weight of it all."

Dante reached out, gently taking her hand, his touch radiating warmth and reassurance. He didn't offer words of encouragement or advice; he simply held her hand, offering his silent support, letting her know that she wasn't alone, that he was there, with her, through the struggles, the frustrations, the triumphs.

"It's alright," he whispered, his voice filled with a quiet understanding that transcended words. "Sometimes, the most beautiful art comes from the most challenging experiences."

His presence was enough. The silent understanding between them, the unspoken words of support and reassurance, were as powerful, as comforting, as any verbal encouragement could ever be. He understood the emotional turmoil she was going through; he saw the reflection of his own struggles in her eyes. He knew the depths of her artistic process, the emotional investment she made in her work. This understanding wasn't just empathy, it was the profound connection of two souls intertwined, two beings who knew each other's hearts and minds with an intimacy that transcended words.

That night, they didn't talk much. But they were together. His presence was a silent promise, a testament to their unwavering love, a reaffirmation of their commitment to each other. He knew that sometimes, the greatest act of support was simply being there, offering a quiet presence, a comforting silence, a reassuring touch. The unspoken understanding between them, built over years of shared experiences, mutual respect, and an unshakeable love, was stronger than any words could ever express.

The following weeks were a testament to their unwavering commitment to each other. They continued to navigate the challenges of their individual lives, but they did so with a renewed sense of purpose and understanding. They consciously made time for each other, prioritizing their relationship amidst the demands of their respective careers. They scheduled dinner dates, even if it was only for a quick meal, carving out pockets of time for intimacy and conversation. They rediscovered the simple joys—a shared cup of coffee in the morning, a walk in the park during their lunch break, a quiet evening at home, curled up with a book or a movie, surrounded by each other's comforting presence.

Their unconditional support wasn't limited to grand gestures; it thrived in the everyday moments, the subtle acts of kindness, the shared smiles, the silent understanding. It was in the way Dante listened patiently as Elena described her creative struggles, in the way he helped her with her studio, carrying heavy canvases, cleaning brushes, organizing supplies, offering his silent presence, understanding her needs without her explicitly mentioning them. It was in the way Elena listened patiently as Dante talked about the challenges in his work, offering insightful advice, unwavering encouragement, and the comforting assurance that she was right there with him, sharing in both his victories and defeats. They were two individuals, passionately pursuing their dreams, yet fiercely intertwined, bound by a love that nourished, supported, and strengthened them both.

One rainy afternoon, while Dante was grading papers, Elena came into the study, holding a newly finished painting. It depicted them, sitting together on a park bench, the sky a stormy grey, rain falling gently around them. But their faces were filled with quiet contentment, their hands clasped together, a silent testament to the enduring power of their love.

"I finished it," she whispered, her voice filled with a quiet emotion, her eyes reflecting the stormy sky outside.

Dante put down his papers, turned to her, his heart swelling with love and pride. He didn't need words; he saw the reflection of their life in that painting. He saw their struggles, their perseverance, their shared victories, and most importantly, he saw their love, as strong and resilient as the storm depicted in the background.

He embraced her gently, his arms enfolding her in a warm embrace. It wasn't just a physical gesture; it was a silent reaffirmation of their love, their commitment to each other, a testament to the enduring power of their shared journey. Their love was more than just a feeling; it was a force, a driving power, a lifeline that carried them through life's storms, solidifying their bond, reinforcing their commitment to an unconditional support that anchored them to each other, no matter the challenges they faced. They had been through so much together, and they knew, with unwavering certainty, that they would weather any storm, hand in hand, their love an unbreakable beacon in the darkness, guiding them on their shared journey, always.

53
DEEPENING INTIMACY

The days that followed were a tapestry woven with threads of quiet intimacy. It wasn't the dramatic, sweeping gestures of romance novels, but rather the subtle nuances of a love deeply rooted in shared understanding and unwavering support. They found solace in the simple act of sharing a cup of tea in the morning, the warmth of her hand in his as they walked through the city streets, the comforting silence that filled their evenings as they worked side-by-side in their respective studios.

One evening, Dante found Elena staring out the window, lost in thought. The city lights cast long shadows across her face, illuminating the subtle lines of worry etched around her eyes. He knew, without needing to ask, that the weight of her upcoming solo exhibition was pressing heavily upon her. He approached her quietly, placing a gentle hand on her shoulder.

"What's troubling you, amore?" he asked, his voice soft and reassuring.

She turned, her eyes reflecting the flickering city lights, and a single tear traced a path down her cheek. "I'm afraid," she confessed, her voice barely a whisper. "Afraid of failure, of not living up to expectations, of… of letting you down."

Dante pulled her gently into his arms, holding her close as she succumbed to the release of her pent-up anxieties. He didn't offer platitudes or empty reassurances. He simply held her, letting her feel the warmth of his embrace, the steady rhythm of his heartbeat against hers. He understood her fears; he had faced his own battles with self-doubt. His love for her was not a blind faith, but rather a profound understanding of her vulnerabilities and a unwavering belief in her strength.

"You won't fail, Elena," he whispered, his voice filled with a conviction that resonated deep within her soul. "Your art is breathtaking, it's powerful, it's you. And I'm here, always. No matter what happens, I'll be here."

That night, they talked, not about the upcoming exhibition, but about their fears, their insecurities, their dreams. They shared their vulnerabilities, laying bare their souls to each other with a level of intimacy that had deepened over time, a trust earned through shared experiences and mutual respect. It was in these moments of shared vulnerability, in the honest expression of their fears and anxieties, that their bond solidified, their love growing stronger with each shared tear, each whispered confession.

Their intimacy wasn't solely confined to emotional vulnerability. It manifested in the physical as well, a tender touch, a lingering kiss, a quiet embrace. These moments, seemingly insignificant in the grand scheme of life, were infused with a depth of meaning, a testament to the unspoken understanding that bound them together. It was in the stolen glances across a crowded room, the subtle brush of their hands as they walked side-by-side, the quiet intimacy of shared laughter, that their love blossomed, growing stronger and deeper with each passing day.

They spent hours in her studio, not just working on her art, but sharing the creative process itself. He would watch as she worked, captivated by her intense focus, her passionate dedication to her craft. He offered silent support, occasionally offering a word of encouragement, but mostly content to simply be present, to share in the magic of her artistic creation. She, in turn, would offer him insightful feedback on his curriculum development, challenging his thinking, pushing him to be better.

One evening, while reviewing a particularly challenging section of his curriculum, he felt a wave of frustration wash over him. He slumped back in his chair, overwhelmed by the sheer complexity of the task. Elena, sensing his distress, gently approached him, her hand resting softly on his arm.

"What's wrong, amore?" she asked, her voice laced with concern.

He explained his frustrations, detailing the obstacles he faced, the resistance he encountered. She listened patiently, offering insightful advice, challenging his perspective, helping him find solutions he hadn't considered before. It wasn't just about finding answers; it was about sharing the weight of his burden, the challenge of his work, the frustration of his struggles. Her empathy, her unconditional support, her intellectual engagement with his challenges transformed the process into a shared journey of creation and problem-solving. It deepened their emotional connection and strengthened their intellectual partnership, proving that intimacy wasn't just emotional vulnerability; it was intellectual engagement, shared challenges overcome together.

As the exhibition drew closer, Elena's anxiety increased, but Dante's unwavering support remained a constant presence. He helped her prepare, organizing her studio, framing her paintings, handling logistical details, taking care of all the mundane tasks that would otherwise distract her from her art. He was not just her lover; he was her confidante, her rock, her partner in every sense of the word.

The opening night of the exhibition was a triumph. The gallery pulsed with energy, the air thick with excitement and admiration. Elena's paintings, raw and powerful, spoke to the heart of the viewers, evoking a range of emotions. Dante, watching her from the sidelines, his heart swelling with pride, saw in her eyes the reflection of the journey they had undertaken together, a journey that had tested their love, refined it, strengthened it, and ultimately brought them to this moment of shared success.

The exhibition was more than just a showcase of Elena's artistic talent; it was a testament to their enduring love, a visual representation of their shared journey, a powerful expression of their profound connection. It was a victory they shared, a celebration of their unwavering support for one another, a reaffirmation of the profound intimacy that bound them together. As the evening progressed, they stood amongst their friends and colleagues, hands clasped tightly, their bond as strong as the love they shared. The success of the exhibition became a symbol of their resilience, their trust, and their unwavering commitment to one another, deepening their intimacy through a shared moment of triumph and celebrating the enduring power of their love.

54
FORGIVENESS AND UNDERSTANDING

The success of the exhibition didn't magically erase the lingering shadows of the past. The wounds inflicted by Marco's betrayal hadn't completely healed, leaving subtle scars on Elena's heart. She found herself occasionally retreating into herself, a fleeting melancholy clouding her usually vibrant spirit. Dante, ever observant, noticed these subtle shifts in her demeanor, the slight tremor in her voice, the way her eyes would momentarily glaze over, lost in a sea of unspoken memories.

He didn't press her, didn't demand explanations or force her to confront her pain. He simply offered his presence, a silent reassurance that he was there, a steadfast anchor in the turbulent waters of her emotions. He understood that forgiveness, like healing, was a process, not a destination, and he would patiently walk alongside her on this journey of self-discovery and emotional reconciliation.

One evening, as they sat by the fire, the crackling flames casting dancing shadows on the walls, Elena finally spoke, her voice low and hesitant. "I still... I still think about Marco sometimes," she confessed, her eyes filled with a mixture of sadness and regret. "I wonder... what if I had made different choices? What if I had seen the truth sooner?"

Dante reached for her hand, his touch gentle, reassuring. "There are no 'what ifs,' Elena," he said softly. "The past is the past. We can't change it, but we can learn from it. And what we've learned is that love, true love, endures, even in the face of betrayal and heartbreak."

He didn't minimize her pain, didn't attempt to dismiss her feelings. He acknowledged her struggles, validating her emotions with a level of empathy that transcended mere sympathy. He understood that forgiveness wasn't about forgetting; it was about accepting, about understanding, about moving forward without carrying the weight of resentment and bitterness. It was about recognizing that everyone makes mistakes, even those we love, and that the capacity for growth and change is inherent within us all.

Elena continued to open up, sharing the lingering doubts and insecurities that haunted her. She spoke about the sense of vulnerability she felt, the fear of being hurt again, the difficulty in trusting completely. Dante listened patiently, offering words of encouragement, sharing his own experiences with betrayal and heartbreak. He revealed his own vulnerabilities, his own fears, his own past mistakes, creating a space where both could be truly seen and understood, without judgment or condemnation.

Their conversations weren't always easy. There were moments of anger, moments of tears, moments of profound sadness. But within these challenging exchanges, a deeper understanding blossomed, a stronger bond forged in the fires of their shared vulnerability. They learned to navigate the complexities of their emotional landscape together, discovering the resilience of their love in the face of past hurts.

Their journey towards forgiveness extended beyond their personal conversations. Dante made a conscious effort to understand Marco's perspective, not to condone his actions, but to comprehend the motivations that drove him to such cruelty. He delved into the details of Marco's past, researching his background, speaking to mutual acquaintances, trying to piece together the puzzle of his character. He wasn't seeking justification for Marco's actions, but rather a deeper understanding of the circumstances that shaped him, the forces that contributed to his destructive behavior.

This wasn't about excusing Marco's actions; it was about contextualizing them, understanding the intricate interplay of factors that contributed to his betrayal. It was about acknowledging the complex nature of human behavior, the myriad influences that shape our choices, the nuanced interplay of circumstance and personality. This understanding, though it didn't erase the pain Elena had endured, helped her to process it, to find a path towards healing and eventually, towards a measure of compassion.

Forgiveness wasn't a sudden, dramatic event, but a gradual unfolding, a slow erosion of resentment, a conscious decision to release the grip of bitterness. It was a process that required patience, understanding, and a profound respect for the complexities of the human heart. It was a journey they embarked on together, hand in hand, their love serving as a beacon in the darkness, guiding them towards a future where forgiveness could flourish.

The understanding they cultivated extended beyond their relationship. They actively worked to build empathy in their professional lives. Elena found herself increasingly patient with her students, acknowledging their struggles and imperfections with a newfound compassion. Dante, in his role as an educator, embraced a more inclusive and understanding approach to teaching, striving to create a learning environment where every student felt valued and supported. Their journey of forgiveness and understanding had profoundly impacted not just their personal lives but their professional endeavors as well.

Their relationship evolved into a deeper, more profound connection, a testament to the transformative power of love and forgiveness. It was a love that had endured the storm, weathered the tempest, and emerged stronger, more resilient, and profoundly more beautiful. The scars remained, subtle reminders of the pain they had endured, but they were woven into the fabric of their love, a testament to their resilience, a symbol of their shared journey, a powerful expression of their enduring bond. Their love was not merely a feeling, but an active process of understanding, acceptance, and unwavering commitment. It was a love that had survived betrayal, healed wounds, and emerged transformed, a beacon of hope in the often-turbulent waters of life. Their story became an echo of resilience, a whisper of hope, a testament to the enduring power of love, forgiveness, and understanding.

Their shared experience transformed their perception of intimacy. It wasn't solely about physical closeness or emotional vulnerability; it encompassed intellectual engagement, shared challenges, and the unwavering support they offered each other. Their partnership became a testament to the idea that true intimacy thrives on transparency, acceptance, and a mutual commitment to growth and healing. They celebrated their successes together and faced their struggles hand-in-hand, creating a strong foundation built on trust, understanding, and unwavering love. The journey towards forgiveness was a testament to their resilience, a testament to the enduring power of their love. It wasn't a quick fix, a simple solution; it was a process, a journey, an evolution of their relationship, a testament to their commitment to each other.

The quiet moments, shared in the warmth of their home, became even more precious, infused with a deeper understanding of the fragility and resilience of the human spirit. The simple act of holding hands, the quiet comfort of a shared silence, became powerful expressions of their enduring love, their mutual respect, their unwavering commitment to each other's well-being. Their love was a tapestry woven with threads of joy and sorrow, success and failure, strength and vulnerability, forgiveness and understanding. It was a testament to the power of human connection, the enduring strength of love, and the transformative potential of shared experiences. It was a love story that transcended the boundaries of conventional romance, evolving into a profound partnership, a testament to their shared journey and the enduring strength of their love. The scars of the past remained, but they were now interwoven with the vibrant threads of their present, serving as reminders of their resilience, their strength, and the unwavering power of their love. They were not merely lovers; they were partners in life, in love, in the journey of forgiveness and understanding. And in that shared journey, they found not only healing but a deeper, more profound love than they ever could have imagined.

55
A TESTAMET OF LOVE

The ripple effect of their healing journey extended far beyond the confines of their intimate relationship. Elena, once haunted by the betrayal and the lingering insecurities it had spawned, found a newfound confidence in her professional life. Her interactions with her students, once tinged with a hesitant caution, now radiated warmth and understanding. She could sense their struggles, their anxieties, their vulnerabilities, not with judgment but with empathy, forged in the crucible of her own emotional journey. She listened more intently, offered support more freely, and celebrated their achievements with genuine joy. The classroom, once a place where she projected a carefully constructed facade of competence, transformed into a space of genuine connection, where she could offer not just instruction but genuine care and compassion. Her students responded in kind, their trust in her growing exponentially, fostering a learning environment characterized by open communication and mutual respect. The scars of her past, far from hindering her, had become unexpected catalysts for growth, transforming her into a more effective, compassionate, and empathetic educator.

Dante, too, witnessed a profound shift in his professional life. His work as an educator was always characterized by a commitment to inclusivity and understanding, but his interactions with his students acquired a new depth, a new level of empathy informed by his personal journey with Elena. He could see the shadows in their eyes, the weight of their unspoken anxieties, the silent battles they fought within themselves. He approached them with a patience and understanding that stemmed from his own experiences with vulnerability and emotional healing. He fostered an environment of open dialogue, where students felt empowered to share their struggles without fear of judgment or condemnation. He created a space where mistakes were seen as opportunities for growth, failures as stepping stones toward success, and vulnerabilities as strengths. His students felt seen, heard, and understood in ways that had a transformative impact on their academic performance and overall well-being. His classroom became a microcosm of the healing and understanding he and Elena had cultivated in their own relationship, a space where vulnerability was embraced, and support flowed freely.

Their influence extended beyond their immediate circle. Their shared resilience, their ability to overcome adversity and emerge stronger, inspired those around them. Friends and family observed their transformation, their unwavering commitment to each other, their ability to find joy and fulfillment even amidst challenges. They became an unspoken testament to the enduring power of love, a beacon of hope in a world often characterized by cynicism and despair. Their story, quietly whispered among friends and family, served as a potent reminder that even the deepest wounds can heal, that even the most profound betrayals can be overcome, and that love, genuine love, possesses an almost supernatural capacity for redemption and transformation.

Elena and Dante found solace in the quiet moments they shared, in the simple acts of companionship that spoke volumes about the depth of their connection. The shared laughter over mundane occurrences, the silent understanding that passed between them without words, the comforting weight of their hands clasped together – these were the moments that nourished their souls and reaffirmed the strength of their bond. Their relationship was not a fairy tale; it was a testament to the power of commitment, resilience, and the unwavering belief in the capacity of love to heal. They acknowledged the scars of the past, but they refused to let those scars define them. They embraced the imperfections, the vulnerabilities, the complexities of their shared history, and in that embrace, they found a love that was deeper, richer, and more profound than anything they had ever imagined.

Their shared journey became a source of strength, a foundation upon which they built a future filled with purpose and meaning. They discovered that forgiveness, far from being an act of weakness, was an act of extraordinary strength, a testament to their capacity for empathy, understanding, and self-awareness. It was a testament to their ability to rise above pain and create something beautiful from the ashes of heartbreak. They learned to celebrate the victories, both large and small, recognizing that growth and healing are not linear processes but rather a series of ups and downs, triumphs and setbacks. Their resilience, their ability to learn from their mistakes, and their unwavering commitment to each other served as a powerful example to those around them.

They understood that true intimacy extended beyond the physical and emotional; it encompassed intellectual engagement, mutual respect, and a shared commitment to personal growth. They encouraged each other's aspirations, celebrated each other's successes, and offered unwavering support during times of struggle. Their relationship was a dynamic partnership, a constant evolution, a testament to the transformative power of love. They learned to communicate openly and honestly, to navigate conflicts with grace and understanding, and to value the quiet moments of shared intimacy. Their love was a sanctuary, a safe haven, a place where they could be completely themselves, flaws and all.

The artistic collaboration they embarked on, initially a means of healing and self-expression, evolved into a powerful symbol of their shared journey. The art they created together reflected their emotional growth, their resilience, their capacity for forgiveness, and the enduring strength of their love. Each brushstroke, each carefully chosen color, each deliberate composition represented a milestone in their journey, a testament to their ability to transform pain into beauty, sorrow into hope. Their art became a reflection of their inner selves, a window into their shared experience, a powerful expression of their enduring love and mutual understanding.

Their story, a testament to the resilience of the human spirit and the transformative power of love, became a source of inspiration for those around them. It demonstrated that healing is possible, that forgiveness is attainable, and that love, in its most profound and enduring form, can conquer even the most devastating betrayals. Their journey serves as a beacon of hope, illuminating the path toward emotional healing, forgiveness, and the creation of a love that is stronger, deeper, and more resilient than any they could have ever imagined. The scars they carry are not badges of shame but rather emblems of their strength, reminders of the journey they have undertaken together, and symbols of the enduring power of their love. Their story is a testament to the enduring power of love, a powerful reminder that even amidst the deepest darkness, the light of love can illuminate the path toward healing, redemption, and a future filled with hope and joy.

56
ADJUSTING TO PEACE

The morning sun streamed through the kitchen window, illuminating dust motes dancing in the golden light. Elena hummed a little tune as she prepared breakfast, the scent of freshly brewed coffee and sizzling bacon filling the air. Dante, already awake, sat at the table, engrossed in a newspaper, the quiet rustle of the pages a gentle counterpoint to Elena's cheerful melody. This was their new normal, a life punctuated by the simple pleasures of shared mornings, quiet evenings, and the comfortable silence that spoke volumes about the depth of their connection. Gone were the frantic phone calls, the hushed whispers, the gnawing anxiety that had once characterized their days. In its place was a calm, a tranquility that seeped into the very fabric of their being.

It wasn't a fairy tale ending, not by a long shot. The scars of their past remained, faint etchings on the landscape of their souls. There were still moments when the memories surfaced, unwelcome ghosts from a life they had painstakingly left behind. But those moments were fleeting, overshadowed by the overwhelming sense of peace and contentment that permeated their lives. They had learned to acknowledge the past without being consumed by it, to honor the wounds without letting them dictate their future.

Their days unfolded with a gentle rhythm. Elena, revitalized by the newfound serenity, threw herself into her work with renewed passion. The classroom, once a battleground for her insecurities, now felt like a sanctuary. She engaged with her students with a genuine warmth, her lessons imbued with a depth of understanding that transcended mere instruction. She could see their potential, their vulnerabilities, their hopes, and she nurtured them with patience and unwavering support. The students responded in kind, their respect and admiration for her growing with each passing day.

Dante, too, found a renewed sense of purpose in his work. He channeled his energy into mentoring students, guiding them through the complexities of life with the same understanding and compassion that he had shown Elena. His classroom became a vibrant hub of intellectual curiosity and emotional support, a space where students felt empowered to explore their potential without fear of judgment or condemnation. He and Elena, in their separate classrooms, were shaping young minds, guiding them towards a future where healing and compassion were valued above all else.

Evenings were spent in a shared embrace, the quiet hum of conversation filling the air. They might discuss current events, delve into philosophical debates, or simply share stories about their day, their words interweaving like the threads of a rich tapestry. Their conversations were laced with laughter and understanding, a testament to the depth of their connection. There was a shared comfort in their silence, too, a comfortable companionship that needed no words to express itself. They would sit side by side, reading, listening to music, or simply enjoying each other's presence, the unspoken connection a silent testament to the resilience of their love.

Weekends were reserved for simple pleasures. Long walks in the nearby park, hands clasped together, their steps falling into a comfortable rhythm. Picnics by the lake, surrounded by the tranquil beauty of nature, their laughter echoing through the trees. Quiet evenings at home, cooking together, sharing meals bathed in the warm glow of candlelight. These were the moments that nurtured their souls, reaffirming the strength of their bond. They rediscovered the joy in the everyday, in the simple things that had once been lost in the whirlwind of their tumultuous past.

The artistic collaboration that had begun as a therapeutic exercise blossomed into a shared passion. They painted together, their styles blending and contrasting, reflecting the multifaceted nature of their relationship. Each canvas became a narrative, a visual chronicle of their journey, a testament to their ability to transform pain into beauty. The vibrant colors and bold strokes reflected their newfound joy, the delicate lines and soft hues spoke of the tenderness and understanding that formed the bedrock of their connection. They exhibited their art in local galleries, sharing their story with the world, not as a tale of woe, but as an inspiring narrative of resilience, forgiveness, and the transformative power of love.

Their friends and family, witnesses to their remarkable transformation, offered their admiration and support. They celebrated their newfound peace, their ability to overcome adversity and emerge stronger than before. The whispers of their story, once tinged with sorrow and caution, now carried a note of hope and inspiration. They had become an example, a testament to the enduring power of human resilience, a beacon of hope for those struggling to navigate the complexities of life.

 One evening, as they sat on their porch, watching the sunset paint the sky with vibrant hues of orange and purple, Elena turned to Dante, her eyes filled with a love that transcended words. "Do you remember," she asked softly, her voice barely a whisper, "how dark it felt sometimes?"

Dante nodded, his gaze fixed on the distant horizon. "Yes," he replied, his voice rough with emotion. "But look at us now, Elena. Look at what we've built."

He reached for her hand, his fingers intertwining with hers. The simple gesture, so commonplace now, was imbued with a profound significance. It was a testament to their journey, a symbol of the strength of their love, a promise of the peace and tranquility that lay ahead. They had emerged from the shadows, transformed by the crucible of their shared experiences, stronger, wiser, and more deeply in love than ever before. Their new normal wasn't just a life free from the shadows of their past; it was a life illuminated by the radiant glow of their enduring love, a love that had healed the wounds of the past and paved the way for a future filled with joy, purpose, and unwavering commitment to each other. The scars remained, but they were now simply a part of the rich tapestry of their lives, reminders of the journey they had undertaken together, a testament to their resilience and the enduring power of their love. The quiet moments, the shared laughter, the unspoken understanding – these were the treasures they now cherished, the building blocks of their peaceful, fulfilling life together. Their love story, once a tempestuous storm, had finally calmed into a gentle, unwavering current, carrying them towards a future brimming with promise and hope. And in the quiet peace of their new normal, they found a joy that was deeper, more profound, and infinitely more precious than anything they had ever imagined.

57
BUILDING COMMUNITY

The quiet rhythm of their new life extended beyond their home. Elena and Dante, having found solace in their shared existence, felt a growing urge to contribute to the community that had, in its own way, offered them a silent support system during their darkest hours. It started subtly. Elena, inspired by her students' burgeoning creativity, volunteered to help organize the annual town art fair. It wasn't simply a matter of setting up tables and hanging artwork; she infused the event with her own passion, personally mentoring some of the younger participants, guiding them through the process of presenting their work, helping them craft compelling artist statements, and encouraging their unique perspectives. She even convinced Dante to contribute a few pieces, showcasing their collaborative art for the first time on a larger platform. The response was overwhelming; their artwork, so deeply personal and emotionally resonant, struck a chord with the community, prompting conversations about resilience and healing.

Dante, meanwhile, took his mentoring role a step further, engaging with the local youth center. He initiated a series of workshops focused on critical thinking, problem-solving, and conflict resolution—skills he'd honed during his own tumultuous past, skills that were now a source of strength and empowerment for the young people he worked with. He found a profound satisfaction in watching these young minds blossom under his tutelage, seeing the spark of potential ignite in their eyes. His empathy, previously a source of vulnerability, now became his greatest strength, enabling him to connect with them on a deep emotional level, guiding them toward a path of self-discovery and personal growth. He brought a level of understanding that surpassed simple instruction, addressing not only their academic needs but also their emotional well-being, addressing the anxieties and insecurities they often faced.

Their involvement in the community wasn't limited to formal settings. They embraced the simple acts of kindness, the everyday gestures that strengthened the fabric of their neighborhood. They helped Mrs. Gable, the elderly woman next door, with her garden, their laughter echoing amidst the vibrant blooms. They volunteered at the local soup kitchen, sharing not only their time but also their warmth and compassion, offering a listening ear and words of encouragement to those who needed it most. They attended local community events, engaging in conversations with their neighbors, learning about their lives, their hopes, and their dreams. These interactions were not merely social engagements; they were conscious efforts to build bonds, to foster a sense of belonging, to contribute to a collective well being.

Elena's influence extended to the school as well. She initiated a mentorship program, pairing older students with younger ones, fostering a sense of camaraderie and mutual support.

She believed in the transformative power of human connection, and this program became a testament to that belief. She also organized workshops for parents, focusing on effective communication and building strong family relationships. Her ability to connect with people on an emotional level allowed her to create a safe space where parents could share their concerns, discuss their challenges, and find support within their community. This fostered a sense of unity within the school, strengthening the bonds between teachers, students, and parents.

Dante, beyond his work at the youth center, got involved in the local neighborhood watch, not out of fear, but out of a desire to contribute to the safety and well-being of his community. He wasn't interested in policing; his focus was on community building, fostering relationships between neighbors and establishing trust. He organized community gatherings, creating opportunities for neighbors to get to know each other, share stories, and build a sense of collective responsibility. These were not simply social events but carefully planned interactions that fostered mutual understanding and a deeper sense of community.

Their collective efforts went beyond individual initiatives; they started collaborating on projects that brought the community together. They organized a community cleanup day, transforming a neglected park into a vibrant green space. They initiated a fundraising campaign to support a local charity, combining their artistic talents with their organizational skills to create a compelling narrative that resonated with potential donors. Their commitment wasn't about personal recognition; it was about making a difference, about leaving a positive impact on the lives of others.

The impact of their efforts wasn't just measurable; it was deeply felt. The community, once a collection of individuals, started to feel like a cohesive unit, bound together by a shared sense of purpose and mutual support. The simple act of sharing a meal at the soup kitchen, volunteering at the art fair, or engaging in a neighborhood cleanup day fostered a sense of belonging, creating a web of connections that strengthened the community's resilience.

Their home, once a sanctuary for their personal healing, now extended to encompass the wider community. It was a place where neighbors gathered for impromptu coffee mornings, where students came for guidance, and where artists shared their creations. The boundaries between their personal life and their community life blurred, reinforcing their sense of belonging and mutual support.

Their artistic endeavors also played a significant role in their community building efforts. They organized art workshops for children, introducing them to the joys of creative expression. They painted murals on the walls of local buildings, transforming drab spaces into vibrant canvases that reflected the community's spirit and vitality. They held open studios in their home, inviting neighbors to experience their creative process, fostering dialogue and encouraging community participation in the arts.

Through their art, they didn't merely depict their journey of healing; they extended an invitation to others to engage in their own processes of growth and self-discovery. Their art became a catalyst for conversations, a space for sharing experiences, and a powerful tool for community building. They hosted exhibitions, showcasing not only their work but also the artwork of other local artists, creating a platform for creative exchange and fostering a vibrant arts community.

The process of rebuilding their lives had inadvertently become a project of community building, a testament to their ability to transform personal trauma into collective strength. Their quiet acts of kindness, their tireless involvement in community projects, their shared artistic endeavors – all these intertwined threads wove a rich tapestry of connection, forging a strong bond between them and the community they had chosen to embrace. It wasn't about fixing a broken system; it was about creating a better one, brick by brick, relationship by relationship, act of kindness by act of kindness. And in doing so, they found a deeper purpose, a more profound sense of fulfillment, and a love that was even stronger, bound not just by their shared history but also by their shared commitment to building a stronger, more compassionate community. Their new normal wasn't just a personal triumph; it was a collective one. It was a testament to the transformative power of love, resilience, and the unwavering belief in the capacity of the human spirit to heal, to grow, and to build something beautiful from the ashes of the past.

58
PERSONAL GROWTH

Elena, ever the insatiable learner, enrolled in a series of online courses, delving deeper into art history and therapeutic techniques. She found a particular fascination with the works of Frida Kahlo, whose resilience in the face of adversity mirrored her own journey. The vibrant colors and raw emotionality of Kahlo's paintings resonated deeply, inspiring her own artistic expression and strengthening her resolve to use her art as a tool for healing and connection. She meticulously documented her learning, compiling a detailed journal of her insights and reflections, a personal testament to her intellectual curiosity and her commitment to personal growth. The knowledge she gained wasn't confined to her personal enrichment; she integrated it seamlessly into her teaching, enriching her lessons and empowering her students to explore their own creative potential with greater depth and understanding.

Her studies extended beyond the digital realm. She sought out mentorship opportunities, connecting with established artists and art therapists, absorbing their wisdom and expanding her professional network. These connections weren't merely professional exchanges; they were opportunities for personal growth, fostering a sense of belonging and mutual support within a wider artistic community. She found herself inspired by the generosity and mentorship of her own mentors, further strengthening her commitment to nurturing the creative talents of others. This reciprocal relationship served as a powerful reminder of the cyclical nature of learning and growth, emphasizing the importance of giving back and sharing her knowledge with others.

Dante, too, embraced a path of personal development. His involvement with the youth center sparked a renewed interest in psychology, leading him to embark on a self directed study of human behavior and emotional intelligence. He devoured books on trauma-informed care, cognitive behavioral therapy, and the science of resilience, seeking to deepen his understanding of the complex challenges faced by the young people he mentored. He started attending workshops and conferences, expanding his knowledge base and refining his techniques. He found that his own journey of healing had equipped him with a unique perspective, an empathetic understanding that allowed him to connect with the youth on a profoundly personal level.

His personal growth wasn't confined to theoretical knowledge; he actively sought opportunities to practice and refine his skills. He volunteered at a local crisis hotline, offering support and guidance to individuals in distress. This direct engagement provided invaluable practical experience, honing his empathy and strengthening his ability to communicate with individuals grappling with emotional turmoil. He learned the importance of active listening, of creating a safe and non-judgmental space for individuals to express their feelings without fear of criticism. He discovered the profound power of human connection, the ability to offer comfort and hope in moments of despair.

Beyond his academic pursuits, Dante sought personal growth through physical activities. He rediscovered his love for hiking, spending weekends exploring the rugged mountain trails that surrounded their town. The solitude of the wilderness provided him with a sense of peace and clarity, a space to reflect on his journey and appreciate the beauty of the natural world. He found that physical activity not only improved his physical well-being but also enhanced his mental clarity and emotional resilience. The challenges he faced on the trails mirrored the challenges he overcame in his own life, reinforcing his strength and determination.

Their individual journeys of self-discovery intertwined and complemented each other. They supported each other's pursuits, celebrating each other's achievements and providing comfort during moments of doubt and frustration. They discussed their respective learning experiences, sharing insights and perspectives, deepening their understanding of themselves and each other. Their relationship, strengthened by their shared resilience, became a source of mutual encouragement and growth. Their home transformed into a space of intellectual curiosity and collaborative learning, a haven where they could freely explore their passions and support each other's aspirations.

Elena and Dante's personal growth extended beyond their individual pursuits. They embarked on joint projects that blended their unique skills and interests. They developed a series of art therapy workshops designed to help young people process trauma and express their emotions through creative expression. Their combined experience in art and psychology provided a unique and effective approach, creating a safe space for young people to explore their feelings and find healing through artistic expression. Their workshops were not merely therapeutic interventions; they were opportunities for personal growth, empowering young people to harness their creativity as a tool for self-discovery and emotional well-being.

Their collaborative efforts further solidified their bond and deepened their shared commitment to community engagement. They discovered a synergy in their approach, their strengths complementing each other, creating a potent force for positive change within their community. They realized that their personal growth wasn't simply a matter of individual achievement but a catalyst for collective growth, strengthening the community around them. Their relationship, far from being a private haven, became a powerful engine for societal betterment.

They established a small non-profit organization focused on supporting local artists and providing art therapy services to vulnerable populations. This endeavor combined their passion for art, their commitment to community service, and their dedication to personal and collective growth. It became a tangible expression of their values, a testament to their resilience, and a symbol of their hope for a better future.

The organization's work extended beyond art therapy. They organized community events promoting mental health awareness, bringing together experts and community members to discuss important issues and provide support to those who needed it most. These events were not simply informational gatherings; they were opportunities for personal growth, encouraging self-reflection and collective healing. The community responded enthusiastically, embracing their initiative and actively participating in their programs. This outpouring of support further validated their commitment to personal and collective growth, confirming the transformative power of their combined efforts.

Their journey was far from over, but they had reached a significant milestone. Their new normal was characterized not by an absence of challenges but by their ability to face them with newfound resilience, informed perspectives, and a deep commitment to personal and community growth. They had learned to embrace change, to adapt to unforeseen circumstances, and to find strength in their shared experience. Their love, forged in the crucible of adversity, had transformed into a powerful force for positive change, shaping not only their individual lives but also the lives of those around them. Their story served as an inspiration, a testament to the enduring power of the human spirit and the ability to rebuild lives and communities from the ashes of tragedy. Their journey of healing had become a journey of empowerment, impacting themselves and leaving an indelible mark on the community they had adopted as their own.

59
SHARED PASSIONS

Their renewed focus on personal growth naturally bled into shared activities. The structured routines of their individual studies gave way to spontaneous adventures, their shared passions weaving a vibrant tapestry into the fabric of their daily lives. Weekends often found them exploring the hidden gems of their adopted town, discovering quaint coffee shops tucked away on cobblestone streets or antique stores brimming with forgotten treasures. These explorations weren't merely sightseeing excursions; they were opportunities for connection, for quiet conversations amidst the gentle hum of everyday life. Elena, ever the observer, would find inspiration for her art in the subtle details—the chipped paint on a weathered windowsill, the interplay of light and shadow on a cobbled lane—while Dante, attuned to human interaction, would engage with the shopkeepers and fellow patrons, his observations enriching his understanding of human behavior.

One particular Saturday found them wandering through a bustling farmer's market, the air thick with the aroma of freshly baked bread and ripe, sun-kissed fruits. Elena, captivated by a display of vibrant wildflowers, found herself drawn to the artistry of their arrangement, the way the colors and textures complemented each other. She engaged the florist, a seasoned woman with calloused hands and a kind smile, in a conversation about the symbolism of flowers, their language transcending words. Dante, meanwhile, chatted with a local honey producer, learning about the intricacies of beekeeping and the delicate balance of nature. Their individual conversations became a shared experience, weaving together strands of their respective passions and adding another layer to their growing understanding of each other. The shared experiences extended beyond casual explorations. They discovered a mutual love for hiking, their weekends often spent conquering challenging trails amidst breathtaking landscapes. The physical exertion provided a release, a space to clear their minds and reconnect with the raw power of nature. It was during these hikes that they would often have their most profound conversations, sharing their thoughts and feelings with a vulnerability that only the vast expanse of the wilderness could foster. The silence between them, punctuated by the chirping of birds and the rustling of leaves, became a space for deep introspection, a refuge from the complexities of their lives. The quiet moments served as reminders of the profound bond they shared, a connection forged in adversity and strengthened through shared experiences.

Their shared passion for community engagement led them to volunteer at a local soup kitchen, serving meals to the homeless and those in need. The act of serving others provided a sense of purpose and fulfillment, a counterpoint to their personal struggles. It was here that they witnessed the resilience of the human spirit, the ability to find hope amidst despair. The stories shared by the individuals they served often sparked conversations that deepened their understanding of the societal forces at play, inspiring further discussions about social justice and their role in making a positive impact on their community. Their work at the soup kitchen was not merely an act of charity; it was a testament to their shared commitment to uplifting those around them and making a difference in the lives of others.

Beyond their volunteer work, their shared passion for the arts extended to attending local theater productions, art exhibitions, and musical performances. They analyzed the plays and artwork, critiquing the performances and discussing the themes explored by the artists. Elena, with her artistic eye, would analyze the composition and color palettes, while Dante, with his empathetic nature, would focus on the emotional depth and the human stories portrayed on stage or through the brushstrokes of the artists. These shared cultural experiences enriched their intellectual life, providing them with fodder for further discussions and deepening their understanding of art's ability to express universal human experiences.

Their shared love for travel blossomed into weekend getaways, small escapes from their daily routines, offering them an opportunity to explore new places and create lasting memories. A trip to a nearby coastal town, with its charming harbor and quaint shops, became a testament to their ability to find joy in simple pleasures. They spent their days strolling along the beach, collecting seashells and marveling at the beauty of the ocean, their conversations ranging from childhood memories to their hopes and dreams for the future.

The evenings were marked by candlelit dinners and quiet conversations, their bond deepening with each shared moment.

One particularly memorable journey took them to a remote mountain cabin, far from the hustle and bustle of city life. Surrounded by the tranquility of nature, they found solace and rejuvenation, their connection strengthening in the quiet embrace of the wilderness. They spent hours hiking, exploring the surrounding trails, and marveling at the vastness of the landscape. They discovered a hidden waterfall, its cascading waters creating a mesmerizing symphony. They shared stories under a sky ablaze with stars, their words whispered against the backdrop of the natural world. This getaway provided them with much-needed respite, strengthening their bond and giving them renewed energy to face the challenges that lay ahead.

Elena's artistic talents and Dante's empathetic nature found a harmonious blend in their joint creation of a community garden. They transformed a neglected patch of land behind their house into a vibrant oasis, cultivating herbs, vegetables, and flowers. This collaborative project allowed them to express their creativity, connect with nature, and contribute to their community. They learned together, sharing knowledge and techniques as they planned and planted, nurtured and harvested. The garden became a tangible symbol of their shared commitment, a testament to their resilience and their shared ability to create beauty from seemingly barren spaces. The bounty of the garden, shared with their neighbors, became a conduit for connection, further embedding them within their community.

Their individual and shared pursuits were not without their challenges. Elena occasionally grappled with moments of self-doubt, questioning her abilities and her worth. Dante, though generally optimistic, sometimes struggled with the weight of his past experiences. These moments tested their bond, but their commitment to each other and their shared passions allowed them to navigate these periods of uncertainty, providing each other with the necessary support and encouragement. They learned that true intimacy wasn't about the absence of challenges but about the ability to face them together, emerging stronger and more unified.

Their new normal wasn't simply a period of calm after the storm. It was a conscious creation, a carefully nurtured space built upon mutual understanding, unwavering support, and a shared passion for life's simple joys and complex challenges. Their shared passions weren't merely hobbies; they were the foundation upon which they built a life together, a life that was not only meaningful to them but also enriching to their community. Their story, still unfolding, became a testament to the enduring power of human connection and the capacity for love to transform lives and heal wounds.

60
CELEBRATING LIFE

The morning sun, filtering through the lace curtains of their tiny kitchen, illuminated dust motes dancing in the golden light. Elena hummed a tuneless melody as she prepared breakfast, the scent of freshly brewed coffee mingling with the sweetness of ripe berries. Dante, already awake, sat at the small kitchen table, sketching in his notebook, the soft scratching of his pencil a counterpoint to Elena's humming. He looked up, his eyes crinkling at the corners as he smiled at her. "Good morning, my muse," he murmured, his voice husky with sleep.

Elena grinned, placing a plate laden with pancakes and berries before him. "Good morning, my artist," she replied, her voice echoing the warmth in his eyes. Their mornings were often like this, a quiet symphony of shared intimacy, a celebration of the simple joy of being together. It wasn't grand gestures or extravagant celebrations; it was the quiet moments, the shared smiles, the unspoken understanding that formed the bedrock of their connection.

Their evenings were equally cherished. After a long day of work and studies, they would often find themselves curled up on their worn couch, a shared mug of tea warming their hands. Elena would read aloud from a favorite novel, her voice a soothing balm to Dante's soul, while he sketched the scenes unfolding in her words, his charcoal capturing the essence of her voice and the emotion of the story. These quiet evenings were a refuge, a sanctuary where they could escape the pressures of daily life and lose themselves in the shared intimacy of literature and art. It was during these moments that they felt most connected, most themselves.

One particular evening, as the rain drummed against the windowpane, they found themselves discussing their dreams for the future. Elena spoke of her aspiration to open her own art gallery, showcasing the works of local artists and giving a voice to those often overlooked. Dante spoke of his ambition to become a behavioral psychologist, helping others understand and overcome their personal challenges. Their dreams were ambitious, yet they felt grounded in their shared commitment to building a life that was both fulfilling to them and beneficial to their community.

Their celebrations weren't confined to the four walls of their home. They discovered a hidden gem of a jazz club tucked away on a cobbled side street, where the sultry notes of a saxophone and the rhythmic thump of the bass drum filled the dimly lit room. They danced close, lost in the music, their bodies swaying in unison, their hearts beating in rhythm with the music. It was in these moments, surrounded by the soulful energy of live music, that they felt truly alive, truly connected.

They found themselves drawn to outdoor adventures, too. Weekend hikes became a ritual, a chance to escape the urban sprawl and immerse themselves in the tranquility of nature.

They explored hidden trails, their footsteps silent on the mossy forest floor, the scent of pine needles and damp earth filling their lungs. They would often pause, breathless and awestruck, by a stunning vista, the grandeur of the landscape mirroring the depth of their love. These adventures weren't merely physical challenges; they were opportunities for introspection, for quiet contemplation, for sharing their innermost thoughts and feelings. It was during these moments that they discovered a deeper understanding of themselves and their connection.

Their celebration of life extended to their community. They continued their volunteer work at the soup kitchen, finding fulfillment in serving others and witnessing the resilience of the human spirit. They joined a local book club, engaging in lively debates about literature and sharing their perspectives with others who shared their passion for stories. They participated in community theater productions, contributing their talents and skills to a creative endeavor that brought people together. Their involvement in their community wasn't just about giving back; it was about nurturing their sense of belonging, strengthening their connection to others, and enriching their lives.

Even seemingly mundane tasks became opportunities for connection and celebration. A shared meal cooked together, a simple act of tending to their community garden, a quiet evening spent side-by-side, each moment woven into the rich tapestry of their lives. Elena discovered a newfound joy in simple acts of domesticity, finding beauty in the ordinary routines of daily life. Dante, in turn, discovered a love for cooking, his culinary creations often becoming a source of shared laughter and appreciation.

One rainy afternoon, while curled up together on the couch, Elena decided to teach Dante how to knit. He initially approached the task with his usual meticulousness but soon found himself captivated by the simple rhythm of the needles and the slow, steady creation of something beautiful. His hands, usually skilled at sketching and drawing, found a new kind of dexterity, a new kind of expression. Elena, watching him, felt a surge of warmth in her chest. It was not just the shared activity, but the way he approached it, with his usual intensity and careful attention, that brought her immense joy. It represented the way he approached their lives together with dedication, and love.

Their life together was a tapestry woven with threads of shared experiences, small moments of connection, and unwavering support for one another. They celebrated life not in grand gestures, but in the quiet moments of intimacy, in the shared laughter, in the unspoken understanding that bound them together. Their love was a testament to the power of shared passions, a testament to the enduring strength of human connection, a celebration of life's simple joys and profound complexities. It was a life built on mutual respect, unwavering support, and a shared vision for a future filled with love, adventure, and the pursuit of their individual dreams. Their story was still unfolding, but each chapter was a celebration of their enduring bond, a vibrant testament to the power of a love that had blossomed amidst adversity and blossomed into a life filled with profound happiness and shared joy. It was, in its own quiet way, a masterpiece.

61
FUTURE PLANS

The rain had stopped, leaving behind a world washed clean and glistening under the pale light of the late afternoon sun. They sat on their porch, two mugs of steaming chamomile tea warming their hands, the silence between them comfortable and familiar. The scent of petrichor hung heavy in the air, a sweet perfume after the storm. Dante traced the rim of his mug with a finger, his gaze drifting towards the vibrant green of their small community garden.

"So," Elena began, her voice soft, breaking the quiet, "we've talked about our individual dreams, but what about us? What does our shared future look like?"

Dante smiled, a slow, thoughtful curve of his lips. "That's a question worth pondering, isn't it? It's more than just the sum of our individual aspirations, isn't it? It's a whole new canvas we're creating together."

Elena nodded, her eyes reflecting the golden light. "Exactly. And it's exciting, terrifying, and exhilarating all at once."

They fell silent again, the quiet punctuated only by the chirping of crickets and the distant hum of city traffic. Dante's gaze returned to the garden, his mind clearly already racing ahead.

"My practice," he mused aloud, "I see it growing. Not just in terms of clients, but in terms of the kind of work I want to do. I'd love to incorporate more community outreach, perhaps workshops on stress management or communication skills. Something that helps people beyond individual therapy."

Elena's smile widened. "That's wonderful, Dante. It's so much you. Remember that time we volunteered at the youth center, and you helped that young boy work through his anxiety about public speaking? That was beautiful to witness."

Dante chuckled. "He's doing so much better now. It's those small victories that make all the difference. And I see myself, eventually, working towards a program that incorporates art therapy. Maybe even collaborating with your gallery."

Elena's breath hitched, a spark of excitement igniting within her. "A gallery featuring local artists, maybe even incorporating therapeutic art programs. That could really work."

"Exactly! A space where people can come together, connect through art, express themselves, and find healing," Dante added. "We could have workshops, events, even a small residency program for emerging artists. Imagine the possibilities."

They spent hours discussing these possibilities, their ideas flowing effortlessly, weaving together their individual dreams into a shared vision. Elena's gallery wouldn't just be a showcase for art; it would be a community hub, a place of connection and healing. Dante's practice would extend beyond individual sessions, becoming a force for positive change in their community. Their collaboration would be the keystone, a bridge connecting art and psychology, creativity and wellbeing.

"And what about us personally?" Elena finally asked, a blush warming her cheeks. "Our own little nest. Do you still see us here, in this small apartment? Or do you envision something...bigger?"

Dante reached for her hand, his touch warm and reassuring. "I love this place. It's our haven, our sanctuary. But I also see us growing, expanding our horizons. Maybe a slightly larger space, a little more room to breathe. A garden, perhaps, big enough to cultivate a bounty of vegetables and herbs."

Elena leaned against him, her head resting on his shoulder. "And what about...children? Have you given that any thought?" she asked, her voice barely above a whisper.

Dante hesitated for a moment, a thoughtful expression clouding his face. "It's something we need to discuss fully," he replied cautiously, "It's not something I ever thought about until now. But it does feel right, doesn't it? Imagine, little tiny feet running through the garden, filling our home with laughter and the chaos of childhood."

Elena smiled, a tender expression softening her features. "Chaos sounds just perfect right now. We've had a bit of a whirlwind romance, we could use some healthy chaos."

They spoke about the challenges, the adjustments, the

potential joys and difficulties of parenthood. They were both aware of the significant changes that family life would bring, the compromises and sacrifices it would demand. But they also recognized the profound love they shared, the unwavering support they offered each other, and the strength they found in their shared vision for the future.

"It's not just about the gallery and the practice," Dante said, his voice filled with a quiet intensity, "it's about creating a life together, a home filled with love, laughter, and adventure. A life where we support each other's dreams, while also building something new, something beautiful, together."

Their conversation shifted to travel. They dreamed of exploring distant lands, immersing themselves in new cultures, expanding their perspectives, and collecting memories to fill their photo albums. They imagined long walks on sun-drenched beaches, the thrill of mountain climbing, the awe-inspiring beauty of ancient ruins. Travel would be a source of inspiration, a way to recharge, and a means to deepen their connection as they shared these experiences together.

They talked about continuing their volunteer work, expanding their involvement in community projects, and making a positive impact on the lives of others. They saw their future not just as a personal journey but also as a journey of service, a path of giving back to the world that had given them so much.

As the sun began to set, casting long shadows across their small porch, they fell silent once more, a comfortable quiet settling between them. They had laid bare their dreams, their hopes, their fears, their aspirations. They had painted a vivid picture of their future, a canvas filled with vibrant colors and subtle shades, light and shadow, joy and challenge.

"It's a lot to take in," Elena murmured, breaking the silence. "But it feels right, doesn't it?"

Dante nodded, his gaze fixed on her face, his heart filled with a profound sense of peace and contentment. "More than right, Elena. It feels like coming home."

Their future was not a fixed destination but an ongoing journey, a path they would traverse together, hand in hand, supporting each other, celebrating each milestone, learning from every challenge, and cherishing every moment along the way. Their story, still unfolding, was a testament to the power of shared dreams, unwavering love, and the enduring strength of human connection. It was a story of hope, resilience, and the boundless possibilities that lie ahead, a future as vibrant and captivating as the life they had already built together. It was a future as rich and complex as their love itself, a masterpiece still in the making.

62
SHARED VISIONS

The following weeks were a whirlwind of activity. Elena, energized by their shared vision, threw herself into planning the expansion of her gallery. She spent hours researching grants, networking with potential sponsors, and sketching out blueprints for a larger space that would accommodate not only more artwork but also the therapeutic art programs Dante envisioned. She secured a meeting with the city council, presenting a detailed proposal that highlighted the community benefits of her project, emphasizing its potential to foster creativity, promote mental wellbeing, and create a vibrant cultural hub. The council members were impressed by her passionate presentation and the innovative nature of her proposal, promising to expedite the approval process.

Meanwhile, Dante was equally busy. He secured funding for a small pilot program for his community-based art therapy initiative. He partnered with a local high school, offering workshops to at-risk students, using art as a medium for self expression and emotional processing. The initial results were overwhelmingly positive. Students who had previously struggled to articulate their feelings found solace and empowerment through creating art. Their improved self esteem and emotional regulation were tangible and measurable, providing concrete evidence of the program's effectiveness. This success fueled Dante's ambition, and he began working on a proposal for a larger-scale program, hoping to secure funding from private foundations and corporate sponsors.

Their individual successes fueled their collective ambition. They spent evenings brainstorming, refining their ideas, and supporting each other through challenges. Elena helped Dante design marketing materials for his program, using her artistic eye to create visually appealing brochures and posters. Dante, in turn, offered Elena advice on structuring her grant proposals, ensuring they were clear, concise, and compelling. Their collaboration was seamless, their shared vision acting as a powerful unifying force.

One evening, while working late in Elena's small studio apartment, amidst canvases, paint tubes, and half-finished sketches, a disagreement arose, a rare crack in their otherwise harmonious collaboration. It wasn't a major conflict, but a subtle friction stemming from their differing approaches to fundraising. Elena preferred a more organic, grassroots approach, focusing on local community support and smaller grants. Dante, however, advocated for a more aggressive strategy, targeting larger foundations and corporate sponsors.

"I understand your concerns about maintaining our integrity," Elena said, her voice laced with frustration, "but we need significant funding to make this happen. We can't rely solely on small grants and donations. We need to think big, Dante."

Dante sighed, running a hand through his hair. "But what

about the risk? What if we compromise our values in the process? We need to make sure the funding is aligned with our mission," he replied, his voice tinged with anxiety.

The tension in the air was thick, palpable. For the first time, their shared vision seemed to be pulling them in different directions. The silence that followed was uncomfortable, filled with unspoken anxieties and conflicting priorities.

Finally, Elena softened her tone, reaching out to take his hand. "You're right, Dante. We need to be careful. But we can find a middle ground. We can seek out funding that aligns with our values, while still being ambitious in our goals. This isn't about compromising our integrity; it's about finding the right partners who share our vision."

Dante nodded, relief washing over him. "You're right. We need a strategy that blends both approaches. We can explore smaller grants to ensure the sustainability of the program and simultaneously pursue larger sponsorships from organizations whose mission aligns with ours. We're stronger together; let's find a solution together."

The resolution of their conflict strengthened their bond, deepening their understanding and appreciation for each other's strengths and perspectives. They spent the next few hours meticulously crafting a comprehensive fundraising strategy that incorporated both Elena's preference for community-based support and Dante's desire to secure larger funding sources. Their collaboration was not merely efficient; it was a testament to their commitment to both their shared dream and their individual values.

Their combined efforts began to bear fruit. They secured a significant grant from a local foundation that supported community arts initiatives, and they landed a sponsorship from a national corporation committed to promoting mental wellbeing. The funding was enough to not only launch their pilot programs but also to secure a lease on a larger space for Elena's gallery, allowing them to begin renovations and construction.

As the construction progressed, so did their planning for the grand opening. They envisioned a gala event, a celebration of their shared vision and a showcase of their combined efforts. They designed invitations, planned the entertainment, and meticulously crafted a schedule of events. The process was a testament to their evolving relationship, a demonstration of their complementary skills and unwavering support for each other.

They even began discussing their personal future. The shared stress of building their combined projects drew them closer. They started looking at houses, small, charming bungalows with gardens large enough to cultivate herbs and vegetables. The conversation about children remained delicate, a topic they approached with careful consideration, acknowledging the profound changes it would bring to their lives. But they both felt a growing sense of readiness, a shared desire to expand their family and fill their home with the laughter and love of children. They knew it wouldn't be easy, but their shared dreams provided a firm foundation for navigating the challenges that lay ahead.

The grand opening of Elena's expanded gallery and the launch of Dante's art therapy program were a resounding success. The event was a celebration of their combined vision, drawing in a large crowd of community members, artists, and supporters. The gallery showcased a diverse collection of local artwork, and the art therapy program generated significant media attention, highlighting its positive impact on the community. It was a testament to their unwavering dedication, hard work, and shared vision.

As they stood together, watching the guests mingle and enjoy the atmosphere, Elena turned to Dante, her eyes sparkling with pride and love. "We did it," she whispered, a smile lighting up her face.

Dante nodded, his gaze locked on hers. "Together," he said, his voice thick with emotion. Their future, once a distant dream, was now a tangible reality, a vibrant tapestry woven from their shared aspirations, unwavering support, and the profound love they shared. Their story was far from over, but it was a story filled with hope, resilience, and the endless possibilities of a future built on shared dreams and unwavering love. It was a future as beautiful and complex as their love itself – a masterpiece in progress, a work of art that was just beginning to take shape.

63
LONG TERM GOALS

The immediate euphoria of the grand opening faded, replaced by the quiet hum of anticipation for what lay ahead. The success of the gallery expansion and the art therapy program wasn't just a culmination of their efforts; it was a springboard. Elena, ever the pragmatist, began to draft a five-year plan, a detailed roadmap outlining their shared ambitions. She meticulously charted projected growth for the gallery, including expansion into online sales, collaborations with international artists, and the potential development of a residency program. Her projections were ambitious, yet grounded in the solid foundation they had already built. She knew that sustainable growth required careful planning, meticulous budgeting, and a relentless pursuit of excellence.

Dante, fueled by the positive impact of his pilot program, was already developing proposals for collaborations with other community organizations. He envisioned a network of art therapy centers across the city, offering accessible mental health support to diverse populations. He had identified several potential funding sources—private foundations focused on community development, corporate sponsorships from companies committed to social responsibility, and government grants geared towards preventative mental health initiatives. He envisioned a future where his art therapy program would not only provide therapeutic support but would also foster a sense of community and belonging among its participants.

Their long-term goals weren't solely confined to their professional pursuits. Their personal lives were inextricably intertwined with their shared vision. They discussed purchasing a larger home, a place that could accommodate their growing needs and offer space for their evolving family. The charming bungalow they had envisioned now seemed slightly too small, a cozy nest that had served its purpose but needed to make way for a more expansive space —a family home. They wanted a garden large enough for children to run and play, a space where they could plant their own vegetables and nurture their connection with nature. They began browsing real estate listings, imagining the laughter of children echoing through their new home, a vibrant symphony against the backdrop of their shared dreams.

The conversation about children was still delicate, a cautious dance around a future that felt both exciting and slightly terrifying. They talked about the potential challenges of balancing parenthood with their demanding careers, acknowledging the sacrifices they would inevitably have to make. They discussed the importance of sharing parental responsibilities equally, ensuring that neither one felt overwhelmed or burdened. They weren't just planning a family; they were strategically designing their future together, ensuring that their partnership remained strong and resilient.

Elena, ever mindful of the potential conflicts that could arise from such a significant life change, suggested pre-nuptial counseling. She didn't want to approach such a momentous step without a clear understanding of their mutual expectations and aspirations. She believed that open communication and clear agreements could prevent future misunderstandings and ensure that their personal and professional lives could flourish in harmony. Dante, initially hesitant, agreed. He recognized the value of professional guidance in navigating such a complex transition.

The idea of professional counseling led them to discuss other aspects of their long-term plans. They realized they needed a comprehensive strategy for managing their finances as they transitioned into this new phase. Elena, with her business acumen, suggested working with a financial advisor to develop a long-term investment plan, ensuring their financial security and stability. They discussed saving for their children's education, planning for retirement, and establishing a robust financial safety net to protect their future.

Beyond the practical considerations of finance and family planning, they also discussed their long-term goals for community engagement. They didn't just want to build a successful gallery and art therapy program; they wanted to make a lasting impact on their community. Elena envisioned establishing a foundation to support local artists, providing grants and scholarships to emerging talent. Dante planned to expand his art therapy program, partnering with schools, hospitals, and community centers to offer affordable and accessible mental health services. They talked about organizing community events, creating spaces for artists and community members to connect, and fostering a vibrant arts scene that would enrich the lives of those around them.

Their commitment to social responsibility extended beyond their immediate community. They began discussing opportunities to use their influence and resources to support international art initiatives. Elena researched potential collaborations with artists from developing countries, seeking ways to promote cultural exchange and artistic collaboration. Dante considered partnering with NGOs to develop art therapy programs in regions affected by conflict or natural disasters, providing therapeutic support to those who had experienced trauma. Their ambition wasn't confined to their city; their vision extended globally, their desire to make a positive impact reaching across borders and continents.

As they laid out their long-term goals, a sense of shared purpose and unwavering commitment permeated their conversations. They weren't just planning their individual futures; they were meticulously crafting a collective narrative, a story of ambition, resilience, and unwavering love. The challenges ahead were undeniable – the complexities of business expansion, the demands of parenthood, the constant pressure of maintaining a successful professional life alongside a thriving personal relationship. Yet, they faced these challenges not as obstacles but as opportunities, chances to test their resilience, deepen their bond, and ultimately, build a life that mirrored the beauty and complexity of their shared dreams.

The process of defining these long-term goals wasn't simply about setting targets; it was a journey of self-discovery and mutual understanding. It was a testament to their evolving relationship, a space where they could explore their hopes, fears, and ambitions without judgment. The discussions were filled with laughter, tears, and moments of profound intimacy, strengthening their bond and deepening their connection. They learned to navigate their differing perspectives, finding compromise and mutual respect in the face of diverging opinions. Their ability to communicate openly and honestly, to articulate their needs and desires, was a testament to the foundation they had built on shared dreams and unwavering love.

The future stretched before them, vast and full of potential. It was a future they would create together, brick by brick, dream by dream. It wasn't a linear path, but a winding road filled with unexpected twists and turns, challenges and triumphs. Yet, they knew that as long as they remained committed to their shared vision, their unwavering support, and the profound love they shared, they would be able to navigate any obstacle that came their way. Their story was a testament to the power of shared dreams, a beautiful and complex tapestry woven from threads of ambition, resilience, and unwavering love – a masterpiece in progress, still unfolding before them, chapter by chapter, brushstroke by brushstroke. Their future was a blank canvas, a world of endless possibilities, ready to be painted with the colors of their shared vision. And they, together, would be the artists.

64

NAVIGATED LIFE'S CHANGES

The pre-nuptial counseling sessions proved unexpectedly insightful. It wasn't just about legal agreements; it was a deep dive into their expectations of marriage, family, and individual aspirations. Dr. Anya Sharma, a warm and perceptive therapist, guided them through exercises designed to unearth unspoken anxieties and clarify their long-term goals. Elena, ever the planner, had meticulously outlined her financial expectations and career trajectory, envisioning a future where her professional success complemented their family life. Dante, initially more hesitant about the specifics, gradually opened up, revealing his own vulnerabilities and hopes for a family life that was both nurturing and stimulating. He confessed to anxieties about the demands of fatherhood and the potential for professional sacrifices, a stark contrast to Elena's carefully constructed plans. Dr. Sharma helped them bridge this gap, facilitating conversations that were both challenging and deeply intimate. They uncovered subtle differences in their perspectives on financial management, parenting styles, and even the distribution of household chores. These weren't insurmountable differences, but rather areas that required open dialogue and a willingness to compromise. Through the therapeutic process, they refined their shared vision, creating a flexible framework that allowed for individual growth and mutual support.

The sessions extended beyond their personal lives, delving into the potential challenges of running a rapidly expanding business while raising a family. Elena and Dante explored strategies for delegating responsibilities, building a strong support network, and managing the inevitable conflicts that would arise from their demanding careers. Dr. Sharma emphasized the importance of clear communication, mutual respect, and a commitment to shared decision-making. They created a flexible schedule that allowed for time together as a couple, time for individual pursuits, and dedicated family time. They discussed employing childcare support, acknowledging that it was an investment in their future and a necessity for their individual well-being. Elena, ever the practical one, researched childcare options, comparing costs, locations, and philosophies. Dante, initially resistant to the idea of outside help, came to appreciate the value of a supportive childcare network, recognizing that it would allow them to maintain their individual professional identities and sustain their relationship. The sessions helped them confront their anxieties about work-life balance, ultimately leading to the creation of a realistic and sustainable plan.

The purchase of their new home proved to be another significant milestone. The transition from their cozy bungalow to a larger family home wasn't just a physical change; it was symbolic of their growing family and expanding ambitions. The search for the perfect home proved to be a journey of discovery in itself, filled with laughter, disagreements, and moments of deep connection. Elena favored a modern, minimalist design with ample natural light, while Dante preferred a more traditional aesthetic with a touch of rustic charm. Their compromise involved finding a home that blended both styles, a space that reflected their individual personalities while creating a cohesive and harmonious living environment. The renovation process, while challenging at times, further strengthened their bond. They spent hours poring over design plans, choosing paint colors, and selecting furniture. They learned to negotiate differences in taste, discovering a shared appreciation for craftsmanship and creating a space that truly reflected their evolving lives together. The home wasn't just a structure; it was a tangible manifestation of their shared dreams, a physical embodiment of their evolving relationship.

The arrival of their first child, a daughter they named Maya, marked the beginning of a new and exciting chapter in their lives. The transition to parenthood was challenging, but they approached it with the same level of planning and collaboration they had brought to their professional and personal ventures. Elena, ever the strategist, researched parenting styles, childcare options, and educational programs. Dante, embracing his role as a father, immersed himself in learning about baby care, happily taking on night feedings and diaper changes. They shared parental responsibilities, creating a balance that allowed both of them to enjoy the joys of parenthood while maintaining their professional commitments. The challenges were many— sleep deprivation, adjusting to new routines, and the inevitable conflicts that arose from fatigue and changing priorities. But they navigated these challenges through open communication, unwavering support, and a shared commitment to raising Maya in a loving and nurturing environment. Their relationship, tested by the demands of parenthood, emerged stronger and more resilient. Their love, previously a canvas of shared dreams, now encompassed the unconditional love for their daughter, adding a vibrant new hue to their shared masterpiece.

The expansion of their art therapy program and the gallery presented new challenges, but also opportunities for growth. Dante's program continued to flourish, attracting collaborations with local schools, community centers, and hospitals. He secured grants from private foundations and corporate sponsorships, allowing him to expand his team and develop new therapeutic programs. Elena's gallery hosted increasingly successful exhibitions, attracting both local and international artists. She expanded into online sales, creating a global market for the gallery's unique offerings. Their success, however, came with the added responsibility of managing a larger team and navigating the complexities of business expansion. They invested in managerial training, fostering a supportive and collaborative work environment. They learned to delegate tasks, trust their employees, and recognize the value of teamwork. Their success wasn't solely about financial gains; it was about creating a positive impact on the community, supporting local artists, and providing accessible mental health services.

The creation of their foundation to support local artists became a tangible expression of their shared commitment to social responsibility. They allocated a portion of their profits to fund grants and scholarships for emerging artists, fostering the growth of local talent. They organized community events, connecting artists with the public and creating a vibrant cultural scene. Their commitment extended beyond their local community; they partnered with international NGOs, using their resources to support art therapy programs in conflict zones and developing countries. Their work wasn't just about personal success; it was about making a positive impact on the lives of others. They demonstrated that professional achievement and social responsibility could go hand in hand.

Their journey was a testament to their resilience, their ability to adapt to life's changes, and their unwavering commitment to their shared dreams. They faced numerous challenges—the complexities of running a business, the demands of parenthood, the pressure of maintaining a successful professional life alongside a thriving personal relationship. But each challenge only strengthened their bond, deepening their love and respect for one another. Their story wasn't a linear path to success; it was a winding road filled with unexpected twists and turns, triumphs and setbacks. But throughout it all, they navigated the obstacles together, always supporting each other, always focused on their shared vision. Their success was not measured solely in financial terms but in the lives they touched, the communities they built, and the unwavering love that bound them together. Their life was a symphony of ambition, resilience, and unwavering love – a masterpiece in progress, constantly evolving, always beautiful. Their future remained a canvas of infinite possibilities, awaiting the next brushstroke, the next chapter, the next shared dream to unfold.

65
EMBRACING THE UNKNOWN

The crisp autumn air swirled fallen leaves around their feet as Elena and Dante stood on the porch of their newly renovated home, a testament to their shared journey. Maya, now a toddler, toddled excitedly between them, her tiny hands clutching a brightly colored leaf. The setting sun cast long shadows, painting the landscape in hues of orange and gold, mirroring the warmth and vibrancy of their lives. It was a moment of quiet contemplation, a pause before the next chapter unfolded. They had achieved so much – a thriving business, a beautiful family, a home that was more than just bricks and mortar, it was a sanctuary woven with love and laughter. But the future remained unwritten, a canvas of infinite possibilities, both exhilarating and daunting.

Elena, ever the pragmatist, had always thrived on planning, on mapping out a clear path toward her goals. But this time, the future felt different. It wasn't a series of meticulously crafted objectives, but a vast, unexplored landscape brimming with uncertainty. This uncertainty, however, didn't fill her with fear. Instead, it sparked a sense of exhilaration, an adventurous spirit she hadn't fully acknowledged before. The years spent building their empire had honed her skills in strategy and risk assessment, but it had also taught her the unpredictable nature of life. The unexpected twists and turns of their journey had shaped them, making them resilient, adaptable, and surprisingly comfortable with the unknown.

Dante, too, felt this shift in perspective. His creative spirit, once confined to the therapeutic world of art, now extended to their life's tapestry. He realized that the beauty of their journey wasn't in the precise execution of a pre-determined plan but in the spontaneous brushstrokes of unexpected opportunities, the improvisational dance of challenges and triumphs. He had learned to trust his instincts, to embrace the unexpected, and to find joy in the messy, imperfect beauty of life's unfolding story. He had always been the more impulsive of the two, but now, his impulsiveness felt balanced by Elena's strategic planning. Their differences, once perceived as obstacles, were now recognized as complementary strengths, fueling their journey with both passion and prudence.

Their conversation that evening flowed effortlessly, a blend of practical concerns and dreamy aspirations. They discussed the possibility of expanding their foundation's reach to other countries, the challenges of balancing their professional ambitions with their growing family, and the potential impact of Maya's education. These weren't merely discussions; they were brainstorming sessions, collaborative explorations of possibilities, and shared visions for the future. They acknowledged the inherent risks, the potential pitfalls, but they did so with a shared sense of confidence, a knowing that whatever challenges arose, they would face them together, as they always had.

The following weeks were a blur of activity. Elena traveled to several countries, establishing partnerships with international NGOs and exploring opportunities to expand their art therapy programs to conflict zones and developing nations. Her trip wasn't simply a business venture; it was a mission driven by compassion and a belief in the transformative power of art. She returned home invigorated, her heart brimming with new ideas and a renewed commitment to their shared vision. Dante, meanwhile, focused on expanding their local programs, securing grants, and developing new therapeutic initiatives. He was particularly passionate about establishing a program dedicated to supporting children affected by trauma.

The challenges they faced were immense. The logistical hurdles of international collaborations, the bureaucratic complexities of grant applications, the constant demands of their ever-growing business – these were all significant obstacles. Yet, amidst the chaos and pressure, they maintained a sense of balance, a shared commitment to their values, and a strong emotional connection. They delegated responsibilities effectively, relying on the capable team they had built, and they made sure to prioritize family time, creating sacred spaces in their busy schedules where they could reconnect, laugh, and simply be together.

Their relationship deepened, transcending the practicalities of their shared ventures. They had built a life together that was rich, complex, and rewarding, and they acknowledged the ever-evolving nature of their love. It wasn't a static entity, but a dynamic force, constantly adapting to new circumstances, growing stronger with each challenge they overcame. Their connection went beyond the shared responsibilities and professional triumphs; it was rooted in a profound understanding, a mutual respect, and a deep, abiding love that fueled their every endeavor.

One evening, as Maya slept soundly in her crib, Elena and Dante sat on the porch, gazing at the star-studded sky. They were no longer just planning their future; they were experiencing it, moment by moment. They had learned to embrace the unknown, not with reckless abandon, but with a courageous acceptance of life's unpredictable nature. They knew that their journey would continue to present challenges, unforeseen twists and turns. But they also knew that they would face those challenges together, their love a steady compass guiding them through the uncharted territory of their lives. Their future wasn't a perfectly drawn map; it was an adventurous expedition, and they were ready for whatever lay ahead, confident in their shared strengths, their unwavering commitment, and their love that had grown stronger with each passing year.

The years that followed saw their dreams blossom into reality. Their art therapy programs spread globally, touching countless lives, and their foundation provided vital support to artists facing adversity. Maya grew into a bright, compassionate young woman, carrying the legacy of her parents' dedication and determination. The gallery continued to flourish, showcasing the works of rising talents, making their mark on the art world and enriching the local community. Their success was not just a matter of financial achievement, but a testament to their values – a legacy built on resilience, compassion, and the transformative power of love and art.

Their journey served as an inspiration, reminding them, and

others, that the greatest achievements are not always the result of meticulous planning, but rather the courageous embrace of the unknown, the willingness to navigate uncertainty, and the unwavering commitment to shared values and dreams. The path wasn't always smooth, but it was beautiful, a mosaic of challenges and triumphs, a story woven with love, resilience, and the unwavering belief in the power of shared aspirations. Their story became a beacon, a reminder that even in the face of uncertainty, the human spirit, fortified by love and determination, can create extraordinary things, building a life as beautiful and vibrant as the artwork they cherished. And as they looked ahead, into a future still unfolding, they did so with hearts full of gratitude, and a deep-seated joy for the adventure that lay before them. Their embrace of the unknown wasn't merely a strategy for success; it was a way of living, a testament to a life lived fully, passionately, and with an unwavering faith in the power of love.

66

THE IMPACT OF THEIR ACTIONS

The fire crackled merrily in the hearth, casting dancing shadows on the walls of their study. Outside, the winter wind howled a mournful tune, a stark contrast to the warmth and quiet intimacy within. Elena sat nestled in a plush armchair, a half-finished mug of chamomile tea cooling in her hand. Dante, across from her, traced the lines of a charcoal sketch, his brow furrowed in concentration. The silence between them wasn't awkward; it was a comfortable companion, a shared space for contemplation.

"Remember that night in Rome?" Elena finally spoke, her voice soft, almost a whisper. The memory, sharp and vivid, flooded back – the narrow cobblestone streets, the intoxicating aroma of espresso, the breathtaking view from the Gianicolo hill. It was the night they'd first truly acknowledged the depth of their feelings, a turning point in their journey.

Dante looked up, his eyes meeting hers, a flicker of understanding passing between them. "How could I forget? It felt like the world held its breath, waiting for us to decide."

Their decision, to build a life together, to take a leap of faith into the unknown, had reverberated through the years, shaping not only their own lives but also the lives of countless others. They'd built their empire on a foundation of shared values, a commitment to art, and a fierce belief in the power of human connection. But with success had come responsibility, a weight of consequence that settled on their shoulders, a quiet acknowledgment of the impact their actions had had on the world.

Elena stirred her tea, the swirling liquid mirroring the complexities of their reflection. "The gallery," she began, her voice thoughtful, "It's more than just a business. It's a community. A place where artists find voice, where passion thrives, and where lives are transformed." She thought of the young artists they'd mentored, the struggling families they'd supported, the lives touched by the beauty and healing power of art. Their impact reached far beyond the walls of the gallery, extending into the heart of their community and beyond.

Dante nodded, his gaze drifting to the sketch in his hands – a portrait of Maya, full of youthful energy and vibrant life. "And Maya," he murmured, "She's the living testament to our choices. The life we've built for her, the values we've instilled in her, that's our legacy, isn't it?"

Their daughter, a reflection of their shared hopes and dreams, was a constant reminder of the ripple effect of their decisions. The dedication to their foundation, to providing art therapy to those in need, was a direct consequence of their shared past experiences and the values they held dear. The sacrifices they'd made, the sleepless nights, the relentless work—all of it had culminated in a future they'd never dared to fully imagine.

Elena traced the rim of her cup, her eyes distant, lost in thought. "There were times," she confessed, "when I questioned our path, when the weight of responsibility felt overwhelming. The risks we took, the sacrifices we made... they weren't always easy choices." She recalled the initial skepticism, the challenges of securing funding, the setbacks and disappointments that threatened to derail their dreams. But their unwavering commitment, their shared belief in their vision, had carried them through the storm.

Dante understood her hesitation. He, too, had wrestled with doubt. The uncertainty of leaving established careers, the financial risks involved, the potential for failure—all these haunted him at various points. But the conviction in their mission, fueled by their shared passion, had always outweighed the fears.

"But look where we are now," Dante said, his voice laced with a quiet pride. He gestured around the room, a sanctuary of comfort, warmth, and success. But the pride extended beyond the physical manifestation of their accomplishments. It was a pride in their resilience, their unwavering commitment, their unyielding belief in the power of their shared purpose.

"The foundation," Elena continued, her voice regaining its strength, "has grown beyond anything we ever anticipated. It's touching lives in places we never thought possible. We've seen firsthand the transformative power of art, the healing it provides, the hope it ignites." She spoke of the children who'd found solace in creative expression, the soldiers who'd rediscovered their humanity through art, the refugees who'd found strength and self-worth through their creative endeavors. The success was not merely measured in numbers, but in the tangible impact on the lives they'd touched.

"And the international partnerships," Dante added, his eyes gleaming with enthusiasm, "they've opened doors we never knew existed. The collaborations, the shared knowledge, the collective effort to promote art as a tool for healing and social change – it's been an incredible journey." He described the challenges they faced, the bureaucratic hurdles, the cultural differences, the logistical nightmares. But amidst the complexities, the sense of purpose, the shared vision, had propelled them forward.

They fell silent again, the comfortable silence filled with unspoken understanding. The journey hadn't been without its shadows. There were moments of doubt, times when the weight of their responsibilities threatened to overwhelm them. There were compromises and sacrifices, moments of conflict and disagreement. But these challenges had only served to strengthen their bond, refine their vision, and deepen their commitment.

Elena smiled, a wistful expression softening her features. "We've built something truly remarkable, haven't we?"

Dante nodded, his voice thick with emotion. "More than we ever dreamed possible. A legacy of compassion, creativity, and the unwavering belief in the power of art to heal and transform." His gaze fell on the sketch of Maya, a tangible representation of their enduring love and the future they'd created together. Their legacy wasn't just a collection of achievements, but a testament to their shared journey, a story etched not just in their hearts, but in the lives they'd touched along the way. It was a legacy that would continue to unfold, a tapestry woven with love, resilience, and the unwavering belief in the transformative power of human connection and the healing power of art. And as they sat together, bathed in the warmth of the firelight, they knew that their journey, though far from over, was a testament to the remarkable things that could be achieved when love, determination, and a shared vision were harnessed together. Their legacy was not only about the art they created or the lives they touched but the example they set, the enduring proof that a life lived with purpose, passion, and love could leave an indelible mark on the world. The wind howled outside, but inside, their hearts were full, warmed by the love they shared and the legacy they'd built together, brick by brick, brushstroke by brushstroke, a masterpiece of a life lived to its fullest.

67

LEAVING A POSITIVE MARK

The embers in the hearth glowed like dying stars, their light painting the faces of Elena and Dante in shifting hues of orange and crimson. The storm outside had subsided, leaving behind an almost unnatural stillness, a quietude that seemed to amplify the unspoken words hanging between them. Elena, her hand resting lightly on Dante's, felt a profound sense of peace settle over her, a contentment born not of idleness but of purpose fulfilled.

Their conversation had drifted naturally from their personal journey to the broader impact they'd had on the world. The gallery, initially conceived as a passion project, had blossomed into a vibrant hub of creativity, a nurturing ground for emerging artists, and a haven for those seeking solace in art's embrace. It wasn't merely a space to display paintings and sculptures; it was a living testament to their belief in the transformative power of human expression.

"Remember Carlos?" Dante asked, his voice soft, a ghost of a smile playing on his lips. Elena's eyes lit up. Carlos, a young, struggling artist they'd discovered years ago, his talent buried beneath layers of self-doubt and despair. They had provided him not just with exhibition space but with mentorship, encouragement, and unwavering faith in his potential.

"His retrospective last year," Elena said, her voice filled with pride, "It was breathtaking. To see how far he's come, the confidence he radiates…it's a direct result of the support we gave him." Carlos's success wasn't just a personal triumph; it was a testament to the ripple effect of their commitment to fostering artistic talent. It was a tangible demonstration that a single act of kindness, a single opportunity offered, could change a life's trajectory.

Their involvement extended far beyond the gallery walls. They'd established workshops in underprivileged communities, offering art therapy to children grappling with trauma, empowering them to express their emotions through creative outlets. They'd partnered with local schools, integrating art into the curriculum, fostering creativity and self-expression in young minds. They had witnessed firsthand the healing power of art, its ability to mend broken spirits and ignite hope in the darkest of places.

One particularly poignant memory resurfaced—a young girl named Sofia, who had been withdrawn and traumatized following a devastating earthquake. Through art therapy, she had gradually found her voice, transforming her pain into breathtakingly powerful images. Her journey, chronicled in the gallery's annual exhibition, had become a symbol of resilience, a testament to the human spirit's capacity for healing and renewal. Elena's eyes welled up, the emotion raw and unfiltered.

"These small acts," Dante said, his voice resonating with

heartfelt conviction, "These seemingly insignificant gestures, they accumulate. They create a momentum, a ripple effect that transcends the immediate. We've become acutely aware of the profound interconnectedness of our actions."

Their commitment extended beyond their local community. Through their foundation, they had established international collaborations, sharing their expertise and resources with artists and organizations around the globe. They'd worked with refugee communities, providing them with creative outlets and a sense of belonging, transforming art into a powerful tool for healing, rehabilitation, and reintegration.

Elena recalled a recent trip to a refugee camp in Greece, where they'd witnessed firsthand the transformative power of art. The children, scarred by displacement and trauma, had found solace and expression through painting, sculpting, and storytelling. Their art, raw and powerful, was a poignant reflection of their experiences, but also a testament to their resilience and their unwavering hope for the future.

"We've learned so much from them," Elena said, her voice thick with emotion. "Their resilience, their capacity for hope amidst unimaginable suffering... it's been humbling." It was in these encounters that they had truly understood the universality of the human spirit, the shared capacity for creativity, and the innate desire to create and connect.

The work wasn't without its challenges. Securing funding, navigating bureaucratic hurdles, overcoming cultural differences – these were all obstacles they'd faced with unwavering determination. There were moments of exhaustion, moments of doubt, moments when the weight of their responsibilities seemed almost unbearable. But their shared vision, their unwavering commitment to their mission, had always carried them through.

"Remember that funding crisis three years ago?" Dante chuckled, the memory light despite the intensity of the situation at the time. Elena laughed, recalling the sleepless nights, the relentless phone calls, the desperate scramble to secure the necessary funds to keep their various projects afloat. But they had persevered, demonstrating their unwavering dedication to their cause.

Their commitment wasn't just about the money or the resources; it was about the impact they made, the lives they touched, the change they inspired. It was about creating a legacy that extended far beyond their own lifetimes. It was about building a world where art wasn't merely a commodity but a powerful tool for social change, a catalyst for healing, and a bridge between cultures and communities.

They'd faced criticism, too. Some questioned their methods, their priorities, their very motivations. There were those who accused them of being naive, idealistic, even self-serving. But they had weathered the storms of criticism, their commitment to their vision unshaken.

The fire had dwindled to embers now, casting long, dancing shadows on the walls. Outside, the moon hung high in the inky sky, bathing the landscape in a soft, ethereal glow. Elena and Dante sat in comfortable silence, the unspoken words hanging heavy in the air, a silent testament to their shared journey, their shared purpose, their enduring love. Their legacy wasn't just a collection of paintings, sculptures, and charitable endeavors; it was a tapestry woven from threads of compassion, resilience, and a profound belief in the power of human connection. It was a legacy that would continue to unfold, generation after generation, a silent symphony of hope and healing echoing through the corridors of time. Their lives, entwined and interwoven, had become a living testament to the potential of human kindness, the transformative power of art, and the enduring beauty of a life lived with purpose, passion, and unwavering love. And as they sat there, hand in hand, they knew that their journey, far from being over, was merely entering a new and even more profound chapter, a chapter where their legacy would continue to grow, to flourish, and to leave an enduring, positive mark on the world.

68
INSPIRING OTHERS

The quiet hum of the night was punctuated only by the occasional chirp of crickets. Elena, nestled close to Dante, felt the warmth of his body a comforting counterpoint to the cool night air. Their conversation, though unspoken, continued in the comfortable silence that had become a language all its own. The legacy they were building wasn't just bricks and mortar, paintings and sculptures; it was a legacy woven from the lives they'd touched, the hearts they'd healed, the spirits they'd ignited.

Their influence extended far beyond the gallery's walls, rippling outwards like concentric circles in a still pond. News of their work, their unwavering dedication to fostering artistic talent and community healing, had spread. Letters arrived daily, some filled with heartfelt gratitude, others brimming with requests for assistance, and still others simply expressing admiration for their commitment.

One such letter came from a young woman named Anya, a refugee from a war-torn country. Anya's words painted a vivid picture of desperation and despair, yet also of a flicker of hope ignited by Elena and Dante's work. She described how their online workshops, translated into multiple languages, had provided her with a lifeline, a means of expressing her trauma and finding solace in the creative process. Anya's art, initially filled with images of destruction and loss, had gradually evolved, showcasing resilience, strength, and a tenacious grip on hope. Her transformation, documented through photographs and shared online, became a powerful testament to the reach of Elena and Dante's work. It illustrated that their efforts weren't confined by geographical boundaries, that their impact transcended oceans and continents.

Another story emerged from a small town in Italy, where a struggling community arts center was on the verge of closure. Inspired by Elena and Dante's model, the local residents had rallied together, transforming their center into a vibrant hub of creativity and community engagement. Their renewed efforts not only saved their arts center but also revitalized their town, creating jobs, fostering a sense of community pride, and giving voice to their shared history and culture. Elena and Dante's actions had ignited a spark, a chain reaction of positive change, spreading from their initial focus to inspire countless others to create their own legacies of hope and renewal.

Their commitment had also touched the lives of established artists. A renowned sculptor, once jaded and disillusioned by the commercialization of art, had found renewed purpose after attending one of their workshops. He spoke of the profound impact of connecting with a community focused on the genuine expression of human emotion rather than the pursuit of fame and fortune. This artist, previously consumed by self-doubt, had rediscovered his passion, finding renewed energy in his work and using his platform to advocate for social justice through his art.

The influence extended to those who had never even met Elena and Dante. Their story, chronicled in articles, documentaries, and books, had become a beacon of hope, inspiring countless individuals to pursue their dreams, to embrace their passions, and to make a positive impact on the world. Their story served as a reminder that even seemingly small acts of kindness, when multiplied by countless individuals, could create a tidal wave of positive change.

Their success wasn't built on luck or chance. It was the result of tireless dedication, unwavering belief, and a shared vision. They'd faced moments of doubt, periods of exhaustion, setbacks that threatened to derail their progress. However, they consistently overcame obstacles, drawing strength from their shared commitment and their unyielding belief in the transformative power of art. Their persistence and resilience became an integral part of their inspirational impact. Others saw in their actions a tangible example that with enough passion, determination, and support, any challenge could be overcome.

The gallery itself had become a living testament to their vision, a space where diverse artists could find support, collaboration, and a platform to share their unique perspectives. It wasn't just about selling art; it was about nurturing talent, fostering creativity, and building a community united by a shared passion. The gallery had become a symbol of hope, a reminder that even in a world rife with challenges and uncertainties, beauty, creativity, and human connection could still thrive. It demonstrated how a shared passion could manifest into something much larger than oneself.

The impact extended into the realm of philanthropy. Their foundation, initially established as a means to support their projects, had grown into a significant player in the international art community, providing grants, scholarships, and resources to artists and organizations around the world. Their approach to philanthropy went beyond simple donations; it emphasized mentorship, collaboration, and sustainable development, ensuring their projects created long-term positive change in the communities they served.

Elena and Dante's success hadn't been without its challenges. Navigating the complexities of the art world, managing a growing organization, and dealing with the inevitable criticisms that came with their high profile – these were all tests of their resilience and determination. But they consistently met these challenges head-on, learning from their mistakes, adapting to new circumstances, and remaining steadfast in their commitment to their shared vision. The path to their success was not a linear trajectory but a testament to their ability to adapt and adjust to the changing environment, making them even more compelling role models.

Elena often reflected on the early days, the struggles and sacrifices they made. The long hours, the financial uncertainties, the moments of self-doubt – these were all part of their story, and acknowledging those struggles only served to amplify the magnitude of their achievements. Their honesty and transparency about the challenges they faced made their success even more inspiring, showing others that the path to achieving one's dreams is rarely smooth.

 Their story resonated not only because of their accomplishments but also because of their humanity. They were not perfect; they had flaws, insecurities, and moments of vulnerability. But it was their willingness to embrace their imperfections, to learn from their mistakes, and to remain true to their values that made them relatable and inspiring. Their vulnerability became a strength, allowing others to see themselves reflected in their journey.

The impact of their story extended far beyond the realm of art. It served as a powerful reminder of the importance of community, compassion, and the transformative power of human connection. Their legacy wasn't simply a collection of works of art but a living testament to the potential of human kindness, the power of shared purpose, and the enduring beauty of a life lived with intention, passion, and unwavering love. The embers of their legacy, glowing brightly, promised to continue illuminating the path for many generations to come. It served as a beacon of hope, a reminder that the world could be a better place, one act of kindness, one work of art, one inspired life at a time. Their story continued to unfold, a testament to the enduring power of love, resilience, and the boundless capacity of the human spirit to create, to heal, and to inspire.

69

A SYMBOL OF HOPE

The news reports, initially focusing on the gallery's opening and subsequent success, evolved. They shifted from detailing the artistic merit of the showcased pieces to exploring the profound social impact of Elena and Dante's work. Documentaries showcased the transformation of Anya, the refugee artist whose journey from despair to hope became a poignant symbol of resilience. Her story, interwoven with others, highlighted the ripple effect of Elena and Dante's dedication—a testament to the power of art to heal, to inspire, and to unite. Their story became more than a narrative about artistic achievement; it transformed into a global conversation about the potential of human connection and the restorative power of creativity.

The media coverage wasn't just celebratory; it also explored the challenges they faced. The financial risks, the relentless pressure to maintain their success, the occasional criticisms from within the art world—all were portrayed honestly and openly. This transparency, rather than diminishing their appeal, amplified their relatability. People saw in them not flawless paragons of success but determined individuals who navigated obstacles with grace and resilience. Their journey became a roadmap for others, demonstrating that the path to achieving one's dreams is rarely straightforward, frequently paved with setbacks and self-doubt.

Their foundation, initially conceived as a means to fund their own projects, grew exponentially. It established partnerships with organizations worldwide, supporting artists from marginalized communities, providing scholarships for talented youth, and funding initiatives dedicated to promoting artistic expression as a tool for social change. The foundation's work extended beyond mere financial aid; it fostered collaboration, providing mentorship and resources to ensure the long-term sustainability of the projects it supported. This commitment to sustainable development set their philanthropic efforts apart, creating a lasting legacy that transcended immediate impact.

Elena and Dante's influence extended beyond the visible realms of art and philanthropy. Their story sparked a global conversation about the importance of community building and the transformative power of shared purpose. The gallery itself, initially a physical space, became a powerful metaphor. It represented the potential for collaboration, the strength that emerges from shared passion, and the beauty that can bloom even in the most challenging of environments. It was a beacon, illuminating the possibilities of human connection in a world that often feels increasingly fragmented.

Their approach to mentorship was particularly noteworthy. They didn't simply provide guidance; they created a supportive environment where artists felt empowered to explore their unique voices, to experiment without fear of judgment, and to collaborate without competition. They fostered a culture of mutual respect and encouragement, recognizing that true creativity thrives not in isolation but in the richness of shared experience. The mentorship they offered went beyond technical skills, extending to emotional support and encouragement, helping artists navigate the complexities of the art world and develop resilience in the face of adversity.

The couple's personal journey, marked by both triumphs and struggles, became a compelling narrative in itself. Their relationship, built on mutual respect, shared passion, and unwavering support, served as a powerful counterpoint to the often-cynical portrayal of relationships in the media. Their love story, deeply intertwined with their professional journey, demonstrated the power of shared purpose and the strength that emerges from a supportive partnership. The enduring strength of their relationship became a symbol of hope, reminding people that amidst chaos and uncertainty, love can endure, offering solace and strength.

 The symbol of hope they represented extended beyond the artistic community. Their story resonated with entrepreneurs, social activists, educators, and individuals from all walks of life, inspiring them to pursue their passions, to overcome obstacles, and to strive for a better world. Their work became a testament to the power of human spirit, a reminder that even in the face of adversity, hope persists, and positive change is attainable. Their commitment to social justice, woven into the fabric of their artistic endeavors, became a beacon for others seeking to use their talents and resources to create a more equitable and just society.

The lasting legacy of Elena and Dante was not solely in the

bricks and mortar of their gallery, the paintings displayed within its walls, or the sculptures that adorned its spaces. Their legacy resided in the countless lives they touched, the spirits they ignited, and the hope they inspired in others. It was a legacy built on a foundation of unwavering commitment, shared passion, resilience in the face of adversity, and a profound belief in the power of human connection.

Their story became a living testament to the potential of human kindness, demonstrating how a single act of compassion, multiplied by countless others, could create a tidal wave of positive change. Their actions demonstrated that even seemingly small acts, when fueled by intention and passion, can have a profound and lasting impact on the world. This ripple effect, extending beyond geographical boundaries and cultural differences, highlighted the universality of human aspirations and the shared desire for a better future.

Their vulnerability, far from being a weakness, became a source of strength. Their willingness to acknowledge their struggles, their moments of self-doubt, and their imperfections made them even more relatable and inspiring. People saw in them a reflection of their own journeys, recognizing that the path to success is rarely smooth, and that setbacks and challenges are an inherent part of the process. This authenticity and transparency fostered a deep connection with their audience, creating a sense of shared humanity and fostering a collective understanding of the challenges and triumphs of life.

Elena and Dante's story resonated because it was not a tale of effortless success. It was a narrative of unwavering commitment, relentless hard work, and unwavering belief in their shared vision. It illustrated the importance of perseverance, the power of collaboration, and the transformative potential of human connection. Their journey highlighted the fact that achieving significant goals requires not only talent and passion, but also dedication, resilience, and a willingness to adapt and overcome the inevitable obstacles that life throws our way. It is a story that continues to inspire and uplift, a reminder that the human spirit, when nurtured and supported, can overcome seemingly insurmountable challenges and create a lasting legacy of hope.

Their impact continued to reverberate long after their initial successes. Their story became a case study in the business schools, a topic of discussion in philanthropic circles, and an inspiration for countless individuals striving to make a difference in the world. Books and articles continued to document their journey, sharing their experiences, their successes, and their challenges. This ongoing dissemination of their story ensured that their message of hope, resilience, and the transformative power of art continued to reach new audiences and inspire new generations.

The foundation they created continued to grow and expand its reach, establishing programs in new countries and supporting emerging artists from diverse backgrounds. The gallery itself evolved, becoming a hub of innovation and creativity, showcasing not only established artists but also emerging talents from around the globe. Their legacy, therefore, was not static; it was a living, breathing entity that continued to evolve and grow, adapting to the changing needs of the world and remaining a beacon of hope for those who sought to create positive change. Their story serves as a powerful reminder that even amidst the darkness, love, redemption, and the enduring power of the human spirit can prevail. And that even the smallest act of kindness, when multiplied by the countless others, can indeed change the world. The lasting legacy of Elena and Dante was not just a story; it was a movement, a testament to the enduring power of human connection, resilience, and the unwavering belief in a brighter future.

70
ENDURING LOVE

The years that followed saw the relentless pace of their initial ascent slow to a more sustainable rhythm. The whirlwind of media attention gradually subsided, replaced by a steadier, more profound appreciation for their contributions. Elena and Dante, however, remained steadfast in their commitment, not just to their art and philanthropy, but to each other. Their relationship, forged in the crucible of shared ambition and unwavering support, deepened with each passing year. It wasn't a fairytale romance, devoid of challenges; rather, it was a testament to the resilience of love in the face of adversity.

Their evenings, once consumed by the demands of building their empire, now held a gentler rhythm. They found solace in quiet moments together, sharing a glass of wine by the fireplace, reminiscing about their journey, their laughter echoing through the spacious rooms of their home, a home that was as much a sanctuary as it was a reflection of their shared success. They discovered the beauty of simplicity, the joy found in the mundane – a shared cup of coffee in the morning sun, a quiet walk through their garden, filled with the fragrance of blooming flowers, a silent understanding passing between them that transcended words. These quiet moments were the anchors in their lives, grounding them amidst the whirlwind of their public accomplishments.

Their love was not expressed through grand gestures or extravagant displays of affection. Instead, it manifested in the subtle details: the way Elena would leave a note on Dante's pillow, a simple message of love and encouragement; the way Dante would anticipate her needs, anticipating her unspoken desires; their shared silences, comfortable and meaningful, a testament to a connection that required no words. Their relationship was a quiet symphony of mutual respect, shared understanding, and unwavering support. It was a sanctuary, a refuge from the storm, a place where they could simply be themselves, without pretense or expectation.

Dante, known for his fiery passion and relentless drive, discovered a new depth of serenity. He found contentment in the simple act of being present in their lives. He learned to slow down, to appreciate the small joys, the quiet moments, the subtle nuances of their relationship. He found that the truest form of fulfillment lay not in the relentless pursuit of success but in the simple pleasures of shared love and companionship. He dedicated more time to nurturing their relationship, finding immeasurable reward in the quiet intimacy of their shared life.

Elena, always the anchor of their partnership, found her strength bolstered by his newfound serenity. She cherished his moments of vulnerability, his quiet confessions of self doubt, his moments of reflection. Their connection deepened, becoming even more profound, not by the conquering of new challenges but by the quiet acknowledgment of their shared journey, the understanding of their shared imperfections. She found her own strength in his newfound peace, discovering that true fulfillment lay not in the accumulation of accolades but in the unwavering love and companionship they shared.

They faced challenges, of course. The demands of their foundation, the ever-present pressure to maintain their success, the occasional disagreements – these were the inevitable currents in the river of their life. But they navigated these challenges not as adversaries but as partners, facing them together, leaning on each other's strength, finding solace in each other's arms. Their conflicts were never destructive, never leading to lasting rifts. Instead, they were opportunities for growth, for a deeper understanding, for a stronger bond.

Their success was not just a measure of their artistic achievements or philanthropic endeavors; it was a reflection of their enduring love, a testament to the power of shared vision, mutual support, and unwavering commitment. Their relationship was the cornerstone of their accomplishments, the quiet force that fueled their passion, and the foundation upon which they built their enduring legacy.

The gallery continued to thrive, becoming a global hub for artistic expression, a space where artists from diverse backgrounds could connect, collaborate, and share their unique visions. The foundation expanded its reach, supporting countless artists, providing scholarships, and funding initiatives dedicated to promoting social change. Their influence spread far and wide, touching countless lives, inspiring countless dreams. But at the heart of it all, lay their enduring love – a love that transcended the fleeting nature of fame, the ephemeral nature of success, and the inevitable challenges of life.

Elena and Dante's love story was not just a tale of triumph; it was a testament to the resilience of the human spirit, the enduring power of love, and the transformative potential of shared purpose. Their enduring love was a beacon of hope, a shining example of a partnership built on mutual respect, unwavering support, and an unyielding commitment to each other, and to the world they sought to improve.

Their legacy extended beyond their accomplishments; it resided in the countless lives they touched, the hearts they inspired, and the dreams they helped to realize. It was a legacy of compassion, of resilience, of unwavering hope, and most importantly, of enduring love – a love that stood as a testament to the transformative power of human connection, and a reminder that even amidst the chaos and uncertainty of life, love can endure, providing solace, strength, and an enduring legacy of hope for generations to come. Their love story became a legend, whispered from one generation to the next, a testament to the enduring power of the human spirit and the magic that happens when two souls intertwine to create something larger, more beautiful, and infinitely more enduring than themselves.

Their story became a source of inspiration for couples worldwide. They were invited to speak at conferences, to share their insights on building successful and lasting relationships. They spoke not of perfection but of perseverance, of navigating challenges together, of finding strength in vulnerability. They shared their secrets not as formulas for success but as guiding principles, emphasizing the importance of open communication, mutual respect, and unwavering commitment.

Their advice was simple yet profound. They stressed the importance of prioritizing quality time together, of cultivating a shared vision, of celebrating each other's successes, and of supporting each other during times of hardship. They spoke of the necessity of forgiveness, of understanding, of acknowledging imperfections, and of cherishing the small moments of joy that make up the fabric of a lasting relationship. Their message was clear: lasting love wasn't about the absence of conflict but about the ability to navigate conflict with grace, understanding, and a steadfast commitment to one another.

Their impact extended far beyond the art world. Their story resonated with people from all walks of life, inspiring them to pursue their dreams, to overcome challenges, and to build meaningful relationships. Their enduring love became a symbol of hope, a reminder that even in the face of adversity, love can endure, offering solace, strength, and a pathway towards a brighter future. Their legacy lived on not just in their art and philanthropy, but in the countless hearts they touched, the countless lives they inspired, and the countless relationships they helped to strengthen.

 Their love was a living testament to the enduring power of human connection, a beacon of hope in a world often characterized by fleeting relationships and superficial connections. It was a reminder that true love is not a fairytale but a commitment, a journey, a testament to the resilience of the human spirit, the unwavering power of shared purpose, and the enduring strength of two souls bound together by a love that defied time, distance, and the inevitable challenges of life. It was a love that transcended the boundaries of art, philanthropy, and societal norms, becoming a symbol of hope, a source of inspiration, and a testament to the enduring magic of love's enduring power. Their legacy extended beyond their lifetime, a continuing ripple effect of inspiration and hope, a testament to the unwavering power of love in a world desperately needing its light.

71
REFLECTING ON THE JOURNEY

The late afternoon sun cast long shadows across the manicured lawn, painting the sprawling garden in hues of gold and amber. Elena and Dante sat on a weathered stone bench, nestled amongst the fragrant lavender bushes, a comfortable silence settling between them, punctuated only by the gentle chirping of crickets. The air hummed with a quiet contentment, a palpable sense of peace that enveloped them like a warm blanket. This wasn't the frenetic energy of their early days, the whirlwind of ambition and relentless pursuit of success. This was the quiet aftermath, the gentle ebb after a tumultuous tide.

Elena traced the delicate veins on a nearby leaf, her gaze distant, lost in a sea of memories. "Remember that first gallery opening?" she murmured, a faint smile playing on her lips. "The chaos, the nerves, the sheer exhilaration... It feels like a lifetime ago."

Dante chuckled, the sound deep and resonant. "A lifetime ago indeed. We were so young, so naive, fueled by nothing but passion and a reckless disregard for the odds." He reached out, his fingers gently intertwining with hers. "And yet, we made it. We built something extraordinary, together."

Their journey hadn't been without its storms. The early years were a blur of late nights, relentless deadlines, and the constant pressure to prove themselves. They navigated treacherous waters, facing doubt, skepticism, and the inevitable betrayals that come with climbing to the pinnacle of success. There were times when the weight of their responsibilities threatened to crush them, moments when the tension between their personal lives and their professional ambitions seemed insurmountable. Yet, through it all, their love had remained their unwavering compass, guiding them through the darkest storms.

They spoke of those challenges now, not with bitterness or regret, but with a quiet understanding, a shared acceptance of the inevitable bumps in the road. They discussed the compromises they'd made, the sacrifices they'd endured, the times they'd stumbled and fallen. But they also spoke of the moments of triumph, the shared victories that had strengthened their bond, the unwavering support that had sustained them through adversity.

"I never imagined we'd be here," Elena confessed, her voice laced with wonder. "Sitting here, in this peaceful garden, surrounded by the fruits of our labor... it's surreal."

"It's a testament to our perseverance," Dante replied, his gaze fixed on her, his eyes filled with an unspoken depth of affection. "But more than that, it's a testament to our love. It's the foundation upon which everything else was built." Their conversation drifted to the people they had encountered along the way — mentors who had guided them, colleagues who had inspired them, friends who had stood by them through thick and thin. They reminisced about the countless lives they had touched, the artists they had supported, the causes they had championed. Their philanthropy wasn't simply a charitable endeavor; it was an extension of their shared values, a reflection of their belief in the power of art and the importance of social justice.

Elena spoke of the young artists they had mentored, their faces lighting up as she recounted their triumphs and successes. She described the impact their foundation had on communities struggling with poverty and inequality, the positive change they had witnessed in the lives of countless individuals. Her voice trembled with emotion as she recounted the stories of resilience, hope, and transformation she had encountered along the way. It was a reminder of the profound impact their work had extended beyond the walls of their gallery and into the hearts and lives of countless individuals across the globe.

Dante, in turn, spoke of the evolution of his artistic vision, his journey from a fiery young artist with a burning passion to a seasoned creator with a deeper understanding of his craft. He reflected on the lessons he had learned about collaboration, compromise, and the importance of staying true to one's artistic integrity, even amidst the pressures of the art market. He acknowledged the struggles and the sacrifices, the moments of self-doubt and uncertainty. But he also spoke of the immense satisfaction he found in his work, the fulfillment of creating something meaningful and enduring.

Their conversation flowed seamlessly, weaving together memories, reflections, and hopes for the future. They spoke of their hopes for their legacy, their desire to continue inspiring others to pursue their passions, to make a difference in the world. They envisioned a future where their gallery would continue to thrive, a beacon of artistic expression and innovation for generations to come. They dreamt of a future where their foundation would expand its reach, supporting even more artists and initiatives dedicated to promoting social change.

As the sun dipped below the horizon, casting long shadows across the garden, a profound sense of peace settled over them. They sat in comfortable silence, each lost in their own thoughts, yet bound together by a shared history, a profound love, and a sense of quiet gratitude for the journey they had shared. They had weathered storms, scaled mountains, and achieved remarkable heights. But their greatest accomplishment, they both realized, wasn't their material success but the enduring love that had sustained them, the unwavering support that had strengthened their bond, and the unwavering commitment that had guided them through the challenges and triumphs of their lives.

Their journey hadn't been easy, and the future held no guarantees. Yet, as they sat together in the twilight, hand in hand, they felt a deep sense of serenity and contentment. They had found not just success but a profound and enduring love that had transcended the demands of their careers, the pressures of public life, and the inevitable challenges of life. Their love was a testament to the enduring power of human connection, a beacon of hope in a world that often seemed shrouded in darkness. It was a love story for the ages, a story whispered from one generation to the next, a reminder of the transformative power of love, and an enduring testament to the resilience of the human spirit. And as the stars began to emerge in the darkening sky, they knew that their journey, though long and arduous, had been worth every step. The memories, the challenges, the triumphs – they were all woven together, creating a tapestry of love, resilience, and enduring hope. Their story was far from over; it was, in fact, just beginning to unfold, chapter by chapter, each new day an opportunity to deepen their bond, to create new memories, to continue weaving their story into the fabric of time. Their legacy extended beyond their accomplishments, reaching into the hearts and minds of those who would hear their story for generations to come, a tale of triumph, resilience, and enduring love. And in that moment, under the starlit sky, they found peace, contentment, and the quiet assurance of a love that would endure, forever.

72

GRATITUDE AND APPRECIATION

The crickets continued their serenade, their chirping a soft counterpoint to the rustling leaves. Elena squeezed Dante's hand, a silent acknowledgment of the unspoken gratitude that swelled within them. Their conversation had drifted to the people who had shaped their lives, the individuals who had believed in them when doubt threatened to engulf them. They spoke of Sofia, the elderly woman who had owned the small bookshop where they first met, a haven of quiet contemplation amidst the bustling city. She had nurtured their fledgling romance, offering sage advice and unwavering support, her kindness a beacon in their early, uncertain years. They planned to visit her the following week, bearing gifts of her favorite books and a bouquet of vibrant wildflowers from their garden.

Their thoughts then turned to Marco, the enigmatic art critic who had championed their work when others remained skeptical. His sharp wit and uncompromising standards had pushed them to be better, his insightful critiques shaping their artistic vision. They remembered his unwavering belief in their talent, even when they themselves had faltered. They decided to organize a small retrospective of his own work, a tribute to his enduring influence and a testament to their lasting gratitude. The exhibition would feature previously unseen pieces, accompanied by a collection of his insightful essays and reflections.

Elena recalled Isabella, the fiercely independent businesswoman who had provided them with their first gallery space, taking a risk on two ambitious young artists with little more than passion and talent. Her mentorship extended beyond the realm of business; she had been a steadfast friend, offering guidance and support during times of personal and professional turmoil. Elena envisioned commissioning a portrait of Isabella, to be hung in the gallery's most prominent space, a symbol of their enduring respect and admiration. The portrait would capture Isabella's strength and unwavering spirit, a tribute to her impact on their lives.

Dante spoke of Professor Rossi, their mentor at the academy, a man whose patient guidance had honed their artistic skills and fostered their creative vision. He had believed in them long before they believed in themselves, providing encouragement and constructive criticism during periods of self-doubt. Dante and Elena planned to establish a scholarship in Professor Rossi's name, providing opportunities for talented young artists from underprivileged backgrounds. The scholarship would be a lasting legacy, a testament to their gratitude and a commitment to fostering the next generation of artistic talent. The application process would be rigorous, ensuring the award would be given to students who showed exceptional promise, mirroring Professor Rossi's high standards and unwavering commitment to artistic excellence.

Their reflections extended beyond their immediate circle,

encompassing the countless individuals who had contributed to their success. They remembered the dedicated team at their gallery, the hardworking staff who tirelessly supported their vision. They envisioned an employee appreciation week, complete with generous bonuses, special outings, and a heartfelt acknowledgment of their contributions to their collective success. Elena and Dante felt a deep sense of responsibility towards their employees, recognizing that their collective achievements were a result of their shared efforts. The week would be a time to celebrate the team's achievements, fostering camaraderie, and strengthening their bonds.

They discussed the many artists they had supported, whose talent had touched their lives. They planned to curate a special exhibition showcasing the work of young and emerging artists, providing them with a platform to share their visions and connect with audiences. The exhibition would be more than a showcase of artistic talent; it would be an opportunity to foster a sense of community among artists and art enthusiasts alike. The opening would be a grand event, bringing together art lovers, collectors, and patrons from around the globe. It would serve as a testament to the power of art to inspire, connect, and transform lives.

Their conversation extended to the countless charitable initiatives they had supported, organizations that were striving to make a difference in the lives of others. They resolved to increase their philanthropic efforts, donating a substantial portion of their earnings to support causes close to their hearts. Their commitment to social justice and environmental sustainability would be a guiding principle in all their future endeavors. They planned to engage in collaborative projects with different NGOs, pooling their resources and expertise to create meaningful and lasting change. They envisioned a world where art and social responsibility intertwined, where the power of creativity was used to create positive change.

As they sat in the deepening twilight, Elena and Dante exchanged a knowing look. Their gratitude wasn't merely an abstract feeling; it was a driving force, shaping their actions and inspiring their future endeavors. Their appreciation for the people who had supported them wasn't confined to words; it was expressed through thoughtful gestures, meaningful acts of kindness, and a deep commitment to giving back to the community. They saw their success not as a personal triumph but as a shared achievement, a testament to the collective efforts of countless individuals who had walked alongside them on their journey.

Their conversation moved towards the future, envisioning new projects, collaborations, and opportunities to support others. They discussed expanding their gallery, creating more space for emerging artists and hosting larger, more ambitious exhibitions. They planned to establish artist residencies, providing a haven for creative exploration and fostering collaboration among artists from diverse backgrounds. Their goal was not merely to showcase art, but to create an environment where artists could thrive, connect, and inspire one another. They dreamt of international collaborations, partnering with galleries and organizations around the world to promote the exchange of ideas and broaden their reach.

The night air grew cooler, but the warmth of their shared gratitude filled the space between them. The conversation subtly shifted, intertwining their dreams for the future with the profound appreciation they held for their past. They reminisced about their humble beginnings, recalling moments of uncertainty and self-doubt. They acknowledged the challenges they had faced, the sacrifices they had made, and the setbacks they had overcome. Yet, these hardships hadn't diminished their appreciation for the journey; rather, they had deepened their understanding of the importance of resilience, perseverance, and the unwavering support of others.

They spoke of the mentors who had guided them, the colleagues who had inspired them, and the friends who had remained steadfast through thick and thin. They acknowledged the countless acts of kindness they had received along the way, the small gestures of support that had bolstered their spirits and reaffirmed their belief in the goodness of humanity. Their hearts swelled with gratitude for every single individual who had played a role in shaping their lives and propelling their success.

The stars emerged, twinkling like diamonds scattered across the velvet sky. Elena and Dante sat in comfortable silence, hand in hand, reflecting on their journey. They understood that their success was not solely their own; it was a tapestry woven from the threads of countless relationships, collaborations, and acts of kindness. Their gratitude was a cornerstone of their being, a guiding principle that shaped their actions, fueled their aspirations, and underpinned their unwavering commitment to creating a positive impact on the world. The gentle night sounds enveloped them, a comforting reminder of the serenity they had found, not just in their success, but in their deep appreciation for the people and experiences that had brought them to this moment. Their story, far from being a singular narrative of triumph, was a testament to the power of human connection, the strength of collective effort, and the enduring importance of gratitude. Their journey, they knew, was far from over; it was a continuous unfolding, a perpetual weaving of relationships, experiences, and expressions of gratitude. And as they sat under the starlit sky, they felt a profound sense of peace and contentment, knowing that their love, their work, and their gratitude would continue to illuminate their path for many years to come.

73

PEACE AND FULFILLMENT

The scent of freshly brewed coffee mingled with the aroma of blooming jasmine, a familiar and comforting fragrance that always marked the start of their day. Elena woke first, sunlight painting the bedroom in a warm, golden hue. She watched Dante sleep, his dark hair tousled against the pillow, a faint smile playing on his lips. The sight filled her with a quiet joy, a deep sense of contentment that settled in her heart like a warm stone. She traced the line of his jaw, her fingers lingering on the soft stubble, a silent affirmation of their enduring love.

She slipped out of bed, the cool morning air a gentle caress against her skin. She went to the balcony, the city awakening below, a symphony of sounds and movement. The distant hum of traffic, the chirping of birds, the laughter of children playing in a nearby park – all blended into a harmonious chorus that painted a vivid picture of life in motion. She inhaled deeply, the fresh morning air filling her lungs, invigorating her spirit. The quiet solitude of the moment was a precious gift, a chance to reflect on the journey they had undertaken, the challenges they had overcome, and the unwavering love that had sustained them through it all.

Their days were now a tapestry woven from simple pleasures: quiet breakfasts shared on their balcony overlooking the city, afternoon strolls through the botanical gardens, evenings spent curled up together, reading or talking about their dreams and aspirations. The intensity of their early years, marked by uncertainty and ambition, had mellowed into a comfortable rhythm, a harmonious blend of shared goals and personal pursuits. They worked alongside each other, their creative energies complementing each other, their artistic visions intertwining to create masterpieces that resonated with audiences across the globe. But their work was no longer a relentless pursuit; it was a joyful expression of their shared passion, a canvas on which they painted their love story.

Their expanded gallery thrived, a testament to their hard work and vision. The walls were alive with color and creativity, showcasing the works of both established and emerging artists. The space was not merely a gallery; it was a vibrant hub, a place where artists could connect, collaborate, and inspire one another. The artist residencies were a resounding success, attracting talented individuals from around the world, fostering a creative environment that buzzed with energy and inspiration. Elena and Dante had succeeded in creating a space where art not only flourished but also served as a powerful catalyst for human connection and creative growth.

They had established the Professor Rossi scholarship, providing financial support and mentorship to promising young artists from disadvantaged backgrounds. The selection process was rigorous, ensuring that only the most talented and dedicated individuals were chosen. They actively participated in the selection process, meeting with candidates, listening to their aspirations, and offering guidance. They saw this as a crucial aspect of their commitment to fostering the next generation of artistic talent, a way of paying forward the kindness and support they had received from their own mentors. Seeing young artists succeed filled them with a profound sense of satisfaction, an affirmation of their belief in the power of art to transform lives.

Their employee appreciation week became an annual tradition, a joyous celebration of the collective efforts and dedication of their team. The bonuses were substantial, but it was the personal recognition, the heartfelt acknowledgements of each individual's contribution that held the most significance. They organized outings, team building activities, and special events that fostered camaraderie and strengthened bonds within the team. They understood that their success wasn't solely their own; it was a collective achievement, a testament to the hard work and dedication of every member of their team. The success of the gallery was a reflection of their combined efforts. They celebrated their triumphs together, fostering a sense of unity and shared purpose.

They continued to support countless charitable organizations, their contributions to social justice and environmental sustainability a testament to their unwavering commitment to making a positive impact on the world. They engaged in collaborative projects, pooling their resources and expertise with different NGOs. They understood that their success had bestowed upon them a profound responsibility, a duty to use their platform and resources to uplift others and make a difference in the world. Their actions reflected their deep commitment to social responsibility, their actions mirroring their words. Their philanthropy extended beyond mere financial contributions; they invested their time and energy in advocating for causes that they cared deeply about.

Their lives were filled with artistic collaborations, a vibrant tapestry of creative partnerships. They had international exhibitions, their art resonating with audiences across continents. Each collaboration presented new challenges, new opportunities for growth, and a chance to learn and create together. Each project reinforced their belief in the power of art to connect people, transcend boundaries, and foster understanding. Their art became a universal language, communicating stories, emotions, and experiences that resonated deeply with individuals from all walks of life.

One particular project, a collaborative mural in a vibrant, underprivileged community, was especially rewarding. They spent several weeks working alongside local artists and residents, transforming a drab, neglected wall into a vibrant masterpiece that celebrated the community's resilience and spirit. The experience was enriching, not just artistically but also on a human level. They interacted with community members, listening to their stories, sharing their experiences, and working together towards a common goal. It strengthened their commitment to using their art as a force for positive change, demonstrating the potential for creativity to inspire hope and foster community building.

Their love continued to blossom, deepening with each passing year. Their intimacy was not just physical; it was a profound connection of minds, souls, and spirits. They were each other's confidantes, their biggest supporters, and their most trusted friends. Their relationship transcended the romantic; it was a profound partnership built on trust, mutual respect, and unwavering love. Their shared life experiences, their collective triumphs and setbacks, had strengthened their bond, forging an unbreakable connection that extended far beyond the boundaries of romantic love.

They spent evenings on their balcony, gazing at the twinkling city lights, hand in hand, sharing quiet moments of intimacy and reflection. They reminisced about their journey, the struggles, the triumphs, and the unwavering support they had received from one another and others throughout their lives. They acknowledged the blessings in their lives, their mutual success, and the peace and fulfillment they had found in their journey together. Their quiet moments together were precious reminders of the depth of their connection, a sanctuary where they could be themselves, fully and completely, without pretense or reservation.

Their future stretched before them, an open canvas of possibilities. They had plans for new exhibitions, new collaborations, and new ways to give back to their community. They knew their journey was far from over, that there would be new challenges to overcome and new heights to reach. But they faced the future with confidence, their love, their art, and their shared commitment to creating a positive impact on the world guiding their path. And as they looked out at the star-studded sky, they knew that their life together was not just a story of success, but a beautiful testament to the transformative power of love, gratitude, and a shared dedication to living a life of purpose and meaning. The peace they found wasn't the stillness of a calm lake, but the gentle rhythm of a river flowing steadily toward the sea a constant, gentle current carrying them forward on their shared adventure.

74

A NEW BEGINNING

The crisp autumn air carried the scent of woodsmoke and fallen leaves, a stark contrast to the heady jasmine of their summer balcony. They stood hand-in-hand, overlooking a sprawling vineyard bathed in the golden light of the setting sun. This wasn't the bustling cityscape they'd known for so long, but the rolling hills of Tuscany, a place Dante had always dreamt of calling home. Their new beginning wasn't just a change of scenery; it was a conscious shedding of the frenetic pace of their lives in the city, a deliberate slowing down to savor the simple pleasures.

The vineyard wasn't just a romantic whim; it was a meticulously planned venture, a culmination of years of dreaming and meticulous research. Dante, with his innate business acumen, had spearheaded the business plan, his passion for Italian wine a driving force behind the project. Elena, ever the artist, had envisioned the aesthetic, planning the design of the tasting room, even creating a series of stunning landscape paintings that would adorn the walls, capturing the essence of the Tuscan countryside.

Their days were now a rhythmic dance between the practicalities of vineyard management and the creative pursuit of their artistic passions. Dante, with his calloused hands, expertly pruned the vines, his movements precise and deliberate, a testament to the years he'd spent learning the art of viticulture. Elena, her fingers stained with the juice of freshly crushed grapes, painted scenes of vibrant sunsets over the rolling hills, each brushstroke a testament to the beauty that surrounded them. Their collaborative spirit, honed over years of working side-by-side in their gallery, seamlessly translated into this new chapter. They weren't just partners in business; they were partners in life, their strengths complementing each other, their passions intertwined.

The transition wasn't without its challenges. Learning the intricacies of winemaking was a steep learning curve, demanding long hours of hard work and meticulous attention to detail. There were unexpected setbacks – a sudden frost, a disease that threatened the vines, bureaucratic hurdles that seemed insurmountable. But they faced each challenge together, their resilience forged in the crucible of their past experiences, their love a steady anchor in the storm.

The initial harvest was a triumphant moment, a celebration of their hard work and dedication. The first vintage, a rich Chianti Classico, was a testament to their passion and perseverance. They held a small, intimate tasting, inviting close friends and family to share in their achievement. The atmosphere was convivial, filled with laughter, shared stories, and the rich aroma of their newly bottled wine. The success wasn't just measured in the quality of the wine; it was the culmination of a shared dream, a testament to their enduring love and partnership.

Their new life wasn't merely about the vineyard; it was about a renewed focus on personal growth and self-discovery. Elena, freed from the pressures of managing the gallery, found time to explore new artistic avenues, experimenting with different mediums and techniques. She rediscovered her passion for sculpting, creating a series of breathtaking clay figures inspired by the Tuscan landscape and its people. Dante, in turn, found solace in the quiet solitude of the vineyard, finding a meditative quality in the rhythm of his daily tasks, a sense of connection to the earth and its cycles.

They found time for the simple pleasures they had always cherished – long walks through the countryside, picnics under the shade of ancient olive trees, evenings spent curled up together, sharing stories and dreams. Their intimacy deepened, nourished by the quiet intimacy of their new surroundings, far removed from the hustle and bustle of city life. Their conversations were no longer punctuated by the ringing of phones or the demands of their professional lives; they had time to truly listen to each other, to appreciate the nuances of their evolving relationship.

Their artistic collaboration continued, but it took on a new form. They created a series of paintings together, a collaborative effort that reflected the beauty and serenity of their Tuscan home. Elena's vibrant colors and expressive brushstrokes complemented Dante's more muted tones and detailed precision. Their works were no longer simply individual expressions but a shared narrative, a visual representation of their shared journey, their interwoven lives.

They also found time for philanthropy, but in a more localized approach. They supported local charities, sponsoring a community center, and mentoring young artists from disadvantaged backgrounds. Their commitment to social responsibility hadn't diminished; it had simply shifted its focus, becoming more deeply rooted in their new community. They understood that their success was inextricably linked to the well-being of the people around them.

Their lives were now a harmonious blend of artistic pursuits, business endeavors, and community engagement. They found fulfillment in the rhythm of their days, in the simple act of nurturing the vines, in the creative act of bringing beauty into the world, and in the quiet satisfaction of making a difference in their community. Their new beginning was not an escape; it was a transformation, a conscious decision to create a life that aligned with their deepest values and aspirations. It was a testament to their enduring love, a celebration of their shared journey, and a promise of continued growth and happiness. The Tuscan sun set each evening, painting the sky in hues of orange and purple, a breathtaking spectacle that mirrored the rich tapestry of their lives, a life rich in love, art, and the simple, enduring beauty of a new beginning.

The vineyard wasn't just a business venture; it became a symbol of their resilience, a testament to their unwavering belief in themselves and in each other. It was a tangible manifestation of their dreams, a place where they could create, nurture, and grow, both personally and professionally. The scent of fermenting grapes, the sight of ripening vines, the feel of the Tuscan earth beneath their feet – these became the elements of their new reality, a reality filled with the quiet joy of shared accomplishment, the comforting warmth of their enduring love, and the limitless promise of a future yet to unfold. The gentle breeze whispered through the vineyards, carrying with it the promise of new beginnings, a promise they embraced with open hearts and unwavering faith in the power of love, resilience, and the enduring beauty of a life lived with purpose and passion. Their story wasn't just about a new chapter; it was about a new beginning, a testament to the transformative power of love, a journey that continued to unfold, painting a breathtaking picture of a life well-lived, a life filled with art, passion, and the enduring sweetness of a love that transcended time and circumstance. Their success was not just in the quality of their wine or the brilliance of their art, but in the richness of their shared life, a life lived with purpose, intention, and an unwavering commitment to each other and the world around them. The future stretched before them, an unfurling canvas of possibilities, inviting them to paint their next masterpiece, a masterpiece not just of art, but of life itself.

75
A LASTING BOND

The Tuscan sun dipped below the horizon, painting the sky in fiery hues of orange and crimson, a breathtaking spectacle mirroring the vibrant tapestry of their lives. Years had passed since they'd first stood on this very spot, the anxieties of their past a distant echo in the tranquil silence of the evening. The vineyard, once a dream, now thrived, a testament to their unwavering dedication and shared vision. Rows of perfectly pruned vines stretched out before them, laden with the promise of another bountiful harvest. The air hummed with the low thrum of crickets, a soothing counterpoint to the gentle rustle of leaves in the evening breeze.

Elena leaned against Dante, her hand resting comfortably in his. The years hadn't etched harsh lines on her face, but rather, had softened her features, adding a depth and wisdom that only time could bestow. Her eyes, the same brilliant emerald green he'd fallen in love with years ago, held a quiet contentment, a reflection of the peace they'd found in this idyllic setting. Dante, his hair streaked with silver, looked at her with an affection that transcended mere words, his gaze carrying the weight of shared history, a history marked by both turmoil and triumph.

They spoke little, their silence a comfortable embrace, filled with the unspoken understanding that comes with years of shared experiences. The memories they'd made together, both joyous and heartbreaking, were woven into the very fabric of their being, binding them together in a bond that defied time and circumstance. They had weathered storms, faced betrayals, and overcome obstacles that would have shattered lesser souls. Yet, their love, tested and refined by adversity, had emerged stronger, deeper, and more resilient than ever before.

Their love story wasn't a fairy tale; it was a complex narrative, filled with shades of grey, moments of doubt, and the agonizing struggle for forgiveness and redemption. It was a story of overcoming past wounds, of confronting inner demons, and of finding solace and strength in the unwavering support of the other. Their journey hadn't been easy, but it had been profoundly transformative, shaping them into the individuals they were today—individuals who had found a profound sense of purpose and fulfillment in their shared life.

They recalled their early days in the city, the whirlwind romance, the heady passion, and the challenges they faced as they navigated the treacherous waters of their careers. They remembered the betrayals, the suspicions, the agonizing moments of doubt and despair, when the very foundation of their relationship seemed to crumble. Those memories were not erased, but they were reframed, their sharp edges softened by time and understanding. The hurt they'd caused each other was acknowledged, not brushed aside, but woven into the rich tapestry of their shared history, a reminder of the strength of their resilience and the depth of their love.

The vineyard wasn't just a place where they cultivated grapes; it was a sanctuary, a haven where they could nurture their love, their hopes, and their dreams. It was a reflection of their shared growth, their evolving partnership, and the enduring power of their commitment to one another. Each vine, each carefully tended row, spoke of their dedication, their unwavering belief in their shared vision, and their resilience in the face of adversity.

Elena's artistic endeavors had flourished in this new environment. Her sculptures, inspired by the Tuscan landscape, reflected her inner peace and her deep connection to nature. She found a sense of purpose in her art, a way to express the emotions she couldn't always put into words. Her canvases, adorned with vibrant hues, were windows into her soul, revealing her strength, her vulnerability, and her boundless capacity for love.

Dante, too, had undergone a transformation. The pressures of city life had been replaced by the quiet rhythm of vineyard work. The soil beneath his feet grounded him, providing a sense of stability and purpose. He'd discovered a contemplative side of himself, finding solace in the solitude of the vineyard, a place where he could reflect on his life and his relationship with Elena. He learned to appreciate the slow, deliberate pace of life, finding a sense of connection to nature's cycles.

Their evenings were spent sharing stories and dreams, their laughter echoing through the Tuscan countryside. Their intimacy deepened, nurtured by the serene beauty of their surroundings, far removed from the noise and distractions of their previous lives. Their conversations were a testament to their enduring connection, a tapestry woven with shared memories, hopes, and dreams. Their love had evolved, maturing into a profound understanding and acceptance.

One evening, as the stars emerged, painting the night sky with their celestial brilliance, Dante took Elena's hand. He looked into her eyes, seeing not only the woman he'd fallen in love with years ago but also the extraordinary strength and resilience she'd shown throughout their journey. He spoke of their past, acknowledging the pain and hurt they had both experienced. He spoke of forgiveness, of redemption, and of the enduring strength of their love, a love that had weathered the storms and emerged triumphant.

Elena's response was not a torrent of words, but a gentle embrace, a silent affirmation of their shared journey and their unwavering commitment to one another. She, in turn, spoke of her own gratitude for their relationship, for the lessons learned, the growth experienced, and the immeasurable love they shared. Their conversation flowed effortlessly, marked by honesty, vulnerability, and an unspoken understanding that transcended mere words.

Their love story was not a fairytale. It wasn't neatly packaged or devoid of complexities. It was raw, real, and profoundly human. It was a testament to the enduring power of love, forgiveness, and redemption. It was a reminder that even amidst the deepest struggles, even when faced with seemingly insurmountable obstacles, love can endure, it can heal, and it can prevail. Their love wasn't just a feeling; it was a choice, a daily commitment to nurture, to understand, and to forgive. It was a living testament to the power of resilience and the enduring strength of the human spirit.

They stood there, hand in hand, as the stars twinkled above them, their silent vow an unspoken promise of continued love, growth, and the quiet joy of a life lived together, a life that had been shaped by trials, yet ultimately defined by the unbreakable bond they shared. The vineyard, bathed in the soft glow of moonlight, stood as a silent witness to their enduring love, a symbol of their triumph over adversity, a testament to the enduring power of love's resilience and the beauty of a life lived with purpose, passion, and unwavering commitment to one another. The future stretched before them, a canvas waiting to be painted, a masterpiece of life itself, created by two souls intertwined, their love story a testament to the enduring power of a love that transcended time, circumstance, and the trials that tested it. Their love, refined by fire, had emerged stronger, more profound, a radiant beacon shining against the darkness, a testament to the enduring power of love's resilience.

ABOUT THE AUTHOR

Kimberly Kogut is a writer whose passion lies in exploring the complexities of human relationships and the resilience of the human spirit. She has always been fascinated by the interplay of love, betrayal, and forgiveness, themes which she herself has gone though and is able to bring into her work. She currently resides in Connecticut and when she is not working as a school bus driver, she spends time writing and creating art, reading, and drawing inspiration from the world around her, spending time with friends, close family and her fur baby Mini Dew. As this being her debut novel, she can make a long-time dream come true as an author, a dream she has had since she was a child.

www.ingramcontent.com/pod-product-compliance
Lightning Source LLC
Chambersburg PA
CBHW020343010826
48973CB00005B/1259